Praise for THE KINGDOM OF LIARS

"An excellent fantasy debut, with engaging world-building and a good mix between action and character. I thoroughly enjoyed the novel and look forward to following Nick's sure-to-be lengthy writing career."

—Brandon Sanderson, #1 *New York Times* bestselling author of The Stormlight Archive series

"A symphony of loyalty, greed, family, and betrayal set in an innovative culture!"

—Tamora Pierce, #1 *New York Times* bestselling author of *Tempests and Slaughter*

"With a smartly plotted story, great world-building, flawed but fascinating characters and plenty of mystery, *The Kingdom of Liars* is a terrific debut."

—James Islington, author of *The Shadow of What Was Lost*

"A richly rewarding fantasy that seethes with mysteries, fused with a mindscrew of a magic system. This, dear readers, is the good stuff."

—Jeremy Szal, author of *Stormblood*

"Nick Martell's debut, *The Kingdom of Liars*, lives up to its name, with so many truths and lies interwoven that nothing is as it seems and surprises lurk across every turn of the page. Michael's tale is nothing if not thrilling."

—Ryan Van Loan, author of *The Sin in the Steel*

"For all the right reasons, *The Kingdom of Liars* resonated with Scott Lynch's Gentlemen Bastards sequence, Joe Abercrombie's First Law, and Brandon Sanderson's Mistborn novels. Highly recommended."

—*SFFWorld*

"An impressive fantasy debut that creates a solid foundation for (hopefully) a much larger narrative to come."

—*Kirkus Reviews*

"This smart, briskly told high fantasy entertains all the way until the unexpected end."

—*Publishers Weekly*

THE LEGACY OF THE MERCENARY KING

THE
KINGDOM
OF
LIARS

A Novel

Nick Martell

SAGA PRESS

LONDON SYDNEY **NEW YORK** TORONTO NEW DELHI

SAGA PRESS

AN IMPRINT OF SIMON & SCHUSTER, INC.

1230 AVENUE OF THE AMERICAS, NEW YORK, NEW YORK 10020

First Saga Press trade paperback edition January 2021

SAGA PRESS and colophon are trademarks of Simon & Schuster, Inc.

For information about special discounts for bulk purchases, please contact Simon & Schuster Special Sales at 1-866-506-1949 or business@simonandschuster.com.

The Simon & Schuster Speakers Bureau can bring authors to your live event. For more information or to book an event, contact the Simon & Schuster Speakers Bureau at 1-866-248-3049 or visit our website at www.simonspeakers.com.

Interior design by Davina Mock-Maniscalco

Manufactured in the United States of America

3   5   7   9   10   8   6   4   2

The Library of Congress has cataloged the hardcover edition as follows:

Names: Martell, Nick, author.
Title: The kingdom of liars : a novel / Nick Martell.
Description: First Saga Press hardcover edition. | New York : Saga Press, 2020. | Series: The legacy of the mercenary king
Identifiers: LCCN 2019047936 (print) | LCCN 2019047937 (ebook) | ISBN 9781534437784 (hardcover) | ISBN 9781534437807 (epub)
Subjects: GSAFD: Fantasy fiction.
Classification: LCC PS3613.A77766 K56 2020 (print) | LCC PS3613.A77766 (ebook) | DDC 813/.6—dc23
LC record available at https://lccn.loc.gov/2019047936
LC ebook record available at https://lccn.loc.gov/2019047937

ISBN 978-1-5344-3778-4
ISBN 978-1-5344-3779-1 (pbk)
ISBN 978-1-5344-3780-7 (ebook)

For my father

THE

KINGDOM

OF

LIARS

THE TRIAL OF MICHAEL KINGMAN

At my trial for treason for killing the king, I played with my father's ring, twisting it around my middle finger. It was one of the few things they hadn't taken away from me when I was arrested. Maybe because they knew it was my father's last gift to me . . . or maybe because no one cared about an old ring. Despite wearing it for the past ten years, first on a chain around my neck and then on my middle finger when I was finally big enough, I never understood why my father gave it to me before his execution for murdering the nine-year-old prince.

My father gave my sister our mother's red scarf, the one she wore every day before the incident that claimed her memories. My brother received my father's favorite book, something he refuses to read, even to this day. But I was given a ring. An extremely unremarkable, once black and steel, rusted ring. When I was young, I thought my father bequeathed it to me so I could sell it to support our family. But after an appraiser revealed it was essentially worthless, I convinced myself there must have been another reason. Looking back, I can only think it was something he had cherished, and he thought I might follow in his footsteps.

My father had been right—in the worst way possible. Now I was the one on trial for killing the king. As if regicide could be inherited from father to son. I wondered how many people thought it was true: that I had killed King Isaac. It seemed obvious—after all, I had been there when he died. I had even heard him plead for forgiveness.

Not that it matters what actually happened. No one seemed to believe me anymore.

Not that most of them should have. Depending on who one asked, I was either a puppet master—with my strings tugging around nobility and commoners alike—or a mindless weapon others could direct without care. Yet, no matter what they claimed, I had only ever done what I believed was necessary, which had been easier in some aspects than others. Particularly when the city was so hesitant to change.

The entire city—no, country—had gone to shit after my father was executed. Hollow owed its foundation and preservation to my family. This city had grown up in the shadow of my ancestors—men and women who were more fantastical and awe-inspiring than any tale of make-believe dragons, of children chosen to rule by God, of bandits masquerading as vengeful demonic creatures, or whatever else was passed around as a bedtime story. Anyone who claimed to be a demon hunter, or god slayer, or divine champion, was a pretender and professional liar. Fools who had flown too high and had not yet been shot down by the moon.

The king wanted Hollow's citizens to forget the truth in favor of a fiction, as if it would make the past easier to swallow. Worse, eager to make my father's betrayal less painful, they blindly accepted the king's medicine.

And forgot everything my family has sacrificed for this country.

We eased the hate against the king. We spoke for the common people. We were the neutral party in all negotiations and never dreamed of taking power for ourselves, content in protecting the citizens from those who had illusions of grandeur. Without us, the separation between the nobility and commoners had grown so much that few could talk with the other without spitting venom, let alone sympathize. It wasn't a surprise refugees had stopped coming here. There was nothing but death, riots, war, and poverty waiting for them. Hollow, the once famous refugee city, was no more. It was just another sign of how our country was preparing to be forgotten by history, only remembered for shattering the moon Celona.

All those problems that would soon be another's to worry about. I was, after all, still on trial for treason. And I knew I would be found guilty, because, for everyone who hadn't been there, the choice was clear. How could they not find the boy who had been found standing over the king's body, blood-splattered with gun in hand, guilty?

Regardless, I am Michael Kingman, and my tarnished legacy will survive, even if my body does not. It will take more than this trial to erase me and my deeds from memory. I understand that now, when before I was always chasing my ancestors' shadows, hoping to be remembered as fondly by history as they were.

Clearly, that wouldn't happen. My story was a tragedy.

Still, here I was, sitting alone underneath a skylight in the middle of the court, with a large half-circle bench in front of me, waiting. Normally, the bench would be filled with the three lucky individuals who would hear the charges and make their decision, but they were still in discussion. Except for the Scales judge, who sat unmoving. I hoped they would hurry up and share their verdict. I was anticipating a bad death.

In all the time I spent waiting, I never turned my head toward the crowd. I could deal with strangers who believed in my treason, but I didn't want to see people I cared about look at me like I was a monster. I was doing this to protect them, even if they didn't know it. That desire kept me focused on the bench and the gold statue of balanced scales behind it.

The morning sunlight peppered through the blanket of snow covering the skylight, warming my aching bones and tight muscles. It was such a simple thing, basking in the sun's glow, that I had taken for granted before I was kept in an endless darkness.

My reverie didn't last long. The door behind the bench opened and out strode the three people who would decide my fate.

First came Gaius Hewitt, Whisperer for the Church of the Eternal Flame, dressed in his church's garb: heavy black robes with a vibrant red lining and flames sewn across the bottom.

Then came Efyra Mason, Captain of the Ravens, serving in place of King Isaac. She wore dented steel plate mail and carried a curved sword. There were seven peacock feathers woven into her black hair, denoting her high rank.

Lastly came Charles Domet, the man who had led me down the

path toward my death. The business magnate wore no smile today, instead picking at his jacket, buttons done up in the wrong holes, black hair disheveled, and wolf's head cane at his side. He was a cowardly contrast to the man I had first met two or three weeks ago—it was hard to tell how long I had been in the dungeons.

Once they had taken their seats to the right of the judge, he began: "Michael Kingman, son of David Kingman, before the jury gives their decision I will ask you one more time: How do you plead?"

The chains rattled as I rose to my feet.

I looked each of them in the eyes. I had not spoken since I surrendered myself, and as much as they'd tried, nothing would get me to utter a single word. This time wasn't any different.

"Do you plead to be a Forgotten?"

I gave no reply. I wasn't a Forgotten. I hadn't overused the nobles' magic of Fabrication until it took all my memories. My suffering and experiences were still mine. They made me who I was: my father's son, inheritor of his legacy. And I remembered everything, now more than ever.

The judge met my unwavering gaze. "Members of the jury, how do you find Michael Kingman?"

Charles Domet rose slowly and read from the piece of paper, his hands shaking, "On the charge of treason of the highest degree, we find Michael Kingman . . ." Domet met my eyes for a last desperate moment, seeking forgiveness. ". . . guilty."

Shouts rose around me. I heard every voice except for my brother's, Lyon. No doubt he was paralyzed in his seat, the nightmare of my father's fate in mind as he consoled my sister, Gwen.

We, the sole surviving members of the Kingman family, knew what would come next better than any. A charge of high treason only had one fate.

Or so I thought.

Moonstruck heroes always seemed to ruin everyone's plans. As the judge pounded his armored hand against the bench, screaming at the crowds to be silent, a man jumped over the barrier that separated me from everyone. He had a flintlock pistol in his hand and reeked of alcohol, likely for bravery. The gun was aimed at my heart. I had no idea what I had done to him, but knew I deserved his hate.

I would have a clean death after all. A better death than any king killer deserved.

"I won't let there be another!" the man screamed. "You will not be remem—"

It would have been a poetic death. Gunpowder made everyone equal, when the strongest Fabricator could be killed with the pull of the trigger . . . as everyone in the city knew far too well.

But, sadly, the poor fool didn't see that the Captain of the Ravens was already in flight. She leaped from her spot on the jury, soaring through the air as lightning crackled around her. She came down right above him, blowing the gun out of his hand with a lightning bolt. As the dust settled and coughing filled the courtroom, a nearby Advocator grabbed the gun before anyone else could.

The assassin didn't even scream when his plan failed, only stared at me. He was on his knees soon after, crying about how much this city had suffered because of me and my father. How he had sought to save it from taking the coward's way out of this mess. The crowd was silent, waiting for what was next.

"Michael Kingman will die when we say he can. As we dictate. After everything he's done, we will not let him go peacefully. We will have justice," Efyra growled. "Judge, what is the penalty for having firearms in Hollow?"

"Death," he said.

Efyra held her hand over the man. "Then let it be done."

It only took a single bolt of lightning out of her palm, aimed at the heart, for the man to die. He blew back into the crowd, smashing into people and their seats. His body smoldered, smoke wafting off it, and the entire courtroom was filled with a foreign, unnatural smell. Something that haunted my dreams ever since this all began.

While others dealt with what she had done, Efyra returned to her seat on the jury with her blade drawn. She laid it across her lap as if daring my siblings to try and save me.

When the chaos settled and the body had been removed by the Wardens, the judge continued my sentencing, "Michael Kingman, we hoped for more from you, of all people. You should know better than this. Despite your father's actions, you are still a Kingman, and our troubled times called for a man who could lead us, aid us. Yet here we are with a king killer instead."

The judge paused for a moment, eyeing the brand for treason on my neck. A gift the king had given me ten years ago after my father's execution. I wasn't ashamed of it anymore. As the judge shook his head, he continued, "I hereby sentence you to death. You will be executed on the steps of the Church of the Wanderer, as your father was before you, in a week's time. May God have mercy upon you."

I wanted to laugh. If only that would-be assassin had waited a little bit longer, he would have got exactly what he wanted.

There was no controlling the noise after that. Behind me, I could hear the Advocators of Scales holding back the crowds. Cheers and clapping and threats became white noise as a Warden came for me. The metal monster wrapped my chains around one gauntlet and dragged me away from the witnesses and into one of the back rooms with tempered ferocity. As I was shoved through the open door, I took my first look back at the courtroom crowd. My sister was at the front, smashing herself against the Advocators, reaching for me.

Dark, the Mercenary, was leaning against a doorframe at the back of the courtroom with his arms crossed. He was shaking his head at me. His dull, smoky eyes silently said I should've known better. He wasn't wrong—I should have . . . yet here I was. What a sad sight I must have been, to elicit pity from a Mercenary.

The door closed and I was separated from the court. I shut my eyes and waited to feel the sun's warmth again, knowing full well it would mean my death.

AN AUDIENCE

You will hear this story as I lived it.

Count yourself lucky to hear a Kingman tell their story. There has been no other account like this. And all I ask from you, in return for the greatest story ever told, is a small favor and to let me live long enough to tell it.

To learn how I earned the title of king killer, we must begin on the night before the Endless Waltz began, the last remnant of my youth.

Not that I ever really had one.

After my father's execution, I spent years struggling to survive in a city that wanted to see shackles on my wrists and my head roll. It might not surprise you to hear that I spent much of my time conning the nobility, which was always easier than it should have been. Even without hiding the brand on my neck or how suspicious my intentions ever were.

And my actions were as suspicious as usual that night I oversaw a duel between my friend Sirash, a former Skeleton, and his target: a rather drunk and rather obnoxious country-born Low Noble who had never been to Hollow before. The mark was so fresh to the city, he hadn't even had time to change into something more befitting of a Hollow noble, and was still wearing layers of clothes that lacked a uniform style or color. It showed everyone how low he was, as if that wasn't evident enough when he called Sirash a copper-skinned savage. The so-called civilized people only did that in the comfort of their own homes.

The Low Noble pointed the flintlock pistol at Sirash, then showed it to his painfully sober brother before peering down the barrel himself. His finger was on the trigger the entire time. Thankfully for him, it wasn't loaded. Not that he was privileged to that information. "Sure you want to do this, Skeleton?"

Sirash didn't reply. We were already past the point of no return, and the nobles were ensnared in our trap. There was no chance they were escaping unscathed.

But that didn't stop the brother from trying. "Adrianus, we shouldn't do this. Guns are still illegal here and the last thing you want is to be seen with one. They'll execute you."

"Adrianus," I said quietly. "I am compelled to inform you that unless you apologize, this duel will proceed. Should you decline, with the Endless Waltz beginning so soon, your reputation will be ruined."

"He's a Skeleton!" Adrianus said. "What could *he* do to me?"

I looked at Sirash. He was sitting calmly on a stone wall, fiddling with the other flintlock pistol I had brought. Since he was masquerading as a Low Noble, he was clean-shaven, wearing long, dark-colored trousers and an almost see-through, partly unbuttoned white shirt. The only odd detail about his appearance was the bone tattoo on the back of his left hand. A remembrance of his past. Much as the rusted ring on my middle finger was for me.

"Look at him. He's clearly risen in society," I said.

"Could he be a Low Noble?" Adrianus asked.

"Maybe. High Noble Morales has added many new families in recent years."

"Even a former Skeleton?"

"Stranger things have happened."

Adrianus considered my words, nodding as he studied the flintlock pistol in his hand.

"Enough of this," Adrianus's brother said. "Forget the Skeleton. We should go and receive the Eternal Flame's blessing for the Endless Waltz tomorrow. High Noble Maflem Braven can protect us from gossip and rumors."

"But what if he names me a coward and the women want nothing to do with me?" Adrianus said, worrying as only an underconfident boy could about those of the opposite sex. "I don't want to please Father and marry Jessi. I want a more adventurous future than breeding horses!"

"What if someone hears this duel and arrests you?" his brother said.

I put my hand on Adrianus's shoulder. "We're in the middle of the Fisheries. There are no members of Scales or the King's Ravens down here unless there's a riot about taxes. Most of the locals are asleep."

"Is . . . is the gun ready?" Adrianus asked.

"Yes," I said. "I've prepared it for you. All you have to do is point and shoot."

"Let us do it," he said. "I'm ready."

Before his brother could protest, I made a sweeping gesture and guided Adrianus into place with my hand on the small of his back. "Listen closely, Adrianus. Instead of the typical ten steps, turn, then shoot, you're simply going to stand a distance apart and shoot. That way no one cheats and turns early. Sound good?"

Another nod as I signaled for Sirash to take his place opposite from him. "You will shoot on three. Aim true." With a final pat on the back, I took my place.

"On my mark!" I shouted. "One! Two! Three!"

They shot. White smoke billowed across them both and they were lost in it for an instant. As it cleared, there was a crash, and Sirash fell to the floor. Blood poured out of his knee and upper thigh, soaking the ground around him. Despite being unharmed, Adrianus screamed and dropped the gun, letting it clatter to the stone.

"Shit!" I was at Sirash's side in an instant, my hand over his knee, staunching the blood. It ran cold over my hands regardless, flowing over the stone around me. "He's bleeding out."

Adrianus stood there moonstruck. "What have I done? I didn't want this. Wanderer, forgive me!"

I checked for his pulse. "Your shot severed an artery and he bled out in a few heartbeats. He's dead."

The noble retched and then puked all over the stone, his shocked brother patting him on the back. Adrianus mumbled to himself as he recovered, and it wasn't long before his mumbles turned to sobs as he repeated to himself, "I killed him. Oh, Wanderer, I killed him."

"I didn't think you'd actually hit him. Why couldn't you apologize!"

Adrianus's brother stepped forward and pointed at me. "No, this is not happening. I knew who you were the moment I saw that brand. You are Michael Kingman, traitor son of David Kingman, and you are going to fix this."

I felt the crown brand on my neck throb, whether from being reminded it was there, or from my racing heartbeat, I couldn't tell. "Fix this? How do you expect me to bring him back from the dead?"

"I don't." He reached into his pocket, pulled out a bulging purse, and shook it at me. I suspected it was a sizable part of his allowance for the Endless Waltz. "You will take this, get rid of that body, and we are never going to hear from you again. Understand?" He sneered at Sirash's body. "I doubt anyone will miss him. If someone does, they can always import a new slave from the Skeleton Coast."

"You want me to cover up a murder for you and your brother?"

He pushed the bag of coins against my chest. "I don't want you to. I'm telling you to."

"If I don't?"

Lightning began to form and crackle around his right arm, saying more than any idle threat could. I hadn't realized he was a Fabricator, though it explained why the moonstruck fools had been sent to Hollow for the Endless Waltz.

I held my tongue as he bundled Adrianus away from the scene, first pushing and then dragging him away by the shirt. Once they were out of sight, I wiped my stained hands off on my shirt and then kicked Sirash in the ribs to signal we were in the clear.

"Seriously? How am I supposed to convince someone you died from being shot in the knee?"

Sirash sat up and grimaced at his dirty clothes. He'd broken a sheep's stomach full of blood for effect during the duel. "Oh, I'm sorry. Next time I'll grab my chest after he points the gun at my leg. We're lucky he aimed anywhere near me. Unlike the last one."

"All I'm asking is for an easy one, so I don't have to come up with some artery in some random place to explain why you dropped dead. You should be grateful I can talk us out of these problems."

"Literally every time you open your mouth, all you do is get us into more trouble."

"Then why am I always the one doing the talking, not the shooting?"

"Because no one would hesitate to shoot you." Sirash grinned at me wickedly. "So, how much did we get?"

I returned his smile and crouched down, emptying the bag of coins in front of us. We began to spread out the gold, silver, copper, and iron, making sure to count as we did. "Almost eleven suns," Sirash said.

"I would have expected more from a noble coming to Hollow Court."

"Must've been poorer than we thought. You should have tried to get Adrianus's allowance, too."

"Maybe if he had less to drink I would have."

We split the take. Sirash took seven suns to cover his expenses and to help his lover, Jean, pay for her tuition at the College of Music. I took the rest—enough to cover my expenses and potentially buy another cure if I haggled the oddity merchants down a bit. With it safely in my pocket, I asked, "How much more do you need for the month?"

"Another three suns. I'm not sure how many more Low Nobles will come to Hollow for this ridiculous courting ritual—"

"Call it the Endless Waltz. We've been doing this for two years now; it has to be second nature if we're masquerading as Low Nobles."

"How much do you need?"

"I don't know. This should cover my mother's medical expenses. I'll talk to Trey and figure out how much more I need tomorrow. I might have to start covering part of his bills while he's indentured to a High Noble family—"

A bell rang out in the city, and we turned our heads toward the sky, looking for the piece of the moon falling from it.

"I can't see it with all this light," he murmured.

Before I had a chance to respond, the city began to darken. Seizing the guns, Sirash and I emerged from the alleyway and looked down the street. The gas lamps that ran down the length of one of the main roads in Hollow held a strong flame within them, burning brightly. One by one they were being snuffed out by the lamplighters, and it was Lights Out in the city. The spreading darkness was accompanied by a symphony of slamming shutters and windows.

"Do you see it?" he asked.

I didn't. Tenere, our smaller moon, was full, its orange-bluish mass clear in the dark, even at a distance. In front of it, much larger, was the ever-broken Celona, its seven major pieces bright and white. They were surrounded by dust and smaller rocks, most of which would eventually hit the world below. The stars around them looked dull and flickering . . . and then I saw the falling piece of Celona. I strained to make out what color the tail was, hoping for red. If it was blue or white, it would mean the end of Hollow, no matter how the king and Scales attempted to stop it.

Their infamous Celona defense system, built to reassure the general public, was little more than a trebuchet. I'd love to see the imbeciles tasked with aiming that thing at a fast-falling piece of the moon try to save Hollow. It would be a show worth watching before the city's inevitable destruction.

"We need to find cover in case a second or third bell starts ringing," Sirash said.

"I can't," I said. "I should have been at the asylum already. Celona be damned." I slapped Sirash on the shoulder and took off, running through the streets, knowing Sirash would find shelter in the sewers, as he always did when the bells rang.

Amidst his laughter, Sirash shouted, "Michael! If you don't take moon-fall seriously, one of these days it will be the death of you! You'd be the bastard that gets hit!"

Doubtful. The Kingman family did not die with whimpers. History was shaped by our births and deaths, and whether I liked it or not, I would be no exception.

THE WOMAN IN
THE ASYLUM

I had never feared the falling pieces of Celona, not like others did. Especially not when only one bell was ringing.

One bell signaled a piece of the moon was falling, two bells signaled that it would fall within the country, three bells meant it would hit Hollow, and a fourth bell meant to expect an earthquake or a wave from the coast. Until I heard that third or fourth bell, I'd keep running.

I ran through the city as fast as I could, heading for the asylum in the Student Quarter near Hawthorn Medical College. The Upper Quarter was like a lighthouse in the middle of a storm: it was never Lights Out there. It was some noble-esque bullshit, since the observatories trying to track the moon-fall were hindered by the light from their district, but few, if any, complained. Too scared they'd be associated with the rebels if they spoke up against the Royals and their High Nobles. I was one of the few who wasn't. After all, what more could they do to me? I was already branded. Whatever I did, my legacy would never amount to more than that of a simple con man.

By the time I reached the asylum, the Student Quarter was dark. A second bell began to ring across the city as I pushed the door open and ran along the cold, stark white hallways. I could hear shouting ahead.

"Get your hands off my mother!" my sister screamed. "You're not throwing her out while the bells are ringing!"

I rounded the corner in time to see one of the asylum nurses dragging my mother toward the exit by her long black hair. Her green eyes were so glazed over, I doubted she even realized. My sister, Gwen, had her hands clenched into fists, exposing the treason brand on the back of her left hand.

"Dustin!" I said, skidding to a stop in front of them. "I have the money right here. Both of you, calm down."

The nurse, a monk from the Church of the Eternal Flame, dressed in a black robe with flame trim, released my mother and gave me a sideways glance. "You heathens are late again! How many times do I have to remind you payment is due at month-end? No exceptions, no charity."

"Does it matter? I have your money."

The nurse fingered through the gold I put in his palm.

"Do you want to bite it? It's real. Now let us get our mother back to bed."

He waved us away dismissively. "As much as I would enjoy throwing you out, I must be faithful to Prophet Hewitt and show mercy. Even toward you heathens who destroyed Celona, God's masterpiece. It'll be five suns next month. My tithe has gone up, and so must yours."

I could see a vein throbbing in Gwen's neck. I wasn't doing much better, but instead of making it worse I said, "Please, our mother needs to get back in her room."

The nurse left without another word, whistling.

"You're late and smell like a bar," my sister snapped. She crouched down and ran her fingers through our mother's hair. "You were supposed to be here hours ago."

"It took longer than I thought to get the money."

"If you could hold down a real job for more than a month, maybe we wouldn't have problems so often. The only reason we've made it this far is luck and the fact one of the other wards routinely takes pity on us. But she wasn't here tonight, and it almost went to shit. As it always seems to."

"I'm doing my best, Gwen."

The bells stopped, and we gave a sigh of relief. It was one less thing to fear, one less thing to worry about.

Gwen motioned for me to take our mother's knees, and together we carried her to her plain room, pallet bed, and itchy blanket. The only comfort in there was a painting of our parents on their wedding day that hung on the wall opposite her bed. We tucked her in and then stepped outside to talk without disturbing her.

"You need to visit more, Michael. She asks about you a lot."

I folded my arms. "About me or our father?"

A pause. "Both of you. But you know how much she needs routine and normality. Your visits always make her feel better."

I bit down on my tongue, hating the position my sister put me in. Unlike me, Gwen had inherited features from both our parents, our mother's thick black hair and sun-kissed skin and the famous Kingman amber eyes, while I was almost a perfect replica of my father. It meant, unlike me, she could weave in and out of public scrutiny whenever she wanted to. Even her brand was obscured by the long sleeves of her asylum uniform.

"Please, Michael? Talk to her before you go. It'll mean a lot to her."

"Fine. I have something for her, anyway." I went back in, sat down on the edge of her bed, ran my fingers through her hair, as she sat up, smiling. "Mother, how are you doing?"

She gave me a tight hug. Or tight as she could when she was all skin and bones. She had done nothing but lie in a bed for so long, her muscle had wasted away. "Oh. David, I've missed you so much. Where have you been? Did you return to the Warring States to meet with the cripple? Or did you have to head to the Gold Coast again?"

"Mother . . . ," I whispered. "It's me, Michael."

Her eyes refocused and grew serious as she stared into mine. "Amber eyes, strong jawline, thin face, messy brown hair . . . Oh, Michael, I'm sorry . . . You just look so much like your father."

She sobbed, and I returned her hug as best I could, silent. My mother, despite not being a Fabricator, had suffered a Forgotten's fate, remembering nothing about her life save the occasional flash of memory of her world before my father killed the prince. Initially we had thought her memories had been manipulated by Darkness Fabrications, but no matter how many Light Fabricators we hired, there was no change. So, shortly after losing our father, we realized we had no parents to rely on anymore.

"Are you doing well? Are you eating well?" she said. "Do you have a woman in your life? You'll be participating in the Endless Waltz soon. Will you attend Hollow Academy, as your father did?"

Sometimes . . . sometimes it was easier to lie to her than share our daily truth. It always upset her, and she wouldn't remember it the following day.

"The Endless Waltz starts soon, and there are plenty of fine women out there you'd love to have as a daughter-in-law. And, yes, Mother, I'll be attending Hollow Academy like Father. How else would I learn how to use Fabrications?"

"Good," she said. "Your father was one of the most remarkable Fabricators I ever saw. I still remember the first Fabrication I ever saw him use. We were in my homeland, at a festival, and he entertained the children with fire he created from nothing. Have I told you how we met, Michael?"

"Mother, you look hungry," I said as she paused for breath. My hands shook as I pulled out a small pouch of Deepwater seeds I'd imported from the Gold Coast. "I have something for you."

She took the seeds from me and began to eat them with the shells still on. According to my research, Deepwater seeds could give the Forgotten moments of clarity. Usually around whatever magical incident had taken their memories. It wasn't a complete cure, if there truly was one, but it might help us uncover a clue as to what had happened to her.

"Mother, forgive me for asking while you eat," I began, "but do you remember what happened to Father?"

She hesitated, and my breath hitched. "What do you mean?"

"With Davey."

Her eyes went wide. "Oh, I do. Oh, God, how could I forget? Davey's birthday is soon! Did your father forget to get his gift? I swear, that man . . ."

A sword through the chest would have been more pleasant than those words. Another failure in a long line of failed cures.

I played with my father's ring, my mind wandering as she told me again how they had met. The story never varied, but sometimes the details would change: this time my father had been a Fire Fabricator, though the time before he had been a Lightning Fabricator, and the time before that he had been a Metal Fabricator. My mother might love telling stories about my father, but it was impossible to tell which of them were true.

Even my own memories told me little of the man he had truly been. The only concrete memory I had was of the night before he murdered Davey Hollow. That night I had crept into his room and found him working on the balcony, piles of papers at his feet. He was always clean-shaven, but he looked so old and worn-out . . . and that night I saw a moment when he paused and looked up at the stars, mid–pencil stroke, and smiled. That moment never fit the narrative of the monster he had been, and I sometimes wondered if I'd invented the memory as a child to cope with everything that followed.

Whether I had invented it or not, I knew nothing about the man my father had really been, and probably never would. All I knew for certain was the title he carried: traitor. Earned after killing the king's son in cold blood.

I promised myself I would never be like him.

I'd rather die than abandon my family.

THE HANGED

My mother told her stories until her eyelids grew heavy. I kissed her on the forehead and left her to sleep, closing the metal door behind me.

My sister was waiting for me.

I rubbed my bare skin. I always felt colder after visiting my mother, as if she had taken the warmth from me as I held her hand. I loved her, and would do anything for her, but it was draining to come here. I don't know how Gwen did it or if it made me a bad son not to come more often.

"Don't you have other patients to take care of tonight?" I asked.

"No. All that's left is staying awake until first light while they sleep."

"Sounds riveting."

"It helps pay for her to be here. So," she said, her voice growing stern. I knew what she was about to say. "Have you had any luck finding the gun?"

"The gun?" I asked. I lifted my shirt to show the two I had hidden there. "I have two right here."

"Angelo won't like that you've stolen those from him again . . . but you know which gun I'm talking about, Michael. The same gun I've been talking about for the past ten years. The gun our father is supposed to have killed Davey with. Have you found it yet?"

"I made that promise when I was ten, to make you stop crying." Back when I openly believed my father was innocent. Years of living in Hollow had shown me how unwise that was.

"You still promised."

"Gwen," I said, looking down at her, "our father pled guilty. Instead of dwelling on conspiracy theories, can we focus on something more productive?"

"Like wasting our money searching for natural remedies to cure being a Forgotten? It's not as if hundreds and thousands of people haven't tried to already. Unless you think you're smarter than all of them."

"Not smarter. More persistent."

She turned her back to me, something she'd done ever since she was a child. "We each have our obsessions. I'll stop mentioning mine when you can give me a good reason for our father to have killed his best friend's son."

"I'm not getting into this, Gwen. I'm tired, and I want to go home." I began to walk away, and she heard and followed.

"Fine," she said, defeated. "There's something else. A job opening here you might be interested in."

I stopped. "What kind of job? Because the last time it was for that Eternal Flame nurse, and I nearly got us both dismissed and our mother kicked out."

"You'd be a companion to an outpatient, making sure he doesn't relapse too badly."

In all the years I'd been visiting my mother in the asylum, I had never heard of anyone improving. I said as much to Gwen.

"It's the first time it's happened while I've been here."

"What's the downside?"

"The patient is High Noble Charles Domet."

I blinked a few times. "No."

I knew the stories about Charles Domet. Some said he was richer than every church, Gold Coast clan, and High Noble family combined. That he wielded more power with a suggestion than my ancestors had with an army behind them. Domet could slap the king in front of all his Ravens and get an apology in reply. And all that was just what everyone talked about in public. The quieter rumors, the ones told behind locked doors with blinds shut, spoke of what he had done to merchants who tried to con him. Eradication was putting it nicely.

"It's five suns a day."

That made me reconsider, exactly as she knew it would. It was a fortune. "How long for?"

"A month. And there's only so much he could do to you in forty-eight days. You'd walk away with two hundred and forty suns."

I could do a lot with that much money. Stop conning nobles for a while. Try a raft of cures with my mother, instead of leaving her a slave to her brief moments of clarity. But it was Charles Domet. There was a reason the job was available, and a reason they were offering so much for doing it. Only a fool kept putting their hand in the fire to check if it was hot.

"Still no."

"Domet's a Fabricator. He might be able to teach you to use Fabrications. Or at least the basics. Maybe then you'd have the knowledge to find a *real* cure for her. We both know those natural cures won't do a damn thing."

"Gwen, you're talking about Domet the Deranged. He once threw a servant out of a window for stealing a spoon. Do you really think it's wise for me, of all people, to interact with someone like that?"

"You're the only person I know who could," she said softly. "Like the king, he rules with fear. But Domet likes to be entertained—challenged, even. That's what you do. Con him into giving you what you want."

I wondered how long she had known about the job, if she had waited for another of my natural cures to fail before bringing it up. It was likely. Gwen was patient, and she always knew what to say, and when, to get the outcome she wanted.

This was the first time she'd ever suggested I could find a cure . . . not that it would change my opinion on using magic.

"No."

"What other option is there? Only magic can cure magic."

"And risk ending up like our mother? Do you want to care for me, too? Because last time I checked, having one patient in the family was hard enough."

I waited for Gwen to retaliate, but, astonishingly, she left it at that. Instead, she held the ends of our mother's scarf to steady her trembling. We were both looking for a way to make lives better, and every day we seemed to crack more and more under the pressure.

How long would it be before we shattered?

When she was calmer, she reached into her pocket and handed me a piece of cloth. "For later. I know you're going to go looking for a fight, and that's been sterilized. You might as well be prepared. Or you could not fight. Just a thought."

I took it from her, kissed her cheek in thanks, and waved goodbye.

———

It was a long walk from the asylum to the Narrows where we lived, and I took the path through the Hanging Gardens. More out of habit than a conscious decision. There were great redwood trees in the park, tall as towers, with branches as thick as my torso. The trees were so grand, their leaves mostly blocked out the sun in the daylight, leaving the park in a perpetual state of gloom. There were newly blooming flowers in the trees, blue and purple, some fat and some skinny, all swaying gently in the wind, hung by some rope around limbs.

I almost walked into three Advocators, the most common members of the private military—Scales—that ruled the city, adding more flowers to the already populated trees. One of them was fitting a noose around a boy almost ten years younger than me, his dead eyes vacant and glazed over. His parents were already in the trees above us, waiting for their family to be reunited.

The boy was already dead—nothing would change that—but I

was still a Kingman and always tried to do as much good as I could in this city. My family had helped King Adrian the Liberator unite Hollow against the Wolven Kings, and I would not let our illustrious family legacy be forgotten because of one rotten Kingman.

"What are you three doing?"

The one with the noose met my gaze as his accomplices continued their work. "Official Scales business, boy. Get out of here, unless you want to join these rebels."

"That child was a rebel?"

The Advocator sounded exasperated. "His parents were. They sold bread to the Rebel Emperor."

"So you killed a baker, a baker's wife, and a baker's boy for doing their job? How were they supposed to know who the Rebel Emperor is? It's not as if you've put out Wanted posters showing his likeness. Could that be because you don't know what he looks like either? That couldn't be the case, could it?"

Another Advocator spoke up. "I think you should leave, boy. Before we string you up with them."

I scratched the back of my head. "I wish I could."

And I punched the closest one in the jaw, sending him sprawling to the ground.

One Advocator tackled me, punching me in the face as I did my best to block his blows. As I fought to throw him off, the third came up from behind and slipped the noose around my throat. A moment later I was in the air, hung by my neck as I clawed at the rope. Every constricted breath was like swallowing molten metal, and my eyes began to water, blurring everything below me.

The Advocators howled with laughter and hoisted me higher and higher into the trees until one shouted, "He's Michael Kingman! Look at his brand! Cut him down! Cut him down! The king will hang us if we kill him!"

I hit the ground with a thunderous slam, in a tangle of rope, and wrenched away the noose. I couldn't tell if my first breath hurt more than it brought relief or if more pain came from the scratches my nails made clawing at the rope. By the time I could focus again, the Advocators were long gone, leaving the unhung boy slumped against the tree.

I crawled my way over and leaned next to him, panting. It was a small comfort, in a way, that no matter what I did, I couldn't be killed quite so easily as everyone else. As a High Noble, however disgraced, I could only be sentenced to death by a public execution, after a trial.

Unless one day the Advocators didn't notice the brand until it was too late and let me hang in the trees like anyone else. I doubted it, but the thought lingered in my mind as I rested in the Hanging Gardens, glad to feel something other than shame or regret, even if that was a searing, burning pain.

THE VISIONARY
ON THE WALL

It was almost first light by the time I slipped through the window
into my room after burying the boy in the garden. I didn't need to be
quiet, since Gwen had the late shift at the asylum and Lyon was on
night patrol for the Executioner Division of Scales, but it was habit. I
cleaned my wounds as best I could with Gwen's cloth but could
barely sleep, my battered body unable to find a comfortable position
that avoided getting blood all over my bedding. I had to settle for a
restless doze, my mind unfocused to the world around me . . . until
my foster father and probation officer, Angelo Shade, stormed into
my room and dumped a bucket of water over me, then said, "Downstairs. Bring my guns, Michael."

I groaned and sat up as he slammed the door behind him. Slowly, with every movement bringing fresh pain, I began to take note of my injuries. I took the swollen eye, a nasty seeping cut over my eyebrow, a raised red welt from where I had been hung, scratches all over my neck, and bruises all over my chest as a victory and headed downstairs. I left the blood-soaked cloth and clothes from last night in a pile outside my room, making a mental note to do the household laundry before Gwen ran out of clean uniforms.

Angelo was waiting for me in the kitchen in his Scales regalia, an old silver-button coat and dark trousers. There was a golden eye sigil on his shoulders to denote he was a part of the Watcher Division. As always, he looked too perfect and too Hollow-esque for an immigrant, all traces of his former culture gone. His short black hair was tidy, his skin slightly tanned, and his trim build showed how little he indulged in rich food.

Only his rings were non-regulation Scales uniform: a glass ring around his left ring finger, a large, bulky golden band around his left thumb, and, on his middle finger, an iron ring with a crown crest. A gift from his wife before her death.

"Guns," he said, pointing to the table.

I put the guns, stolen from his office yesterday, down.

"You realize they could execute you just for carrying those, right?"

I nodded. We had done this enough to know nothing he could say would change anything.

"What was it this time, Michael? Protecting a fair maiden? Standing up against injustice? Or did you provoke another fight with Advocators as they did their duty?"

"Advocators. In the Hanging Gardens."

"What will you do if they report you? Or, worse, if you run into Lyon one night?"

"I'd probably punch him first," I said. Seeing his grey eyes narrow at me, I took advantage of the lull and said, "Can you help me stitch the cut above my eye?"

Angelo knocked his ring against the table. "Yes, but I can't be late. You'll have to come to work with me. Unless you're willing to wait for Gwen to stitch you up. She's working a double shift."

I cursed: I'd have to go with him, rather than waste my day indoors, waiting for Gwen, or wandering the city with an open wound. I followed my foster father through the trapdoor and onto the rooftops.

We walked single file across the planks of wood that spanned the small gaps between the buildings of the Narrows toward Angelo's outpost on the city's battlements. The planks creaked and bent with every step we took but never broke, and for that I was grateful. I could only imagine the stories if a Kingman fell from the sky. The old ladies who lived in the district would be the angriest. If I fell from up here, I'd take out most of their clotheslines and get blood on their freshly laundered clothes when I hit the stone.

It would be an ironic way to go, after everything I'd survived.

Closer to the wall, the planks were more secure and led to a ladder that would take us to the top of the battlements. I wasn't looking forward to the climb: the wall was twice the size of the nearby buildings. But at least I wasn't free-climbing it, as I'd done years ago on a stupid whim. I had no desire to repeat the feat; my muscles had ached for weeks.

When we reached the edge of the wall, Angelo turned back with one hand on the ladder and said, "Do you remember the only rule we have on the battlements?"

"I don't think I could forget if I turned into a Forgotten, since you come home angry every night because some imbecile private didn't remember."

"Humor me."

As a drop of blood trickled down the side of my face, I said, "No need to be mute, just don't salute."

Tragically, Angelo climbed the ladder without praising my response. Once he reached the battlements, I followed him up, and for the third time in my life I saw the world beyond Hollow.

There was patchwork farmland, with long lines of wheat and corn alternating with pastures for cows and horses and enclosures for goats and chickens. At the edge of my vision I could see that the rebel army encampment had doubled in size since I had last been up here. They had even begun to dig ditches to make their position more defensible. More worryingly, dozens of Low Nobles' banners now flew beside the rebels' closed red fist. I wondered how long it would be before a High Noble joined forces with the rebels, and how the king would respond.

As for what was beyond, I could only rely on the stories my parents had told me to imagine what was out there. In my mind I could see the Sea of Statues off the Gold Coast and the frozen desert to the north, where pieces of Celona never fell. My nose could smell the spicy lamb dishes served on the streets of Goldono, and my feet could feel the black sand beaches of Eham. But after Angelo tapped me on the shoulder, my daydream disappeared, and all that remained was the rebel army and a few Watchers playing cards at a table on the battlements.

Angelo prodded the nearest soldier, "Private Thornwood, get me a medical box, a glass, and alcohol from the barracks."

The private glanced at me. "Should I get a medic too, sir?"

"No, they have enough to deal with. I'll do this myself."

"Yes, Commander Shade." The private ran off, forgetting to button his coat before he did.

The other four Watchers knocked their knuckles against the table to acknowledge his arrival. It was the only subtle sign of respect members of Scales could do without making Angelo a target.

"Sergeant Calder," Angelo said, before sitting down at the table. "Night report."

"No advance by rebels to the west, sir. Farmlands are still secure. Our spies remain in place, but the rebels didn't send out a scouting party last night. Low Noble Bartos may have joined the rebellion; his banner was seen flying over their encampment."

"I'll inform the Commander. She won't be pleased. More Low Nobles from the other cities seem to be joining the rebellion every day." A pause. "When does our next supply caravan arrive, and who's escorting it in?"

"Midday, sir. Orbis Company, and a few local Low Nobles are accompanying them."

"Do we know which ones?"

"Unclear, sir."

"When did Scales resort to hiring Mercenary companies to protect the caravans?" I asked.

One of the soldiers chuckled to himself, and Angelo answered, "The rebels won't attack Mercenaries. No one wants to provoke them after Regal Company sacked the city of Vurano. There's a reason that massacre ended the Gunpowder War."

"And why companies are hired to storm cities and kill kings and emperors," one soldier added. "Just last year Orbis Company was credited with sinking a half dozen of the Palmer's battleships."

"Didn't even need a full company to do that," another said. "No offense, Commander, but I'm running with my tail between my legs if I ever see one of them charging me."

There was laughter around the table. My foster father even smiled.

If Hollow was desperate enough to work with Mercenaries, those fucking leeches, this rebellion must have been more serious than the public knew. Maybe that explained why they were hanging more people every day. It was easier to crush every trace of rebellion than fix the problems that had started it.

"Are the rebels expected to besiege Hollow soon?" I asked.

This time none of the soldiers would look in my direction. Thankfully for them, their colleague returned with the supplies Angelo needed, and he dismissed them with an order to do one last lap around the area before getting breakfast. None of them argued.

Angelo took the bottle of vodka in his hands and poured a sizable amount into the glass. "Drink. This will hurt."

I downed it in a single gulp, coughed, and blinked the tears out of my eyes. "Ready."

Angelo dabbed my cut clean with alcohol, chastised me for wincing, and began to stitch it. "You shouldn't mention open war in front of my soldiers, they're nervous enough as it is. Do you know how long it's taken me to get them to laugh up here?"

"It was just a question." I groaned as the needle went through my skin.

"A stupid question. Those on the front lines don't like to be reminded they could die soon."

I grabbed the bottle of vodka and took another drink from it. It did little to ease the pain. "That sounds like you're expecting the rebels to attack soon."

Angelo leaned back in his seat, leaving a piece of thread hanging down over my eye. "Of course I am. Good commanders worry about everything. Just like good foster fathers. Have you figured out what you're going to do with the rest of your life yet? Or are you set on this imbecilic path to martyrdom?" He eyed the welt around my neck.

After all my years living in Hollow, I had no idea what or who I wanted to become. The only thing I was truly good at was taking a beating and ignoring the pain that followed.

While I wanted to blame my father for my indecision, it's not like I had spent my childhood learning a trade like Gwen had. No, I had spent it whining about my family's legacy and how my father had ruined our lives, reducing us to beggars and criminals.

I had always assumed I would inherit the family business and become as legendary a Kingman as my ancestors. It had taken me ten years to admit that wouldn't happen, and now I had nothing to show for my hope but empty pockets, useless skills, and the enduring desire to redeem my family.

But, looking back, I couldn't say I would have done anything differently. I had spent much of my childhood searching for a cure for my mother. It hadn't made a difference yet, but at least I hadn't given up, as most did when their loved ones became Forgotten. Family looked after family, and I wouldn't stop until she was cured.

But another swig of vodka was the only answer I gave to his question.

He finished a stitch. "Take an apprenticeship on the Gold Coast. I have a few friends who would take you on. Especially if Granen was flooded by a moon-wave last night, after that piece of Celona hit the ocean. You'd be worked hard, and the conditions are rough with the unpredictable tides, but in a few years you could be a journeyman. Or even a knight. They still have them down there."

As sensible as that was, I couldn't do it. Even if Gwen and Lyon could pay for my mother's medical expenses alone, I wouldn't abandon her until I found a cure. Maybe then I could seek out a life without feeling indebted to my family's name.

"Any other ideas?"

"You could be a city messenger," he said, less delicate with the needle than before. "Post always has to be delivered. Or join one of the guilds . . . Wouldn't make you a noble, but you'd be close."

"My goal is to be farther away from the nobility, not closer."

"Honestly, given how childishly you act, it's shocking to hear you have any goals at all—"

I kept my silence about curing my mother. I knew it was a foolish dream—one he would ridicule, but one I wouldn't want to give up until I had tried everything. Until I knew there was no hope for her.

"—and don't feel indebted to this city because of that brand on your neck or your last name."

A pause. "What if I can't help it?"

"Then, when the rebels attack, join me on the battlements. Either you'll die a hero or live long enough to see you can never redeem your family in the eyes of the king."

If there was no chance at redemption for my family, then what was I supposed to do?

Who was I, if not a Kingman?

"There," Angelo said, cutting the thread. "Done."

"Thanks, Angelo."

He rose from his seat with a smile. "It's why I'm here. But if you steal my guns again, I'll throw you out on the streets. No more second, or third, or fourth, or fifth chances. I'd be in as much trouble as you if they were traced back to me. Understand?"

A nod.

"And in thanks for my remarkable healing skills, you're going to make breakfast every day next week. Fair?"

"Fair." It was well worth the price. A few infections had taught me as much.

"Still planning on going to the stadium to celebrate Kingman Day today?" Angelo asked.

I touched the stitches to see how tender the cut was. Which only seemed like a stupid idea after I'd done it. "Haven't missed one yet. I'm seeing a friend first, though. Are you cooking tonight?"

"No," he said, tidying away his supplies. "You'll be on your own. Nothing fresh, but there's plenty of pickled food in the pantry."

I groaned. Pickling was a hobby of Angelo's, and he liked to ex-periment. Suddenly skipping breakfast this morning was fine; I'd need to be hungry later. I waved goodbye and went in search of Trey.

There was a whole world waiting for me if I abandoned my fami-ly's name. But, for now, I had a friend waiting for me and an execu-tion to attend.

Maybe tomorrow I'd stop fearing the future.

THE LIVING LANTERN

Even though Trey lived on the east side of Hollow with tweekers and thieves, he worked on the Isle surrounded by scholars scared of ripping paper with their delicate fingers.

It was normally impossible to get a job outside of one's quarter. But since Trey worked to organize a blind Archivist's personal records, she didn't care where he was from, only that he did his job well. If Trey could read and write fluently, it would have been perfect. But there were words that he had never learned or heard before—having taught himself how to read and write with partially burned books found in the trash—so I spent a portion of my mornings helping him.

Today was no different.

I entered the Archivist's house and joined Trey in the basement, where he had dozens of papers spread out in front of him. He had a pencil in one hand, the other fisted, ready to pound the table when he was stuck. Based on how much was on its side or teetering, he'd had a frustrating morning.

"You're late," he said.

I took a seat opposite him. Even though we looked different— him lanky, quick, and of mixed race, whereas I was broad, muscular, and light-skinned—we were brothers more than Lyon and I were anymore. Maybe because our disagreements didn't devolve into shouting matches. Family was supposed to be able to do that, too.

As Trey cracked his knuckles, I took the paper he was working on and scanned through it:

> *On the fortieth day of the seventh month, a piece of Celona,*
> *fallen when the moon was at its apex, was retrieved from*
> *the Iliar mountain range. Our initial attempts to discern its*
> *message were futile, but eventually a child was able to relay it*
> *to us:*
>
> > *"Enough with the past, let it die with them."*
>
> *Once we had recorded the hidden message correctly, we*
> *placed it in our vault for safekeeping. Archivist Laetia, you*
> *and your assistant, Trayvon, would have to come to us to see*
> *it yourself. As promised, we are transcribing our work on why*
> *only a select few can hear the messages. May this aid your*
> *endevors.*
>
> > > *The Institute of Amalgamation*

"I see Archivist Laetia is still obsessed with the pieces of Celona. Please tell me she doesn't actually believe they're messages from God like the fanatics do."

"I don't know what she believes," Trey said, adding the paper to a pile and scribbling a note to himself. "We don't talk about that."

"Aren't you curious?"

"Not curious enough to ask and risk losing my job if our beliefs don't match. You know how Archivists are. They only see the world their way."

"If you left, you could always con nobles again with me and Sirash."

"And leave Jamal alone all night? No, thanks." Trey pushed a piece of paper back to me. "What do you think?"

"You spelt 'endeavors' wrong. You're missing the *a* between the *e* and *v*. Use 'pursuits' instead."

"No, it's better if I use the same language as the Archivist, in her reports. Was that the only mistake?"

"Your name was spelt wrong, too. It's an *e* instead of an *a*."

Trey cursed a few times and scribbled something out with his pencil. "We can leave once I'm done with this. The Archivist is letting me go early so I can participate in the selection process for the High Noble Fab armies."

"I thought you'd have more work today."

"I've been here since first light and I'm only finishing now. You're still planning on spending the day fishing with Jamal, right?"

"Of course."

"You swear you're not going to Kingman Day?"

"After what happened last year? Not a chance. Where is Jamal, anyway?"

"Visiting our ma's grave."

I held my tongue as I watched Trey clean up his workstation. As he did, I couldn't help but glance at some of the pages. His notes were so clear and concise, no one would have been able to tell that a few years ago he was completely illiterate. Except recently he had started making obvious mistakes with words that should have been impossible to forget. His name the most obvious. There was only one logical answer.

We'd crossed over the eastern bridge on our way to the graveyard when I finally said, "You've been tinkering with your Fabrications again, haven't you."

He opened his mouth to respond, then furrowed his brow and said, "What gave me away?"

"Everything you've written for the past week has had your name misspelled."

"I was hoping you wouldn't notice that."

"What were you thinking?"

Trey held up his hand and a steady glow of light came off it. "I know that my specialization is light, but I can't control it most of the time, and I need to. Otherwise I'm nothing but the world's least useful lantern."

"Tinkering with them by yourself is dangerous until you know the basics. Why not wait until you've joined one of the High Noble Fabricator armies?"

"Because they won't teach me unless I sign an eight-year contract to do their bidding in exchange. I don't want to live with those self-righteous High Noble pricks for that long if there's another way. Especially not when I just want to learn how to control my Fabs and move on. I don't want to be remembered . . . I just want to live without fear." A shrug. "So I experimented. Even tried to find a book about it."

As we passed a group of children play fighting with sticks and rocks, I said, "Everyone wants to be remembered."

"Not me."

"You're lying, but, regardless, you can't go your entire life unconsciously using Fabrications. You'll be a Forgotten before you're twenty-five—and in the army you could be trained by twenty-six."

"But once I know how to control my Fabs, I never have to use them—and I think I've almost got it. It has something to do with how I see the world. The glow occurs when I imagine things lighter in my head. Although I can't figure out what's going on with the shadows—"

"Is your freedom worth more than your life?"

Trey stopped. "Besides my brother, my freedom is all I have."

"And is it worth more than your brother? What would he do if you forgot about him? It may just be words now, but it won't be forever. No one is that lucky. Find a teacher and learn from them before it's too late."

Trey glared at me, but we continued walking. "I wouldn't have to teach myself or join one of the Fab armies if Hollow Academy was still open."

"Blame my father for dying. Or the king for getting rid of it instead of finding someone else to oversee it."

"The king has always been incompetent. But running the acad-emy was a Kingman family responsibility. So it seems reasonable to blame the only Kingman I know." He said it with a grin.

"You going to blame me for shattering Celona next?"

"Thinking about it."

"Then maybe I should yell at you for being a moonstruck—"

"Can you let it be? I took your advice once already and applied to join the Fab armies. The selection process won't conclude until this evening," Trey said. "I need to go. No doubt, unless I show up early, they'll say I'm late and reject me."

"Fine," I said, wondering if that was the whole truth or whether it had something to do with Trey having no desire to see his mother's grave. We'd reached the graveyard's iron gates, and going further would take him out of his way. "Want me to bring Jamal to Margaux Keep afterwards?"

"Please. I promised we'd get some chicken after my interviews, no matter what happened. You're still planning to spend the day fish-ing, right?" He was always overprotective of his little brother, double-checking what he'd be doing.

"Yes."

"Thanks, Michael. Catch a redfish for me." Trey slapped me on the back and took off for his interviews, while I passed through the gates and started to walk down the hill through a sea of graves to find Jamal. He was sitting cross-legged in front of a recently disturbed patch of dirt, in the shadow of a destroyed stone tower. As usual, his stuffed dragon was with him. It was his most prized posession, and he took it everywhere.

"How's your mother?" I asked. Jamal was darker and shorter than

Trey, but their eyes were the same. One day I hoped to have as close knit a family as they did.

Jamal kicked at the dirt. "Still dead, but I wanted to know where she was. Makes me feel better." He checked behind me, to be sure Trey wasn't hidden from sight, then perked up and said, "We're still going to the colosseum for Kingman Day, right? And the execution?"

"Obviously."

Before either of us moved, Jamal looked back into the sea of graves behind us. "Oh. Do yah want to visit your da while you're here?"

I didn't look back. "No, he isn't going anywhere."

If I had to see a Kingman who'd disappointed me, I'd rather it be my executioner brother than my child-murdering father. At least when Lyon killed people, I could pretend they deserved it.

THE CHAINED
EXECUTIONER

"Do you know who's being executed this Kingman Day yet?"

"Not this year, no."

I only ever knew if I went to a bakery the day before. They were always gossiping about the latest noble drama there, and I never truly cared. Either the person being executed for treason was a rebel or they weren't . . . and the fact that their guilt wasn't always that clear made me feel sick. As did the Royals and High Nobles who had turned a day once meant to celebrate my family into the day my brother stood in front of a crowd and executed others.

The High Nobles didn't even attend, always preferring to watch from a distance.

"It's Low Noble Philip Grossman."

I knew him. Sirash and I had conned him a few weeks ago, when he first arrived in Hollow for the Endless Waltz. He'd been one of the easiest targets, and his aim was atrocious. During the mock duel, his hands had shaken more than a wet dog trying to get dry.

"What's the charge?" I asked.

"Transportation of firearms from New Dracon City to Hollow with the intent to sell," he recited carefully.

"Low Noble Grossman oversees grain farmers. I doubt he's smart enough to smuggle guns into Hollow. Let alone sell them."

"The Royals wouldn't charge him with treason if it wasn't true."

"If you say so," I said, letting the conversation go, knowing Jamal saw these executions more as a form of entertainment than a representation of justice. Probably because he and Trey had grown up hating and envying the nobility. It had taken Trey years to call me a friend, and longer still before he let me meet his brother.

"Trey will be fine today, you know."

"I know. I've just been worried about him ever since your mother died. He seems to be handling it . . ." I trailed off, unable to find the right word.

"Ma was always addicted to Blackberry," Jamal said. "He's protected me from her outbursts, the stealing, and the rest of it. When she died . . . I don't know, I think he's trying to find his place in the world. We survived the East Side; now he has a chance to do more than that."

Something else Trey and I had in common, unlike my actual brother. He may have bowed to the nobility, but I never would.

"He won't tell me how she died," I said.

"Me neither. Just that she died like she lived: alone and only caring about herself."

"Didn't she steal food from you two when you were young?"

"Every day."

"Then I suppose she deserved her fate. Just like my father," I said as we neared the large crowds for the execution.

Kingman Day used to be held in the Great Stone Square on the Isle or in front of the castle in the Upper Quarter. But since it became a spectator event where rebel nobles met the ax, they had decided to hold it somewhere the nobility never went. Luckily, no one on the East Side cared, seeing it as a business opportunity. The children, in particular, were always selling pointy rocks, rotten vegetables, and fresh dung in such large quantities, it made me wonder where they got their stock from. Aside from the dung, it certainly wasn't coming from their own district: the Militia Quarter had been stripped clean of anything that could turn a profit.

The Militia Quarter was one of the oldest districts in the city, having been built back when Hollow was founded. The buildings were a motley mess of different materials, having been hit by moonfall more often than any other part of the city. Everything in the quarter was misplaced and run-down, from the broken cobbles that could pierce shoes to the cracked and pothole-riddled roads. Sirash and his brother worked in one of the bakeries—although, as it was Kingman Day, the baking was all done in advance so they could enjoy the festivities.

I was thankful there were no masks depicting my ancestors this year. The ones meant to look like my father didn't, and still made me angry. As part of the day, an Archivist was regaling the crowd with a stupidly detailed list of all the historical mistakes uncovered in the past year, deciding what the truth truly was. When it became clear they weren't going to slander my family again this year, I ignored the rest of the scandalous noble drama.

"We should get a good spot for the execution," Jamal said. "I want to hear the rebel's last words. I want to know if he feels remorseful for what he did and who he helped in his last breaths."

Usually they just cried.

"You don't want to get food rations?"

Jamal shook his head. "If I show up with rations later, Trey won't be able to pretend we went fishing. We've been enjoying the king's diet lately, and I wouldn't want to ruin a terrible thing, you know? Besides, the line is too long. By the time we got up there, all the bread would be gone."

"Do you want something to throw?"

Jamal took a few rocks from his pocket with a smile. "Brought my own! The children always charge so much for them. We only charged an iron trite a stone, but now they cost two! It's a robbery!"

"Jealous?"

"Yes," Jamal said with a roll of his eyes. "Since Trey is trying to learn how to use Fabs. When are you going to?"

"I'm not."

"But you're a Kingman! You have to catch lightning like the Unnamed Kingman could!"

"You can't catch lightning. Fabrications don't work like that. At best you could create some lightning of your own if that was your specialization, but—"

Jamal shushed me. Loudly. "Let me have my Kingman stories. Hearing them from my ma was the best. And if I have to be friends with the lamest Kingman ever, let me at least pretend you might be a legend one day."

"You only want me to be a legend to get into the stories yourself."

"Yah," he said. "Best chance to be remembered by someone other than you and Trey."

I rubbed my arm. "I'm still sorry you're not a Fabricator, Jamal."

"Me too. But it makes sense. Trey's only a Fab because his dead-beat father was a High Noble. My father was a fisherman. Not a drop of magic in his blood. Sadly, not all men are created equal."

"I—"

He looked up at me, serious now. "Don't feel sorry for me. I may not be a Fab, but you are. So you should learn how to use them. Then I can be remembered, too."

If only it was that simple. My ancestors were titans, insurmountable by any mortal . . . and the older I got, the less it seemed the three of us could ever be remembered as fondly as they were. Or, if we would be a generation without greatness, only remembered for allowing the Kingman name to survive when it should have died with my father.

"Weren't we going to meet your friend and his brother?" Jamal said after I had grown quiet.

"They're saving us seats in the colosseum."

"Close to the stage?"

"Not too close. I don't want to accidentally end up in line for the ax."

"I'd save you."

"Oh, would you? You'd charge through the crowds and fight the Militia?"

"Obviously," Jamal said as he flexed his muscles. "They'd have to send Ravens to slow me down."

"Of course they would."

"Don't believe me? Just wait. If you're ever in trouble, I'll save you. That's a promise. I'll even bring Trey."

I had a hard time containing my laughter. "Trey? Never. It would take nothing short of a war—where you were in trouble—to get him into the public eye."

Jamal glanced at me. "I'd at least try. Maybe he'd agree if I begged."

"I'll believe it when I see it."

We made our way through the crowds and into the colosseum, which was a marvel of stone construction, taller than the walls that guarded the city and maintained as perfectly as the High Noble keeps. Some Archivists claimed it had been built before the Wolven Kings lost control of Hollow, but I had always doubted that. It didn't show hundreds of years of wear and tear. If anything, it looked new.

Most of the crowd had gathered around the stage in the center of the colosseum. We went up the stairs toward the top instead. Sirash and his adoptive brother Arjay waved us over. Arjay had two loaves of bread and a bag of candied nuts in his hands.

"You two took your sweet time getting here. We were worried you'd miss it," Sirash said as we sat down. "You forget the way?"

"Michael was late," Jamal said.

Arjay snickered. "Nothing unusual, then."

Sirash handed Jamal his own bag of candied nuts, to the boy's excitement, and he and Arjay began to compare their bags. I gave Sirash a nod of thanks and he smiled in response. He knew from experience how important small luxuries were to those who had very little.

"What are the chances of us conning another noble before the Endless Waltz begins?" he asked.

"Minimal," I said. "Though two Low Nobles are arriving today from the outskirts."

"Do you know their names?"

I shook my head. "We'd have to be lucky to find them."

"We're rarely lucky." A pause. "Winter is going to be rough this year. Especially if the supply caravans into Hollow get less frequent."

"I'll help when I can. I'm always around to nick wood from the nobility's gardens."

"Like you have a choice," he said, nudging me with his shoulder. "Family looks after family."

"Always." A pause. Gwen's suggestion had been at the back of my mind all morning. "Sirash, if I had the chance to help a lot of people, but it meant I had to compromise my beliefs, should I do it?"

"You just said a lot, and nothing, all at the same time."

"I could earn a lot of money by working for a High Noble."

"Which one?" he asked.

"Domet the Deranged."

"Shit," he said. "Do you want to get a drink later? That won't be a quick conversation."

"Yeah, I'd like that. Thanks, Sirash."

Before I could steal some candied nuts from Jamal, my brother was climbing the stairs to the executioner's block, dressed in black with a serrated great-sword in his hands. He had a list of names tattooed on his right arm, a record of all the nobles he had executed so someone would remember them. He had the names of his lower-class victims, peasants and merchants, on his back. I'd never seen it, but I suspected there was little unmarked skin left.

Lyon stood in front of the block, flanked by a monk from each church ready to record the rebel's last words. He faced the crowd and let the point of his sword hover above the ground. As he looked down, the treason brand above his eyebrow was exposed for every-one to see, so there was no mistaking that the nobility had made a Kingman their puppet.

With my brother in place, his noble victim would arrive quickly. Sure enough, I heard vegetables and rocks splatting against flesh be-fore I saw him. The crowds cleared a path for him and his escort as they pelted the rebel with everything they had.

To give him some credit, he didn't scream or curse the crowd as some did. He only wept, softly and steadily, with every step he took. I got a better look at him once he reached the platform: similar in age to me, bruises plentiful under his loose rags, and eyes that had long since abandoned hope.

His female Scales escort chained him to the executioner's block as my brother stepped forward, cleared his throat, and then said, "I am here on behalf of King Isaac to execute Low Noble Philip Grossman on charges of treason, smuggling, and improper handling of financial records. Low Noble Grossman, do you have anything to say?"

Low Noble Grossman tried to compose himself for a moment and then, in a strained voice, said, "I didn't do it. I didn't do it. Tell my parents I didn't do it. Tell them to remember me. Please. Please . . . I don't want to be forgotten. God, be merciful. I don't want to die. Please. Please . . ."

Lyon raised his sword above the noble's neck. "You will not be forgotten. Your name will live on, even if your body does not."

My brother was efficient—he had been executing people for years—and he severed the noble's head in one clean strike.

There was a splatter of blood and a thump as the head dropped into the basket, followed by that lull of noise that always came after a death, before the crowd started hollering and cheering, Jamal one of the loudest.

Lyon cleaned his sword with careful, precise movements and dropped a rag over the basket to hide the head. He picked it up and was gone before the escort who had led the noble to the block had recovered from the shock of seeing an execution.

"Lot of blood this time," Jamal said.

"There's always a lot of blood," Sirash stated.

"You'd think they'd find a less messy way to do it," Arjay said.

"The blood is the least of today's worries," I said darkly, getting to my feet. With the excitement over, we joined the mob descending the stairs and began to leave the colosseum.

"You don't think the rebels would be stupid enough to attack Hollow, do yah?" Jamal asked.

"How can they not?" I countered. "How many rebels do we execute or hang every week? A dozen? Two dozen? How long before we've killed so many they—"

I didn't finish my sentence.

A man with the rebel's symbol of the closed red fist painted onto his face and a sword in his hand emerged from the crowds. He cut down one of the monks in a fluid motion and shouted: "Long live David Kingman!"

The rebel closed his eyes and tilted his head back before exploding into a brilliant blue flame. I was frozen as I watched it happen, wondering why a Fabricator turned rebel, and hoping Jamal and Arjay were still behind me.

When his fire touched the stage, multiple explosions rocked the pristine colosseum and the twisted and broken streets of the Militia Quarter beyond. As we were blown back, the colosseum cracked and crumbled around us. The people trapped inside screamed desperate, pained wails as thick black smoke covered everything. Angelo had been right. The rebels had come to destroy this city, as they had Naverre. The last thing I remembered was being thrown by the blast, my face skidding across the shattered stones, wondering what death would be like.

FAMILY

My ancestors weren't waiting for me in the afterlife, only darkness.

Had I been left in nothingness for the lies I had told and the dishonorable acts I had performed to survive? Was my father somewhere close by? If I had to be punished, could I at least be punished with family? It would make it easier. And maybe I could finally ask him why he had murdered Davey. I wanted to know. Simply so I could know if I idolized the wrong man.

My body hurt. And that confused me; I had always assumed there would be no pain in death.

It made sense everyone had been wrong about that. Who wanted to think death would bring more pain? Life is cruel enough. I hoped Jamal, Sirash, and Arjay were still alive. I hoped they were safe. I was fine with dying if it meant they would live. At least then I could claim to be as selfless as my ancestors.

Someone was calling my name. How was someone calling to me when I was dead?

Michael. Michael.

I knew that voice. Was it my father? No. Different. Younger. Scared. Did they need me?

Michael. Wake up! Please!

My family still needed me.

I took a breath, and it burned.

NOBODY

I choked on the sharp smell of burnt hair, sulfur, and shit mixed together. I was sprawled out on the ground with clumps of sharp stone lodged into the side of my face. I twitched my fingers. Then my toes. And then flexed my muscles. Dull pain washed over my entire body as my vision blurred into focus.

There were dozens of bodies around me. Some were blackened with burns or had been blown apart, while others were bent at odd angles, as if they were trying to test how flexible they were. But the worst were the ones who still had their mouths open, having died screaming. Ash and dust dribbled out of their mouths like blood, and their eyes had been stained grey. I scrambled backwards, rolling away from my previous position.

I tried to focus on what I had woken up to, but the sheer carnage of everything around me was too much. I couldn't stop shaking as I brushed the dust and rubble away, replacing it with a sticky streak of my own blood instead. I could still see it with my eyes closed as I tried to regulate my breathing and ease the pain in my head and think clearly again. I was hurt beyond anything I had felt before. The dull pain rocked my body when I tried to stand and sent me wobbling back against the stone pillar.

It was one of the few things that were still standing, most of the colosseum having collapsed in on itself after the explosion. I must've landed, or fallen, into the underground corridors beneath the colosseum. They had been condemned over a decade ago due to flooding, and with only scattered rays of light that came in through the cracks to guide my path, I doubted they had gotten safer since.

I had to find Sirash, Arjay, and Jamal. If there was anything I could be thankful for right now, it was that my executioner brother would be safe. He never lingered after the executions, preferring to get some distance between him and the bloodthirsty crowd in case they ever turned their attention from dead rebels to former nobles. We had always shared that fear.

But the others had been caught in the explosion, too. They should have been down here with me, surrounded by bodies, ash, and rubble.

They wouldn't have left me behind. They weren't like that.

Unless the blackened bodies I saw were them.

I did what I had to. I searched all the bodies around me, wading through . . . through what remained of these people, wondering if I would come across a charred stuffed dragon or the body of one of my friends first.

I spat what I could onto my hands in a foolish attempt to clean them. It didn't work, but it calmed my stomach down after what I had done. My friends hadn't been among the bodies where I woke up, so I continued my search, screaming out their names as I did. The broken corridors were veiled in a thin layer of dust and crushed rocks, and everything smelled like garbage left out in the hot summer sun for a week.

I examined each and every body that littered the ground, hoping for survivors. Some were hunched over against walls and broken columns, an outline of ash around them, and some were simply lying on the ground like dolls scattered across a child's bedroom floor. Then there were others who were in their final moments. I stayed with them until they passed, most too far gone for me to do anything but hold their hand and hear their last words. I made sure I left them in the most respectful positions possible. Selfishly, I was filled with relief every time I found out they weren't Sirash, Arjay, or Jamal, and yet struck with a numb grief that I couldn't do more to help them. It made me feel like a hypocrite.

Since I had woken up, I hadn't seen anyone else as lively as me. Only the departed and soon-to-be. How had Hollow survived the Gunpowder War if the enemy was capable of this level of destruction? Could any of us survive when the entire rebel army decided to attack Hollow? If they hadn't already.

"You there! Stop!"

I turned toward the voice and saw the female escort from the execution striding toward me. She was as coated in mud and ash as I was, strands of her hair stuck to the dried blood on her neck, her electric-blue eyes stark against the grime. Judging from her expression, I must've looked as lost as I felt.

"State your name."

Everything sounded muffled. I opened my mouth wide and my ears popped. It felt as if someone had stabbed me in the forehead. I nearly puked.

The woman repeated her orders.

"Michael," I said, and nothing more.

"Michael what?"

I gestured at the devastation around us. "Why does that matter?"

"Either comply or I'll arrest you."

I couldn't stop myself from laughing, and she didn't appreciate it. "What're you going to charge me with? Treason? For not telling you my last name? Do you see what's happened? We need to work together. Who cares who I am?"

"Are you Michael Kingman?"

It would have been easy to lie to her. If she was asking, she clearly didn't see my brand. Maybe all the grime and blood and dirt was obscuring it. I could have said a hundred different names and been a hundred different people. Yet, after what I had heard that rebel shout—whose name he had used as a rallying cry for this war— there was only one person I wanted to be. Even if I should have been anyone else. I would not be ashamed of who I was. Even if the world told me I should be.

One rotten apple didn't mean the entire tree had to be cut down.

I clawed at my neck until whatever was there flaked off and revealed what was underneath. Then, so there was no mistake, I turned so she could see the crown brand. "Whether you believe me or not, I didn't help the rebels do this. I was just here to watch my brother perform that noble execution. Then I got separated from my friends because of the explosion. Have you seen any survivors?"

Astonishingly, she backed down. "There aren't many. They're gathered up there." The woman pointed to the ceiling above us. Which, from where I was standing, looked as if it would collapse onto us at any moment. I was even less reassured by the water that dripped down from it.

"Thank you."

"Don't thank me yet," she said. "We're trapped down here. Some unstable parts of the colosseum caved in and blocked off the exit everyone else used."

"And you threatened to arrest me?"

"There's a different way out, but I'll need your help."

"Maybe start with that part next time."

"I just wanted to know who I was working with."

Without giving me time to ask her name, the woman with electric-blue eyes turned her back on me and walked over toward a pillar that had fallen at a drunken angle. There was a pool of water around one end, while the other pointed toward a hole in the rubble that was allowing daylight to shine through. It was the first unobstructed glimpse of the sky I'd seen since the collapse.

"What do we need to do?" I asked.

"Do you see the opening above the column? Launch me up there, then I'll pull you up."

"That's ridiculous. It'll barely support my weight, let alone both of ours. And how do I know once I lift you up you won't just leave me behind?"

It was her turn to laugh. "Do you want to get out of here or not?"

I didn't have any other option. Thus, once I had mentally prepared myself, I began to climb on the fallen pillar. It wobbled and creaked with every step I took on it. As I neared the crumbling end I watched as chunks of it fell away and into the water below, and it was an effort to look up at the opening overhead. I could get her up there, but I doubted there would be much time, if any, for her to pull me up. I'd have to jump, grab her hand, and hope for the best.

"Ready!" I shouted down to her.

Like a messenger before a long run, she shook out her legs and stretched her arms, backed up a little, and then sprinted toward the pillar. I braced myself as she reached the other end as she leaped . . . and then, as if carried by the wind, she floated through the air. With one light step on the column that nearly sent me into the water, she rose even higher.

It was as if she was flying.

I knew what I had to do. I cupped my hands together, ready for her foot, and pushed her up toward the ledge the best I could. Her chest hit the lip of the hole, hard, and I thought she'd slip and fall into the water. But after a moment's winded struggle, she swung her hips and pulled herself up and over.

She vanished as the pillar beneath me continued to wobble.

She left me. I knew I couldn't trust Scales. Not after I told her the truth. I'd have to—

Then she was back. Lying flat over the edge, she reached down to pull me up. It was easy, and soon I was at her side again.

"You didn't tell me you were a Wind Fabricator. No regular person could have jumped like that," I said.

"You didn't need to know," she replied, rolling away from the edge to stand in front of me. "All I needed from you was a boost."

"Thank you for not leaving me behind."

The woman didn't respond at first, giving me a sideways glance instead. "Don't thank me. I did leave you for a moment there. Good luck finding your friends."

The Scales woman left me sitting near the opening, confused.

––––––––

It was much more stable up here than in the corridors beneath, aside from the massive holes in the floor. But they were easy enough to avoid, and I was able to find my way out of the collapsed section and into daylight.

For a city that had been founded with such promise, it was hard for me to stomach how far it had fallen when I gazed upon the destruction.

The colosseum was in ruins. Half still stood while the other half had collapsed into the ground, as if sucked in by a sinkhole. There was a huge crater where the platform and the densest part of the crowd had been. The stage itself had been blown in half, burnt and torn pieces of cloth caught against pieces of wood. It was the only sign people had been here at all. In the heart of the blast, the dead had been burned so badly they had formed a weird grey-and-black construct. Carrion crows picked at it with a quiet efficiency.

Past the shattered colosseum, the rest of the Militia Quarter hadn't fared much better. The trees in the immediate area had either been set aflame or snapped in two, only their splintered stumps left behind. The closest buildings had been reduced to piles of stone, and small fires littered the area like weeds. It was also so, so quiet I could hear the buzzing of flies one moment, and then so loud the next that my thoughts were drowned out by swords clashing and gunfire.

Where were the rebels? Where were the survivors? Where were the reinforcements?

Where was anyone?

Despite all the destruction, I noticed a small group of people huddled a little bit away from the colosseum. There were maybe a dozen of them, and I squinted, hoping to spot my friends. I picked and slid my way across the unstable rubble as fast as I could, careful to avoid the most dangerous areas, and then ran to the grouping.

Jamal, Arjay, and Sirash saw me coming before I reached them. When we reunited, I scooped Jamal up in the biggest hug I could as I ruffled Arjay's hair. Sirash just smiled, and life felt right again. They all looked as dirty and bruised and shocked as I was, but otherwise fine. Jamal's stuffed dragon was still in his pocket, and I was thankful he hadn't lost it. Enough had gone wrong today.

"Sorry I'm late," I said, with a half grin.

"We were coming back to look for you," Sirash replied.

"What happened?"

"Rebels," Arjay declared.

"Besides that."

"We got separated in the explosion," Sirash said. "I tried to catch you before you fell, but I couldn't. It was chaos after that. The blast destroyed the central arena, and without that foundation the colosseum disintegrated around us. Rebels disguised as Advocators were waiting outside to cut people down as they escaped. Not many survived."

"How'd you all?" I asked as I put Jamal down.

"We did what we do best," Jamal said. "We hid and waited for all the lunatics to stop killing each other."

"It helped that the Militia led a charge against the false Advocators and distracted them from us civilians," Sirash explained.

"Does that mean the Militia drove off the rebels?"

All three of them looked at each other. But it was Jamal who said, "No. I think they're all dead. The rebels shot at them as they charged. When the Militia retreated, the rebels followed. Last we saw, the Militia Headquarters was on fire."

"So this is an active war zone and the rebels are winning?"

They all confirmed my statement with a nod.

"Then we need to get going before any more rebels show up," I said.

"There's no need to go anywhere," an Advocator interrupted. He had a nasty wound on his forehead and his front teeth had been knocked out. "Scales will send help soon. Let us do our jobs and remain here for now."

"I'd rather take my chances. Especially if some of the rebels are disguised as members of Scales."

The Advocator shook his head and mumbled something rude but didn't argue further. He returned to bandaging someone. Besides us, there were maybe ten other survivors.

"There are rebels everywhere. How do you plan on getting out of here?" Sirash asked.

I grabbed a sharp stone and sketched a makeshift map of the east side of Hollow in the dust. "We're right in the middle of the Militia Quarter. The Ravens or Scales will block both bridges to the Isle and the eastern gates once they hear of the attack. So we have three options: the Rainbow District, the cemetery, or the wharf."

"The Rainbow District is blocked off, too. Some of the others tried going up there but got turned away," Jamal said with a nudge toward his home district, off in the distance.

"I think we should split up," I said. "We'll be less likely to be seen in twos."

Sirash agreed with me and then pointed at my makeshift map. "Arjay and I will take the wharf and then find Jean. We'll have to swim, and I'd rather not be responsible for Michael drowning today."

I grumbled to myself. "I'll learn how to swim eventually."

Jamal's face was serious. "That leaves us the cemetery, where the walls are as tall as eight full-grown men. How are we going to get over them and onto the battlements?"

"The wall is climbable. It'll be tough, but I think I know a place that shouldn't be too bad. And once we're on the battlements, my foster father will protect us."

An uneasy silence fell over us all. Our plan was dangerous and risky and based on limited information, but what else could we do?

"Are we doing the right thing?" Sirash asked. "Should we wait? We haven't seen any rebels since the initial attacks. Heard them, but—"

"I knew it!" the Advocator shouted, cutting Sirash off. "I told you all Scales would send reinforcements! Look! They even sent the Wardens! We're saved!"

A group of twenty or so people were walking toward us. They were dressed almost exactly like Wardens normally were: full dark-colored plate mail, curved-horn helmets, and massive spears across their back. The only thing missing was their stark white capes. It was part of their uniform, and they wouldn't go out anywhere, let alone a battle, without them.

"You thinking what I am?" I asked Sirash.

He nodded. "Time to go. Be careful out there."

"You too." I held my open palm out. "See you on the other side?"

Without hesitation Sirash took my hand and said, "See you under the stars."

I tried to warn the other survivors, but when it became clear they weren't listening, I grabbed Jamal's hand and we ran away before it was too late. We only ran faster when we heard their screams. I told myself I would have been braver if Jamal wasn't with me.

Jamal and I moved quickly and quietly through the district, avoiding anyone in a uniform and hiding whenever we heard yelling— or heard wails suddenly go silent. It helped that the rebels had no need for stealth, some of them even chanting about useless kings, corrupt nobility, the price of bread, and the need for the commoners to take back what was owed to them. I took their ideals less seriously every time I passed a body in the streets. If they wanted a revolution and a restructuring of power, killing the people who never had power to begin with wasn't the way to do it. It would happen only when the country moved on from that useless King Isaac, his Ravens, the surviving prince and princess, and all the High Nobles.

When we passed through the iron gates into the cemetery, I let go of the breath I had been holding while we had snuck through the district. The worst of it was over. With no people or property in here, there was no reason for the rebels to be here. Luck, for once, was on my side as we delved deeper into the unkempt areas of the cemetery. On our way to the wall, we'd have to pass by my father's grave.

Jamal held his stuffed dragon tightly. "I hope Trey doesn't cancel our chicken dinner plans because of what happened."

"He might. Or he might want to celebrate that we're both alive."

"Don't think I can remember the last time he was ever happy about something."

"What about that time he found a gold sun in the street?"

Jamal made an exaggerated sound of surprise. "Name another. But it's not like you're any different. When's the last time you've been happy about anything? Besides not going into an orphanage after your father was executed."

He wasn't wrong. My siblings and I had been relieved when we were put in Angelo's care almost immediately after our father was executed. No matter how useless the king was, even he knew it wouldn't be safe for us if we were still in public after the Kingman Keep riots. Those riots had killed enough . . .

"Michael," Jamal said as he tugged at me, "there's a problem."

"What're you—"

Then I saw what he meant. There were two rebels standing near my father's grave as another knelt in front of it, almost as if she was in prayer. A ridiculous thought or act for anyone who knew my family well enough. The Kingman family had been at war with God since Hollow had been founded.

We hid behind a dead tree. "What are we going to do, Michael?"

Something poked me in the back, almost in reply, and I felt hot breath on my neck. "You're going to raise your hands, nice and slow, and walk toward the others. Unless you want an iron ball in your spine."

I did as I was told, moving slowly toward the other rebels around my father's nameless grave in a field of weeds. Jamal followed me, even if a gun wasn't pointed against his spine, and his struggling and squirming drew the others' attention to us.

"Lookee what I found!"

A thin, pale man with the rebel symbol shaved into the side of his head smiled. "What're you doing? We don't need hostages. Wait, is that . . . ? Check the left side of his neck. Look for a brand."

"His neck?" the brutish rebel questioned. He grabbed my head and twisted it, exposing the crown brand. "I caught me a traitor! Best day ever!"

"Not just any traitor. That's Michael Kingman, the perfect replica of the great one."

The rebel was giddy. "I caught Michael Kingman! And look, his brand really is in the same spot as my tattoo. I should've believed you two. This must be a sign from God what we've done today is just."

The pale man approached me. He smelled like citrus despite all the mud and blood that covered his exposed skin. He squished my cheeks and covered my mouth with his hand. "Oh, having a Kingman is better than a sign from God. Em, come see him for yourself."

"You will never be forgotten and neither will your Sacrifice," the woman in front of my father's grave muttered, eyes closed, before walking over to us, as graceful as a dancer. A bold silver scar ran from below her right eye, along her jawline, to the bottom of her head and then disappeared beneath her high-collared shirt. She was gorgeous, in the most frightening way possible. "Michael, how long has it been since we've last seen each other?"

I had no idea who this woman was. I repeated that sentiment to her in a much more colorful way.

She giggled, and it made me shiver. "Oh, Michael. Always the rebel. Even before we existed. Have you come to join us?"

"I'd rather die."

She ran two fingers gently along my jawline. "So stubborn. You know, you look so much like your father. Are you sure you don't want to join us? Together we could restore the Kingman legacy."

"Restore the legacy? You're murdering innocent people. I don't think you get what my family stood—"

The woman grabbed my collar and pulled me closer. "We're the only ones *left* who understand. Our role in society is not an easy one, but it is necessary. We are here to rid the world of a tyrant whose regime will never end. Without this public spectacle, he would remain elusive, holed up in his fortress, indulging in wine and memories. But now we've done something he can't ignore. He will have to act or risk losing everything he has built. And then, once we have the opportunity, we'll bring about the next generation and eradicate any trace of the old."

"You really think you're going to get close to the king? After this?"

"Our goal is within sight. It's a shame you're as blind as the others. We could have been great together." She turned my head from side to side, examining me. "But maybe it's too soon for you to join us. I wonder . . . how much of your childhood do you remember?"

"Lady," I growled, "please shut the fuck up."

Another giggle, higher pitched than the last one. The other rebels even joined in, only stopping when she did. "I always suspected you didn't remember. I wonder what caused it . . . Was it a Darkness Fabrication? Or did you use your own Fabrications and lose the memories in the process? So many options. But there's still hope so long as you don't suffer the same affliction as your mother."

"I have no idea what you're talking about. I've never used Fabrications, I remember everything, and don't you fucking dare mention my mother again."

"Did I strike a nerve?" she asked with a smile. "You see, Michael, if you truly remembered everything, you'd be with us, fulfilling your father's wishes. Haven't you ever wondered why a Kingman killed a Royal? A child Royal, no less?" She put her hands behind her back and leaned close. "I'll tell you if you say my name."

When I didn't respond, she said, "Such a shame. I would ruin the surprise, but I'm worried it might do more harm than good. Thankfully, we'll meet again. Once you've remembered why your father truly killed the boy prince." She turned her back to me and waved goodbye. "But just so you don't forget this, kill the nobody."

My scream was drowned out by the gunshot, and Jamal's eyes went wide as he crumpled in place like wet paper, a bloodstain spreading across his back. The rebel behind me cackled, still holding the smoking gun as I threw my elbow back into his face and heard a crack as his nose broke. I turned and tackled the rebel into a tree and heard another crack and hoped it was his back. The pale rebel yanked me off him and then threw me against the ground next to Jamal, his friend's gun pointed at my chest. The woman hovered around me.

"Leave him," she ordered. "A Kingman is too valuable to waste, and I don't want him to die until he remembers who I am and why we fight."

They left me in that field of weeds in front of my father's grave, holding Jamal's body in my arms and begging him to wake up . . . saying it over and over and over again until the sun was low in the sky and Scales found me holding his dead body.

_____

Scales took us to some building that was too fancy and clean and structurally sound for us to belong in. They took Jamal away from me, despite my protests, and put me in a room that was dark and cold, and let an auburn-haired woman clean and bind my injuries while she hummed a lullaby to me . . . It was only after she left, taking her soothing lullaby with her, that the weight of what happened fell on my shoulders. I had Jamal's stuffed dragon clenched in my hands and wondered how I was going to tell my best friend his brother had died in front of me. And that I had been powerless to stop it.

The Wind Fabricator from the colosseum found me. She was closer to my age than I'd realized and dressed in the typical military uniform of the Executioner Division of Scales, the only differences between her uniform and that of an Advocator were that hers was colored white instead of purple, was incredibly dirty, and she had an emblem of two axes crossed over each other instead of the standard gold scales. There was also a gold crown insignia on her lapel, signaling her participation in the upcoming Endless Waltz.

"Michael," she said, without the typical iron in her voice that I expected from members of Scales. "My name is Naomi Dexter. We met earlier in the Militia Quarter after the explosion. I'm here to collect your statement. Are you ready?"

I nodded. My throat hurt. From screaming, from begging Jamal to live. I wondered what my voice would sound like when I spoke again.

"What happened?"

"Rebels," I croaked.

"I can't hear you."

"Rebels," I said louder. "They killed him."

"Can you tell me what happened?"

"There were three of them," I said as she opened a notebook and began to take notes. Did she have that the entire time? I hadn't seen her enter with it. "One of them looked like a bruiser, probably has a broken nose . . . maybe a broken back. The second was pale and sickly and smelled of citrus. The last was a woman, with a scar that covered most of her face."

"Tell me more about the man who smelled like citrus."

"What about him?"

"Anything. A name or place or a passing thought. Anything he said about their plans. Anything that could help us capture him."

"If I knew anything important, I would tell you," I said, voice straining. I was holding back tears, just thinking about what had happened in the graveyard made me remember Jamal and . . . and . . . and . . .

Naomi put her pencil down on the desk and reached across to take my hands in hers. They were warm despite all the grime. "I know this is difficult to talk about, and I'm sorry about your friend, Michael. These rebels have taken a lot from all of us. I . . . I don't like to talk about it much, but they killed my mother in Naverre. Ever since then I've made it my goal in life to stop these people from hurting anyone ever again. So, please, can you go over what they said to you? You're one of our best leads right now, and, truthfully, you might be our only hope at stopping them once and for all."

I steeled myself and exhaled. I scrounged my memory for anything that might be helpful so this could never happen to anyone else ever again. "The pale man barely spoke to me. But the woman—"

"Stay on the pale man." She squeezed my hand. "What did he say to you? Tell me the specifics. Maybe something that doesn't seem important to you will mean something to me."

"Others were there. Why are you so interested in one man?"

"Because reports in the past led me to believe that was the Emperor, the rebel leader. Do you know anything about him or not?"

"No, I don't. I'm sorry."

Naomi let go of my hands ever so slowly before leaning back in her seat, arms crossed. "They left no other witness. Did they give you any reason to explain why you were allowed to live?"

"They said because I was a Kingman, and too valuable to kill."

"Why would you be too valuable to kill?"

"I don't know," I said, head pounding.

A silence, and she made another note. "Be honest with me, Michael. Are you working with the rebels?"

"What?" I responded. "How could you ask me that? I'm a Kingman, and Kingman don't kill—"

"Children?" she snapped. "Your father might disagree."

"I am not my father."

"The rebel who triggered the explosion did so in your father's name. You were there, and you left the colosseum to meet the Rebel Emperor at your father's grave. That's beyond a coincidence."

"I go to Kingman Day every year. I was there with my friends. We were trying to escape, when we were caught in the attack . . . I was trying to protect Jamal and get to the battlements. We were caught by the rebels by accident and they—"

Naomi leaned closer to me, and there was something in the way she looked at me that I couldn't quite determine. "The future doesn't look good for you, Michael. You left your district to be a part of an attack in your father's name. You refused to come with me for questioning. You have minimal injuries, as if you knew where to be when the explosions went off. Your mysterious, potentially rebel friends are nowhere to be found, and you've admitted to being at a meeting with the Rebel Emperor. You're a rebel. Admit it."

I had underestimated her. Badly. "Is this why you helped me get out of the ruins? To frame me for the attack?" I couldn't help but smile at my own naïveté. "Did your mother even die in Naverre?"

"Would you even believe me if I said no?"

Before I could respond, the door behind Naomi flew open, and my foster father stormed in. "Naomi, I told you no one was to question Michael Kingman without me in the room. Leave before I decide to file this foolish slip of your judgment as insubordination."

She stood, chair screeching behind her, and saluted Angelo. "Sir, he was about to confess—"

"Don't make me repeat myself."

Naomi left the room, eyes and head down, while Angelo took her seat. "Days like these make me wish I hadn't given up drinking. Anything you want to tell me?"

"I was only trying to protect my friend. How much trouble am I in?"

He drummed his fingers against the table. "It's difficult to say. It looks suspicious on paper, compounded by your meeting the Emperor, and Naomi is keen to place the blame on you. Only that boy's death shows your innocence . . . though it would help if a family member could confirm you were friends. I should've been here sooner. I'm sorry, Michael."

"Lyon?" I asked.

"Safe. Worried but safe."

"Did they attack you on the wall?"

"No, they snuck into Hollow somehow. The fighting was confined to the Militia Quarter."

My mind felt fuzzy, so all I did was nod in response. "What happens now?"

"You won't be held. I've convinced my superiors to put you on probation for a month. Like how it was when you first came to live with me. But if Scales finds any evidence to suggest you're working with the rebels—or if you're caught fighting, robbing, trespassing, or even refusing their questions—they'll arrest and then likely execute you."

"By hanging or by cutting off my head?"

Angelo slammed his closed fist against the table. "Will you take this seriously, Michael? They could charge you with treason!"

I already had the brand on my neck; getting charged for it

wouldn't matter. And at this point my brand, and my infamous family, had already kept me alive more times than I deserved. It was only a matter of time until someone noticed it too late—or didn't care when they did. I'd been hung from a tree, caught in the middle of an explosion, and held at gunpoint in the past day and only had bruises, burns, ringing ears, and cuts to show for it.

Except . . . except now I was to blame for Jamal's death. I'd been looking after him. Would Trey ever be able to forgive me?

Angelo moved from his seat and gave me a hug, a warm, tight embrace I needed in that moment. "It'll be all right, son. It'll be all right. It wasn't your fault."

Angelo stayed with me until the tears had dried up and I could speak complete sentences again. He was there for me in that moment and made the pain bearable. It was something my father had never been able to do. Not after he chose ambition over family. With no other reason to keep me there and more work to do than ever, Angelo showed me where Jamal's body was and then escorted me out of the building—Scales Headquarters, I discovered—and released me back into the wild.

There was normalcy in Justice Hill, and only the black smoke across the river indicated what had happened to the colosseum and the Militia Quarter. Just the sight of it was enough to make me want to crawl into bed and never leave.

But, I couldn't. I had to keep moving forward.

It was time to change things. I'd become a pawn for nobles and rebels, and an obvious scapegoat for Scales . . . and my battle to protect my family month to month for ten years had left me with nothing but an everlasting hatred for those in power. If I truly wanted to contribute to the Kingman legacy and be remembered, I had to figure out how to protect myself.

And even though I didn't like the risk of learning how to use Fabrications, I would have to know how to use them. Because maybe, if I did, things in the graveyard with the rebels would have gone differently. Maybe Jamal would still be alive.

If I was lucky, maybe I'd even be able to find a magical cure for my mother's condition. Or determine why I didn't remember that rebel woman.

But before I could learn how to use Fabrications, I had to find Trey.

Armed with a stuffed dragon, I made my way to Margaux Keep.

THE FORGOTTEN BOY

Despite being born on the wrong side of the river with a skin tone that made him feel isolated no matter where he was, Trey had survived for eighteen years on his own. For more than a decade he'd had his younger brother at his side—the only thing worth a damn his parents had ever given him. And he was only interviewing to join a High Noble Fabricator army to give Jamal a better life. He would never be the same once he heard what had happened.

I was frightened he would go after the rebels, using his untrained skills, and lose his memories of Jamal in the process. That fear was ever-present as I made my way to Margaux Keep to find him; it wasn't news that should wait. Trey deserved to know, and to hear it from me.

Thankfully for me, anyone could watch the selection process for the High Noble Fabricator armies so long as they paid to get in. Thus, despite the fact I looked like a tweeker, in bloodied, dirtied clothes, the female guard took my silver moon and let me enter the keep. Although anyone could attend, I couldn't imagine that included the traitorous Kingman children. So I kept my head down, hid Jamal's stuffed dragon in my pocket, and did my best to avoid anyone that looked too important.

Which was hard to do. The public spaces were filled with the High Noble families in attendance for the selection process—even the Braven family, which was odd, as they generally only participated in religious events. Everyone who wasn't a High Noble was a merchant, a foreign ambassador, a high-ranking member of Scales, or a Mercenary.

It was clear that if Kingman Day in the colosseum was to entertain the commoners, hand out survival rations, and watch rebels die, then the selection process for the nobility was defined by excess. The hallways were lined with long tables stacked high with the kinds of rich, decadent food that Angelo would have a hard time turning down. There was even a fountain filled with wine instead of water at the entrance, and everyone was dressed in colorful silk or lace or leather, tailored in the latest fashion—which included short capes for some asinine reason. Maybe I had always misunderstood this event; I had assumed it was a test to gauge Fabricator aptitude, not a party.

I was clearly wrong, but only when I reached the ballroom did I see the true horror of what was going on.

There was no test or evaluation by master Fabricators . . . This was a fucking auction. The applicants were standing on display, being poked and prodded and ordered to show off their skills. Those from Low Noble families wore their sigils. Those who lacked a noble title wore a thick metal chain on one of their wrists instead, and I hated to think what that was meant to signify.

As I searched for Trey, I couldn't help but watch as different Fabricators demonstrated their abilities on the main stage. I saw a commoner Wind Fabricator conjure up a gust of wind to make capes and dresses flutter wildly. Then I saw a Low Noble Fire Fabricator summon a ball of fire and juggle with it like he was a jester. There was even an Ice Fabricator who created an elegant dress for a marble statue. If it weren't so barbaric, treating these Fabricators like attractions and auctioning them off, I might have been in awe of their gifts.

When an auction-goer wanted to bid on a Fabricator, they called over a strange person in a ridiculously tall hat. From what I saw, the going rate for a Lightning Fabricator who already had some control was roughly two hundred suns, while a Lightning Fabricator with barely any control was triple that. I couldn't help but wonder where the money was going, because none of that was going to end up in Trey's pocket.

The Low Nobles were treated differently from the commoners. Most of them seemed to already have a position guaranteed in the armies of the High Nobles their families pledged allegiance to, and rather than being visibly confused and nervous, they attempted to convince other families how useful they would be to drive their price down and their position up. Their specializations were the biggest leverage they had. The High Noble Solarin family was actively avoiding any Fire Fabricators, while the Bravens were talking only to them.

It sickened me to be in there, so it was a relief to see Trey in one corner, alone on a raised platform. I was stunned that he was still participating in this monstrosity; I wouldn't have been able to bear it.

Before I could say anything to him, one of the men in the pointy hats along with two High Nobles—one from the Andel family and another from the Castlen—made their way over to Trey. I held back and waited for them to leave.

"This is applicant fifty-five," the pinhead said. "Born on the East Side in the Rainbow District. Mother passed recently, and his father is unknown and likely the source of him being able to use Light Fabrications. Reserve price is eight hundred suns."

High Noble Andel crossed his arms as he looked Trey up and down. "Does the applicant have any combat experience?"

"Minimal, High Noble Andel. Hand-to-hand primarily."

"A shame," he said. The High Noble pinched Trey's biceps and almost got rewarded with a backhand. "Plenty of muscle. A few months with the Weapon Master should make him good enough to wield a sword. But I'd want him to specialize soon after. Maybe with a mace or short spear."

"Why waste such a remarkably rare Fabrication specialization on combat training?" the other High Noble questioned. "Have him begin training at the Hawthorn Medical College immediately. If the applicant shows promise, marry him into one of the Low Noble families under us. Keep his talent close by."

Trey exhaled and closed his eyes as the High Nobles continued to squabble about his future. When he opened his eyes, he saw me and said, "Michael? What . . . Are you . . . wait, where's Jamal?"

I had rehearsed the words over and over and over again until saying them should have been as easy as breathing. But seeing my friend's face had knocked them out of me. Wordlessly, I held Jamal's singed dragon out to him.

He took the dragon from my hands, seeing the dried blood on it. "Where's my brother?"

"Rebels attacked the Militia Quarter," I said, my voice shaking. "Attacked Kingman Day. I tried to protect him, but . . . but . . ."

He had the dragon in a death grip. "Where is my brother?"

The tears wouldn't fall down my face, but my eyes were red and my throat ached all the same. "Scales Headquarters. They have his body there. Trey, I'm so sorry. I'm so sorry."

"Applicant," the pointy-hatted man said as he snapped his fingers, "show us your Light Fabrications. We need to make sure you're not lying about your specialization."

Trey wobbled, eyes glazed over. Had the High Nobles not heard what just happened?

"Applicant. Get on with it already," he repeated.

Trey muttered something to himself.

"Applicant!" one of the High Noble's shouted. "Are you blind? Deaf? Either show us your Fabrications right now or—"

"My apologies, High Noble," Trey declared, standing straight. "I'll show you my light."

The sun was dimmer.

Everything went white, Trey's wails and sobs all that could be heard.

"Trey!" I screamed through the light, my face flushed and body warm.

The light vanished in an instant, but I had to blink repeatedly to regain clarity.

Trey broke there and then, folding over as he clutched the dragon, as if it would disappear if he let it go. His performance had drawn a different kind of crowd now. Even the High Nobles who had been interested in him backed away, perceiving what had happened as uncontrollable recklessness. Out of the corner of my eye, I saw a girl in a red dress with an Endless Waltz patch part the horde to get a better view, watching carefully. Others in the crowd had already turned away or were openly mocking Trey, and she gently but firmly turned a few away from the scene.

When Trey, huddled on the floor, could form words again, he said, "Why? Why would they kill him?"

I was helpless before his grief and told him everything. The attack, the explosion, our escape through the quarter and into the cemetery, the rebels' careless ruthlessness . . . even, in my shock, because I blamed myself for Jamal's death, the rebel's final words: that I lived because I was a Kingman and that I was too valuable to die until I remembered everything.

I had barely finished when he uncoiled like a whip and punched me in the jaw, and only as I landed on my ass, him standing over me, face neutral, did I realize how it must have sounded.

"I trusted you. You were my friend. And you're the reason my brother is dead." Trey seized me by my collar and held my face close to his. "I lost everything because of you."

"Trey, please, let me explain."

"Explain what? Explain that my brother's life wasn't as valuable as yours? That he deserved to die so you could live?"

"Trey, that's not what I—"

"Shut the fuck up!" he screamed. "My brother is dead! And it's all your fault, you High Noble prick!"

"Treyvon Wiccard!" The girl in a red dress was approaching us. "The way you're acting is not becoming of a Fabricator for a High Noble family. The auction is almost over, so get yourself under con—"

"As if I care anymore. I only wanted to know how to control my Fabs because of my brother," he said, choking on the words. "I could only survive *this* to give my brother a better life. But now? Now I refuse to bow to anyone.

"Michael," Trey continued, facing me, the crowd around us no longer of interest to him, "I will avenge my brother. You're responsible for my brother's death. You destroyed my family. So I will destroy yours, and your precious legacy. You will be the last Kingman."

It wasn't befitting for a Kingman to beg, but I did anyway, desperate for my friend to forgive me. "Trey—"

"Do you hear me, Kingman?"

"Are you finished, Treyvon?" the girl in red demanded. "After this outburst, what High Noble family do you think will take you in their army and teach you how to use Fabrications?"

"I can still think of one that would." Trey looked down at me. "Goodbye, Kingman. Enjoy the time with your brother and sister while you can."

Trey stormed away, hugging Jamal's stuffed dragon. I would have followed him, but I couldn't stop shaking and I doubted I could find the words that would make any of this better. If there were any at all.

Maybe with some time to grieve he wouldn't be so angry . . . but if our positions were reversed and Gwen had died, would I be able to forgive him?

I had no chance to ponder it. The girl in red dismissed the crowds with a flick of her wrist as she went to my side, kneeling next to me even if it meant staining her dress. She spoke quickly and softly.

"Are you well?" she asked. "What happened? Why did he threaten you?"

"I'm fine," I lied. "It's between us. No one else."

"I see," she said. "While I would have preferred different circumstances, it is good to see you again, Michael. Even if I do wonder why you ignored all my attempts to contact you."

Still in a daze, I said without thinking, "You are who, again?"

She slapped me. Hard. Hard enough to forget what had happened between Trey and me and focus on her instead. The girl in red was biting the bottom of her lip with her nostrils flared. Both of her fists were clenched, and I thought she might hit me again.

"Would you like to try that again?" she asked.

"Not if you're going to slap me again."

She didn't. This time she whacked my stomach and I returned to the ground. I had never been hit that hard. It left me breathless and wide-eyed, and it wasn't even a punch.

"We were childhood friends before you disappeared after your father's execution. I thought we were best friends, but you vanished, cut us all out, so clearly I was wrong. What, did you think your old life ceased to exist after your father died?"

I mumbled something, squinting at her, hoping her appearance would trigger my memory. She was shorter than most Hollow-born women, had three stars tattooed behind her left ear, and there was something about how her brown hair was twirled upward in a messy bun that seemed familiar. Was it similar to one of the styles Gwen sometimes put her own hair in?

"Don't try to claim that you've forgotten me because of Fabrications either," she said. "Treyvon would have mentioned it, or someone would've noticed if you used them involuntarily. Almost all Fabrications are visual in nature."

"Besides the ones that aren't, which I still wouldn't know about."

"Do you want me to hit you again?" she asked.

I didn't, so I considered my next words carefully. Despite having no idea who she was, I said, "I'm sorry."

"For?"

"For everything. I'm sorry I don't remember you and therefore didn't contact you at all for all those years."

She folded her arms, clearly expecting more.

"It's been a struggle to survive since my father died. My life was destroyed in a day; everyone seemed to turn against us—especially after the riots in Kingman Keep. It never occurred to me to think anyone else that didn't share a last name with me was affected—that anyone was worried about us or wanted to find us. I know that doesn't explain why I don't remember anything about you . . . but I'm willing to start over if you are. I'm not sure you'll like who I am or can be around someone you thought a friend when they can't remember you, but if you're up for it, so am I."

Her expression changed; she blushed and avoided my gaze. "I . . . I think I owe you an apology, too. I shouldn't have hit you. Your comments caught me off guard and I reacted badly. I thought time had healed those wounds, but in the end I was once again an insecure eight-year-old girl who thought she had been abandoned. I am very embarrassed, to say the least."

"We all have our moments."

"Yes, we do." The girl in red hit her cheeks lightly, regaining some of her composure. "Anyway, would you like to go somewhere more private and begin anew? My duties here are nearly over, and there's a lot to talk about after ten years."

"I would love to, but after what just happened with Trey, I—"

"Oh my God, I am such a selfish prick. I completely forgot, and—"

"It's fine," I said. "Really. But I need to go deal with things. We'll talk another time."

"Yes. Go. Another time."

After giving me a quick, awkward hug, she left me and returned to the Fabricator auction. It was only after she was out of sight that I realized I never got her name or really had any idea who she was. Just like the rebel woman.

It was beginning to become clear to me that something had happened to my memories. But why was I only noticing it now? Had it happened recently? Or had it happened a long time ago? Or was I just being conned by someone? Two in one day couldn't be coincidence . . . could it?

I didn't know.

Regardless of how much my heart ached for Trey, there was nothing I could do to help him until he had time to grieve. But there was something I could do, and it meant not squandering an opportunity Jamal had always been envious of.

It was time I paid Gwen and High Noble Charles Domet a visit in the asylum.

THE REGRETFUL MAN

"You need a bath," Gwen said. "I could save the water for you if you want."

I shook my head as I stood in the door to one of the inmates' rooms, watching my sister wash a fully grown man with a sponge and a bucket of water. The man was sitting in the middle of a ring of candles, focused on making sure no drops of water put the flames out. Which seemed unnecessary, as there were candles on every surface of the room, from the floor to the desk to the bed. And where there was no candle, dried wax was in its place.

"It's been a long day," I said.

"Who was it this time? Advocators? Wardens? Evokers?" Gwen looked down at her patient. "Blackwell, raise your arm, please."

The man did exactly as he was told, eyes fixed on his candles.

"Rebels," I said.

She looked up at me, sponge in one hand, holding Blackwell's with the other. "Rebels? Where?"

"They attacked the Militia Quarter. Jamal and I got caught in the cross fire. I'd tell you which cuts and bruises were from last night and which were from today, but I don't really know . . . Jamal is dead. They killed him."

In shock, Gwen dropped Blackwell's hand and it fell into the water. The splash extinguished a few of the candles and sent the man into a panic. "My light! Oh, God. They'll come for me if it's dark." With no warning, his hands became gauntlets of fire, making Gwen swear and jump back as he lifted one shaking hand and held it over the wick of each candle in turn until it ignited.

"I can't deal with this right now," Gwen muttered as she dried and dressed Blackwell. After she was out of the room and the door was locked behind her, she had a flurry of questions: "Rebels? Is that what that black smoke across the river is from? My employer said the noble they were executing for Kingman Day got out and had caused a scene. Are you well? Are Lyon, Angelo, and Trey safe? Did you see the rebels in person? Did you fight them? Wait. You went to Kingman Day! What were you thinking after what happened last year?"

"Angelo is safe—frantic but safe. Haven't heard from Lyon, but Angelo said he was worried but well. Trey is . . . I don't know how he is. I told him what had happened and he . . . he . . . he snapped." The tears wouldn't come. No matter how much they ought to have. "I failed him. I should have protected Jamal from them . . . As for why they did it or what they were after . . . I have no idea. It seemed like they just wanted to kill people."

Gwen drew her scarf up over her mouth, a habit she'd had for years, muffling every word that followed. "I didn't expect them to attack the city. I thought the king would've dealt with them by now."

"He's had seven years to deal with them after they annexed Naverre. Their numbers are increasing and they're running wild in the countryside. I'm not surprised they got into Hollow. I just didn't think it would be today."

"Do you . . . ," she began, hesitating. "Do you think Scales will start a conscription?"

"After one attack on the East Side? Doubtful. They don't know enough about them: not who the Rebel Emperor is, how many of them there are, where they're located aside from Naverre and the encampment near the walls, or even what their goals are. It would be too soon for a conscription."

She let out a deep breath in relief. "Good. Good. So, not that I question your brotherly affection, but why are you here?"

"Charles Domet."

A raised eyebrow. "What about him?"

"I want the job."

"No fucking way. You *actually* want the job?"

I rubbed the back of my neck. "Yes."

She was shocked, beyond being able to hide it on her face. After a few heartbeats her shock turned into acceptance . . . and I had the cold shock of realizing I knew nothing about this job except for the pay—and that I hoped Domet might teach me to use Fabrications.

"Then you should talk to him about it." She looked me up and down again. "Maybe tomorrow, after you've had—"

"No. I should do this tonight."

"Why?" she asked. "You must be exhausted after what happened. Don't you need to rest?"

I didn't know how to tell her the truth. That what had happened in the Militia Quarter and graveyard had changed me. That I was scared more people I cared about would get hurt. That I wouldn't be able to rest until I knew I could protect my family. I had already lost Jamal, and maybe Trey; I couldn't lose anyone else. No matter how badly my body screamed for a reprieve, I had to keep moving forward. So I lied.

"I need something to focus on," I said. "The worst thing I can do is sit in my room alone thinking about Jamal. It'll only make his death . . . his death harder to accept. This way I'm productive."

"Michael, I don't—"

I put a hand on her shoulder and smiled. "I'm fine, I promise."

I didn't lie to Gwen, and she didn't lie to me. It had been that way since our father was executed. So, despite the obvious signs that should have shown her I was anything but fine, she accepted my truth.

Love was blinding sometimes.

"It wouldn't hurt to talk to him tonight," she conceded. "His paperwork would have to be completed before he left anyway. You would be able to rest while that was filled out."

"Then there's no harm." I made a sweeping gesture. "Lead the way."

The asylum was one of my least favorite places. I hated how the walls seemed to close in on us the further we made our way inward, twisting and contorting as the slabs of stone it was built around became more and more distorted. It was like being in an underground dungeon. The eerie scratching didn't help either. When my mother had come here, I'd thought an asylum would be filled with moaning or screaming or noise. But this one wasn't, and it always made me more paranoid to be in it—as if one of the doors would open and I'd be dragged into a room and be a silent prisoner here forever.

It wasn't long before Gwen stopped in front of a metal door with the number 27 engraved on it.

"First," she said, and she emphasized each point by holding up a finger, "you know Domet is rich. No one knows how or why. Almost all of the nobility have debts to him, and if they don't currently, they did in the past. Second, being here has had no effect on his social power or presence in the Hollow Court. Someone will likely host a party for him when he's released. Lastly, he's an alcoholic. You can't stop him from drinking—just make sure he doesn't die."

"Is that why he's in here?" I asked. "I didn't think the asylum dealt with addiction."

"It doesn't. But it's the only explanation I ever found for his stay."

Gwen reached for the key ring that hung from her belt, picked out one that resembled canine teeth, inserted it, and then opened the door with a loud crunching of tumblers. There was a flash of light, and I looked away until my eyes adjusted, and began to understand who and what Charles Domet was. His room was beyond elegant, with a plush white carpet, a large feather bed, and a cabinet stocked well enough to rival most bars in the city. The light that had caught me off guard came through a large window directly in the middle of the wall. It was the first window I'd seen in the asylum.

Charles Domet sat in a big pink chair reading a book with a half-empty bottle of rum and a wolf's-head cane at his side. He had the refined look of a High Noble, the build of a farmer, and a breathtakingly fierce gaze. He set his book aside with a snap. "Gwen, darling, how are you today? Who have you brought with you?"

She curtsied to him. "I'm doing well, High Noble Domet. This is my brother Michael."

He grabbed his cane, levered himself up, and limped closer to us, favoring his right leg. We were of equal height, yet he seemed to overshadow me with his presence alone. "An honor, Michael King-man. And if will you excuse my bluntness, what brings you to see me today?"

My sister answered for me. "He's here about being your companion once you leave the asylum, High Noble Domet."

"Excellent! No offense, my dearest, but I was getting quite bored of the atmosphere in here. And it's a little cold, or is that just me?"

"It *is* cold, High Noble Domet. The weather has brought great-coats back into style."

Domet put a hand on my sister's shoulder. "Much obliged for the tip. But, Gwen, my dear, they will follow my fashions. Not the reverse. Michael, let us be off. There is plenty I want to do with my newfound freedom."

Elegantly, Domet sidestepped us and left the room. Gwen and I followed, caught off guard by his sudden departure.

"High Noble Domet!" my sister exclaimed. "I haven't explained my brother's duties yet."

He didn't even glance back. "No need, my darling. I've done this before, I will explain on the way. He can always check with you later. Come along, Michael, we are very, very late already."

"What about the paperwork? Or your things? What should I do with them?"

High Noble Domet flicked Gwen a gold sun. "Handle it for me. I'll send the staff a crate of wine as an apology for my sudden departure. And leave the things where they are: Who knows when I'll need another vacation?"

I glanced at my sister. She mouthed an apology and shooed me after him, so I followed Domet out of the asylum. He threw money at anyone who questioned what he was doing, destroying the asylum's rigorous safety procedures without care. Once we were outside, he gripped the sides of his coat, closed his eyes, and took a deep breath. "Smell that, Michael? It's fish guts, sulfur, and bad perfume. Hollow still stinks, just as I remembered. Except for the sulfur—it wasn't as strong when I was younger."

I didn't know how to respond. I had expected him to say the city smelt like freedom or berries or something nice, not to be truthful about it. From his reputation, he didn't sound like the honest type. "Are you going to tell me what the terms of my employment are?"

"No," he declared, and headed for the Upper Quarter. With no other option, I followed.

We walked in an even silence, which meant he never shut up and I never spoke. Domet found all manner of topics intriguing and was perfectly capable of carrying the conversation all by himself. He discussed politics, religion, and even how he was thinking about creating his own brand of wine. Frequently throughout the walk he would take a flask out from his jacket and drink from it until his breath turned pungently sour.

Before we reached the Upper Quarter, he forced a flower stand to open as I waited a few paces away beside a scarred cobbler fixing a pair of shoes. Domet must have examined every single flower, asking the florist to add one type to his bouquet and then asking him to remove it moments later. It took so long I could've asked the cobbler to deal with my torn-up boots. I was close to falling asleep by the time Domet made his choice. He set off again with a bouquet of Moon's Tears and morning glories—the sunrise and sunset flowers.

"What are those for?" I asked. "Are they for a lady?"

My question was met with a chuckle. "Not *a* lady, *the* lady."

Any of my other questions after that were met with a curt response. As we passed through the gates to the Upper Quarter—the Advocators who guarded them barely noticing I was with Domet—I realized it had been years since I was last there. Unlike other parts of the city, which still showed the damage from the Gunpowder War of a quarter century ago and the scars from weekly moon-fall, the Upper Quarter was immaculate. The air tasted sweet, the buildings were uniform, and the cobblestone pathways were smooth compared to the sharp stone that filled the rest of the city. A constant reminder that they were distinct from the other parts of the city. Seemingly superior.

As we approached the city walls, Domet led me down an alley and into a courtyard that held the shrine of Patron Victoria. Tucked away between tall buildings, it was a green and mossy nook in a stone-and-brick jungle. At the heart of it stood a patchwork temple on a small island surrounded by murky water, with a single marble walkway leading out to it. I had never seen one of her shrines so beautifully preserved before. They were usually broken-down and decrepit, much like the elderly followers Patron Victoria seemed to attract.

Domet stopped before crossing the bridge, seeing a pair of delicate silver sandals on the marble. "It seems the Lady already has a visitor."

"So?"

He glanced at me, the lines in his face deepening into a frown. "So we must wait for them to finish. It's unlucky for both parties to interrupt another's time with Patron Victoria."

"But it's fine to take a flask into the shrine?"

Domet took the flask out of his pocket and gulped down whatever remained. Afterward his lips were glistening. Shaking the flask, he said, "There. Done. No more."

"Are you ever going to explain why we're here or what I have to do with you for this job?"

"I suppose I should explain. You will visit me at my house in the Upper Quarter—the redbrick one opposite Conqueror Fountain with amaranth in front of it—every day for the next month and check I've not died with a bottle in my mouth. I'll give you your five suns every day for that. Easy money."

"That's it?" I asked.

"That's it," he reaffirmed.

"Why not tell me that in the asylum?"

Domet touched his hand against his chin. "I suppose I wanted some company. You can leave if you wish." He rummaged in his pockets until he'd pulled out five gold suns and handed them to me.

"I'll see you tomorrow, Michael Kingman. Show up whenever, I'll either be drinking or sleeping."

I weighed the coins in my hand. It was so much, and for doing so little. There must've been a catch. I just couldn't see it, lost within the con he was ensnaring me in. But, tempted as I was just to walk away, I needed more than money from him. "You're a Fabricator, right?"

"Why?"

"I want to learn."

Domet rolled his eyes. "Join one of the High Noble Fabricator armies."

"I can't . . . I tried to join a few of them and they all rejected me," I lied. "They all claimed the king would have their heads if they helped a Kingman learn how to use Fabrications. But you're Charles Domet. No one tells you what to do . . . even the king."

That elicited a smile from him. "You actually tried to join some of the armies? Interesting. I didn't quite expect that."

"Are you that surprised? My brother joined Scales despite being a Kingman."

"Yes," Domet said, "but the nobility didn't give him an option. They needed a dog on a chain to show the commoners no one was above justice. I would've thought you to be too proud to seek out help from the nobility."

"I do what I must."

"Enlighten me: Why do you want to learn? Magic isn't quite what the stories claim, you know. One mistake, and you can become a Forgotten. The price is rarely worth the payoff, when there are so many better ways to get what you want."

"I'm aware," I said. "But I don't have any other choice. With everything that's going on in the city, I need to know how to protect my family." I thought of the rebel woman specifically. "Whatever the cost."

"Do you mean that, truly?" he said quickly. "Whatever the cost? What about attacking your adversaries before they could strike against you? Would you go that far to protect those you cared about? If so, we can make a deal, Michael. A favor for a favor."

My face felt flushed. I had worked so hard to ensure I was in debt to as few people as possible . . . and now I was considering entering an agreement with High Noble Charles Domet, a behemoth even among the other High Nobles. But I had to try for my family. And if it didn't work, I'd have done everything I could. Jamal would be proud of me then. "What do you want?"

"Enter the Endless Waltz—not for a political marriage, Michael—but to uncover the truth about your father. I know he was set up by a Royal or a High Noble; I just don't know which one. Oh, don't look so shocked. I didn't end up in the asylum because I was drinking or from memory loss . . . It was to silence me. I was getting too close to the truth."

Who had enough power to silence Domet? Let alone put him in the asylum? It seemed impossible—as did his assertion that my father had been set up. He was lying . . . right?

The whisper of bare feet on marble interrupted my thoughts, and I turned to see a young woman, just a year or two older than me, wearing a short dark-blue dress with her frizzy black hair falling to her shoulders.

"High Noble Domet. I wasn't expecting that you would be released from the asylum so soon. I apologize if I kept you waiting to see Patron Victoria."

"There's no need for apologies, Chloe. I have nowhere to be, though I thought you and your mother followed the Wanderer's teachings."

Chloe glanced away to the right, caught off guard. "We do . . . or my mother does. I don't know what I believe yet. I take the Ravens' test tomorrow and hoped seeing Patron Victoria would calm me."

My eyes widened. This frail-looking woman wanted to join the King's Royal Guard? Compared to Ravens I had seen, Chloe was a leaf in the wind.

Domet awkwardly patted her on the back. "I have the utmost faith in you. You're Efyra's daughter, after all."

I held my tongue, hoping my thoughts were not visible on my face.

"We will see," she said, catching my eyes and changing the subject. "And who is this, High Noble Domet? I'm unfamiliar with your companion."

Domet stepped between us. "High Noble Chloe Mason, let me introduce you to—"

"Michael Kingman," I interrupted, standing straighter. "Youngest son to David Kingman."

"My mother told me about your family," she said.

"Before or after she executed my father and took his place by the king?"

She met my gaze levelly, only the sounds of nature and the city around us. "Not all of us were raised on the same stories," she said with a tight smile. Then: "You must excuse me. The Ravens' tournament starts early tomorrow, and I have much to do before then. I wish you well, Michael Kingman." Chloe slipped into her silver sandals and began to walk away. "I hope we meet again on better terms."

When she was out of sight, I returned to Domet and said, "Explain."

"I thought it was clear. Your father was framed for the murder of Davey Hollow by a Royal or a High Noble. If you help me prove it, I'll teach you how to use Fabrications."

"Do you have any proof?"

"Beyond circumstantial? No."

"Why should I believe you, then?"

Domet extended his arms, as if welcoming me in for a hug. "That's the beauty of it, Michael. You don't have to. All you need to do is investigate for me, and if I'm wrong, then it is what it is. Help me and I'll give you five suns a day for a month, teach you the basics of Fabrications, and you know what? I'll even get your mother out of that asylum and placed somewhere she'll be properly cared for. It would be a new start for your sister, too—free to be something, not just pay the bills."

My heart felt like it was going to burst. I had expected nothing when I agreed to take the job, and Domet was offering me everything. "Why do you care about my father and what happened to him?"

"Years ago I made the mistake of remaining silent when I shouldn't have. I knew your father was innocent . . . but I wasn't in a position where I could defend him. Too much wine and vodka made me weak. No one would have believed me. But now I've recovered and can do something about it." He took a deep breath. "I can't die until I've made up for my inaction back then. Some days I worry my mistake may have been the catalyst of our country moving from a global power to a forgotten mess."

"Alright, but why do I have to join the Endless Waltz? If they wouldn't let me join a Fabricator army, why would they let me join something much more prestigious?"

"You let me worry about those details. I'll get you into it one way or another. And isn't it obvious why you have to join the Endless Waltz to investigate what happened? We live in a country where the nobility has access to magic that takes away their memories, and then you have a king, scared of how he'll be remembered once he's gone, censoring history to paint him and his decisions in a better light. The truth about your father is locked away in his memories. Thus, only one option is feasible: you're going to steal them while pretending to take part in the Endless Waltz. It will give you all the access and opportunity you need."

I backed away from him, light-headed. "This is insane. You're insane. Do you realize what I'd face if I participated in the Endless Waltz? Let alone attempting to steal from the king?"

"You'd be claiming your birthright. Are you a Kingman or a coward?"

I was a survivor, and returning to the world of the nobility wasn't surviving. It was charging headfirst into a fire. But he was offering so much in return: care for my mother, freedom for Gwen, the chance to use Fabrications, and money. Could I really turn it all down?

"I'll do it on one condition," I said.

Domet gestured for me to continue.

"If something happens to me, you take care of my friends and family. You swear they won't have to worry about a thing for the rest of their lives. That includes my mother, Gwen, Lyon, Angelo, and my friends Sirash, Arjay, Jean, Ja—" I gulped. "And Trey."

"Deal." Domet offered his hand. "Do you want a blood oath, or will my word suffice?"

Blood oaths were a pointless gesture and had been broken so many times in Kingman history that someone's word was more valuable. Especially a High Noble's.

"Your word is fine."

We shook on it. And just like that, it was too late to worry about what I had agreed to.

THE MAN WHO CAME
THROUGH THE WINDOW

I left Domet at the shrine. I had never been one to care for deities, or prophets, or patrons, or God, and he didn't seem to mind, preferring to spend as long as he wanted without worry.

Not that I truly suspected he would care about me if I had chosen to wait.

On my way home I stopped by the public baths in the Student Quarter, since they were the only ones open past Lights Out. It was nearly abandoned, most people preferring to stay inside after everything that had happened on the east side of Hollow. It took me a long time to clean all the blood, mud, sweat, and dust off me, and even longer to get all the shards of glass and stone lodged under my nails out. Afterward they looked as if I had bitten them to the nub.

No one else was home when I returned, so I did the household laundry, ate as much pickled food as I could stomach, and was in the middle of wondering if I should go look for Trey, when Sirash banged on my window. I opened it and he tumbled in frantically and straight into a hug. I was thankful I hadn't lost him, too.

"Jamal?" he asked as we separated.

"Rebels shot him."

"Oh, Michael. How's Trey handling it? How are you?"

I filled Sirash in, a wave of nausea overwhelming me as I did.

"Michael," Sirash said ever so slowly, "I'm sorry."

Before tears could form, I asked, "Jean? Arjay?"

"They're fine for now, but I need your help." Sirash's gold-flecked green eyes were darting back and forth.

"What happened?"

"After the attack on the Militia Quarter, all of the refugees have been temporarily moved to the Rainbow District. There's plenty of abandoned houses, but there's more tweekers than ever, and people are getting into fights over nothing. Shit, there's even rumors spreading that some tweekers have begun working together. I need to get Arjay out of there." He barely paused to take a breath.

"How can I help?"

"I need money," he stated. "There's a place for us in the Fisheries. Not perfect, but only dimmers live there."

"How much do you need?" I said, pulling out the suns Domet had given me. "You can take this. I don't have any immediate bills. And if you can wait a few days, I can give you more."

Slowly, Sirash took the coins out of my hand. "Thank you, but I can't wait for it to get worse. I have to get out of there tonight."

I had never seen him this flustered before. Whatever was going on in the Rainbow District had him scared, which took a lot for a former Skeleton. "How much more do you need?"

"Because it's so sudden, in addition to yours, I need another fifteen suns. By midnight."

I cursed in quick succession. "How do you expect to get that much in a single night?"

"There's a two-man job tonight that will do it."

I had never heard of a job with such a payoff. We rarely ever made that much conning Low Nobles, and Sirash had always vetoed selling Blackberries after seeing the child tweekers in the Rainbow District. I asked him what the job entailed.

"It's for a Mercenary."

Before Sirash even finished the word, I said, "No. Not a chance, Sirash. I was caught in the Militia Quarter today and I'm on probation. They'll arrest me if I do anything that could possibly be linked back to the rebels. Working with a leech definitely counts."

"Michael, please, I wouldn't be asking if I had any other option. I found a stash of Blackberries in our house that belonged to Arjay. I don't know if he's selling or using or whatever, but I'm worried if I don't get out tonight, he'll get caught up in something terrible soon."

I paced and cursed in my room at the same time. As a Kingman, since our actions more often than not became history, my siblings and I were taught about the world when we were young. We learned a lot about the neighboring countries—the five Warring States that had once been a united empire, the Gold Coast, and New Dracon City—and enough about the countries that were farther away—

Eham, Goldono, Azil, the Thebian Empire, the Skeleton Coast, along with others—so we were familiar with the basics of their cultures. But we had spent more time learning about Mercenaries and their Companies than we had on all the countries combined. We learned about their formation, how they had become infamous, and how their Companies had become nomadic city-states, unable to be prosecuted by any noble, king, emperor, prophet, or God.

Needless to say, they were fucking terrifying and I didn't want a thing to do with them.

But with my thoughts still on Trey, I couldn't do anything else but support Sirash.

"Do you know what the job entails?" I asked.

"It's a transfer of information from one party to another. I'm not sure whether we would have to steal or deliver it."

"Depending on what the information is, it could be treason."

"I'm aware."

"Sirash," I said, "this is by far the stupidest thing we've ever thought about doing. Are you sure there's no other option? There's nowhere else you could stay for three days while I get the rest of the money?"

"Not unless your foster father is willing to host us."

Which he wasn't. Three mouths to feed, excluding his own, were enough to make money scarce. Having two more mouths, even for a few days, was enough to have a lasting impact on us for months to come. Even if I promised to pay Angelo back, it would still take me days to get his permission after explaining the situation and who Sirash was. Especially since the only members of my family who knew he existed in my life were Gwen, Trey, and my mother.

"If things begin to go wrong with the Mercenary, you run," Sirash said. "And if it comes to that, we'll meet up again in six days to make sure nothing can be traced back to you while you're on probation. Good?"

"Good."

With an agreement, we climbed through the window to meet Sirash's Mercenary.

Sirash hadn't mentioned that we were meeting in what remained of Kingman Keep, my old home on the Isle between the eastern and western sides of Hollow.

For generations, Kingman Keep had been a beacon, its light seen from anywhere in the city. These days, a veil of obsidian entangled Kingman Keep with only the stars left to shine a light on it. Even the nearby streets and houses had been abandoned by the knights and servants it had once employed. Which was a statement; that people would rather live on the east side of Hollow than in the shadow of Kingman Keep. The building itself had suffered during the riots, the holes badly patched with discolored wooden planks. Only the observatory at the top had escaped being broken, gutted, burned, or looted. Instead, it had endured years of neglect to become another damaged memory of the past.

Nature had tried to fix what man had wrought, and half of the keep was covered in the pale white light that came off the Moon's Tears and their vines. All it did was make it look more decrepit and lonely, as if it were ruins waiting to disappear. But even if I wanted to forget about it, I couldn't. Kingman Keep sang me to sleep every night, with the screams of those who died in the riots over ten years ago still burned into my mind.

"You didn't tell me the job was in there," I declared as we approached the servants' entrance on the side of the keep.

"Sorry," he mumbled. "I knew the Mercenary would be bad enough. Didn't think you'd ever agree if you knew we were meeting here."

"Why? Just because the last time I was here was during the riots? Where I watched so-called friends try to kill me in order to better their suddenly bleak positions in society? Did you think I wouldn't want to relive those memories?" A pause. "Because you'd be right."

"Do you want to leave?"

"Yes," I said. "But I won't abandon you. Just tell me the truth next time."

"Sorry. I was desperate."

I tried to let my irritation go as we saw a man ahead, waiting for us.

The Mercenary was disheveled, his long black hair fell to his shoulders and a heavy beard covered his face. His eyes were a smoky grey and he was dressed for a harsh winter, but it was easy to see that he was tall and bulky, more muscle than fat.

"Evening, gentlemen," he boomed. "Are you two the wonderfully generous con men assisting me tonight?"

I kept my eyes on the Mercenary, not even glancing toward Sirash. He hadn't told me he had already accepted the deal before consulting with me about it. Another convenient omission. Did he not trust me?

Sirash cleared his throat. "We are. You must be Dark, from Orbis Company. Can you tell us more about the job?"

"Of course! We're meeting with two people in there. One of them I'll probably kill and the other I'll torture for information. Or maybe I'll let them live. I haven't decided yet. Sometimes I like to improvise. Once I get the information from them, you'll be required to take it somewhere. But I'll tell you where once we have it."

"You're lying, right?" Sirash asked.

"No," the Mercenary said with a smile, rocking back and forth on his heels. "Someone's going to die tonight, and it won't be me. Might be one of you, but that remains to be seen."

I stepped closer to the Mercenary. "Did you truly think we were going to go along with murder?"

"Of course. I—" Dark cut himself off, staring at me instead. "That mark on your neck. You're Michael Kingman, aren't you?"

"If you're asking, you already know the answer."

"I suppose I do," he said as he looked me up and down. His tone and posture changed—they were firmer than before—but that often happened when people found out who I was. It didn't bother me. Even if he was a Mercenary. "I'll consider this good fortune: a Kingman finally returns to his keep. Let's head inside. We wouldn't want to be late."

"Are you truly planning on murdering someone?" I asked.

"Yes," he said. "If you two don't want to be involved, you can leave. But I imagine that if you didn't need money immediately, you wouldn't be here. So let's skip the part where you'll both give me a reason about why you must do this that makes you out to be a better person than me. We're all selfish monsters—the only difference is some of us are more honest about it than others."

Neither Sirash nor I said anything in response as Dark placed his hand on the lock and it began to freeze over. With his other hand, he hefted the hatchet that swung from his belt and shattered the lock. Shards of metal fell to the ground like glass. Dark yanked the door and held it open for us.

"Keep your heads low. Try to earn that money in there."

The three of us entered my old home, cold as a crypt. The dust and cobwebs had taken the place of the servants, the rusted steel replaced the knights, and bloodstained stone was the only reminder that people had once chosen to live in this place. We strode down the corridors where guardsmen had once stood with honor, prepared to fight to the death for the Kingman family, and into the great hall.

Time had reduced it to a hold for soot and scorched stone. The balcony's wooden barriers had charred away, and the archways were falling apart. The stained glass windows that had once been the envy of all the other High Nobles had been smashed, leaving only shards of red and grey glass to show they had ever existed. The high ceilings that had once made the keep so imposing and grand only filled it with a darkness that wrapped the keep in its tight embrace. As I stood in the center of the room, I looked around, fully expecting that if I closed my eyes, it would return to its forgotten splendor where shadows didn't exist and everything was as immaculate as it looked in my childhood memories.

"Where's the war room?" Dark asked me.

"It's over there," I said, nudging my head to the farthest room on the right.

"Then let's get moving."

A step ahead of him, I took the heavily plated door's handle and pulled as hard as I could. The metallic screech of unoiled hinges echoed off the walls and made the hairs stand up on the back of my neck. Dark shoved me aside and entered the room, Sirash close behind him.

There were two cloaked men waiting for us behind the cracked war table in the middle. Dark, Sirash, and I took our places on the other side, staring them down. The only light came from behind them, casting their features into darkness.

"Do you have what we asked for?" the one on the left roared, chest puffed out.

"Which one of you contacted me?" Dark asked.

The man on the right gave a nod.

"Thanks." Dark pulled out a revolver from his coat and shot him in the chest. The white smoke washed over my face with the stink of sulfur as the echo of the shot hung in the air. The man looked puzzled for a moment and then crumpled to the floor, dead. "What were you asking, again?"

Stammering, the man said, "Y-You killed him? He contacted you!"

"And now he's dead. I'm assuming you have the real information. He's got the fake version, right? Hand it over before I start hacking off your fingers. I'm not very patient."

The shaking survivor placed a large brown envelope on the broken table. Dark nudged my shoulder for me to collect it, and I did as I was told, my eyes fixated on the pool of blood forming beneath the dead man. Envelope in hand, I returned to Dark's side, only then understanding what he had meant about us all being monsters, some just more honest than others.

Dark took out a letter from his jacket and tossed it to the survivor. "Might want to dispose of that body. Evokers don't take too kindly to murders in Hollow."

We were back in the great hall before I spoke. "You killed him."

"I told you I was going to," he said casually.

"Why?" Sirash asked.

Dark stopped. "Would you feel better if I told you the man I killed was a murderer, rapist, and dog kicker?"

Neither of us responded.

"Well, he wasn't," Dark declared. "He was probably a decent man. Had a family, friends, maybe a girlfriend or boyfriend, or a wife or a husband, and he was on the wrong side of things tonight. He put his faith in people that couldn't protect him, and I was just protecting myself. Neither of you should be shocked: I told you at the beginning of this what I was going to do. It's not my fault if you thought I was lying."

"Just pay us and tell us where the envelope needs to go," Sirash said levelly.

I couldn't look at Sirash. We'd never done anything like this before, no matter how desperate things had gotten. I hoped it was worth it.

Would I be willing to go this far to protect my family and its legacy?

"Fine," Dark said. "Let me see the envelope and then I'll—"

"Drop your weapons and raise your hands so I can see them! We will shoot if you don't!"

Shouts filled the great hall as a cascade of lanterns sparked to life in unison along the walls, and troops poured from every entrance and exit. We were surrounded in an instant. I couldn't see how many people were around us, as the shadows seemed to double the presence they had in the room. I quickly lifted my shaking hands and the envelope into the air, then glanced toward Dark. He was shaking his head and rubbing his brow.

"These senile imbeciles," he sneered. "They sent Advocators to arrest me again?"

My heart felt lodged in my throat, and all I could see in the darkness were the glimmering tips of the bolts, aimed at us from the upper floor. We were fish in a barrel.

"Who is in command here?" Dark shouted.

A voice came from one of the balconies that wrapped around the room. "I am Franz Russel, lieutenant of the Executioner Division of Scales, here to bring you to justice for the multitude of crimes you have committed in our fair city. Lay down your weapons, Mercenary, and we will not immediately kill you where you stand."

"Under what law or prophet do you think you have the right to try to arrest me?" Dark asked. "I am a Mercenary. I stand outside the law, and if you have charges to level against me, you can politely take it up with Orbis Company. They might use your complaint to wipe their asses. It's a great honor."

"Lay down your weapons and leave Hollow for good or we will shoot!"

With a big smile on his face, Dark muttered to us, "When it begins, don't move, or I can't guarantee what will happen. And, Kingman, if you value your life, then don't let go of that envelope. Understand?"

We nodded. We had no choice but to do as we were told. Me especially. If Scales caught me working with a Mercenary . . . well, I doubted they would be content with just arresting me. I hoped they'd let me choose where I wanted to have my head cut off. In front of the castle would allow me to curse the king one last time, but on the steps of the Church of the Wanderer would be more consistent with the family legacy.

I wondered if my brother would kill me himself.

"You have all made a grave mistake tonight," Dark explained. "You may be members of Scales, but right now you're nothing more than vigilantes in the darkness. Your king can't support you unless he wants a war against every single Mercenary company on the continent." He bared his teeth. "So I'll save everyone the trouble and kill you all myself."

The hall was plunged into darkness, as if all the light had been banished, and it began.

Even though my eyes were open, I couldn't make out what was happening. None of my childhood lessons about Mercenaries had prepared me for this. I was only able to pick out bits and pieces of the battle amidst the chaos, my senses overwhelmed. Claws scratched at the stone walls as the screams intensified. Bolts whizzed through the air and smacked against the floor and walls. Lightning crackled, ice shattered, stone crumbled, and metal snapped against metal. The heat in the room fell and rose in such sharp contrasts that at one moment I was sweating and the other I was shivering. The only thing that was constant were the screams for help from the Advocators as orders were being shouted.

"Who do you think you are to try and ambush me?" Dark shouted, his voice rumbling.

My eyes finally adjusted, and I *saw* what was happening. The darkness and the shadows seemed alive in the great hall, taking shapes of twisted hands and the silhouettes of people, creeping and dancing along the walls like water running through cracks. Advocators, in a flash of lightning, were swinging their swords against the shadows, the metal slipping through them as if it were mist. Others were thrown screaming off the upper floor before a distinctive *crack* echoed off the walls.

Dark was at the heart of it all, his hands orchestrating the movements of the shadows and darkness within the keep. His eyes were wild, lost within the picture he was painting, the shadows his instruments and the screams his music. This was the destruction a single Mercenary could create. I couldn't even imagine what Vurano had looked like when it had been attacked by an entire company of them.

"Michael," Sirash said, crawling beside me. "You need to go! You can't be caught here!"

"Sirash, I can't—"

"Go!" he bellowed. "I'll take care of myself and it's my fault you're here! Go!"

Dammit. I did the only thing I could: I ran, my patchwork boots slipping across the floor as if it were ice. I scrambled for the nearest door, my old room, and slammed my shoulder into the door. The frozen, rusted hinges snapped, and I fell with the heavy door to the ground.

The Mercenary saw me. His eyes were burning red like a tweeker's. "Michael!"

With the door beneath me, I ran over it and through my cobweb-covered room toward the exit. I smashed through the window, envelope in my left hand and right forearm covering my eyes. The glass created a thousand small cuts in my skin as it shattered.

When I landed, there was no salvation, only a crossbow pointed at my chest.

———————

"No sudden movements, or I'll shoot," my assailant said.

I stood up slowly with my hands raised. That was when I realized who it was: Naomi, the ambitiously cruel girl who had lied about her mother's death.

"Michael Kingman?" she said, almost lowering her crossbow, and then with more iron in her voice she continued, "Michael Kingman, it is with great pleasure that I—"

"Wait! You have to let me go."

She hesitated, if only to humor me, slightly lowering her crossbow. It was aimed at my gut instead of my chest. It wasn't much better. "What?"

"Let's make a deal. In exchange for letting me go and pretending you never saw me tonight."

"What could you offer me?" she asked, her disgust evident. "Arresting you right now would make it quite easy to convince others you were working with the rebels. I'd be a hero."

"A hero for a day," I said. "Arrest me here, and tomorrow I will go down in history as the Rebel Kingman. While you'll be forgotten—no matter how hard you try to remain relevant—overshadowed by what I've done. Or you can work with me and experience what it's like for the world to know your name."

The glint I had seen in her eye was back, sharper than before.

Pressing my luck, I pointed to the crown patch on her lapel. "That means you're participating in the Endless Waltz, right? Well, so am I."

At long last she lowered the crossbow. "You can't be."

"No one knows yet. It's going to be a surprise. But, either way, for someone who lacks a noble family name like you do . . . well, I think you should let me court you during the Endless Waltz. Even though I'm a traitor, it'll still raise your position. High Nobles will look at you differently. They'll see you as a potential partner, rather than another commoner trying to rise above their position. And imagine the reaction, the attention, if you spurn my interest in you."

Naomi tapped her finger against the crossbow. "Why should I trust you?"

"You'll have to take my word."

"Your family's word has been worthless for years. I need something tangible as collateral." Her eyes fell on my father's ring. "That ring. I want that."

I put my hands down. "No."

I'd rather be shot than give up my father's ring.

"You're not really in a position to argue with me," she said. "Is that ring worth your life? I'll even be nice and give it back to you once I see you at Ryder Keep for the Endless Waltz. Consider it a loan if it makes you sleep better at night."

As I played with my father's ring, the screams from inside Kingman Keep had disappeared. One side had won, and I really had no desire to find out which. Having seen me run, I doubted Dark would be any more merciful than Scales.

Dammit, I didn't have any other choice.

I slid my father's ring off my middle finger, hesitated, and then put it in her hand. "If you lose that ring, I'll find your house and burn it down to the ground."

"Noted," she said with a roll of her eyes. "I'll see you soon, Michael Kingman. Don't be late to the Endless Waltz."

I sprinted away from her and Kingman Keep. I didn't stop running when it was out of my sight, or when the ringing in my ears stopped, or even when I felt blood trickle down my arms from the cuts left by the broken window. Only when my breath faded, my legs tightened, and my fingers were numb did I stop and find a seat on the curb outside of the last place anyone would ever find me.

Only then did I realize how well I had followed Dark's instructions. His envelope was still in my hand, with deep creases where my fingers had held on to it for dear life. I set it down beside me, wiped the sweat off my brow with shallow breaths, and ran through the night again in my mind. I was an accomplice to a murder, didn't get the money Sirash desperately needed, and was an eternal failure who couldn't protect himself, let alone his family.

Then there was what Dark had done in Kingman Keep. He had used both Ice and Darkness Fabrications, but every rule I knew about Fabrications said that was impossible. Fabricators only had one specialization. Yet I had seen him break the rules, and I had no idea how or why yet.

I hoped Sirash had escaped. I hoped he was safe, but since it would be days before I could see him in person, all I could do was hope. Then there was the deal I had just made with Naomi, a girl who I knew absolutely nothing about except for her name and the fact she had my father's ring. My finger felt naked without it.

And I had just stolen from a Mercenary, who was most likely going to kill me for what I had done, even if I hadn't meant to.

Curious as to what we had risked our lives for, I opened Dark's envelope and pulled out a random piece of paper enough to read a line in the middle of the page: *It should be noted in the report that David Kingman was arrested without problems.*

"Michael."

Shivers went down my spine. Had Dark found me?

It was my brother, Lyon. I shouldn't have knocked on his patrol house's door before trying to collect my thoughts.

"Michael? What're you doing here? It's late."

One thing I had learned from conning nobles was how important it was to always have a backup plan. Especially when the person who held my fate in her hands had already shown herself capable of twisting the truth to fit her desired narrative.

I needed an alibi for tonight.

And my executioner brother was going to give me one.

EXTENDED FAMILY

"You want *what*?" my brother said as he paced in front of me. "How much trouble are you in, that coming to me was your best option?"

"Enough. But not so much I'd go to Angelo. I wouldn't be here at all if I wasn't on probation. I got into a little trouble tonight and need an alibi. Just in case."

"Just in case? That doesn't make me feel any better, Michael. I've told you to stop coming to the executions months ago. I knew something like this would happen eventually. That rebel who yelled our father's name only made it easier for them to frame us."

"And I told you to stop acting like the nobility's lapdog and ruining what little respect we still have in the city."

Lyon ignored me as I sat on the curb, Dark's envelope rolled and stuffed in my back pocket before he could see it. His treason brand was stark, right above his eyebrow, since the king decreed as the oldest his had to be the most visible.

"Get up."

"Are we going somewhere? No, thanks. I'm tired and want to go back home. I just need you to—"

Lyon glanced at me and I was silent. "You want an alibi or not? This will give you one that will be more than just my word to protect you."

"And where is this mysterious place you're taking me to?"

My brother didn't respond, tugging me to my feet instead. "You'll see soon enough."

"Have I mentioned that—"

"Unless you're about to thank me, I don't want to hear it."

As I followed my brother through the streets—only stopping to wash the blood off—I barraged him with questions that were met with short answers, a few words at most and a sentence if I was lucky. It was only when we were near the Upper Quarter that my questioning became more frantic.

I had always feared that his noble-dog façade wasn't a lie. That one day he might turn against my family after seeing how far he could advance without me, Gwen, and our mother holding him back.

"Why are we in the Upper Quarter so late at night? What're you hiding from me?" I asked.

My brother didn't even give me a one-word answer this time, walking into a long, low building that seemed out of place. I followed silently into a plainly decorated room, a few chairs scattered about it. One of them was occupied by a blond-haired boy my age wearing black-and-yellow-striped nightwear and reading a book, using his finger as a guide. He looked like a bee and smelled of smoke and embers. Something about him nagged at the back of my mind, and I wasn't sure why.

"Kai, it's Lyon," my brother said, approaching the stranger. "Is Kayleigh still in there?"

The boy nodded. "They were finishing up. They will be done in a few minutes. You may join them if you desire."

"Is someone going to explain to me what's going on?"

Lyon ignored me. "I'll be right back. Kai, make sure my brother doesn't leave."

As I cursed at him, Lyon went through a door on the other side of the room, closing it behind him. With little else to do, and needing an alibi, I took a seat beside the boy.

"Did you get dragged out of bed or something?" I asked.

"I was in a hurry this morning and made a mistake. Thought I grabbed other clothes and didn't realize I was in my nightwear until I left my home. I suppose I should be glad they are presentable rather than threadbare and full of holes."

"How'd you manage that? Can't you see the difference? Are you bli—"

The boy turned to me, and he was. His eyes were the color of murky water, and I finally glanced at his book and saw each letter had bumps, allowing someone to determine what letter they were reading by touch. He was blind, and I had made a joke about it.

"I am so sorry," I exclaimed, almost choking on my own breath. "I was just trying to make a joke. I am so sorry."

The boy didn't respond.

"Could we start again? I'm Michael." I paused, then added, "Michael Kingman. Pleasure to meet you."

He closed his book. "I'm Kai Ryder. I'm surprised I haven't seen more of you since your father's execution. The Kingman family was never good at hiding. They're usually on the front lines when a conflict arises."

"Yeah, well, it's hard to be anything more than a traitor's son when the only interaction my family has with the nobility is through my brother when he executes them," I said. As quietly as I could, I took Dark's envelope from my back pocket, opened it, and very slowly began to investigate the contents, curious if I could find more about my father. Since I was stuck here waiting for my brother, I might as well take advantage of the fact that the only person with me couldn't see.

Did that make me a horrible person? Maybe.

There was a glass ring at the bottom of the envelope. I pocketed it, then took most of the papers in hand and began to read, continuing a conversation with Kai at the same time.

I think I'm going to die today.

    Everyone's heard stories about Mercenaries when they go to war, but nothing could have prepared me for this. The Mercenaries of Tosburg Company are besieging Hollow Academy. All the teachers have been killed . . . they died getting us into the Hollow Library. We have barricaded all the doors and windows, but I don't know how long we can last without help. Word has been sent to the king and Malcolm Kingman to raise the armies, but I don't think they'll get here before the Mercenaries break through. Even if we gathered all the High and Low Nobles' guards and knights, I doubt we would stand a chance against a Mercenary company. This place will be my grave. I know it. My only consolation is that when someone finds this they will know what happened to us . . . I don't want to be forgotten.

"Do you have a plan for the future?" Kai asked. "If you can't aid the Royal Family as your ancestors did, what are you going to do? Do Kingman know how to stay on the sidelines of history?"

"No idea," I said. "What do you hope to be? Is someone in your family a Fabricator?"

As he replied, I returned to reading, saying something every now and then so he didn't catch on to what I was truly doing.

It's been a short amount of time since I last wrote. The Tosburg Mercenaries have us surrounded. They haven't attacked yet, but all the students are growing restless. There is no sign of any help coming. I think we may be on our own, though no one is brave enough to admit it yet. We all keep saying Malcolm Kingman will come for us, with an army behind him. I've been trying to keep everyone calm and they seem to be buying it, but . . . but I am terrified of what will come.

I don't want to die like this.

❧

No one believes anyone is coming to save us. The Ryders and
the Low Noble families under them charged into battle and were
decimated. I've seen people die before . . . but not like that. It
was a massacre. They were crushed like ants. The Mercenaries
mounted the knights' heads on pikes around the library.
Antonio Ryder was among the fallen. The Mercenaries kicked
his head around before placing it with the rest and Alexander
isn't taking it well. He's demanding blood and I've been trying
to calm him down, persuade him to wait until we have backup.
But it's hard to convince someone who's staring at his older
brother's head on a pike. He'll snap, sooner or later.

I have no idea what I should do next.

But if Malcolm Kingman is coming for us, it will take time.
Strategies will be built, and he'll gather double the number
of troops he thinks he needs to guarantee a victory. Sadly, the
longer it takes, the less likely there will be a positive outcome for
us. I just wish I understood why these Mercenaries haven't made
any demands yet. Is there something we're missing here? Are we
just bait? What are they after?

⤜⤛

I figured it out. I know why Tosburg Company is here.
They're after something in the Archives! The Archivists
have been silent throughout all of this, and only started talking
after I slammed one of them against a wall. The Mercenaries
want something called The Journal of the Archmage. *They*
won't tell me what's in it, but it doesn't matter. I have leverage
now. I know what those leeches are after. I'm not waiting

around for them to kill us anymore. This is my war, and I'm going to win it.

❧

I've met with the leader of Tosburg Company and told him that if they don't retreat, I would burn The Journal of the Archmage. He was pissed and threatened to cut off my cock and feed it to my friends while I watched. Obviously, we didn't reach an honest agreement. As if there was any chance of that anyway. More importantly, I know where his troops are gathered, and we're preparing to attack. We've speculated that we have roughly the same number of students as they do Mercenaries. They have a lot more experience than us, and I'm the first to admit attacking them verges on suicidal, but we've all agreed it's better to die on our feet than sit idly by for our executioners to arrive. William and Alexander are already talking about how they plan to change everything. They want to reform the government, the army, the noble families—all of it. They won't die here, I'll make sure of that.

I have a plan.

I've been spreading rumors that the ground the Hollow Academy Arena was built on is a hot spot for Fabricators and that if we make a stand there it will elevate our powers. It's nonsense, but I need to lure the Mercenaries into the arena and couldn't think of anything else to tell the students. Was I supposed to tell them that the arena is the only place on campus that we can surround them in? Or that if we don't, we'll be killed? No, this is better. Let them believe in a lie. Let them find strength in it. Few of them know that some of the Mercenaries are Fabricators, too.

At first light, the vanguard and I will draw them into the Hollow Academy Arena, where William and Alexander will be waiting with the students and Archivists who choose to fight with us. Alexander will be with the archers in the stands. William will be waiting to ambush the Mercenaries. The vanguard will take the brunt of the battle, and I hope the others get to us before the Mercenaries slaughter us all.

There's a good chance this will be my first and last battle . . . Most of the vanguard won't survive this . . . We're few in number, as no one was forced to join. Everyone who volunteered did so knowing the risks. They're the bravest people I'll ever know. Alexander and William both tried to join, but I told them they couldn't. There aren't enough people with leadership experience to command the other students, and they're needed elsewhere. They need to live. For the future of Hollow.

In case . . . in case this is my last day . . . I want there to be some record of my life. That's why I'm leaving these messages in my favorite book in the library. Ma . . . Da . . . Sis, if you're reading this, know what I do here is to protect everyone. I'm the only one with the military experience to command the vanguard. I learned from the best. I can't leave the protection of Hollow to someone else.

I hope we meet again, be it tomorrow or on the other side. I hope you'll be proud of me, no matter what happens.

I love you all, never forget that.
So, please don't forget me.

I flipped to the next page, but it was blank. There was no clue to what Dark wanted from these pages, and they didn't contain the line about my father and Davey either. The only Kingman mentioned was my grandfather, Malcolm.

All that stood out was the mention of *The Journal of the Archmage*. Was Dark after it, as his Mercenary brothers had been? What was so special about it that they attacked Hollow Academy and the library to get it?

I tuned back into Kai just in time: "—and that's what I want to do once I learn to control my Sound Fabrications. I think I can make a difference, even if I did lose my sight when I was young. That's actually why my eyelids are open instead of closed like they would be for someone who was blind since birth. In case you were wondering."

There was another paper left in the envelope I hadn't read yet. "How'd you lose your sight? Was it an accident?"

Kai shook his head slowly. "I used my Fabrications as a child. It was for a good cause . . . I saved a friend's life. It just cost me a lot to do it."

"What? I thought Fabrications only cost memories. How can they take away your sight?"

"Excuse my bluntness, but you are thinking too simply. There are many types of memories: of how your body moves, of how your organs work, and your memory of how events occurred being some of them. How terrible is that? That someone could use a Fabrication one day and forget how to walk the next."

Maybe I didn't understand the cost of Fabrications like I thought I had. It could be more than losing the memory of how someone looked or how an event unfolded. Considering the deal I had made with Domet to learn how to use them, I hoped the power would let me protect those I cared about like it had for Kai.

"Yeah, definitely terrible," I said. "Since you're a Fabricator, are you going to join a High Noble Fabricator army and fight the rebels?"

As he spoke, I read the final document. I had searched every public library and collection for a glimpse of some record of my father's trial. None of them had anything that even mentioned him; his past and accomplishments erased from history. Except for this.

David Kingman, right hand to the throne, was found in the room where David "Davey" Hollow was murdered, holding—as surgeons later confirmed—the gun that killed him.

Henceforth, the deceased will be referred to as Davey Hollow to avoid confusion between Davey Hollow and David Kingman. The bullet extracted from the body had a crown held by a pair of hands scratched into it. It is not the Kingman family's sigil—being the open palm presenting a crown—but it has enough similarities to be deemed suspicious and presented as evidence.

We have been unable to locate the manufacturer of the gun or bullets, and the initial suspicions that it came from New Dracon City were quickly disproved. Further reports will be made when we discover where the gun was manufactured.

Due to its unique caliber, design, and sophistication, we have faith that we'll be able to track it down eventually. No one with such advanced technology could hide it forever.

It should be noted that David Kingman was arrested without problems: he didn't run or attack those who discovered him, which speaks in his favor.

David Kingman was found by two of our primary witnesses: Kendra Blackwell, one of the King's Ravens, and Colton Blackwell, her husband and heir to the Blackwell Low Noble family. In their testimonies, they both reported entering the Star Chamber as the murder took place. As neither David Kingman nor Davey Hollow had any reason to enter the Star Chamber that day, there is still much speculation as to why either was there. David Kingman later claimed he was there to meet a man named—

"What are you reading?" Kai asked.

I looked at him, snapped back into the moment. "What?"

"What are you reading?" he repeated. "You've been reading the whole time and I wondered what it was."

The door opened and my brother came in with a woman on his arm. She was beautiful and looked very much like Kai, with her dark-blond hair in an updo and small diamond studs in both her cartilage and her earlobes.

It was only then that I recalled who the Ryders were. They were one of the oldest High Noble families in Hollow, their only competition for the title being the Kingman family. I still had no idea why

Lyon and I were here, and it was starting to worry me as I saw how calm my brash brother was with the girl on his arm.

"Michael," Lyon said, "this is Kayleigh Ryder, Kai's older sister. She's also . . . uh, I'm not sure how to say this, but . . . she's my . . . or she'll soon be my—"

"Wife. The word he's looking for is wife." She pressed one hand down over her stomach. "And the mother of his child."

I didn't hear anything after that. The world had gone silent as I watched High Noble Kayleigh Ryder's lips shape polite nothings. My brother stood next to her, blushing and rubbing the back of his head every so often. Refusing to believe what I had just heard, I struggled from my seat and screamed, "You're really bringing another Kingman into this city, Lyon? Are you mad? You're really going to damn another innocent with our cursed last name?"

I couldn't stop myself, words coming out of my mouth unfiltered. "Kayleigh, don't have this child. You're making a mistake. Even if it doesn't end up branded like we were, it'll still be doomed the moment it learns about the Kingman legacy. There is no freedom for those who share our blood, and the pressure to be as flawless as our ancestors is . . ." I gulped. ". . . suffocating."

They all looked at me in shock. My face felt hot and I knew my words were unforgivable, but it was the truth and I couldn't take them back. I stuffed Dark's papers and ring back into their envelope and left. Alibi be damned.

I'd gone less than a block before my brother caught up with me, grabbed my shoulder, and punched me in the face. It sent me to the ground. As Lyon stood over me, he said, "What the fuck was that, Michael?"

"What the fuck is wrong with you, Lyon? Doesn't our family have enough problems without you getting a High Noble pregnant?"

"The pregnancy may not have been planned, but I still love her! I don't care if she's a High Noble and she doesn't care if I'm a Kingman! I have the right to be happy, Michael. I don't want to spend the rest of my life taking care of . . ."

I returned to my feet. "You don't want to care of who, Lyon? Me and Gwen? Because it's been years since you've had to give either of us anything. We take care of ourselves. Or were you talking about our mother? Don't want to be burdened by your Forgotten mother anymore? Tired of contributing a portion of your lapdog pay to house her in an asylum?"

"Don't make me out to be the villain, Michael. I took care of you all for years while you and Gwen were too young to do anything except cry about losing our father."

"What are you saying, then? That you've done your time and you can wipe your hands of her?"

"She's never going to get better, Michael. Whatever happened to her mind is permanent. We have to accept that."

"So we should abandon her? Our father always said family was the most important—"

"Our father was a traitor!" he screamed at me. "That bastard murdered a child and cursed his children with these brands. I'm done with him and the Kingman legacy. Unlike you and Gwen, I'm trying to move on, to find my own place in the world. This is the start of that."

"And I guess we're just obstacles to your new life?"

"We're family," he said. "But eventually, like me, you'll see that all we can do for our mother is make sure she's comfortable and that our father deserved what happened to him. He destroyed the family legacy, and that doesn't mean we're responsible for fixing it."

"Kingman don't abandon family."

Lyon shook his head and turned his back to me. "None of us have been true Kingman since he was executed. We won't lead the king's armies, we won't be sent all over the world to foster relations with other countries, and our generation won't be remembered as anything more than bystanders. It's time you accepted that . . . and until you do, don't come near Kayleigh or my child. We'll be your alibi if you need it, but we've already agreed our child will be born a Ryder, not a Kingman. And once it's socially acceptable for me to do, I plan on renouncing the Kingman family name and taking hers."

"That's the coward's way out."

"Then I will be remembered as the Cowardly Kingman, and I will wear that title with pride. Just as the Heartbroken Kingman wore hers." A pause. "I just want to be a good father and husband. No matter the cost."

"You know what happens if you walk away, right?"

"Yes," Lyon said. "But you always wanted the legacy on your shoulders, didn't you?"

My brother left me as he'd found me earlier in the night, sitting on a curb somewhere in the west side of Hollow, alone and flustered. Now I had an alibi, but I had destroyed my relationship with my brother. And if he was serious about taking the Ryders' last name, I would soon be the heir to the Kingman family.

How would history remember me?

As I began to calm down, my thoughts still on my family, I took out the page I'd been reading.

David Kingman claimed he was in the Star Chamber to meet
Shadom, a pseudonym for an unidentified High Noble famous
in the East Side for their generosity. Uncovering their identity
will be a primary focus of this investigation.

End of Part 1 of the report concerning the murder of Davey
Hollow, Heir to Hollow. —Evoker Division leader, Idris Ardel.

I looked at the page in disbelief. Domet believed my father had
been framed by a High Noble, and now I had independent information suggesting it was possible. I had a duty to investigate—no matter
what Lyon said about our father's guilt.

It was time I cleaned up the Kingman family's tarnished legacy.

THE FABRICATOR AND
THE HISTORIAN

In Hollow, a good baker could tell someone the district news about who was pregnant, who had been hanged in the past week, and where to get illegal goods in the time it took them to wrap a loaf of black bread to go. And since the Fisheries had the best bakeries, that was where I went for news of Sirash.

"Sorry, Michael, Sirash ain't here," Becca said. "Isn't even set to work until next week. I can let him know you were looking for him when he comes in."

"No, it's fine," I said. "Was just hoping to ask him a quick question."

She put a loaf of rye bread on the counter. "Sorry I couldn't be of more help. But—"

A voice yelled from the back of the store. "Becca! Ask him about the thing!"

"I was just about to, Da!" Turning back to me, she lowered her voice. "Michael, we got a lot of people asking about the rebels, trying to figure if they should hunker down or make a break for greener pastures. Have you heard anything from your fake da that might help them make a choice?"

"Low Noble Bartos's banner has been seen flying over their encampment."

She rolled her eyes and leaned closer. "I knew that already. Anything else?"

"Not really. Sorry."

Her face fell. "Shame. It'll be a penny, then."

I put a bronze penny in her palm and then took the bread. "If I hear anything, I'll make sure to tell you."

"You better. Wanderer guide your path, Michael."

"You too, Becca."

With the loaf of bread in hand, I left the bakery. Gwen was waiting outside for me.

There were five days left until I could check up on Sirash in person. Or was it six? He hadn't been clear on whether yesterday or today would be day one. All I wanted was a glimpse of him, to know that he was well.

"Not there?" Gwen asked.

"Not there."

"Doesn't he work at bakeries all over the city? He might be closer to home."

"He was planning on moving to the West Side. Thought there

would be a chance," I said. I tore the loaf in two and we walked toward the Upper Quarter, eating as we went. "How long have you known about Lyon and his future child?"

"Since Kayleigh suspected. He needed to talk to someone, and you and Angelo weren't really options."

I couldn't blame him, given my reaction last night. "You're fine with it all?"

Gwen pushed a few strands of hair out of her eyes and behind her ear. "If you're asking me if I'm fine with him having a child, then I am. He can take care of himself. If you're asking if I'm fine with how he's been acting recently toward our family in general . . . I'm not sure I have an answer for that yet. Not that I think you reacted well either, Michael. Family supports family even when they disagree."

"Tell that to Lyon," I exhaled. "Sorry. That was petty of me. I'll apologize to him when I see him next."

"And to Kayleigh."

"And to Kayleigh. My anger got the best of me, but . . . I don't know . . . it's one thing to condemn our father, but he's condemning all our ancestors and our mother, too. They deserve more than that, after everything they've done for this country."

"They do. Hollow wouldn't have been founded without them. We know that, but how many others do? Unless you study history or listen to us, it's hard to think of them as anything more than relics of the past," Gwen said as we reached Refugee Plaza, where the roads that went to the Upper Quarter, Sword District, and the Hollow Asylum diverged.

There was normally a bustling market here, with overpriced

goods sold to desperate travelers, but today it was oddly deserted. There wasn't even someone from the Hyann High Noble family that oversaw the merchants in attendance today, only an auburn-haired woman paying her respects to the refugee statue in the center. This market had been losing significance as travelers stopped coming to Hollow, preferring to visit New Dracon City instead. Not that I could blame them. All things considered, New Dracon City was superior to Hollow . . . well, except for the fact their rulers were as ruthless and corrupt as Mercenaries and deserved to be buried alive in a shallow grave.

For most in Hollow, hatred for New Dracon City ran deep, because everyone remembered what they had done to our country in the Gunpowder War . . . but for us remaining Kingman it was inherited. Their rulers had murdered my grandparents, my aunt, and the Queen at the time under the pretense of peaceful diplomacy. That was hard to forgive, and I doubted we or our descendants ever would.

As we neared the end of the plaza, I saw two Sacrifices notice us out of the corner of my eye. Both gathered their things and left in a hurry. I didn't point them out to Gwen, and she didn't notice them herself. We all had something that reminded us of what we had lost . . . and Sacrifices were hers. She blamed herself for their fate, even though Lyon and I didn't.

"With everything going on with Lyon, I've been thinking about my future more," Gwen said. "A long time ago I decided that I would participate in the Endless Waltz when I was of age if I felt I had no other option. Even though I'm a Kingman, as a woman, they're more likely to let me in than you or Lyon. For most participants, a disgraced Kingman is still better marriage material than a commoner, a merchant, or a Low Noble."

That surprised me, and I did little to hide the shock on my face. "You'd be condemning yourself to a political marriage if you did that, Gwen."

"Potentially," she said. "But what else can I do? Neither the Ravens or Scales will take me, no High Noble will accept a Kingman into their Fabricator army, and unless I get lucky and apprentice to a doctor, my medical career ends in the asylum. And as much as I enjoy working as a blacksmith twice a week, masquerading as a boy all day is tiring. At least as a noble's wife I wouldn't have to hide." Gwen sighed loudly and dramatically for emphasis. "You'd think after the Mother Kingman created the Ravens, women would have more options than we do. Our next ruler will even be a Queen! But I can't be anything more than a wife."

"If you weren't restricted, what would you do?"

"It doesn't matter if I—"

"Humor me."

Gwen stuck her tongue out at me.

I ruffled her hair and she swatted my hands, cursed, and then attempted to fix what I had ruined. As she did I said, "Fine, don't tell me. But you're a Kingman, and a Kingman can do anything. Do what's best for you, Gwen. I'll take care of our family."

"You can barely take care of yourself, let alone the family's legacy."

"I'm doing better than you may expect."

That made her laugh. "Why don't you become an Archivist? Then you can ensure the Kingman family isn't forgotten. After everything we've been through, that would be enough."

We parted ways after that, so she could see some of her friends before her shift at the asylum started and I could see Domet before it reached midday. This was the first of my days being his companion, and I had no idea what to expect.

I didn't get hassled as I made my way into the Upper Quarter and toward Conqueror Fountain, its half-broken statue of one of my ancestors in the center of it another reminder of how far my family had fallen. Despite promising that it would be easy to find, Domet's redbrick house blended in with the lavish houses around it. If it weren't for the amaranth in front of it, I would have passed it dozens of times without realizing. There was no doorman, so I hopped up the steps and tried the door myself rather than tug the bell with a potentially hungover man inside.

The house was immaculate. An expensive pink-and-white marble floor complemented the deep azure walls and framed paintings on display by every master that ever was. I expected to have a servant intercept me, but I saw no one, and as I made my way deeper into his house, I heard two people in the middle of a quiet conversation.

I couldn't understand anything that they were saying until I made my way into the middle of Domet's living room. He was spread out on a divan in a silk robe, an empty bottle of vodka in his hand and another on the floor beside him. His companion, an old man with a potbelly and mismatched eyes wearing the robes of the Church of the Eternal Flame, was in an armchair beside him.

"Michael!" Domet exclaimed. He attempted to rise, got tangled in his robe, and then returned to how he had been. "You're late! Where were you?"

"We didn't decide on a time for me to be here, and it's not even midday."

"I thought we did," he grumbled. "Doesn't matter: you're still late, and there's plenty to do today."

"Right."

I wondered if he had even slept yet. I suspected not. It was still early to be so drunk.

Domet's companion waddled over to me. "I do apologize for Domet. He's an old friend, so, when I heard of his release, I took the opportunity to catch up. I'm afraid we've been drinking since last night. The poor man needed a release after those dreadful conditions in the asylum."

"I didn't think Domet had friends."

"No, he has plenty. There's a whole group of us, but throughout the years we don't get to see each other quite as often as we once did. One of the downsides of growing up. There never seems to be enough time," the man said. "My apologies! I haven't introduced myself yet. My name is Rian Smoak, Scorcher for the Eternal Flame. As you may have noticed, I'm not quite as intense as my brethren, since I spend most of my time as a—"

"Dragon!" Domet screeched as he surged up, only to collapse back onto the divan in a fit of laughter.

We both looked at the drunk man cackling on the divan. With a sigh, Rian said, "What he's trying to say is that I'm a Dragon *Historian* for the Church of the Eternal Flame. I swear to the Eternal Flame, he does this every time."

"Dragons aren't real," I countered. I hated when adults tried to claim they were; it was childish at best and foolish at worst.

To my surprise he agreed. "You're quite correct! They're not. I study the various myths about dragons in different societies to understand how the creature we know from the stories came to be. Most of the legends can be traced back to the Toothless Wyvern, a large and mostly harmless herbivorous lizard that could glide through the air for long distances. Farmers blamed them, rather than bandits, for carrying off sheep and destroying their crops, since the Dukes were more likely to compensate them for the damage. Bandit activity is the most likely explanation for the monstrous fire-breathing dragons we love hearing stories about." Rian spoke quickly and rarely paused, like a small child who had been allowed to talk about his favorite topic.

"I've never heard of a Toothless Wyvern before."

"No surprise there," Rian said. "They went extinct around the time Celona was shattered. I believe they were more or less blind and needed the light from both moons to forage. Without Celona, their extinction was guaranteed. It's a shame, but that's nature for you. Everything dies eventually."

"Nature didn't shatter the moon, though," Domet interrupted. The jovial drunk had vanished in a moment.

"It could have," I said.

"That's not what the Archivists say."

"The Archivists twist history so it's only remembered as they want it to be," I said without thinking, face flushed. "They aren't reliable anymore. And, regardless of what they say, my family couldn't have shattered a moon. No Fabricator is that powerful."

"Since when have you been an expert on Fabrications?"

"I'm not. But it's quite the coincidence that Archivists just happened to find proof that my family shattered Celona a year after my father was executed."

"Their evidence came from ancient Eternal Flame doctrine. Some dedicate their life to preserving and reading it," Domet said.

"Anything is possible with enough time and determination."

Rian glanced between me and Domet. "I think I shall take my leave. You two seem to have a lot to talk about, and I don't like being reminded of the fanatics I deal with every service. Michael Kingman, a pleasure to meet you. I hope Domet treats you well. If you ever want to talk about dragons, please do find me at my church. Domet can give you the specifics."

With that, the fat old man left. After Domet heard the door shut, he stood up from the couch, cracked his back, and then made his way over to the liquor cabinet to pour himself another drink.

"How are you going to teach me about Fabrications if you're so drunk you can barely stand?"

"Calm yourself, Michael," he said as he dropped a cube of stone into his glass. "Only one of those bottles over there held vodka. Please, do you really think that's what I'm like when I'm drunk? I'm a functioning alcoholic, not a child."

"Then why—"

"Fake it?" he said. "Because when you're in a position like I am, people rarely give you anything for free. But they do have a tendency to spill all kinds of interesting information if they think they're taking advantage of me. When they think I'm drunk, they tell me what I need to know in exchange for some useless tidbits they think I've mistakenly let slip."

"But he said he was your friend."

Domet took a sip from his drink. "I don't have friends—only accomplices and enemies. You'd be amazed at how often they change sides. Now, sit at the table. We have much to do before the Endless Waltz begins."

I didn't know what to make of Domet. Every time I had some insight into him and his goals, he seemed to change in an instant. If I was going to continue working for him, I'd need to have clarity—or risk ending up as one of his enemies by mistake.

Once we had taken a seat, Domet reached under the table and brought out a small square box. He opened it with a click and hid the contents from me as he rummaged through it. "For some reason—I suspect because he likes to fluster the Court—the prince moved the date of the Endless Waltz up to tonight and we need to get you prepared for it."

"The first event is tonight?"

A nod. "My tailors are working as fast as they can to get you proper dressings, so there's no need to worry about that. But there are other things we need to prepare for. What do you know about the Endless Waltz?"

"It's the nobility's courting process. Or has it changed in the past decade?"

"It's changed. Roll up your sleeves and hold out your arm. I need a blood sample," Domet said, a syringe in his hand.

"No, what're you doing with that—"

"We don't have the time for stupid questions. Either do what I say, or leave." Domet pushed my sleeve out of the way, tied a tourniquet around my arm, and tapped the veins professionally before he inserted the syringe right below my biceps. He filled it with blood, and then took the needle out of my arm and handed me some gauze to cover the wound. He set the syringe down next to his box and fiddled with a few vials of liquid, pouring a few drops of each into a copper bowl, then said, "I'm testing your blood to see if you're a Fabricator. No point in attempting to teach you if you're not one. Your mother wasn't, which means there's a chance you aren't either."

"Is Lyon a Fabricator?"

"The Executioner Division doesn't think so, but their reports also say he was never tested. If he is one, he's done a remarkable job hiding it," Domet muttered. "Now, listen closely: I'm only going to explain the Endless Waltz once.

"It changed after your father's death," Domet began. "What once was an organized set of challenges among the noble debutantes, designed to develop alliances—romantic or not—based on merit and ability not position or wealth, has devolved into a mad scramble for power. Over the years the Corrupt Prince has twisted it into a test. Only those who prove themselves to him are deemed worthy of entering the Hollow Court, whatever their status. Those who fail may try again the following year or, in a few cases, are stripped of their titles and banned."

"So it's no longer about courting?"

"No, it's about the Corrupt Prince consolidating his claim to the throne. The Endless Waltz still encourages the formation of relationships, but it's also an opportunity to show the older generation which upstarts are going to be the best to work with in the future. For you to get an opportunity to steal the king's memories and prove your father's innocence, you'll have to earn an invitation to the king's birthday party. It's the final event of the Endless Waltz, where the most successful young nobles and their new partners are introduced to the full Hollow Court."

"So I have to impress a Royal to be let into the full Hollow Court?" I asked.

"Not just any Royal: the Corrupt Prince, one of the vilest Royals there has ever been. You'd be in a stronger position with the princess, since she's the Royal you've been bound to protect since birth. But who knows where she's off to these days. The court hasn't seen her in years."

"There's no chance this will work. The Corrupt Prince won't let me in on principle."

"Don't give him a choice. The Endless Waltz has three events"—he paused with his vials and potions to tick them off as he spoke—"a reception at Ryder Keep, a hunt in the King's Garden, and then a concert by the renowned singer Red. That's three opportunities to impress and ally yourself with every young noble you can. Ensure that the prince can't reject you from the Hollow Court without dividing his own supporters. Because even if he's in a better position than you, he can still be held accountable and face pressure from the other High Nobles. Not so much the Low, obviously."

"So," I said, drawing out the word, "I need to impress the other nobles around my age, get an invitation to the king's birthday party, and then steal the king's memories so we can prove a High Noble set up my father for the murder of Davey Hollow?"

"Essentially."

I stared at him. "You realize how crazy this sounds, right?"

"This is the only way we'll get close to the truth."

I reached into my pocket and pulled out a page from Dark's

envelope. "What about this? I found this last night and it seems like a good place to start. There are names in there that we could question about what happened."

Domet snatched it from me. "What is this?" He read it over, silently. "Where'd you get this? This is all classified information. Even I would have difficulty getting it."

"I accidentally stole it from a Mercenary."

"You did *what*? What are you doing interacting with a Mercenary? Do you realize how much you could have put at risk if you were caught?"

"I wasn't. But this information is good, isn't it?"

"No, it's not. It tells us nothing except the Evokers were investigating a High Noble that used the pseudonym Shadom. Even the other names here are useless. The Raven mentioned was burned alive with the other nobles in Naverre years ago; her husband, Colton Blackwell, vanished from noble society shortly after, and no one has seen Idris Ardel since he left for Goldono years ago."

I took my paper back from him, grumbling. He'd be even less interested in the handwritten account of the battle at Hollow Academy. "Say I do get invited to the king's party and find his memories, what are we even looking for among them?"

"We find out why your father pled guilty. His motive was never revealed to the public, and I've always suspected that it holds the key to finding whoever framed him. The truth can't be hidden from the world, or denied, if we have a record of the king's memories . . . no matter how much he wants history to be remembered his way."

His plan didn't sound too terrible. Because most nobles used Fabrications and risked losing memories on a daily basis, they had systems

in place to record the most valuable information. The system depended on the person: tattoos, journals, paintings, and other things that
were harder to misplace. If we compared the king's version of history to
his memories . . . well, it would certainly separate fact from fiction.

"You'll also need this for tonight," Domet said, pushing a large
book across the table to me.

I began to flip through it: a compendium of handwritten notes
about every noble in the country, from Kai Ryder, the blind High
Noble, to Adrian the Liberator, the first King of Hollow. There were
even a few scattered passages about those in power outside of Hollow.

"Did you write this?"

"Do you always ask such obvious questions? Have it memorized
for tonight."

There were hundreds of pages, a dozen on each king or queen
alone. It would take me all day to read it, let alone memorize anything in it. "I'll need more time than that."

"We don't have such luxuries," he said. He moved the copper bowl
filled with a strange liquid in front of me and then took the syringe in
his hand. "Ready to find out if you're a Fabricator, Michael?"

After a pause I said, "Yes."

I didn't know what I expected as Domet squirted my blood into
the clear liquid. At first nothing happened. My heart felt like it was
about to burst from my chest as we waited, insecurities that I might
not be a Fabricator returning after years of pushing them to the back
of my mind. Then my blood in the bowl began to move, twist, and
spiral upward out of the liquid into a spiderweb tower of blood.

"Does that mean I'm a Fabricator?" I whispered.

Domet huffed and took a sip from his drink. "Obviously. If you weren't, nothing would have happened. Although this test doesn't tell us what kind of Fabricator you are. It'll take some time to determine what your specialization is. But that's a problem for another day," he said, and then rose from his seat.

"Aren't we going to figure that out?" I asked as I followed him.

"We don't have the time. You need to memorize that book and I need to make sure the preparations for tonight are complete."

"You're going to send me up against the nobility with no idea how to use Fabrications?"

Domet looked over his shoulder. "You have the book. If you get into a fight during the first event, teaching you how to be a Fabricator would be foolish—you'd be a Forgotten by the end of the week. Learn some control, Michael. Fighting should be the last resort, not the first."

I didn't argue with him further. All it would do was waste time and leave me even more unprepared for the first event of the Endless Waltz. And I had other tasks I still needed to do without arousing Domet's suspicion. After he gave me my five suns and a few scattered notes on the basic principles of Fabrications to review, then told me where and when to meet him later, I took the book off the desk and said, "Wait."

"Wait?" he said in a condescending tone. "We don't have time for your hesitation, Michael. You need to learn—"

"Don't I need the ceremonial blessing before I can participate in the Endless Waltz?"

"The ceremonial blessing? Unimportant. High Nobles attend without it all the time. And you are a Kingman. Kingman have never been known for being friendly with the churches. The nobles will understand."

"But wouldn't it be helpful? It might improve how they perceive me."

"I didn't think you'd ever consider it."

"So long as you keep to your end of our bargain, I'll do whatever I need to."

"Interesting," Domet said, hand on his chin. "The Church of the Wanderer won't bless you—not after your public displays of criticism. The Church of the Eternal Flame might, but . . . considering you're a Kingman, they might insist on inducting you into their order, and we can't have that."

"What about your friend Rian?"

"Rian? Rian. Yes, he might do it. If I had known you'd consider it, I'd have asked him. He will require something in return, but I have an idea what will satisfy his monstrous appetite."

Domet penned a quick letter to Rian, sealed it with his wax mark, and then handed it to me. "He's in the Church of the Eternal Flame in the Upper Quarter. Take a left once you leave my house and keep walking straight until you find it. It glitters too much for you to miss it. Hide your brand and tell the first monk you see that you're there to confirm a shipment of books for Scorcher Rian. They should take you straight to him. Understand?"

"Understood."

I left after that, hiding my smile from him. I had no desire to conform with the nobility by seeking a blessing from a church. No, I was after something more important.

I was after Domet's secrets.

THE EXTINGUISHED

Given what I knew about Domet, finding someone who considered him a friend was too great an opportunity to ignore. I didn't trust him or believe that he would keep his end of our agreement, and I needed to know more about the man before it was too late. Rian was my best opportunity to learn more about the egomaniac I was working with.

When the glittering church came into view, I took a deep breath and readied myself.

Despite my feelings about the Church of the Wanderer, most—myself included—agreed that the Church of the Eternal Flame was the more corrupt of the two primary religions in Hollow. It was hard to disagree when their cathedral was decorated with more gold and gems than were found in the royal vault.

The multi-spired cathedral was the second-highest building in the Upper Quarter, after the royal castle. I had always thought it was representative of their arrogance—that they would only let themselves be beat by those who ruled the entire country—and my experiences with them had done nothing to alter that.

Rumors said the church was attempting to gain more power in Hollow, as they had on the Gold Coast, and that unless the king acted soon, it wouldn't be long before the Church of the Eternal Flame was inextricably entwined with the nobility and the Royals alike.

Luckily for me, most of today's congregation was busy with a ceremonial bonfire directly outside the church, so when I gave my lame excuse for visiting Rian, I was taken directly to him by a monk who then hurried back to the service. He didn't even pause to call me a heathen or heretic, which was unexpected even with my brand hidden by my collar. They seemed to be able to sense it most days.

As I knocked on the door to Rian's study, I could only hope I wasn't making a mistake coming here and that I could learn something about Domet without losing too much in return.

"Enter," he called, and I opened the door.

I was caught off guard by his study. Every space that wasn't occupied with furniture had hoards of books in its place, except for a very tight and orderly path to the desk. It smelled of books, ink, and tobacco smoke.

"Michael!" the Scorcher said as I entered. "I'm surprised to see you so soon. I didn't expect a visit until after the Endless Waltz.

Excuse the mess: I'm attempting to track when and where the Eham myths about sea behemoths began. What can I do for you, my friend?"

I didn't know where to stand or sit, so I stood awkwardly in the doorway. "Domet sent me here to get a blessing before I participate in the Endless Waltz."

Rian laughed so hard his belly shook. "Michael, as much as I would love to—"

I held up Domet's envelope and said, "He even gave me this, to convince you . . . but I want information about Domet instead."

"Information about Domet?"

"Everything I know about Domet makes me think he'll betray me once I'm no longer useful. So I need to know what he cares about."

"I consider Domet a friend," Rian said. "Why would I help you?"

"Because Domet doesn't have friends—only accomplices and enemies. And everyone's designation changes frequently. Yours included."

"You've been listening to him. That's dangerous. But I might be able to help you—for a fee. In addition to that letter."

"What fee?"

"I want a promise that if you ever meet someone with two Fabrication specializations, you'll—"

"Like the Mercenary?" I said, unthinking.

"What?" Rian jumped to his feet, his chair screeching behind him and knocking over a few stacks of books. "You've met one? What was their name? Did you meet them in Hollow? Did you *see* them use two specializations of Fabrication, or did they simply brag that they could?"

I had assumed Rian was talking about Dark without using his name. Based on his reaction, I wasn't so sure.

"Yes," I said. "I know of someone who proved they have two specializations."

Rian turned away from me, mumbling something. "Their name? Did you catch their name?"

"First, tell me what Domet cares about," I countered.

"Absolutely," he said with a predatory smile. "Domet only cares about one thing: the Shrine of Patron Victoria. He protects it as a father would his child. He's even gone as far as to pay tithes to both churches to leave it alone. It caused quite the controversy here, since our tenets only allow us to acknowledge worship of our prophet and God. But money can change many opinions."

"That shrine?" I said. "That's all? No secret bastard or romantic companion? No siblings or parents? A shrine?"

"If you're doubting what I said, then you don't know Domet. His parents are dead, he has no siblings, and I have never seen him kiss someone, let alone sire a child. That shrine is everything to him."

If Domet broke our deal, I had no idea how to hold a shrine over him. Would the other High Nobles even care if I shared his secret? I'd come up with something if I had to.

"The name," Rian growled. "Who is this Mercenary with two Fabrication specializations?"

"I never met them myself," I lied. "I heard about them from my foster father. He said Scales had a run-in with a Mercenary who used two types of Fabrications against them in Kingman Keep. It was recent. Their records might have the name."

"You said you knew them."

"I said I knew *of* them."

"If you've lied to me, Domet will hear about this conversation."

"Based on what I know about Domet, he might be proud I took the initiative to learn more about him."

"Possibly," Rian said as he returned to his seat. "Excuse my manners, but I have work to return to and information to validate. You know where I am, and I'll make sure Domet believes you've been blessed by our church. Don't forget to leave the letter, Michael."

Armed with the information I'd wanted—and with a record of a blessing assured but the actual blessing avoided—I left, dodging members of the Church of the Eternal Flame as I did. As I walked, I opened Domet's book and started reading as much as I could about every noble who might be in attendance tonight, his notes jogging my hazy memories about the nobles of my generation.

Surprisingly, Advocators who would normally dog my path home turned a blind eye to a boy with his nose in a book. Perhaps they mistook me for a scholar, since the poor rarely had books of their own. The best we managed were the tomes of propaganda handed out by criers, but most people in the Narrows ripped them for toilet paper.

With most of the day ahead, I did the only thing that made sense. I found a spot by the river to settle down and began to memorize as much as I could about the High Nobles, keeping an eye out as I did for anyone who might be the girl in red or the rebel woman, wondering who they could be and why I couldn't recall them.

THE CORRUPT PRINCE

"Name the children of the Ryder Family descending in age," Domet ordered, marching alongside me toward Ryder Keep.

"The eldest is Kayleigh 'Kylie' Ryder, my brother's future wife," I said. "Next is Katrina 'Karin' Ryder, the current two-feather Raven. Then Kyros 'Kai' Ryder, the blind boy who will be participating in the Endless Waltz with me. Lastly, there's Jonathan 'Joey' Ryder, a sickly mute who is never seen in court unless his entire family is present."

"Good." Domet adjusted the collar on my costume for tonight. He claimed that I had to look the part to return to the Hollow Court, but the outfit just made me look like a fool in a paper crown, sitting on a glass throne.

But I'd said I'd do what it took to uphold our deal, and I could masquerade as a sheep in front of a wolf if it got me what I wanted in the end. Domet had questioned me about his notes, smacking me in the head if I made a mistake, while his tailors made last-minute alterations and dressed me. He seemed to believe success depended on knowing my peers, but I knew nobles: no matter how often they liked to pretend they were honest, they rarely were. I had survived worse than them in the last ten years, while they had sat in their keeps, protected and docile.

"Tell me their symbol, and their parents' names and positions in society," Domet ordered.

"Their symbol is a black dragon over a golden background. Alexander Ryder is the High Noble of Health. His wife is Alecia Ryder, born Maple, and she's a midwife to the High Noble families."

"What government positions do the Andel, Castlen, and Braven High Noble families oversee?"

"Agriculture, Development, and Guild Labor, in that order."

"Excellent. You might pull this off. If you hold your tongue when you should." Domet adjusted his jacket as we approached Ryder Keep. "Do you remember the plan? I can only get you so far. You'll have to do most of it on your own."

"Don't engage with the Corrupt Prince," I recited, "but impress the High Nobles. Convince them I want to restore my family's legacy. And avoid any merchants that might be there. No offer they can make me will be worth it."

"Exactly."

We were at one of the side entrances to Ryder Keep, the one closest to the ballroom where the first event was taking place. We had arrived late on purpose, so when I returned, it would be a public spectacle. This entrance also only had two guards outside of it, and according to Domet they were loyal to him instead of the Ryder family. It made me wonder how many others were loyal to Domet in secret.

"Once you're in the ballroom, your participation in the Endless Waltz will be announced," Domet said. "There may be some backlash, but you're a legitimate participant and your paperwork is in order, even if it won't be seen by officials in the castle until tomorrow morning." The guards had seen us and were prepared to usher me in.

"Anything else?"

Domet shook his head. "Don't give them any indication of what we're truly after."

"Wouldn't even consider it."

Domet put both of his hands on my shoulders, squeezed, and then shepherded me into Ryder Keep with a gentle hand and a few words of encouragement. It was a straight line from this entrance to the ballroom, and I couldn't get lost if I wanted to. With every step I took I debated retreating down the stairs and away from all of this. But I was a Kingman, not a coward.

My family needed me to do this. My mother needed a cure for whatever magic plagued her mind, and Gwen needed to have a future to look forward to that didn't lock her into a loveless political marriage. I'd do this for my family. Lyon be damned. He couldn't run away from our family's name, no matter how much he wanted to.

We had to embrace who we were. We were Kingman, and this was our city.

I pushed open the ballroom doors and walked onto the balcony that overlooked it, the light above me bringing out the red and grey in my military-style jacket. In my family colors there would be no mis-taking who I was. No one had worn them together since my father's execution.

"Announcing Michael Kingman to the Endless Waltz!" a herald shouted from below, all eyes turning toward the balcony.

There were gasps, and curses, and sighs, and murmurs as I made my way down the stairs toward the main floor. Most of the participants of the Endless Waltz were dressed in bright colors to represent their households. Those that weren't were in blue and gold to honor the Royal Family. All the men were in military uniforms, useless stylized armor, or religious robes, while the women were in ball dresses, the length of their gloves indicating their status: to the wrist for the Low Born, to the elbow for the High Nobles, and past that for the princess and queen. If they were in attendance. The only exceptions were the Eternal Sisters of the Church of the Eternal Flame, who wore their trademark black flame-trimmed scarves around their arms like veils.

The crowd parted before for me as I made my way over to the only people that I recognized. Kai and the girl in red were at the same table. The girl in red was visibly shocked to see me. Kai, on the other hand, was all smiles.

"What'd I miss?" I asked.

"Quite a lot," the girl in red declared.

"Supper, for example," added Kai.

With my heart still pounding from my return, I asked, "Kai, are we good after last night?"

The girl in red raised an eyebrow as Kai said, "We are. You could have handled it better, and that's on you, but others in my family think . . . similarly. They're just more civil about it."

That made me feel even worse. Lyon probably wanted some support, and I had become yet another voice attacking him. But I couldn't dwell on it when I could do nothing. I asked, "Have you seen the Corrupt Prince yet?"

"No," Kai said. "Typically, he only shows up for the hunt in the King's Garden."

I hoped that would be the case. It would give me some time to earn favor with the High Nobles before he could do anything to hinder me.

I turned to introduce myself to the boy sitting with them, but the girl in red tapped his hand away. "Don't bother. He's my date. I doubt he will be around much longer."

Flustered by her bluntness, I turned to the other participants. The stir caused by my arrival had calmed, though a few were still visibly distraught by my presence, the members of the Church of the Eternal Flame in particular. I couldn't wait until they discovered that their church had blessed my attendance. I scanned for Naomi among the crowd—I doubted she had chosen to withdraw or had arrived late—but I didn't see her.

"Michael Kingman! In the flesh!" a copper-skinned man said as he approached. He had the coloring of the lucky chosen in Goldono to the west. His blond hair and beard were immaculately groomed, his body was tall and thin, and his clothes were loose and flashy as was normal in his home country. Nothing in Domet's book had suggested citizens from Goldono would be in attendance, nor did it warn me of the olive-skinned Azilian man or the Skeleton Coast slave at his side. The Skeleton's bone tattoo covered half his face, far more prominent than Sirash's.

The Goldani gripped the sides of my shoulders and kissed both my cheeks. "I thought you and your family were extinct! I could barely contain my excitement when you appeared out of nowhere like a Waylayer! I had to come over and share my pleasure with you."

"Thank you, but I'm sorry. It's been a few years since I was in the political landscape and I'm not quite as familiar with you as you are with me."

"Michael! My deepest apologies: sometimes my excitement gets the better of me. I am Zain Antoun, ambassador for the Goldono Gold Vein Casino," he said. His hands moved with every word. "This is Lucca Azil."

The Azilian man bowed rather than shake my hand.

"Don't be concerned if neither of them talk," Zain stated. "Lucca needs more practice communicating outside of his family. You know how Azilians are. Great at the arts and agriculture but all the social skills of a toddler. Wait till you see him try to interact with a woman. And this is my Skeleton."

The Skeleton shook my hand but didn't say anything.

"Does he not speak Common? If it helps, I know a few words of—"

"Oh, no, no," Zain interrupted. "He knows Common, but he doesn't have a tongue." He laughed. "I got rid of it years ago. He had such a terrible rural accent. Couldn't stand it, so I gave him a choice: either get rid of the accent or I will. But whatever he did to fix it didn't work, so I was forced to take action myself."

"Well," I said through gritted teeth, "it's been a pleasure to meet you and your friends, Ambassador Zain. But I hope you are aware of

Hollow law while you're here and are respectful of your Skeleton. There haven't been slaves in Hollow for generations."

Zain slapped me on the shoulder as he laughed. "Oh, Michael, I love your sense of humor. We both know what everyone in here thinks of those who have been deemed Sacrifices. Sadly, as much as it would please me, I shouldn't take up too much of your time. You're a living legend, and I'm sure others long to speak with you, although I do have one question for you before I depart: Of all your ancestors, which are you proudest of?"

I'd never been asked that before. "Probably the First Kingman. They set the standard we all followed for generations. For one person to have that much of an impact on the world speaks volumes to what kind of person they were. If I could be half as heroic, I'd be happy."

Zain turned to the Azilian and said, "I told you it wouldn't be the Explorer! Biased fool! Remarkable choice, Michael. A quite remarkable choice."

Zain left, and it was as if he'd been a barrier between me and the rest of the nobility. Others began to approach and make conversation.

First was High Noble Claire Castlen, her family famous for its size. The High Noble Castlen family's primary exports were their children, who were wed away to various powerful families throughout the continent. A Kingman, I suspected, might make a nice addition to their collection. Then Dara Hyann, a High Noble a few years older than me who wanted to bemoan the rebellion for hampering trade. Mercenaries were too expensive, Eham was trying to undercut us, and New Dracon City was taking longer to respond to inquiries than they had in the past. It was so interesting, I only had to stifle a yawn twice.

Dara was followed by a flurry of people from every noble family, High and Low, wanting to be reacquainted, including the Solarin, Morales, Braven, Cottonwood, and Bodkin families. High Noble Cyrus Solarin wanted the two copper pennies he lent me as a child back—which I remembered but refused to admit—while Low Noble Primrose Bodkin wanted to show me her new tattoos. All seventeen of them. Both were shocked when I turned them down.

Ambassador Zain always stayed close to my side, chiming into conversation whenever he saw fit. And as conversation after conversation was filled with laughter and charm, I slowly began to see that not everyone hated the Kingman family following my father's betrayal.

While everyone was distracted with an Ehamian merchant's wares, I found myself beside the girl in red and a wine fountain. Her date was nowhere to be seen, and I asked what happened to him.

"He left when it became clear that even though our parents had been interested in an arranged marriage, I wasn't, and nothing he could say would change that." She ran her finger over the rim of her wineglass. "My father wants me married within the year, and I've been sabotaging all his attempts at matching me with someone. My date tonight was, sadly, another casualty."

"Marriages usually take years to arrange," I said. "How many aspects of the courtship would you have to skip to be married within a year?"

"All of them. Save for the memory tattoos," she said. "But he worries if I don't get married soon, it will . . . Wait, Michael, do you know my name?"

I could feel the heat creeping up my face as she laughed.

"I promise I'm not going to hit you again. To be honest, I'm rather sick of who I have to be right now and would rather be anyone else. So, until you remember my name or who I am, could I pretend to be someone else with you? Someone who doesn't worry about arranged marriages or noble politics? And if you never remember, that's fine. I know I'll have someone at my side who will never judge me on my title alone."

"Only if you don't judge me for what my father did."

"I never did," she said as she raised her glass. "To beginning anew."

I clinked glasses with her. "To beginning anew."

We drank together with smiles on our faces.

"So, if I don't know your name, what am I supposed to call you?"

"How did you refer to me up to this point?" she asked.

"The girl in red."

"But I'm not wearing . . . oh, I was in Margaux Keep." A pause. "What a mouthful. Can't you think of anything—"

The Corrupt Prince arrived.

I heard him before I saw him, which was remarkable in its own way.

"Where's the Kingman?" he bellowed as he strode in, one heavy footstep after another, silencing every conversation. The crowd parted for him, as it had for me, and he ignored the fact that none of his nobles bowed to him. Respect and fear were not the same in Hollow.

The Corrupt Prince was a giant of a man, well over six feet tall, all muscle and bone. He wore his family's colors, blue and gold, a golden crown adorned with every gem imaginable on his head, hidden in the tangles of his red hair, a distinguishing trait of the Royal Family. The Corrupt Prince stopped in front of me, and his Throne Seekers arrayed themselves behind him.

His Throne Seekers were the nickname everyone had given to the company he kept. None of them hid their desire for power within the country and wished for the Corrupt Prince to take the throne from his sister when the king passed. Everyone knew his intentions, even me, before I had decided to return. No matter what, I would always be at odds with them, considering my oath to protect the princess. It made me wonder what she thought about him and his friends.

I recognized a few of the Throne Seekers with the help of Domet's notes. There was High Noble Gael Andel, a leech upon society, and High Noble Sebastian Margaux, the black sheep of his family and half brother to Danielle Margaux—whom I had expected to see here tonight but hadn't so far. To my disappointment, Naomi and Trey were with him as well, both looking out of place: Trey because of his ragged clothes and permanent scowl, and Naomi as she was the only woman. My father's ring was on her finger.

Seeing Trey made my chest hurt. He had sworn to destroy my family and I had hoped he had spoken in anger, but keeping company with the Corrupt Prince suggested otherwise. I could only hope his grief didn't cloud his judgment and make him do something he'd regret. He gave me a look I couldn't interpret. With the Corrupt Prince in front of me, I couldn't spare the time to puzzle it out.

"Kingman," the monster said, showing me his teeth.

"Adreann," I said, looking up at the Royal whom Gwen was bound to protect.

"I am surprised to see you here."

"As a High Noble participating in the Endless Waltz, I can't say the same."

"Since when have traitors been allowed to participate?" He tapped the sword at his side.

"I may have the brand, but I'm still a Kingman. And Kingman are allowed everywhere."

He laughed, and his Throne Seekers joined in awkwardly. When he stopped, so did they. "How is your sister? You should have brought her with you. I've heard she has become quite beautiful, and I would love the chance to admire her in person. It is my right, after all. She is still bound to serve me."

"Bound to protect. She's not a slave, Adreann."

"Protect. Serve. Is there really any difference?" Before I could reply, the Corrupt Prince leaned in close to me and whispered into my ear, "Your father murdered my brother. You are not welcome here, traitor."

The Corrupt Prince stepped back, red in the face, and began to pace. We'd drawn an audience, including Kai and the girl in red, to see an encounter between a Kingman and a Hollow. The last time this happened, a Hollow had died. Many in the audience likely hoped for a similar outcome tonight. It was no secret what people thought of him.

The Corrupt Prince raised his hand. "Everyone," he said, his voice loud enough to carry throughout the ballroom, "I decree, here and now, that anyone who consorts with Michael Kingman will be barred from Hollow Court when I am king."

"But you'll never be king," I said. "Your sister will inherit the throne, and as a High Noble I have the right to participate in the Endless Waltz, regardless of your opinion. You can't force me to leave."

"I am the Prince of Hollow and can do whatever I want. I am in charge here, Kingman."

"You are not, Prince Adreann," Kai said, emerging from the crowd. His steps were careful, calculated, but lacked the hesitation that others who were blind had. "This is my house and you are both guests here. Do not incur my family's wrath. And, Prince Adreann, as my father has just agreed to found a new hospital in Braven, as a favor to the king, I suggest not making an enemy of the Ryders tonight."

The prince spat at Kai's feet and the crowd went silent. If anyone but the prince had done that, a dozen Low Nobles under the Ryder family would've stepped forward to defend their liege's honor. But since it was the prince, none dared. "Fucking Kingman sympathizer."

Kai put his hand over his heart. "We of the Old Blood do not forget as easily as you, it seems. There must always be a Kingman in Hollow."

The Corrupt Prince roared and threw back his fist. Before I could move, a flash of gold dashed in front of me, and the Corrupt Prince's fist slammed into the girl in red's open palm, right before Kai's cheek, with a loud clang.

"Prince Adreann," she said, "please don't allow us to monopolize your time."

"Do you stand against me, cripple?"

"Never, my prince."

A warning bell sounded throughout the ballroom.

The Corrupt Prince and the girl in red backed away from each other, and people began to move toward the large windows all around the ballroom to get a look at the sky. As a second bell began to sound, guests started to express their concerns.

"This is the second one in a week."

"Can anyone see its tail? What color is it?"

"Has one of the main pieces finally fallen?"

"We need to find sanctuary!"

"Can Ryder Keep protect us from a piece of Celona?"

Kai climbed a few steps of the grand staircase, fingertips on the banister, and turned toward the crowd. "Honored guests! Do not fear, Ryder Keep is one of the most heavily defended keeps in Hollow. A red-tail piece of Celona is no match for its walls."

"What about a white-tail one?" a Low Noble shouted.

"We have an underground bunker for those who wish to use it. Any who do, please follow me."

Almost all the nobles participating in the Endless Waltz followed Kai out of the ballroom and to the bunker he had spoken of. The Corrupt Prince and his Throne Seekers remained, along with Zain, his Skeleton, and the Azilian. The girl in red stayed with me, and with fewer people crowding around the window I was able to make out the red tail of the piece of Celona that was falling. Hollow wouldn't be destroyed completely if it hit, but it could still do a lot of damage.

The Corrupt Prince began to laugh as he stared out the window. But before he could say anything, a third bell began to ring. It was official: a piece of Celona would be hitting Hollow tonight. There would be chaos in the streets soon, perhaps even looting in the markets or the Commerce District. My brother would be out there protecting the guilds with Scales. Gwen would be with my mother. I had no idea where Angelo would be; probably with his soldiers on the battlements, laughing at the sky.

"Would you like to make a wager, Kingman?"

Everyone turned toward the Corrupt Prince.

"What kind of wager?"

"Is it not obvious? A piece of Celona will hit our beautiful city soon. If you can bring it back to me, I will refrain from speaking out against you during the Endless Waltz."

Pieces of Celona were incredibly valuable. The metal created powerful blades, decorative hilts, and astonishing jewelry. And, if children's stories were to be believed, they also whispered the lost history of the world to those who held them. Or, if you believed the churches, they carried messages from God.

I'd be fighting against the city if I agreed to the wager.

"If I can't bring it back?"

"Then you resign from the Endless Waltz."

The girl in red stepped forward and said, "Why would he agree to that? He already has the right to participate."

"The odds are heavily against him," Zain agreed. "I wouldn't bet on it, and I bet on everything."

"He has nothing to gain from the wager," she continued.

"Let me put it this way," the prince said. "If you choose not to accept my proposal, my father will hear that you threatened me tonight."

I felt ill. It was an obvious lie, but I doubted the king would believe me no matter how many witnesses I had. A connection to the rebels be damned, the king would call for my execution before first light.

"Well, what do you say, Kingman? Do we have a wager? Or are you willing to risk what my father will do if I whisper half-truths to him?"

The top of a building in the distance was pulverized, the piece of Celona crashing straight through it as stone rained onto the streets. There was a blinding flash of light through the windows, followed by a thunderous roar that made the entire keep shake. A piece of Celona had hit Hollow.

"Do you have an answer for me, Kingman?" the Corrupt Prince asked when the shaking ended.

He was smarter than I gave him credit for. He may have been a brash bull who thought only of blood and sex, but making this wager was smart. If I succeeded, I brought him a piece of Celona for almost nothing. A small improvement in my reputation within the Hollow Court at most. If I failed, I had to drop out of the Endless Waltz and he could claim whatever he wished about me. And if I refused his wager . . . well, even I didn't want to test my luck with the king aiming at me.

"I'll get the piece of Celona. Ambassador, can you facilitate the wager?"

Zain rubbed his hands together. "This is what I live for. The wager is thus: If Michael Kingman can bring Prince Adreann the piece of Celona that just fell, the prince agrees not to speak out against Michael for the duration of the Endless Waltz. If Michael fails, he withdraws from the Endless Waltz. Do you both agree to the terms of the wager?"

"Yes," we said in unison.

"Then let Lady Luck pick a winner and Master Fortune benefit us all. The wager is live."

The Corrupt Prince threw his arm over Zain's shoulders. "Ambassador, let us get a drink and share stories while we wait. I would love to hear more about the Vakacha in your country."

Zain's face lit up and the two of them walked away, the Throne Seekers close behind. Naomi winked at me over her shoulder and then showed off that she still had my father's ring. I felt naked without it, like I was an impostor attempting to be a Kingman—though, as I was busy making deals with High Nobles and wagers with princes, I was behaving more like my ancestors. But one of these days my luck was bound to run out.

Trey didn't even glance at me.

I didn't want to put someone else in danger tonight, so I left Ryder Keep quickly, before the girl in red could volunteer to come with me, and scanned the sky to confirm where the piece of Celona had fallen. Smoke was rising upward from the Isle, so I headed toward it in search of the only thing that could appease a prince.

THE RECLAIMER

I had initially feared that the piece of Celona had struck Kingman Keep and I would be forced to return to my former home once again.

It hadn't.

It was worse.

It had hit the Church of the Wanderer, the impact blowing out one of the massive stained glass windows that detailed their prophet's journey to the stars. It had stood right above the main entrance, and hundreds, if not thousands, of small stained pieces of glass littered the stone steps.

Looters had already descended on the place, fighting to collect as much glass as possible before the monks could stop them. I had passed more on the way here, carrying torches and weapons; I tried to sidestep and ignore them, but there were too many. People pressed in from all sides, jostling and screaming for the piece of the moon within the church. Fights broke out in the horde, and the street was spattered with more blood with every moment that passed. I was only a little closer to the church when I stepped over the first body, facedown on the stone.

A flintlock pistol went off nearby, and those closest ducked in fear. Others swore at the gunman, scrambling for his gun before it could be reloaded.

I took advantage of the confusion to head straight for the church door. It was old and massive, a reminder of the days when doors like that were necessary to keep out invaders and not simply a choice of style. Dull spikes covered it without rhyme or reason.

There was no point knocking for admittance. It would be locked and barred until their next service, whether devotees requested entry or not, and they definitely wouldn't let me in. Everyone in Hollow had an opinion about the Kingman family, and the Church of the Wanderer was no different. They might not claim we were heretics, as the Church of the Eternal Flame did, but they distrusted us and that was mainly my fault.

I hadn't held my tongue often when I was younger.

It didn't matter now. Seeing no other option to get in, I joined the group who were already trying to climb the walls, heading for the broken window to gain entrance to the church. I climbed up the door, pushing and kicking at anyone in my way, and scraping my ankles and calves. My hands started finding comfortable grooves in the aged spikes on the door and I could pull myself up, my feet find-

THE KINGDOM OF LIARS   185

ing firm footholds. It was an effort, but the lethal spikes were tightly enough packed to make it possible. At the top of the door, I pulled myself up over the lip and then into the frame where the stained glass had been.

I took a deep breath once I could stand again and looked down at the people below me. Some had followed me up. Not wanting to draw more attention from those below, I slunk through the shattered glass pane, careful not to cut myself on any of the rainbow icicles that remained.

I hadn't been inside the Church of the Wanderer since I was a child, and I was surprised to see it hadn't changed. Dozens of wooden pews ran down the length of the church with a central aisle leading to a podium and the massive, faceless statue the church was famous for. Almost everyone had their own theory on what it represented or what it was meant to symbolize, but I had never cared and never listened.

Below me, white-clad monks with head scarves were running in all directions. Many of them were busy barricading the main entrance with wood and stone and fortifying the other external doors. Others clustered around the faceless statue, deep in prayer, or examined the damage done by the piece of Celona. It had come to rest behind the statue near the lockless door, in a deep impact crater that had shattered or cracked everything around it.

Slowly and quietly I crept around the edge of the church, looking for a place to descend. Climbing the door had been very straightforward; inside, the stone was smoother and lacking deviations I could use for handholds. It forced me to hug a pillar and slide less than gracefully down it. When I was on the floor, I hid in the shadows behind the pews, hoping the monks were too distracted to spot me. With the looters ahead of me drawing their attention, and those that had followed me in now appearing at the broken window, they were busy holding intruders at bay in one end of the church with their staffs and the backs of their hands. Once I reached the podium unseen, I went to my belly and crawled past the monks in prayer toward the piece of Celona.

Moments later I had it in my hand, my body resting against the base of the statue. It was unnaturally smooth, small enough to fit in my palm, and glowed eerily, as if it were filled with dying fireflies. I had never seen one in person before and was rather underwhelmed for something so sought-after.

"Michael Kingman," a voice said behind me.

I turned and saw an old man with salt-and-pepper hair standing over me. Age had given him a slow pace and a slight hunch, and he kept his fingers woven together in front of him. The Reclaimer.

Shit.

"Yes?" I said.

"I am surprised to discover you so devout as to be here to pray after moon-fall. Especially after the comments you made."

"Don't you think it's rather petty to remember the criticism of a child?"

"Yours were hard to forget," the old man said. "You nailed a different letter onto our door every single day for a year. If you want to reminisce, I saved the best ones."

"Yes, well, sadly, I don't have the time. Places to be, new friends to make, letters to write, you know how it—"

The old man stood in my way, holding out his hand.

"I'm not giving it to you willingly."

"I'm aware," he said, and then nudged his head to the side. Three monks had appeared with crossbows aimed at me. They must've been watching me from the moment I entered the church. Why they'd waited until now to shoot me was a mystery.

"Isn't killing against your oaths?"

"God understands self-defense."

Because of course they did.

"I'm not handing it over," I said. "You'll have to shoot me. I need this. My future depends on it."

"If you truly needed it, it would have landed in front of you. God sent it here so we could hear his message. Please, Michael. Do not make this end in bloodshed."

I paused and glanced around the church again. I wouldn't get far if I ran, let alone fought. I'd never escape with the piece of Celona with all these eyes on me. It would require some subtlety. I made a show of dropping my shoulders in defeat.

"Fine," I said, and held out the piece of Celona. "I'll go. But could you at least help me get out of here? I'd rather not leave the way I came in."

The old Reclaimer put the piece of the moon into the pockets of his robes. "Follow me, I'll show you to an exit where you won't have to deal with anyone."

The old man brought me toward the door that led to the cellar as the other monks watched with suspicion. As we entered the damp tunnel, he took a lantern from the wall and we walked together in the gloom. I tripped on my first step in the cellar and fell against the old Reclaimer. He caught me and then patiently helped me back to my feet despite the stream of curses that flew out of my mouth.

"Apologies, Michael. I should have warned you it's slippery down here."

"I should have been more careful," I grumbled. "I don't suppose now that we're alone you'll consider giving me the piece of Celona back?"

"No, I won't. Whether you agree with our teachings or not, everything has a path. While you may think it's the end of yours without the piece of Celona, I can assure you it's not. The Wanderer will guide you back onto your path in due time. Even if you do not realize."

I tried not to groan. I would rather have fought my way out of the church than get this lecture. It was one of the many reasons I stayed clear of the overly pious. Domet was the closest I had come to in years.

"In exchange for our forbearance in light of your attempted theft, I would ask something of you."

"I'm not attending a service here—not after what you all did to my father."

The old man sighed as if he were about to deflate. "No, I would not ask that of you."

We were at the exit, a trapdoor to the surface.

"Then what do you want?"

"For you to let your hatred of this church die with me," he said. "I was the Reclaimer who allowed your father to be executed upon our steps, and it was a mistake. I've regretted it for the past ten years. We had always been neutral in politics, but . . . but I was driven by ambition unbefitting someone of my rank. It was my mistake, Michael. Not that of the church."

"So?"

The Reclaimer looked me in the eye. "So please let this church begin anew with your family once my journey is over. Your brother and sister—"

"Lyon and Gwen are not me. And I am not them. Don't think otherwise."

"Then maybe one day I can earn your forgiveness."

"Try asking God, because you won't get it from me."

I left through the trapdoor without another word, the bite from the cold air prickling my skin.

I'd emerged far from the church at the end of the Great Stone Square, the exit obscured by bushes and trees. The crowd of looters had grown since I had entered, the fire from their torches and the glints of their blades as abundant as the stars in the sky above. Many were howling for the church to open their doors and surrender the piece of Celona. I could see monks guarding the shattered window, others beginning to patch the gaping hole with wood and nails.

It was such a shame that all the looters were wasting their time. I pulled out the piece of Celona I had pickpocketed from the Reclaimer when I had fallen against him. It was a little heavier and bigger than anything I was used to stealing from Low Nobles, but I had done it nonetheless.

Maybe I should have cared what was going to happen to the church more, now that I had what everyone was after, but I didn't. The Church of the Wanderer would survive, as it always had, with or without my intervention. It could burn to the ground for all I cared.

With the piece of Celona tucked safely back in my jacket, I started back to Ryder Keep. Maybe I could stop somewhere along the way and see if it spoke to me. For the moment, though, as far as walks went, this one wasn't the worst I had ever had the pleasure of taking. My path wound along the riverbanks of the Isle and across the western bridge, a steady mist rising from the water and trees lining the path.

As I crossed the bridge I saw clouds pass in front of the only visible moon tonight and slowly obscure the starlight, and suddenly everything became colder and darker. The mist seemed to slowly creep toward me as if it were reaching for my ankles, and the lantern light flickered and went out, plunging the bridge into an endless night. And ahead of me, emerging out of the mist, I saw two figures in the middle of the bridge, blocking my path.

They wore little more than rags, which made me appreciate the clothes on my back—until I noticed the hefty pieces of wood they were wielding. Behind them was a more elegantly dressed figure laden with gold chains and a fur-lined cloak. My breath was white and wispy as it escaped my lips.

"You're going to make my life worse, aren't you?" I asked, still some distance from them.

"Give us the stone!" the one on the left demanded, in a voice as rough as the water flowing down the river.

"Excuse me?"

"Moon stone! We saw you leave! It's in your pocket!" the right-hand one, a woman, shrieked.

My cold hands found solace in my pockets, one hand holding the piece of Celona tightly. The river ran beneath me, the flow of the water a steady sound I could focus on. "I think you're mistaken."

The woman made a clicking noise and turned to the elegant man behind her like a child would their mother.

With a sigh he said, "Why don't we check your pockets to make sure?"

"I don't think so, but thank you for asking first."

"I apologize if you thought you had a choice. Either let us, or my associates will smash your skull in and then check."

There were enough people out to get me in this city that someone could have sent them after me, but it seemed more likely these were simple bandits who'd seen a chance to grab a piece of Celona.

"As tempting an offer as that is, I think I'll just go back the way I came, and you can forget you saw me," I said, taking a few steps backwards.

There was a clanking on the cobbles behind me, and two more visitors in rags blocked the other side of the bridge. They were armed with weapons, rusted steel instead of wood.

So much for running away.

The elegant man said, "Have you decided which option you want to take yet?"

"I think so. Oh, before this begins," I continued, "just so I'm aware, none of you are working for a Mercenary, the Corrupt Prince, or a man named Trey, right?"

They turned their heads slightly to steal a glance at each other, confused by my words.

"Take it from him," the elegant man said, his face expressionless.

All four rushed me at once. I dodged the first swing from a rusted sword but took the second and third hit from the wooden weapons in my stomach and back. I was pummeled, despite my best efforts not to be, as I moved toward the edge of the bridge. Not wanting to die like this, I did the only thing I could.

I vaulted the barrier and dove into the river.

Water surrounded me. I flailed in any direction, attempting to find the surface again. Instead my feet found the bottom, my boots sinking into the mud. Bubbles escaped my lips and I pushed off the bottom hard, swimming frantically. My head broke through the surface and I inhaled, lungs burning.

My head bobbed in the water, struggling to stay afloat. The current began to quicken, running faster downstream as I flowed with it. Water crashed over my head, forcing me down, then brought me up and slammed me right back down in a torturous formula. My lungs might as well have been filled with barbed wire, with every breath bringing as much pain as it did relief.

The waves continued to batter me until my head fell beneath the surface and didn't break again. My body sank to the bottom as if it were made of lead. At the bottom of the river Jamal, Gwen, Kai, Domet, Naomi, Dark, Lyon, Kayleigh, Chloe, the Corrupt Prince, Trey, Angelo, Sirash, and the girl in red were all waiting for me. They stood around me in a circle, almost as if they were preparing to hear my last words. Their eyes had all been replaced with black voids. But even so, their mere presence was more than enough to comfort me.

As the last bubbles left my lips, I no longer shivered. Instead I felt warm, so warm, warmer than I had ever been before. My body felt light, as if it were being carried on the backs of clouds. The pain in my body vanished along with any worries or fears.

I had never felt so at ease as I did in that moment, accepting my fate.

There was a crash as a black mist of nothingness broke the ranks of everyone I knew. Jamal and Sirash dispersed in a haze as the black nothingness cut through them, and it surrounded me, tugging at my chest and arms. The pain returned soon after, slapping me out of the world that had formed around me in that time. I screamed and screamed with no voice except for the gurgles of water filling my mouth and nose. I screamed for my warm world. I screamed for the solace I had found. And I screamed knowing I would never find it again.

My throat was raw and I was colder than before. The night's air was making me shiver in place of the river water. I coughed harshly, rolling over to my side before throwing up water back into the river. The stones on the road felt like hot knives in my back.

A girl with wet hair was kneeling beside me, panting. Her electric-blue eyes were staring at my own. "Michael! Michael! Wake up!"

It took me a moment to recognize her, but I only knew one girl with eyes like that: Naomi Dexter of Scales. Coughing, I reached into my pocket and fumbled for the piece of Celona, hoping it was still there. I pulled it out a moment later, and it shone in the pale moonlight.

"Michael, what happened to you?"

I could only groan.

THE BOY AND THE WOLF

After pulling me out of the river, getting me back on my feet, and wrapping me in a smoke-stained cloak, Naomi led me through the streets of Hollow, headed toward someplace she claimed would be able to take care of me. In all semblance and reason, I shouldn't have been alive. I had coughed up so much water in the minutes after, I'd been unable to stand, let alone walk in a straight line. My eyes were glazed over and I was cold, so cold. It pervaded my entire body, from the tips of my fingers to the core of my heart, leaving me in a veil of uncertainty and doubt, my imagination mixing with the truth to form some hybrid creation. It made me wonder if this was how my mother lived every day.

I remember walking down the streets of Hollow, my right arm

slung over Naomi as she berated me with questions. They blended together in my ears, merging into the soft sounds of her sweet, crisp voice. It reminded me of a long-forgotten lullaby I had heard as a child that made my chest feel light, allowing me to drift away to somewhere I was always warm.

Lost within my memories of that lullaby, my mind wavered. I staggered into a building's wall and collapsed against it, fighting the urge to vomit. While I fought to keep my stomach's contents in place, Naomi was screaming at someone as the wind picked up around us.

As quickly as that began, things changed. One moment we were in the streets of Hollow and the next we were in a small room. I was lying on a stiff bed, devoid of most of my clothes except for my underwear, blankets up to my chin. Naomi was sitting in a chair next to me, dabbing my forehead with a wet cloth. The moment after the cloth touched me, it would become drier than sand, grating my forehead, peeling away layers of skin.

Suddenly there were two people standing over me with lanterns and tongs. One lifted the arm I wasn't using as the other examined it. "Type three–class infection here, sir," the holder said.

The other man traced the muscles in my arm with ink as if marking me for a butcher. "Shame, really," the other said. "No hope of recovery?"

He shook his head and dropped my arm. It hit the ground with a heavy thud. "Negative. Burn and mark it."

"Gladly." They grabbed the blankets at the foot of the bed and brought them over my head. It was a wave of infinite darkness that crashed over my face, drowning me. I screamed and screamed, but my voice was caught in my throat. The darkness veiled me, forcing me to accept its will. The cold returned, stronger than ever, and I lay there helpless, once again submitting to whatever my fate would be.

No.

That wasn't how it had been.

I opened my eyes, warmer than before, and pushed the upper half of my body up, forcing the darkness to retreat. The room around me shattered like broken glass. Cement and nails and stone crumbled away until eventually it was only me and the bed I was on in the middle of a wooded area. Climbing out of the bed was harder than I thought it would be, my knees barely as strong as wet paper. The trees around me were thick and sprawling, roots entangling everything around the trunks while the leafy tops were completely out of view. Even if it was daytime, I wouldn't know. Shadows inhabited this place as if they were born into it and had never needed to fear the sun.

I stepped on a broken branch and it dug into the sole of my foot, drawing blood. Cursing, I jammed my thumb against the wound, blood running over it, dyeing it dark and red.

The woods seemed alive with nature's music. Leaves rustled around me, the wind spinning them upward around my bed like a cyclone, only to ebb away and reveal a well-dressed boy. He was much shorter than me, with a circular birthmark on his temple and muscle he hadn't grown into yet. An unfinished iron crown was hidden in the tangles of his messy auburn hair, and a sigil that depicted a palm holding out a crown was sewed onto his shirt, over his heart. I couldn't place the symbol in that moment, so my eyes latched onto it, trying to find it among my memories. All I remembered was my father and our family.

"Where am I?"

The boy held his small finger up to his lips. "Too loud."

More quietly, I repeated my question.

"This is where angels come to be feasted on by wolves. Where daemons hide in plain sight, advocating they are the good people in the grand scheme of things. Where dreams come true, legends are born, wars are started . . . and where the Endless Waltz ends."

"Right," I said, drawing out the word. "Who are you?"

"Who are you?" the boy mimicked with a smile.

"Michael Kingman."

"A name does not make the man, just like a lie does not tell the full story. Usually you have to read or hear it twice to fully understand." The boy picked up a rock and held it out to me. "This is a diamond. Do you see?" Before I could protest, the outer shell of the stone peeled away and it began to glimmer and shine, even in the absence of light. "You perceive yourself as clever, but you're just like that rock."

"Oh, do I mature when I'm under pressure?"

"No," he declared. "You're lying about yourself to the world. You're a child who's never grown up. But, unlike me, you can change that. If you stop complaining so much."

"I'm a child? Do you realize what I've had to go through since my father was executed for treason? The abuse I've had to suffer from the nobility because he killed the prince? I've survived when everyone wanted me dead."

The boy shook his head. "You sound like a music box, repeating the same refrain. 'Pity me. Feel bad for me. Don't kill me. It's not my fault. Blah, blah, blah.' You need to grow up already. Are you a Kingman or not?"

Off in the distance of the woods, a howl pierced the silent night. The trees swayed in the wind as birds cawed before escaping into the sky. The boy stood unwavering. "Did you know humanity used to fear the woods? Now we fear the city. Don't you find that strange?"

"No," I said. "Cities have people in them. What does a forest have?"

The howl returned, more bloodthirsty than before. When it faded away, two beady red eyes appeared to the right of the boy. "Animals," he said. "A forest has animals."

A smile came to me. "I'd be more intimidated if this wasn't just another one of my nightmares."

The boy began to evaporate into steam, vanishing into the cold night air. With his last words he simply said, "Get your shit together already."

That pair of beady red eyes began to creep forward. Leaves crunched and twigs snapped as heavy breathing filled the air. With every step, more and more of a wolf became visible. It was a massive animal, black with streaks of grey. Its teeth were stark white, completely unfound in the real world. The wolf stopped in front of me, crouching down as it bared its fangs.

My feet were planted down on the ground. I curled my toes, digging them into a mess of grass and twigs and dirt. "I'm not scared of my nightmares," I said. "My life is scarier."

Its jaw dropped into a grin.

And I returned it. "Go away."

It leapt. The wolf slammed its paws into my chest, overpowering me as its teeth snapped for my neck. It clawed at my chest and forearms, stripping the flesh off me in long, thick sections. I kicked and screamed until the wolf ripped out my throat.

Dying wasn't new to me. I had an understanding that it would come for us all one day; all that differed was the time. It was oddly comforting in a way. It was the only time nobles, Royals, and commoners were the same. We all walked into the darkness at the end, meeting whatever waited for us. There were some days that I thought it would be the only time in my life I would be at peace.

The wolf left me staring at the sky with cold, fixated eyes.

It was a shame I didn't die.

I had shrunk, half the size I usually was. My body moved on its own, taking me down a hallway, fingers moving with the grooves on the wall to feel all the prickly bumps. At the end of the hallway I found a door and pushed it open, entering a bedroom. Against the far wall was a massive feather bed draped in red-and-grey sheets. Only the right side of the bed was disturbed, the left side smooth and flat. Portraits and paintings covered the walls, yet all the faces were blurred as if mist clouded them from my sight. The carpet under my feet was soft and fluffy. My toes clung to it. This was the most realistic nightmare I'd ever had.

"Are you sure it has come to this?" my father said from the balcony.

I turned to him, inching closer to the glass doors. There was no one else on the balcony that I could see. Was he talking to himself?

"There must be another way!" he shouted, a red flush coloring his face. "People will listen to me! I could have dealt with this if you had come to me sooner."

My shadow began to dance on the walls, spinning and doing flips around the exit to the balcony. A slow, deep growl began to fill my ears. It sounded like the wolf.

My father sat down on the edge of the balcony looking out onto the city. His normally neat brown hair was a mess, strands standing at all angles. "No, I refuse. There is always another way. The prince doesn't need to die."

My dancing shadow steadied to the right of the doorframe, its bright red eyes watching me. Just like the wolf.

"Da?"

My father jerked around to me, his eyes red and puffy. "Michael?"

I awoke with a jolt, covered in sweat. The stiff bed I had been placed on was as damp as if I had lost my bladder during the night. Had I dreamed all of that? What had just happened to me? My memories were blurry at best. The details were blending together. And the last part of that dream with my father . . . I hadn't dreamed of him in years, my nightmares normally focused on the Kingman Keep riots.

Gathering my sanity, realizing I'd been stripped to my underwear, I looked around and, surprisingly, discovered I was in my own room in the Narrows. There was half a loaf of stale bread and a bowl of cold soup on the bedside table, old enough that it had developed a thin film of grease. I tore off a piece from the loaf, stirred it into the soup, and popped it into my mouth.

I could have made my own bread in the time it took me to chew it well enough to keep it down. Which, sadly, was fairly normal when it came to Angelo's cooking.

The girl with the electric-blue eyes was sleeping in a chair next to me. She had curled herself up under a thin blanket, her brown hair falling over her forehead like strands of thread. If I didn't know better, I would have thought it was cute. Was she waiting for me to wake up?

As much as I didn't want to disturb someone while they slept, I needed answers—like where my piece of Celona was—so I slammed the bottom of my fist against my bedside table, loud enough to wake her.

Naomi scrambled, jolting awake as the blanket slid off her and onto the floor. Her words in response were barely audible mumbles, but she had the piece of Celona in her hands.

"How'd I get here?" I asked as I chewed on another piece of stale bread. It may be old food, but it was food. Couldn't let it go to waste.

It took her a few moments to wake up properly, but then she said. "I dragged you here."

"How'd you know where I lived?"

"You told me."

"Why were you even there?"

"I left shortly after you did," she said. "I was going to act as your guardian from afar in case you ran into trouble . . . but by the time I caught up with you, you were already in the middle of a fight. Only thing I could do was get you out of the river."

"The Corrupt Prince didn't send them after me?"

"No. He would never work with people like that. They were random bandits."

"Are you working for him?"

"Do you really think I would save you if I was?"

Well, that answered that.

I threw my legs over the side of the bed. "Is any of my family home?"

"Commander Shade was. He stayed with me until your chills went away and then went to work. Told me to do the same, but I wanted to stay until you woke up."

No doubt he would have a lecture and some choice words waiting for me whenever I saw him again. I hadn't told him that I was participating in the Endless Waltz, and I doubted having a woman drag me back home while I was delirious was how he wanted to find out.

"Why'd you stay?" I asked. "I doubt it was for the good of your reputation."

She looked downward and laughed slightly. "I doubt my father would care one way or another. He never was one for following the rules of what was acceptable in noble society. And I stayed because you're still useful to me in the Endless Waltz. I can't have you drop out so soon. Without you, I wouldn't be so close to the prince."

At least she didn't pretend she liked me.

"How long have I been out for?"

"Little less than a day," she said, arms crossed. "It's almost evening again."

"Shit!"

I went to my feet, wobbled, but caught myself before I fell. My body felt weak, stagnant, but I had to stand, so I did, everything shaking. Only for Naomi to push me back onto my bed with a roll of her eyes.

"Relax. You look as bad as you feel. Take some time to rest," Naomi stated. "It wasn't as if there was a time limit on when you had to deliver the piece of Celona."

"And show him what he tried to do worked? No, he gets it now."

"How do you plan on doing that? It's not as if he's still in Ryder Keep."

I hesitated. "Where is he, then?"

"No idea. But I know where he'll be tonight. He's having a small party with his Throne Seekers to celebrate the fact you seem to have lost your wager." A sickening smile spread across her face. "It would be the perfect opportunity to show yourself and claim victory."

"Why are you helping me?"

There was a knock at the door, and Naomi took the opportunity to answer it rather than my question. When she returned, she had a large parcel and a small cloth sack that jingled in her hands.

"These are for you," Naomi said, handing them to me. "Man at the door said you'd know who it was from."

I opened the cloth sack first and found five suns within, confirming my suspicion. Inside the parcel were fine clothes, almost identical to what I had worn to the first event and ruined after jumping into the river. There was a note on top of them that read *For Your Meeting Tonight*.

Domet.

But how he had figured out what had happened to me, where I lived, what I needed to do . . . Who was I kidding? It was Domet. He had already proven he had eyes everywhere. This was nothing for someone like him. If anything, I was amazed he didn't come see me himself to make sure I hadn't run away.

"Secret admirer?" Naomi snickered.

"Jealous?"

"Not even a little."

"If you say so."

"Now, if you'll excuse me, I need to go and get some work done," Naomi said. "I'll take you to the Corrupt Prince when I'm back."

"What am I supposed to do in the meantime?"

She had her hand on the doorframe as she looked over her shoulder. "Rest."

I remained upright until I heard her leave. Despite wanting to do something—anything rather than sit in this bed and recover—I found myself struggling to stay awake. All the stress and exhaustion from everything that had happened recently finally hitting me. So, for once, I rested, and hoped the city wouldn't collapse in the meantime.

A GAMBLER AND HIS FOLLY

We heard the Corrupt Prince before we saw him, something I was beginning to suspect would be a trend. He was nestled deep within the Poison Gardens, playing with fireworks before they shot into the sky and exploded in brilliant colors. Ambassador Zain and the Throne Seekers were with him. Only Trey was absent. A few women had joined them, but, given how lightly clad they were, I doubted they were there for the conversation. Naomi stayed behind at the gates to the gardens, not wanting to be seen at my side.

I hobbled into the clearing, the piece of Celona shining in my hand. Everything still hurt, despite taking so much time to recover. But this wasn't the time to show weakness. "Adreann, you just lost a wager."

All the laughter stopped. Only Zain looked amused as Adreann Hollow moved a girl off him so he could stand. "What?"

I held it up. "I have the piece of Celona."

"Well, well, you retrieved it. Not my preferred outcome, but I have always wanted a piece, and a wager is a—"

He went for the piece of Celona, but I snatched it out of reach. "I think you misunderstood the wager, Adreann. I never had to give it to you, only bring it to you."

"Which implies that it will be given to me."

"It implies nothing. You should have been specific."

The Corrupt Prince breathed out of his nose. "If you won't give it to me, then I'll simply take—"

Ambassador Zain stepped forward, a smile on his face. "My dear prince, I'm afraid Michael is correct. The deal never specified you would be given the piece of Celona, only that Michael bring it to you."

"Which implies—"

"Which is precisely what he has done, Prince Adreann. Words are words, and they were your words and are clear as day. If you must rely on an implication, then you were not sufficiently clear. As arbiter of the wager, I declare it won by Michael, and Adreann will keep to his end of it. So says I, Zain Antoun, ambassador for the Goldono Gold Vein Casino."

I patted the Corrupt Prince on the shoulder. "Pleasure doing business with you, Adreann."

As I walked away, enjoying his fury, I could feel the heat coming from him. "One more bet."

That made me stop. "What?"

"One more bet. You can participate, unopposed, in the Endless Waltz and I won't whisper a word to my father. The new bet would be your piece of Celona against the deed to Kingman Keep. Or do you enjoy living in squalor in the Narrows, Kingman?"

Something was wrong. Why was Adreann so determined to have a piece of Celona? I'd thought this a throwaway wager, and Gwen had never mentioned the Corrupt Prince being interested in Celona while they were children. He had never even liked stargazing. My curiosity was making it hard to say no. The piece of Celona had no particular value to me—other than its sale value and its usefulness in annoying the Corrupt Prince—so the chance to win back Kingman Keep was tempting. Could I ever forgive myself if I turned this wager down?

"What's the game?" I asked.

The Corrupt Prince snapped his fingers and one of his Throne Seekers brought over a pair of chairs, a table, two cups, and a lot of dice. We were seated opposite each other, and Ambassador Zain began to separate the dice into two equal groups. "This is a Goldono game. We teach it to children so they can learn the importance and danger of dear Lady Luck. The rules are simple: Each gambler shakes their dice, and then upends their cup. Whoever has the highest score wins the round. The best of three—not the highest total score—wins."

"This is just luck. There's no skill to it," I said.

"Oh, there is skill, Michael," Ambassador Zain said. "The purpose of this game is to teach children when to stop gambling, so if you believe Lady Luck will not favor you, you may walk away at any moment. The wager between you will be nullified. Do you both understand the rules and agree to the wager: a piece of Celona against the title to Kingman Keep?"

"Yes," I said.

"Yes," the Corrupt Prince echoed.

"Then let Lady Luck choose her winner, and Master Fortune benefit us all. The wager is live."

We both picked up our cups and began to shake them against our palms. The rattle filled the Poison Gardens as all eyes were on us.

"Why the interest in Celona, Adreann?" I asked.

"We live in a country more besieged by the moon than any other. Who's to say I've not long been curious about Celona?"

"My sister."

The Corrupt Prince slammed his cup down on the table. "She should learn to keep her mouth shut unless I direct her to open it."

I put my cup down. "Why? Does it bother you that she knows you as well as you know yourself? That she knows your weaknesses? Your strengths?"

"Reveal!" Ambassador Zain commanded.

We did. The Corrupt Prince had twenty-one points, while I had twenty-three.

"Kingman takes the first round. Reset and shake again when ready."

"Your sister knows nothing about me," the Corrupt Prince spat as we shook again. He didn't hesitate to begin. Almost as if the piece of Celona was worth more to him than anything else.

"Then enlighten me. Why the interest in Celona?"

"Why would I tell the son of a child-murdering traitor anything?"

"Are you ashamed—"

"Shame is a foreign concept to me."

The Corrupt Prince put his cup down on the table, and moments later I followed.

"Reveal!"

I had twenty-one points against the Corrupt Prince's twenty-seven.

"Prince Adreann takes the second round. Reset and shake when ready. Final round."

"This is it, Kingman. Are you ready?" the Corrupt Prince asked with a devious smile.

I tapped my fingers against the table, then slowly loaded my dice back into the cup. It was suddenly clear, as if my name had been called in a crowded room: I knew I would lose if I continued. My pride had dragged me into the game, and I wasn't willing to give the Corrupt Prince anything without knowing his intentions.

Kingman Keep wasn't worth it. Without our legacy restored, it was merely a museum for memories.

"I'm leaving," I said as I rose from the table.

"Sit back down! Roll the dice!" the Corrupt Prince shouted.

"No, I'm done. I know when to walk away."

"Don't you want Kingman Keep back?"

"I have no use for it."

The Corrupt Prince exhaled through his nose, face turning red. "History repeats itself. You ran when Davey tried to talk to you about a piece of Celona before he was murdered. Do you remember the morning before Davey died, Michael?"

I did. I'd spent the morning in a haze, having been unable to sleep that night. Sword practice with Lyon, Gwen, and the Royals had been disastrous, all of them defeating me with ease. Our studies had been little better, my mind unable to find the answers the tutors had been seeking. In fact, it had been such a bad morning, I'd decided to skip the rest of my obligations in favor of exploring the castle.

No one found me until nightfall. I had returned from my adventures and snuck into the kitchen to find something to eat, and heard what my father had done. It had been my last day of innocence. For years I had wished for a redo, so I could have found out with others, because from then on, the weight of my family's legacy had been on my shoulders and mine alone.

None of which I was going to say to the Corrupt Prince.

"You weren't with us the night before, when a piece of Celona fell, so I'll tell you what happened," the Corrupt Prince began. "It struck in the Royal Gardens, and Davey rushed out to see if they truly spoke. He swore it did, but your father took it away before I or my sister could hear it too. Davey claimed it said the eldest had to die for the country to flourish. He thought it was funny . . . but, sure enough, he was murdered the next day."

"Goodbye, Adreann."

"Run away again! Your father will always be a child-murdering traitor. All that can ever change is why. Was he a fanatic? A lunatic? Obsessed with power? One day we'll know."

I kept walking away, and when they thought I was out of earshot I heard the Corrupt Prince scream that the party was over and order everyone out. I should have been pleased to win our bet and ruin his evening, but his story was stuck in my head and I didn't feel like a victor. He'd wanted to put me in my traitorous place. Why else tell that story but to make me feel guilty and ashamed of my father?

I should have walked away to begin with.

Naomi was waiting for me outside. "How'd it go?"

I held up the piece of Celona. "Well enough."

"I can see that. You realize he'll still come after you—indirectly."

"I'd expect no less," I said. "I'll take my ring back, though. Your position in noble society is currently higher than mine, and I've more than held up my part of the agreement we made while you had a crossbow pointed at my chest."

"Have you?" she said, twisting my father's ring around her finger. "I'm not so sure. You've barely given me anything, and I've saved you from drowning in a river. If anything, I think I should hold on to it for a little longer. Besides, you'll need to know what the Corrupt Prince is planning, won't you?"

"Aren't you with the Throne Seekers? What do you gain out of telling me what the Corrupt Prince is planning?"

Naomi brushed her hand against my cheek. "I'm guaranteed a win. It's as simple as that."

Abruptly, I had the feeling Naomi could be significantly more dangerous than the Corrupt Prince. At least I knew where he and I stood, but with her . . . I'd have no idea what she wanted until she either embraced me or stabbed me in the back. Or did both. I'd never met someone ambitious enough to con a Royal and blackmail a Kingman at the same time. I'd have to be careful.

"Once the Endless Waltz is over, I want my ring back."

"Fair," she said, walking away with a wave. "But, for now, I like how it looks on my finger."

"So do I. But I'm surprised, Naomi. Don't you want to know if a piece of Celona speaks?"

Naomi kept walking. "I've listened already. It's quite interesting. Don't worry about escorting me home, Michael. There is nothing in this city that scares me."

As I watched her walk away, I couldn't help but shiver. There were plenty of things in this country that scared me. There were probably things in this city that scared the king and his Ravens, too. But not her.

I turned my attention to the stupid rock that caused so such trouble, to see if it spoke for myself. I held the piece of Celona up before my eyes, uncertain how I was supposed to hear it relay its secrets, and stared at it for a few moments, concentrating on the stone and the warmth that accompanied it, wondering if they could truly be messages from God or if it was a story made up by someone over the generations—

The message came like the wind, subtle and rustling off in a distance, until it was strong enough for me to hear it fully. In a deep, formal voice, I heard the words:

"The king's man is a traitor. Cut off his head."

A FOSTER FATHER

I didn't try to run away from Angelo in the morning. Trying would have been in vain, since he was up before first light and waiting for me in the kitchen. Even more surprising than his early rising was the fact he was cooking bacon, something he had never done in all the years he had been my foster father.

"Bacon?" I asked suspiciously as I entered the room.

"Bacon," he said.

"Wasn't I supposed to cook breakfast?"

"You can start tomorrow."

I took a seat at the table with Dark's envelope in my hand, thankful I had left it at home before the first event. The river would have destroyed it otherwise. "What's the occasion?"

"Well," he said, "it was supposed to be a celebration of sorts, but considering Gwen is already gone for the day—"

"Already? It's so early. Gwen normally doesn't wake up until midday if she can help it."

Angelo scraped the sides of the pan, the bacon continuing to sizzle. "She's starting another job. Or applying for one. But, as I was saying, this was meant to be celebrating Gwen working for the asylum for three years, Lyon having a child, and—"

"You knew about that? Was I seriously the last person to find out?"

"Will you stop interrupting me, Michael?" he barked over his shoulder. "This was meant to be a celebration for all of you. We don't indulge often, and I wanted to recognize how you've all matured recently. Sometimes I barely recognize the people you're becoming."

Angelo took the pan off the stove and moved it onto the table. He handed me a fork and took another one out of a drawer for himself. "But that doesn't mean I don't want to talk to you about the Endless Waltz."

I had assumed as much. I speared a piece of burnt bacon out of the pan and put it into my mouth. It was fatty and smoky and wonderful.

"Honestly, Michael, are you sure this is the best decision for you to make?"

I waited until I was done chewing. "I don't know. But it's the one I made."

"What do you hope to gain by participating?"

"A better future for myself and our family," I said. "Last night I was one roll of the dice away from reclaiming Kingman Keep." None of it was a lie. Working with Domet had already offered me so much, including more trouble. But soon my family would be taken care of for the future, and maybe, if I was lucky, our family's legacy would be restored, too.

Though, after listening to the piece of Celona last night, it had all started to seem unlikely. Its words had been stuck in my head, a nightmare I couldn't escape from. Especially when I was uncertain what had spoken to me. It had sounded like the wind and I refused to admit it was a message from God. But whatever or whoever the words belonged to, its message was clear.

The Kingman is a traitor. Cut off his head.

Those words could only be about one person.

"You know what you're risking, right? The nobility doesn't play fair," Angelo said. "If they get the chance to destroy you, they will. They might even come after our family, too."

"I won't let that happen," I said, taking more bacon.

"What makes you think they'll give you the opportunity to fight back? If they realize you're on probation, what's to stop them from inventing a connection to the rebels—or, worse, framing you—and then watching alongside the city as you get executed?"

I held my tongue. I doubted Angelo would be reassured to hear I had Domet on my side, who could prevent the nobility from discarding me too easily, or that I'd won a wager against the Corrupt Prince last night, which ensured a little safety. Participating in the Endless Waltz was dangerous.

"There's nothing I can say to dissuade you, is there?"

I shook my head. "I'm sorry. I'm doing this."

Angelo leaned back in his seat. "Have I ever told you why I wanted to foster you three?"

"Not really."

"I have issues with some of the nobility," he declared. "Which is probably no great surprise to you. We all do. But in my youth I saw what they did to those below them and it . . . repulsed me. That raw, uncontrollable hunger for extravagance. Regardless of the cost. After what happened with Davey, I saw your father as the pinnacle of noble arrogance. That the Hollow Court had been foolish enough to think that the one they held so high was exempt from the greed they all thrived on. When I was at the execution, I expected to cheer for the death of a monster. Instead, I saw a man full of regrets who just wanted to make sure his children were taken care of when he was gone."

Angelo twisted the rings on his fingers. "I had lost my wife and our unborn child some time before that, and that unfettered love resonated with me. So I went to my commander and asked to foster you three, away from all the cutthroat politics. Maybe it's my fault that we didn't have much over the years and you've felt this is the only option you had left . . . but what if I could offer you an alternative to the Endless Waltz?"

I looked up at him.

"I received a letter from an old friend yesterday. He's interested in taking you on as a steward for a Gold Coast clan. He's willing to teach you everything he knows from swordsmanship to sailing. With time you may even be able to become a knight for the household."

"Angelo, we talked about this—"

He held up a hand. "He's willing to take in your mother and Gwen, too."

A cold sweat overcame me. Right up until this moment, I had

believed Angelo thought our mother was dead. None of us had ever told him otherwise, letting the rumors that she had died in the King-man Keep riots go unchallenged. Stammering, I asked, "How?"

"How did I learn she was alive? It was an accident. I went to visit Gwen in the asylum about a year ago and asked for the King-man in residence. Imagine my surprise when they didn't take me to Gwen."

The bacon had lost its flavor. "Why didn't you say anything?"

"Honestly? I didn't know how to. I felt like I was invading an aspect of your lives that you didn't want or need me involved in. Even if we're family, I know we're not related by blood, and there are some things I will never understand because I lack the Kingman name. But recently I feel like I have to intrude to protect all of you from that legacy."

"What are you offering me exactly?"

"A way out of Hollow. My friend will take the three of you in on the Gold Coast. The king and the Royals can't get you there, and you'll be able to live in peace far away from Hollow politics and grudges. He would have taken Lyon, too, but . . . he's found his own place in Hollow. Even if it's not as a Kingman."

I didn't know how to respond.

Angelo's offer was as good as Domet's—maybe better—for far less risk. I would be safe. My family would be safe. I wouldn't have to worry about Gwen's hatred of the Royal Family and what she might do one day. My mother wouldn't have to live in secrecy and shame for the rest of her life, and I could continue to investigate ways to cure her. It was as close as I could get to a perfect life, and all I had to do was forsake the slim chance of redeeming my father.

The voice from the piece of Celona repeated in my mind.

The Kingman is a traitor. Cut off his head.

"Who knows," Angelo laughed, "maybe I could come, too. I don't miss the flooding, but the food and scenery were divine."

"Angelo, this is all . . ." I trailed off into nothing.

"Think about it." He stood and put his hand on my shoulder. "You have time to consider what you want to do. But once you're in the king's sight, your options will be severely limited."

"I know," I said, much less confident in my choices.

"No matter what you choose, I'll be here for you, Michael. Always remember that."

"Thank you."

A nod and then he cleared his throat. "One last thing, Michael. About that girl who brought you back here . . . How much do you know about her?"

"Naomi? Not much. Why? Do you know her?"

A pause. "I read Naomi Dexter's application to Scales years ago. I probably still have a copy of it somewhere, though it's classified, so you wouldn't be able to look at it even if I remembered where it was." He glanced toward a pile of papers on the kitchen table. "Be careful around her, Michael. She's ambitious."

I nodded, understanding what he meant.

"I'm going to get changed for work. Finish the bacon off for me, will you? And make sure everything is back in its proper place."

"Of course."

With a smile, Angelo left me in the kitchen. The moment he was back in his room, I searched through his papers for any mention of

Naomi. Most of it was half-written letters, invoices, and an estimate for a painting of his late wife.

Then I found her evaluation.

Naomi Dexter has made multiple applications to the Raven and Scales. Inadmissible to the Ravens, having failed the first stage of the exam, this is her third attempt to join the Scales—this time with the considerable influence of her father: Bryan Dexter, Commander of the Evoker Division. It should be noted that her mother, Evie Browne, was a victim of the Heartbreaker serial killer, and since her death Naomi has focused on opportunities to protect the citizens of Hollow.

She is clearly bright and capable. I suspect she is a formidable liar, most likely taught by her father, and is a highly adept Wind Fabricator who could be an asset to the Scales. She is evidently ambitious and may only embrace a position in Scales as a means to her own ends. But, in this interviewer's opinion, Naomi Dexter should be invited to join Scales in either the Executioner or Warden Division. With guidance, and so long as we are sure her objectives are aligned with ours, she has leadership potential. In any instance where this may not be the case, she should be confined to a role in which her skills can be put to use but she has no influence over her colleagues.

Naomi's evaluation for Scales only confirmed my suspicions about her. And proved she had lied to me about how her mother had died. I'd have to be even more careful around her and figure out what she truly wanted before it was too late. With one report to Scales, that she had seen me at Kingman Keep, she could have me arrested and potentially dead by first light. Or maybe dusk, depending on the king's mood.

I put all the papers back the way I had found them, gathered Dark's envelope and hid the piece of Celona, ate the rest of the bacon, cleaned up the kitchen, and then left the house before Angelo was done getting ready for work. It was still early and I had a lot to do. Including visiting Domet.

On my way I stopped at a bakery near the Hanging Gardens and once again discovered nothing. It only made me worry about Sirash and his family more, but with the Militia Quarter destroyed and the East Side still in chaos it made sense he might not be able to travel far. I kept telling myself that reassuring lie as I walked to the Upper Quarter.

Everyone I passed seemed to be huddled around fliers or chatting in skittish groups. The city seemed quieter than it usually was, silenced for the first time in generations. There were even fewer Advocators on patrol. It was unsettling.

By the time I arrived at Domet's house, I had grown even more concerned with what was going on within the city. The Upper Quarter resembled a graveyard, the songs of birds the only thing that floated through the air in this city of stone. Domet was waiting for me on the steps of his house in his natural state, cane in one hand and a bottle of rum in the other.

"Did you hear the news while you were slacking off in bed, Michael?"

"Are we going to war with New Dracon City again?" I joked.

"No," he said. "Scales caught the Rebel Emperor. They have him in custody and are setting a date to try him for high treason."

"What?"

He took a swig from the bottle. "Did I stutter?"

"How? When?"

"Rumor says they caught him shortly after the attack on the Militia Quarter but have kept quiet about it until now."

I remembered the man who smelled of lemons from the graveyard. The man who was responsible for the fall of Naverre and for killing Jamal. I hoped it was true and that this rebellion would be over soon. I was tired of seeing innocent people hang for their supposed crimes against the government.

"When's the trial?"

Another swig. "Day after the king's birthday celebration. The king wants the entire Hollow Court to witness it."

"You don't seem very pleased they got him."

"Heh, I am. But I'm worried what will happen when the nobility lacks a common foe. The Old Blood will remember their vows, but the New won't. If war can be credited with anything, it's bringing people together."

"Thousands have died because of the rebellion."

Domet stood slowly, shaking out his legs once he was standing. "And thousands more will die if the nobility begin to fight against each other. Hollow used to rely on the Kingman family to curb the ambition of the nobility, and focus on the greater good. That won't be the case this time. But that's a problem for another day, and there's work to be done, Michael. I've already heard that you made a good first impression on the nobility when you were at Ryder Keep. Several small fortunes were made betting on you. But we need even better results in the second event."

"How are we going to do that?"

Domet drained the bottle and left it on the steps. "The second event is a hunt. I have no idea what you'll be hunting, but in case it's something exotic, it's best if you're prepared."

"You're finally going to teach me?"

"Yes," Domet said dryly. "It's time you learned how to use Fabrications."

THE RAVEN

We descended the stone stairs slowly and carefully, trying not to fall over our own feet in the dim light or slam into the other patrons. Charles Domet pulled and pushed me away from the crowds of flushed nobles, directing me toward a corner.

My head spun, and I had to grab the nearby railing and reorient myself. We had gone underground, only to emerge on top of an old building reinforced with scraps of metal and wood. Stalactites hung from the ceiling and stalagmites popped up from the natural ground around the ruins. The air was damp, and there was only enough light to see the immediate area, with movement just out of sight in the gloom. When I finally got my bearings, I looked down.

It was less a building, more an underground arena. The open

square at the bottom of the long, slick walls was paved in broken stone slabs, many splintered upward like blooming flowers, and surrounded by a moat of cloudy, stagnant water that looked green in this light. The stained floor had seen its fair share of blood, and the audience gathered on balconies surrounding it, the rich and the poor rubbing shoulders, all drinking and hollering for entertainment.

Domet rested his elbows against the stone railings. "Have you heard of this place?"

I shook my head as I watched two plainly dressed men clink their glasses in a toast and drink. I thought I knew the unsupervised side of Hollow, but I'd never heard of an underground arena and was fairly annoyed I didn't know about this place before. I could've made a fortune fighting, or at least a fortune getting beaten up.

"This is the Shattered Stones," he said. "It was built over Wolven King ruins and has a fabled history drowned in blood. A prince died here once. We're lucky there's an event today— you'll learn a lot. Pay attention and answer my questions when I ask them. Don't make me repeat myself."

"I'm not some moonstruck fool."

"That's yet to be proven." Domet took a sip from his flask. "It's about to begin. Don't miss anything."

A man dressed exuberantly in blue and gold walked out onto the balcony that projected over the arena. His natural voice boomed out: "Ladies and gentlemen! Welcome to the Shattered Stones! Today we have a rare treat for you: a Raven Bloodbath!"

The audience hooted and howled with excitement, pounding their feet against the wooden floors until they vibrated. As the announcer waited for things to calm down, I asked, "What's a Raven Bloodbath?"

"The final test for those who seek to become a Raven for the king. This is where they are born. In the darkness, surrounded by bloodlust."

That sounded too poetic to be true. Before I could ask another question, the announcer continued, "You know the stakes, now let me introduce you to the combatants! First, the defending champion, hailing from the darkest pits of Goldono, a criminal who has clipped the wings of three other would-be Ravens: the Fletcher!"

A lanky copper-skinned man stamped through one of the entranceways and into the arena. Half of his chest was covered with metal, with the rest covered in thick black body hair. A huge red scar ran from his chin down to his navel, and he dragged a great battle-ax behind him, the metal screech filling the arena. The Fletcher ignored the cheering crowd and licked his lips, eyeing the other doorway.

"Tell me his first mistake," Domet ordered.

After a pause, I answered, "He's dragging his ax along the floor. One side of it is probably duller than the other."

His calm nod was the only response I got as the announcer continued. "And now the challenger herself, Chloe Mason!"

I remembered Chloe. She'd been in the shrine when I visited with Domet. She'd been surprisingly delicate, and we'd made some snide remarks at each other. Nothing too serious or noteworthy.

If I hadn't heard her name, I would never have known it was her.

Her face was gaunt, eyes sunken, and her skin seemed to hang from her face. She was thinner and stumbling, barely able to walk in a straight line as she dragged her bare feet across the ground, the shattered stones cutting them to ribbons, blood documenting her path. Behind her came an armored woman, three peacock feathers woven into her hair.

"What happened to her?"

"The Ravens' test," Domet said flatly. "This is the final portion. In preparation for this, they endure so much hazard and torture that most call it inhumane. The candidates are kept in cells in complete darkness without food or water between tests. If they give up, go mad, or die, they fail."

"Why would someone do that to themselves?" I asked, thinking of Naomi's file.

Chloe was stopping every few steps to catch her breath. She looked barely alive, a skeleton wearing clothes. She was willing to do this for the chance to risk her life for a city . . . for a king she owed nothing to. It made me uneasy.

"Does she have any chance? That man is twice her size and he's breathing without pain. Is this designed so that she'll fail?"

"No," he said. "She's expected to win. That's today's lesson. By the end of this fight, Michael, you will see the strength of a Fabricator. Watch and learn."

By the time Chloe reached her mark, the crowd had grown restless and hungry for violence. People came here to see blood, and if they didn't get it soon, the loser would lose more to quench the crowd's thirst.

The announcer cleared his throat and began to rile up the crowd. "Who's ready to see a Raven Bloodbath?" The crowd started to pound their feet against the floor again. "The rules of the battle are simple: the winner is the first to spill their opponent's blood over the shattered stones! No ring-outs, no tapping out, no nothing but the sweet sight of blood hitting the floor will do! Let the Raven Bloodbath begin!"

Fletcher lifted the great ax above his head and swiped at Chloe. She swayed to the right, the steel just missing her. The clang of the metal echoed through the arena as Fletcher continued to lift the ax, then bring it down. Chloe began circling him, dodging every attack, but never making one of her own. It almost seemed like they were dancing.

"Clever girl," Domet said, leaning toward the arena. "Tell me what she's doing."

The dance continued, Chloe circling as the Fletcher kept driving forward. If any of his blows landed, he would cut her in half. The Shattered Stones arena was already covered in their bloody footprints. "She's wearing him out."

"She's already exhausted—tiring him won't help her. Try again."

I rubbed the spot where my ring should have been and watched closely. When he wasn't putting all his strength into lifting his ax, Fletcher always dragged it along the floor, and he seemed reluctant to swing it left or right, preferring to let gravity drag the ax down toward her. "The ax is too heavy for him," I said. "He shouldn't be using the weapon."

Domet gave me a curt nod. "If he were using any other weapon, this fight would be over. She knows that, but he doesn't. What would you do with that knowledge if you were she?"

Chloe was faster than the enemy, but weaker. If she was hit, even once, it was over, and she was unarmed. "Do you know what her Fabrication specialty is?"

"Lightning."

"Why not just hit him with a bolt of lightning to the chest, then? One and done."

Chloe continued to dance around Fletcher. He was slowly beginning to drive her toward the water. There might be no ring-outs, but it was unlikely she had the strength to swim if she fell in.

"And expose what type of Fabricator she is? First lesson." Domet turned to me, dragging the side of his palm along the stone barrier. "Less than a quarter of the Hollow population are Fabricators, and among those who are, maybe half are skilled. What can you gather from that information?"

"That there's a woman down there fighting for her life?" I said. Domet gave me a flat look. "I don't know."

He sighed and returned to the fight. "Knowledge is power when it comes to Fabricators. Knowing your opponent is a Fabricator is one power, and knowing what kind of Fabricator they are is another. Spellborns, in particular, will avoid revealing their ability for as long as possible and then overwhelm their opponent when they have an opening."

"Spellborn?"

He made a disapproving noise. "That's a lesson you're not ready for yet. Prove to me that this wasn't a mistake agreeing to teach you. Tell me what she's doing right."

I paused. "She's remaining calm."

"Why is that important?"

"Because when Fabricators get emotional and they use Fabrications, they risk snapping."

"Which is?"

"An overemotional state of heightened Fabricator ability that leads to an increase in memory loss. It almost always happens before someone becomes a Forgotten."

"Good. You do know something. But the fight isn't over yet. Pay attention."

Chloe had been driven to the edge of the arena, swaying left and right to avoid the ax. She had yet to fight back. Teetering on the edge, she spun, dragging her foot over the water before bringing it up and kicking it at Fletcher's face. He flinched, then snarled as a few droplets of water ran down his cheeks. That was when Chloe attacked.

Her arms electrified with a snap. *Whap. Whap. Whap.* Three arcs of lightning hit Fletcher, forcing him backwards. His great ax clanked to the ground as the metal hit stone and Chloe pressed her advantage, life returning to her face every time a bolt of lightning hit. *Whap. Whap. Whap. Whap.* Fletcher had his forearms across his face.

That wouldn't save him.

Whap. Whap. Now Fletcher was at the edge of the arena, slightly shaking from the lightning strikes. Something was wrong, though; he was acting as if he hadn't felt pain before, cowering almost theatrically.

With his heels over the water, Fletcher gave a grin and began his counterassault. He smacked his open palm against the bare side of his chest. Instantly, his body began to harden, condensing and toning as if he were shaped out of metal. Every scrap of fat on Fletcher turned into straight, lean muscle. The crowd's hollering took on a new, louder pitch than before as Chloe's face fell. With every pounding footstep he took toward her, the crowd grew more and more bloodthirsty.

"Fletcher's a Metal Fabricator," I muttered.

"And a strong one," Domet said. "Our potential Raven underestimated him and showed her cards too soon."

Chloe was being forced back again, Fletcher moving step by slow step toward her, baring his teeth. When she was close enough, she began to kick more water onto the arena, mixing with the blood that already covered the shattered stones. But with a body reinforced by metal, Fletcher didn't even seem to feel it.

"Any idea what she's doing, Michael?"

Obviously it had something to do with her Fabrication and the water she was splashing onto the arena. But it wouldn't mean much unless she somehow got him to deactivate his Fabrications. Reinforcer Fabricators relied on their improved ability to withstand pain when their Fabrications were activated. A little lightning wouldn't hurt him now, so I had no idea what she was trying to do, and didn't respond to Domet's question.

When Fletcher had her cornered, he threw a punch at her. She dodged it, only to misjudge the distance, lose her balance, slip, and then fall into the murky green water. At the sound of the splash, the announcer screamed, "The Raven is down! The Raven is down! Has Fletcher done it again? Will we see another Raven's wings clipped here tonight?"

The bubbles on the surface of the water dwindled away, Chloe nowhere to be seen. Fletcher knelt over the edge and, like a bear trying to catch a fish, stuck his hand into the cloudy water in search of his prey. Two hands emerged from the water, grabbed Fletcher's toned wrist, and dragged him into it. The Metal Fabricator sank into the water. There was no chance he would float.

Silence hung over the arena, the audience holding its breath, waiting for one of them to emerge.

It was Chloe who, drenched from head to toe, put her hands on the edge of the arena first. With shaking arms she hauled herself back into the arena, wet clothes clinging to her, and staggered to her feet. She held an electrified hand over the water as Fletcher surfaced, no longer using his Fabrications.

The crowd began to chant, "Finish him! Finish him! Finish him!"

Chloe turned to the Raven that had escorted her out to the arena. She was met with a curt nod.

I looked away.

Fletcher's screams were deafening until they simply stopped, an interlude before the cheering.

The crowd began to holler and clap in earnest as the announcer took the stage. "It seems we have a victor! And the king has his newest Raven: Chloe Mason!"

Chloe went to her knees, dripping wet, in exhaustion. She wept as a Raven bound a peacock feather into her hair and helped her up so she could bask in her victory.

"She won."

"She did," Domet said. "Can you guess why I brought you here today?"

"I don't know. This hasn't helped me learn how to use Fabrications at all."

"Hasn't it? All Fabricators can do is transform energy from one form to another. Fire Fabricators nowadays have the same power as they did decades ago. I'm sure Fletcher has faced Lightning Fabricators before. So why did he lose when he was clearly the healthier and stronger of the two?"

"Chloe was smarter."

"Yes!" he shouted, slamming his fist down. "And that, Michael, is always the answer. Good Fabricators know how to shoot fire out of their hands, or call down lightning, or cloud memories, but *great* Fabricators can make a Fire Fabricator burn himself."

"So if I'm going to use Fabrications, I have to be smart?" I clarified.

"Not smart. Clever. You need to learn how to think and fight like a Fabricator. Never reveal your Fabrication unnecessarily, be three steps ahead of the opponents you know about, and two ahead of the dozen that you don't. It's the long con that wins in the end, Michael. The people who do things worth remembering are the ones willing to wait decades to achieve it. That is what I'm trying to teach you today: How to use them doesn't mean how to summon the skill. It means how to wield it once you have. It means balancing every strike with knowing the potential cost."

"So what if I know the principles of war, if I don't know how to wield the weapons?"

"It's better to learn the rules than suffer the consequences for breaking them, Michael. You can't ask for forgiveness with this."

"But how do I actually use Fabrications?"

Domet tapped his cane on the floor. "Let's get out of here. This place is too stuffy for me."

As we left the Shattered Stones, I looked down over the arena. Chloe was crying into her hands, the peacock feather bright against her wet tangles of black hair. I hoped she was happy, having accomplished her dream. For a second I thought I saw Gwen in the crowds, gloved and with her hair pulled back into a ponytail, but the woman was gone when I looked again—and if I didn't know about this place, Gwen couldn't either.

The narrow stone steps weren't nearly as bad going up as they had been coming down. With one hand on the cool wall, I made my way up into the cold autumn breeze and the turning leaves.

———

Domet and I walked side by side toward his house.

"Teaching you how to use Fabrications isn't as simple as waving a wand, muttering certain words, or moving your hands in a certain way. It's a physical process within your body," he began. "And everyone's body responds and acts differently depending on what their specialization is."

"So where do I begin?"

"Well," Domet said, "there are certain things we can gather based on what's happened in the past. Combat Fabrications are the most visual in nature and are hard to miss when used involuntarily, so, since you've not done anything extraordinary in a fight so far, we can assume you're not one. By the same measure, you probably don't have a Reinforcer Fabrication like Smoke, Metal, or Sand."

With a hand on his chin, Domet continued to ramble. "There's a chance you could be a Light or Darkness Fabricator and showing it in a very obscure way. You could have a rare Fabricator specialization like Shadow. That would be much harder to determine."

"What's a Shadow Fabricator?"

"They have the ability to copy, essentially. Shadow Fabricators can mimic another Fabricator's specialization after coming in physical contact with them."

That sounded like a power that I could use to protect everyone I cared about. It would be impossible to know how to counter me if I could steal my opponent's specialization and use it against them.

"How would I be able to tell if I was a Shadow Fabricator?"

Domet stopped and held out his wrist. "Steal my specialization."

I gripped his wrist and waited. And waited. And waited. "Am I supposed to feel something?"

"Is your body doing anything differently?"

I let go of his wrist. "No."

"Then I suppose you're not a Shadow Fabricator."

I grumbled as we walked on. "I just don't understand how I'm supposed to know what my type is, or where to begin, or anything."

"Listen to your body, Michael. All Fabricators use their specialization involuntarily before they learn how to control it. You're no different, you just don't recognize how you use it yet."

"I always thought there was a more refined way to learn how to use Fabrications. This seems scattered."

"There was a formal process once, but after Hollow Academy was shut down that knowledge was kept secret. Twelve Fabricators still know it, and all but one of them are employed by the High

Noble families to train their armies. We don't have the time to recruit one to teach you."

"Guess not. What is using Fabrications like for you, then?"

"It's like taking a deep breath in and then exhaling it."

Trey had described it as attempting to lighten the world around him. But what was it for me?

I stopped and looked at him. "What is your specialization, anyway?"

Domet chuckled, and it surprised me when he didn't reach for his flask. "Michael, you just learned never to share your Fabrication specialization until it's absolutely necessary . . . so why would I tell you?"

"Because you're supposed to teach me how to use Fabrications."

"And I've taught you everything you need to know. The rest is up to you. Listen to your body, Michael. Fabrication is as much anatomy as it is magic." Domet dropped five gold suns into my palm. "I have things I need to take care of, so we'll part here for the day. Visit before first light tomorrow. You'll need to be ready for the hunt. Don't do anything stupid tonight."

I watched him limp away, with a thousand thoughts within my head. Had my body been trying to tell me something for years and I'd been ignoring it? If I figured out whatever it was, would I be able to use my Fabrications? I didn't have any answers, but I wouldn't give up. I'd learn how to use Fabrications, and soon. If only I had listened to Trey.

Only after Domet was out of sight did I remember my other questions for him: about Dark having two Fabrication types . . . and why I would have forgotten two women from my past. I'd have to ask tomorrow or still be clueless the next time I dealt with any of them.

As I stood in the shadow of a tree, I ran my hands over my arms, trying to get warm. It was only moments before a warmth covered my body, easing the coolness from the breeze. This was the first time in days that I didn't know what to do next. Would meditating for the day help me use Fabrications, or should I do something else? What was the most practical use of my limited free time?

Lyon and Trey wanted nothing to do with me, I had no new leads for natural or magical cures that could help my mother, and Gwen was . . . somewhere. She hadn't been home and her shift in the asylum didn't start until early evening. Sometimes she seemed to vanish and it was impossible to find her until she wanted to be found. I had no leads to find Dark, and though I could go search for Sirash and his family on the East Side, if Dark was still looking for me, then I didn't want to lead him to them. I hated not knowing if Sirash was well, but he wouldn't want me to get arrested instead of waiting a few days to hear from him.

Truly, the only thing I hadn't prepared for, to some extent, was what would happen whenever I ran into the Mercenary again. I wouldn't be able to avoid him forever, and eventually he'd come for me to reclaim his papers. I'd have to have a countermeasure against him for when he did. And the only things I knew about him were the contents of the envelope he had killed for: the first page of the investigation of Davey Hollow's murder, a glass ring, and some handwritten notes about a battle where a Mercenary company had been after a book called *The Journal of the Archmage*.

If Dark was like his fellow Mercenaries, maybe he was searching for *The Journal of the Archmage*, too . . . and if I could find it, well, maybe I'd have something to prevent him from trying to kill me whenever we ran into each other again. Not that his last negotiation had gone terribly well for the opposing party.

Since I didn't have any other bright ideas to fill my day and didn't want to waste it meditating, I took off toward the Hollow Library to search for a book that might save my life. To get it, all I would have to do was barter with a madman obsessed with destroying my family's legacy.

THE KING OF STORIES

The Hollow Library was huge.

There were bookshelves everywhere. Where they didn't line the walls or fill the floor with stacks, the great wheels on each side of the bookcases ready to inch them along their tracks, there were tables and chairs, groaning under even more piles of books. Above it all, the painted ceiling depicted two dragons, one silver and the other black, circling around the skylight. The gorgeous colors had dulled and cracked with age, darkening everything beneath it in turn. At the very center of the foyer, beneath the skylight, was a curved redwood table with an Archivist, the caretakers of the written words, sitting at it. She had her red hood drawn up, her face almost completely obscured.

As I approached the table I said, "Hello. Could you help me find a book?"

"Certainly," the Archivist said, putting her scroll aside. "Are you a noble or a member of Scales?"

"I'm—"

"The library is restricted to their use. I'm sorry, sir, you won't be able to use the library. We have rules that can't be broken for any—"

I moved my collar so she could see my brand. "I'm Michael Kingman, and I've come to barter. Information for information."

Archivists claimed that, by nature, they were neutral in all manner of politics and rebellions and war, only ever desiring to preserve the true history of Hollow, always attempting to separate fact from opinion. Which was hard to do in a country where the rulers could lose their memories in an instant.

They had hounded me for a decade to share information about my father. Lyon and Gwen had both talked rather than spend years avoiding them. I never had, recognizing it as one of the few pieces of leverage I had against people in the city, and I knew I'd need something from them at some point. I just hadn't expected it to come so soon. I had always assumed I would use it when I was old and grey, to make sure my family was remembered the right way.

The Archivist gave me a cautious look. "They'll want to know about your father."

"That's fine, so long as it's not about the murder."

She paused, and then said, "What do you want in return?"

"Unlimited access to *The Journal of the Archmage.*"

That surprised her, and I wasn't sure why. What was one book among thousands? It took her a few moments to compose herself, and then she said, "The Recorder will have to authorize the exchange. Follow me."

The Archivist rose with an unexpected briskness and walked at a pace that I struggled to keep up with without jogging. I followed her, weaving through the movable bookshelves and down four sets of stairs, the temperature dropping every time we went further underground. There were Archivists everywhere, huddled in corners and behind wooden desks, though none of them glanced at us as we passed. The only light came from long translucent pipes that ran the length of the ceiling. I didn't know how they worked, but it made sense to have an alternate light source: they would be moonstruck to allow open flames near all these books.

The Archivist led me to a door in a corner of the floor, unlocked it with a big iron key from the collection on her belt, and we entered the room.

A young man with a receding hairline and a nose that had been broken at some point was working at the only table. He was in an Archivist's red hooded robe, and I recognized him immediately. His name was Symon Anderson, the self-proclaimed King of Stories. We had met before.

"Recorder," the Archivist said, "Michael Kingman requests an exchange. Information about his father, excluding the murder of Davey Hollow, in exchange for unlimited access to *The Journals of an Archmage*."

He scribbled a last word, looked up from his papers, and nodded. "I'll allow it. Once you take a seat, we can begin the exchange." The Archivist left as Symon carefully folded away his work and rummaged for a specific journal in his bag, and I took a seat opposite him. "How long has it been, Michael?"

"Years," I said. "Let's skip the pleasantries—last time negated any chance of sympathy between us. If there was any left after what you wrote about my family."

"I told the truth."

"You twisted everything my family has ever done to fit your perception. It was one thing to condemn my father for what he did; it's another thing entirely to claim that my family controlled the Royals from the shadows since this country was liberated. You even went after the Mother Kingman, after all she did for Hollow."

"There are numerous inconsistencies in the reports about her life, and I did what any self-respecting Archivist would do: shared my discoveries with my peers and the nobility."

"You blamed my family for shattering the moon! Was that for pure academic purposes, too? Or one of a more personal nature?"

The Recorder smiled, showing a gap between his front teeth. "History will prove one of us right, and considering I decide what is reality and what is fiction in Hollow, I would be surprised if I were the one proven wrong. For now, be thankful only the Church of the Eternal Flame stands behind my assertions—though I suspect the Royals will, too, soon."

"You'll need more proof."

A chuckle. "Do not fear, Michael. I'll find some eventually."

I held my tongue from saying all the colorful insults my mind had come up with for him. "How many questions do you want in exchange for unlimited access to *The Journal of the Archmage*?"

"Four."

"Two. And none about my father murdering the prince."

"Three. Two now, not about the murder, and one—with no restrictions—to be answered in the future."

I hesitated. "Deal."

"Excellent," Symon said. He took up the quill, dipped it in ink, and held it ready. "First question: Where was your mother born?"

I wasn't expecting that. "No idea. She always deflected the question when asked. All we know is that something forced her to flee after she met our father."

Symon grumbled to himself as he recorded what I said. "I was hoping you might know what your siblings did not. Waste of a question." He flipped through his book to another page. "We know your father was either a Darkness Fabricator, a Shadow Fabricator, or a Light Fabricator. Do you know which he was?"

"No. I don't remember ever seeing my father use Fabrications. But my mother once claimed he was a Fire Fabricator."

"Would you be willing to submit to a Light Fabrication to ensure your memories weren't tampered with, so I can judge the validity of your answers?"

"Don't believe me, Symon?"

"No," he said. "Not when it concerns your father."

"Fine, get a Light Fabricator in here."

Symon held his hand out and a concentrated light began to form in it. I felt my mouth drop. Symon wasn't a noble, so it had never occurred to me that he might be a Fabricator. One of his ancestors must've had noble blood; it was the only reason he'd be able to use

Fabrications. Maybe it also explained how he'd become a Recorder so young, having such an advantage in separating the truth from a false narrative.

My entire body felt warm as Symon rose from his seat and walked around the table. "If you experience any pain, then tell me at once. Pain means your mind has been affected by Darkness Fabrications. Understood?"

"Here I was thinking that pain was from your voice."

Without warning, he pressed the ball of light against the side of my head. I don't know what I expected to happen, but when nothing did, I knew that we were both disappointed for different reasons. I still felt warmer than usual, but it definitely wasn't pain. After studying me for a few moments, Symon collapsed into his seat.

"I wasn't expecting you to be of sound mind, Michael. I was sure you had been affected with Darkness Fabrications." He rubbed his eyes. "Maybe I've spent too much time reading."

I was just as surprised. Being afflicted with Darkness Fabrications could have explained why I had forgotten the rebel woman and the girl in red; my only remaining theory was that I had used Fabrications inadvertently as a child and those memories were the price. But how could I have used them so much unnoticed? How emotional must I have been for my childhood memories to be so fragmented? Questions for another time.

"That's everything," I said. "Unless you want to use your third."

"No," he said. "I won't use the third question until I'm absolutely certain I'll get an answer I want."

"Where's *The Journal of the Archmage*?"

The Recorder blinked a few times in surprise. "Right here. We're in the Archmage Room, Michael. You're surrounded by them."

Dark's papers had never indicated *The Journal of the Archmage* was more than a single book. There were stacks of them in here, the top of each shelf labeled by year. There were easily over a thousand journals.

"The Archmage Room contains all of the first-edition copies of the journals he's written since his teenage years. His apprentice delivers them every month once they've been copied. Commentaries are shelved above the journals themselves. Is there a particular event or a certain person's commentaries you're looking for?"

Dark's notes hadn't mentioned a specific volume of the journals. "How many of them are there?"

"About fifteen hundred by our last count."

"When was that?"

"Maybe five years ago. Truth be told, the Archmage's apprentice is the one who usually deals with this room. All the Archivists have keys to the room to keep it well maintained, while I use it whenever I want to avoid meetings in my office."

I moved to the leftmost shelf and pulled out a random book. "This isn't right, is it? This is dated over a hundred years ago. Who was the previous Arch—"

"There has only been one," Symon said as he gathered his belongings from the table. "His earliest journals are on the left, through to the most recent on the right. He became Forgotten about halfway through . . . though we believe, as a side effect of his Fabrications, he is unable to die. I believe he's about one hundred and twenty-seven years old. What's with that look? Are you truly surprised someone could become immortal? Fabricators can create fire from their fingertips and a tempest with their breath. Immortality isn't as far off as one might suspect."

"Why would the Royals allow an Immortal to live in our city?"

"Besides being unable to kill him? The Archmage is a necessary evil. Who else is willing to sacrifice their memories to research the uses and limitations of Fabrications? The Royals need him, and since he doesn't engage in politics, they allow him to do what he wishes. I imagine something would be done about him if he had any other aspirations."

I was still too shocked about what was in front of me to process the ramifications of what the Recorder was saying.

"And despite being a Forgotten for years, he still researches and writes these journals?"

"Keeping these journals is the king's only demand of him. He's in charge of all the hospitals; we'd be set back decades if he disappeared. These journals are a preventive measure, a little security. And, from what I understand, he doesn't mind, since he still rereads his old journals, making notes in them about why he did certain things. Anything too valuable or important to risk is tattooed onto his body. But that's common enough for Fabricators."

I suddenly wondered, since I was learning how to use Fabrications, what my first tattoo would be.

"I'm surprised," Symon said, books in hand. "Didn't you know about all of this before you asked to see them?"

"No. Not at all."

That elicited a laugh from him. "Well, good luck, Michael. I'll make it known that you have access to this room, per our agreement, though the rest of the library will be off-limits to you. You don't need any special identification. Your brand is proof enough of who you are. May the Wanderer help you find whatever you're looking for in here."

The door closed behind him, leaving me alone with over a thousand journals of a man who had achieved immortality.

Was Dark seeking immortality? Had he wanted the notes because they contained a clue or cipher to identify a particular volume? And why had the Mercenary company wanted these books all those years ago? Had they known it would take a lifetime to read them all?

There were small gold plaques over some of the shelves, indicating which books were in the section. Some of them were very specific, like *The First Ten Years as a Forgotten*, while others were more general. One plate read *The Rambling Years*. And among more than fifteen hundred journals, one of them might indicate what an entire company of Mercenaries was willing to attack the Hollow Library for—what, years later, another Mercenary was willing to kill just to get a clue to. Logically, any of the journals after the battle weren't going to have whatever these Mercenaries were looking for. But how many did that eliminate from fifteen hundred? A few decades' worth? I wouldn't be able to read all of these in a few weeks, or even over a few years. How long would it take for me to gain basic familiarity with the journals to even separate the important information from a Forgotten's ramblings?

Where should I even start? Was it best to start at the beginning and learn the entire story of this man's life? Or was it better to find the battle and work my way backwards? Or should I start with my father's execution and understand how the Archmage felt toward my family first—if that even mattered in this search.

There were too many variables. Too many factors I had a poor grasp of to think of an effective, methodical approach.

So I did the only thing that seemed sensible. I picked a journal at random, flipped it open, and began to read.

They brought me another apprentice today after Yellow left a few weeks ago. I would say I miss her, but it is a relief to finally be able to find things in my office again without her trying to organize it all to suit her needs and ruining everything I had carefully arranged. Everyone just assumes because I'm a Forgotten I can't remember where I put my files, but they're wrong! Most of the time. And when I can't, my routines bring me back. Amazing how, even when the mind falters, the body finds a way. Almost like it's trying to fix the gap in our memories for us.

We never really understand how much our bodies take care of us. Like a mother or a father does. I'll have to instruct this new apprentice—Green, I think I'll call her—how I like my things and not to touch what isn't hers. I can never find good help anymore. Maybe one day I'll be allowed to work alone again. Whoever first suggested I needed an apprentice should've been fired themselves. Did I fire them? I think I did. I should've. I must've. I wouldn't have let a moonstruck fool like that work for me. I'll make that Green's first assignment. To find out whether I fired the fool or not. At the very least it'll get her out of my way. I need to focus on my research. There's still too much I haven't learned.

I closed the book and put it back on the shelf: nothing important. I chose another from the *Experimental Years* section and tried again.

I must tell the king and Malcolm Kingman what I've discovered.
For generations we thought we understood the limitations and
specialization of Fabricators. It turns out we only knew the
most basic rules and theories, and that concerns me more than
I can admit. After studying Fabricators who manifested their
abilities alone, without instruction, I wonder if Fabricators are
born with their specialization already determined or if nature
has a role in determining it. Further research is required before
I can make a public statement to Hollow Academy. Either way,
there is a much wider range of specializations than we ever
thought possible.

In Braven, I have received reports of a blind woman with
a Sound specialization and a blacksmith manifesting a Smoke
specialization in middle age.

In Vurano, I have received reports of a set of identical twins
with the ability to Nullify and Copy other specializations.

In Naverre, I have received reports of a feral boy with
a Wood specialization and a sickly young man with a
specialization that we've deemed poisonous for now until we
come up with a better term.

In—

I closed the book when I realized the list of Fabricator specializations went on for another three pages. It was interesting, but not what I was looking for right now. I went further ahead in the timeline toward my father's execution and picked another journal at random.

Recently, we've increased the number of hospitals in the Hollows from one per city to roughly four in the capital, two in the other major cities, and a few clinics spread through the outer regions where the farmers populate. I've had to travel more than I wanted to be sure we have competent doctors and nurses in each, and a few days ago I had to make an impromptu visit to Naverre, in the north, to deal with a doctor promoting bloodletting in place of proper medical treatment. His incompetence cost the life of High Noble Katherine Naverre and that of her unborn child to poison. If I had been quicker, perhaps I could have saved her.

We must continue to expand and to share medical knowledge to save more lives. If only people understood how important this was to the greater good. Everything in Hollow seems to be about power. Some days I yearn for the years before the Medical College was founded, when it was just me and my research. Though I know Isaac is glad we're continuing his father's legacy, working to aid the general populace. Supposedly he told me as much last I saw him, and Orange, for some reason, won't stop telling me about it every time we've arrived in a new area. I swear I'm going to send him for some rare herbs one of these days and leave him in the forest. No doubt his noble father would object—shout at me, or challenge me to some duel, or whatever these fools do nowadays when they seek justice. In fact, I might just do that. It would be entertaining. Especially if we were near the ruins of Vurano . . . and I would adore some peace and quiet to do my research. I really need to get better apprentices.

Still nothing of value. As I reached for another book, I paused. Instead of taking just one, I picked out a journal from each section and then brought the towering pile of books to the table. It might take a lifetime to read all of them, but I had to start somewhere, and whining about the insurmountable odds against me wouldn't help.

So I began to read, and read, and read, and read.

THE HUNTERS

I was late, very late to meet Domet the morning of the hunt.

I had been awoken by yelling, which wasn't anything new, really. Usually all that differed was the source, rotating through the various members of my family. But what was unique about this morning was that the shouting had come from an Archivist, who had found me sleeping on a pile of books. Fearing for their integrity, she had shoved me out of my chair while screaming at me for being careless. We were in agreement when I realized I had spent most of the day reading and then fallen asleep in the Archmage Room overnight. With little time to waste, I hid Dark's envelope in a journal called *The Dragon Fallacy* and ran for Domet's house.

My stomach wouldn't stop gurgling, my throat felt like I had swallowed sand, and every muscle in my back was angered by my choice of sleeping arrangements. I had no time to do much to hide the fact I had just woken up. No doubt Domet would notice and chastise me when he did. Worse, on my way I took a wrong turn and was forced to backtrack. It was a stupid mistake, since I had grown up running through the city's streets, which made me even later.

Sure enough, as I approached Domet's house, I saw him waiting on the steps.

"What happened to you?" he asked.

"Spent the night in the Hollow Library reading."

"Why?"

"Tried to learn more about using Fabrications," I said. It wasn't a complete lie: the Archmage had detailed some of the various methods people used to focus their Fabrications. I had tried them, but none of the suggestions had worked for me.

Domet looked me up and down. He was dressed a little less formally than normal, in a simple black shirt and trousers and a wide-brim cap. "You can't go to the hunt looking like that."

"It's a hunt, not a ball."

"When have I ever given you an indication that the hunt is any less important than the ball? Just because the nobles are going to kill a beast today doesn't mean they won't do it with style and finesse, and we can't have you mistaken for the animal."

"Do you want me to head back to my home and change? If I'm lucky, I might be able to get into a bath somewhere."

"No," Domet declared. "I'll do it myself. Come, I've fixed worse in the morning before."

And he meant it. He had me in a hot bath with pumice and vanilla soap and orders to scrub everything in minutes. When my skin was pink and stinging, Domet threw in hunting clothes that fit a little too well for chance to be a factor. He even made sure none of the holes in my boots would rip or tear while we were out there. Once he was satisfied with what he had created, we headed off to the King's Garden. He muttered dire things about haircuts, and I ate.

Hollow Castle was a marvel of construction by every standard, a towering feat of stone and bridges that was nestled on the west bank of the river. It had stood for over a millennium, and every new king or queen had added or updated something until it was an amalgamation of differing styles that somehow worked with each other. The left side was tall, pointy, and ornate, with more flying buttresses than necessary, while the right side was clean, simple, and sturdy, without a single stone out of place. It held more secrets and mysteries than all of Hollow combined—the result of a few paranoid kings and over-eager architects—and I had wanted to discover them all as a child. The best thing I had ever found was an empty vault littered with star-shaped fruit and a door without a way to open it. My own personal hideout.

But the King's Garden was something else entirely. More magical than impressive. Tucked behind the castle, it seemed to stretch for miles and contained every tree and creature imaginable, from winterbloom and wisteria to roses and raven's tails. Except for Moon's Tears, of course. They grew only in very specific places and couldn't be transferred, nurtured, or raised from seeds. Why they were so hard to grow was one of the great mysteries of Hollow.

As we passed through the glittering gates to the Gardens, Domet stopped me and said, "Are you ready for this? There will be nobles from the previous generation at this event, too."

"What? You didn't mention that."

A pause. "I thought it best you didn't know until it was required. I don't think the king or his Ravens will be here, but . . ."

"But there's a chance?"

Domet stared straight ahead. We could hear laughter and music deeper within the Gardens. "A slight chance. I personally doubt it, which is why I never mentioned it. From the gossip I've heard, I'm to be the most important High Noble in attendance, aside from the Corrupt Prince."

"If it was necessary, could you protect me from him?"

"No," he said bluntly. "The older nobles and I won't be participating in the hunt that you all will. If anything, I expect us to have some novelty hunt, maybe a few birds or a boar with a broken leg. The Corrupt Prince will be with you. It's a blessing, in that it allows me to spread the good word about you to the others. The longer he's distracted, the better of a chance we have of you getting invited to the Hollow Court for the king's birthday party."

"I guess I'll distract him, then," I said.

"Without getting killed or maimed."

I looked at Domet. "It's a ceremonial hunt—it's controlled. How could I get hurt? There will be hundreds in attendance today."

"What makes you think that, if he wants you dead, he wouldn't try during a hunt?"

"We have a deal. He won't interfere during the Endless Waltz. There were witnesses."

"He won't need to. Hunts are hunts, and people get injured on them all the time. And the more exotic a creature you'll be hunting today, the more likely an accident becomes. Besides, he has plenty of Throne Seekers eager to please him."

"I'll be careful."

Domet laughed as he limped on. "You have all the arrogance of your ancestors. Give me a few minutes before you follow. Let's not have them suspect we're working together."

I loitered for longer than necessary. Part of me longed for the simple days when money was my biggest worry. It had been a shitty life at times, but it had been mine, and it had always been easier with friends and family at my side. Now someone always seemed to be pulling my strings. I tried not to linger on those thoughts for too long before making my way into the garden. The guards at the gate didn't stop me or ask for identification as they might have in the past, my brand enough to vouch for who I was and why I was here. By now I suspected every noble knew what I was doing.

But what I hadn't suspected was the sheer size of the hunt. I had never been allowed to attend one as a child, always having to stay in the castle with my siblings and the other royal children while our parents pranced around in the garden. So only now, with the hunt within my sight, did I begin to understand the danger Domet had hinted at. There must have been more than fifty tents decorated with the various noble sigils, dozens of horses of all colors and breeding, and hundreds, if not thousands, of weapons in the area. Whatever we were hunting, it sure wasn't a boar with a broken leg.

The sight of the hunt was overwhelming, and I had no idea where I was supposed to be. I began to wander the grounds, but instead of being productive and finding the girl in red or looking for the Ryder sigil, I reminisced of summer days spent with the royal children. We used to play tag on these very grounds. Lyon and Davey had always chosen to run in the open, while the princess liked to climb trees. Never content to be outshone, I had always gone after her instead of easier targets like my sister and the Corrupt Prince. They had been too young to realize that bushes didn't hide laughter as well as they did their faces.

It had been such a carefree childhood. What I wouldn't do for that life to return.

My wandering feet carried me past a few lingering looks from Low Nobles who had once served my family to a golden tent with a banner of a black dragon flying above it. I had found the Ryders. With few other options and fewer people I could pretend to be friendly with, I entered the tent, sparing a moment to hope neither Kayleigh nor Lyon would be inside.

They weren't. But Kai was, with three dogs at his side and a frail boy sitting beside him. The boy wore loose clothes that were almost the same shade as his pale face. His hair was thinning and light as snow, with small gold streaks scattered throughout it. He had a wooden dragon in his hands and made roaring noises as he flew it through the air. Based on Domet's book, I assumed this was Joey Ryder, the sickly mute, if the rumors were to be believed. Upon entering, the three dogs sprang to their feet and ran up to me, sniffing and watching me closely.

"Who's there?" Kai asked.

"Michael Kingman," I said as his dogs continued to inspect me. "Did I sneak up on you?"

Kai clicked his tongue and immediately all three of the dogs sat down, none of them taking their eyes off me. "Yes, but only because all the noise outside makes using my Fabrications difficult. Anyway, what're you doing here, Michael?"

"Didn't know where else to go. Not like I was going to have a tent of my own."

And it wasn't like I was going to find Domet's tent either.

"I should have realized that," he said. "Do you need anything? I'm happy to share with my future brother-in-law." He said the last part with a smile.

"Can you call your dogs off me first?"

"I have. My father just trained them to stare at people. Makes most folk uncomfortable."

That was an understatement. I edged between the dogs and joined Kai at the small table. His brother was still amusing himself on the ground. "That's Joey, right? He's not participating in the hunt, is he?"

Kai shook his head as he handed me a plump waterskin. "No, my mother will be picking him up soon. I look after him in the morning so she can sleep and so my father won't be late for his meetings with the king."

"That's nice of you."

"Family looks after family. And it helps me delay determining what I want to do with the rest of my life. No one questions me if I say I'm my brother's caretaker and learning alongside our Fabricator army for the time being."

"You don't know what you want to do with your life?"

Kai chuckled to himself, then began to put on mail and gauntlets. Whatever the joke was, I seemed to have missed it. "I'm the third-born of the family, so my options are limited. Kayleigh will become the family matriarch. Karin is a Raven. I have to find a way to live up to that standard. Somehow."

"Any idea how?"

"No," he said quietly. "My uncle joined the Church of the Wanderer and tells me I could do well there, but I don't think I want to. I have a feeling I'd only be known as the blind monk if I did that. Which isn't really a title I want."

"Understandable."

A nod. "I'm sure I'll figure out what I want sooner or later. Until then I'll participate in the Endless Waltz and learn as much as I can about Fabrications and politics."

"Not a bad idea." It was better than any plan I had ever come up with before meeting Domet. "Do you know what we're hunting today?"

"No, but it's going to be something big. Last year it was a longtooth tiger from the Warring States. The prince was apparently disappointed that it killed only five guards and an overeager Low Noble."

Clearly, Domet was right. Agreement or not, the Corrupt Prince would be coming after me today. I'd have to be more careful than I initially thought. "Is there anything I should know about hunts? I've never been on one before."

"Don't be a hero. Heroes die in Hollow."

"Simple enough. Anything else?"

Kai cracked his back. "Not really. We'll be behind the lancers and the pikemen. So long as you don't break formation, run up, and attack the beast, you should be fine. I'll stay with you, so if something does go wrong, I'll see it first."

"That's a joke, right?"

"Obviously. I'm blind. You can laugh when I make fun of my sight, Michael."

"I can?"

"You can. Like I said, I don't want blind to be my only label. It's a part of me, but it's not the only thing about me. I'm more than my disability."

"Noted."

Kai moved over to a rack of weapons. "Do you need something for the hunt?"

"I do," I said as I moved to his side to get a better look at all the weapons. There were plenty of options, from hatchets and great-axes to maces and spears.

Kai picked a trident off the rack for himself and then asked, "Sword?"

"No. Don't know how to use one."

Kai turned his head so I could see his cloudy eyes. "That's a lie. I know how good you are with a sword."

"No, I don't—"

"You fought in plenty of tournaments as a child, and you won a fair amount of them, if my memory is correct. Which it is."

"That's—"

"Do I really need to bring up the Kingman Family Swordsmanship School? It was renowned before the fall. More so than any of the other High Nobles' save the royal one."

"Fine," I mumbled. "But I don't use them anymore. I'd rather have something else."

"Why walk away from a skill like that?"

"My father taught me everything he knew about swordsmanship. After he was executed, it seemed wrong to keep using what he taught me. So I haven't since, and I doubt I ever will again."

There was a silence between us, aside from the sounds Joey made as he played with his toy and the panting from the dogs.

"You're not your father," he declared. "You're a Kingman, not a traitor."

"There's little difference nowadays." I picked up a wooden kite shield without a sigil on it. After fiddling with the strap and buckle to make sure it fit, I slung it on my back. "Thank you for this. I think I'm going to go explore the grounds some more. Is there anywhere I need to be?"

I could tell Kai wanted to continue talking but dropped the subject for me. "No. The Corrupt Prince will sound a horn to gather everyone when the hunt is about to begin. Do you need anything else? Armor? A weapon that's not a shield?"

"No," I said. "A shield will be fine, and armor just slows me down."

Kai left it at that and scooped his little brother onto his lap. His dogs watched me leave with the same focus they had when I entered. It was a little bit brighter out now, and even more people had arrived. There was one group in particular who were louder than anyone else. I followed the noise out of curiosity, hoping to see who they were and what they were doing.

As I came closer, I discovered that the loudest group consisted of people participating in the novelty hunt, and that they were drinking heavily. A dozen wooden kegs were lined up, allowing anyone who had a receptacle to fill it to the brim with beer. Domet and Ambassador Zain were by the kegs, laughing and drinking with another dozen people, a full tankard in everyone's hands. Neither of them noticed as I walked past and found a place to sit while I watched people come and go.

I saw a lot of the nobles listed in Domet's book. There was the obsidian-skinned Ata Morales, the head of the newest family to gain High Noble status, replacing the Naverre family. An assortment of the Page and Cutter families were there, two of the many families that had formerly pledged their loyalty to the Kingman family. There were even a few Sacrifices mingled in with the crowd, following various nobles around like sheep. Lastly, I saw the Corrupt Prince on a massive white horse, his Throne Seekers and two Ravens trudging behind him on foot. Naomi was nowhere to be seen, which made me wonder if she was as invested in him as she had first seemed. However, Trey was with him, though, and saw me instantly, even hidden by the crowds of people.

The moment the Corrupt Prince's back was turned, Trey walked over to me. "Michael."

"Trey," I said, standing. "Are you—"

Trey opened his jacket so I could glimpse the flintlock pistol hidden there. He closed his jacket moments later, no smile or flicker of expression on his face.

I hadn't expected him to listen to me, but I hadn't expected him to bring a gun to the King's Garden either. Without Jamal, he was acting on instinct, his mind clouded with emotions. That never ended well.

"Are you insane?" I asked, hands slightly raised in defense. "If anyone sees that, you'll be hanging before midday."

"Jamal is dead," he said, voice fluctuating in pitch. "I don't care what happens to me."

"But I do! I know it was my fault, but let me be there for—"

"I could kill you," he stated. "I could steal that guard's sword and then stab you through the heart with it. The Corrupt Prince would probably make me a noble for doing it. Jamal was always jealous of them. He always wanted a feather bed of his own. He deserved better."

"Trey, let me explain and then you can do what you want."

He chuckled to himself. "If the positions were reversed and I got your sister killed, would you pause for excuses?"

I lowered my hands. "No, I wouldn't."

"At least you're honest."

"I'm not sure there are many who agree with that." A pause. "What happens now, Trey?"

"I will have my revenge, Michael," he said. "But not today. Killing you here would be pointless. When I choose to get my revenge, it won't be a waste. It will destroy your family and your legacy."

Trey turned his back to me and began to walk away.

"Trey," I said. He stopped walking but didn't look at me. "Do you want to know who killed your brother? Because, even if I was responsible, you know it wasn't me."

"Who was it?"

"One of the Rebel Emperor's close associates. A brutish man with a tattoo on his neck. I may have broken his back after he shot your brother."

"Would you be able to recognize him if you saw him again?"

"Absolutely."

"Good," he said, and then walked back over to the Corrupt Prince's side.

I had no idea what he was thinking. Grief had changed him. Maybe one day we would be able to talk again, or find peace. I hoped it would be before he lost all his memories trying to get revenge.

I missed my friend. I didn't have many, and I didn't want to lose him.

It wasn't much longer before Kai and the girl in red found me, both dressed for combat and clad in heavy leather instead of the cloth I wore. Kai carried a trident and a net slung over his shoulder, while the girl in red carried a battle hammer. Judging by the way she held it, she was clearly more experienced with it than I was with a fork.

None of us talked as we waited for the hunt to begin, more focused on tracking the Corrupt Prince's progress, strutting around as if he was already king. I could only imagine what it must've been like to see him grow up into the beast he was now.

It made me feel for Gwen, who had always wondered if the Corrupt Prince might have been different if they had grown up together, if she could have prevented his transformation. The rumors about the princess, saying she was a decent person, were a small comfort to me, even if she wasn't around much anymore. But I had a hard time holding that against her. Soon the crown would be atop her head, and she would never know freedom again.

The Corrupt Prince blew a bone horn, the sound drawing everyone's attention. It was nearly as loud as the bells that rang when a piece of Celona was falling. Everyone gathered around him, just as his horse released a copious volume of pungent droppings at close quarters.

"Welcome, ladies and gentlemen, to the hunt of the year!" he shouted, circling his horse so he could see everyone. "For those of you participating in the Endless Waltz, you are in for the time of your life! And potentially, for a few of you, it may also be the end of your lives. Unlike other places where they hunt boar or stag or rabbit or pheasant, we only hunt the best. Of course, those not participating in the Endless Waltz will have the option to hunt a boar if they're more interested in the food and drink than bloodlust. Correct, High Noble Domet?"

Domet lifted his full tankard with a large smile. "I'm already on my second and have no intention of slowing down. Let any that dare come drink with me while the nameless fight for glory."

His response elicited a few laughs from the crowd, but as he drank deeply I began to see how Domet had amassed such power in the Hollow Court. He wasn't combative, but he was tactical. And his battlefield encompassed the keg at a party. I wished I could see it firsthand to get a better understanding of him.

"For those who will be hunting with me, let me explain," the prince said. "Our target has already been released further into the garden, with a Raven and a Mercenary keeping an eye on him to ensure he doesn't do too much damage to my father's precious plants. Before I ruin the surprise, any guesses what we'll be hunting today?"

"A mammoth!"

"Two long-tooth tigers!"

"A family of bears!"

"An elephant!"

"Wrong!" he shouted, with a sweeping gesture atop his horse. "Today we embrace the oldest tales and traditions and hunt a dragon!"

I snorted. Loudly. Just at the moment a complete silence had fallen across the crowd. Almost everyone turned toward me, suddenly the subject of their attention, and the Corrupt Prince caught my eye with a huge smile.

Shit.

I had just given him an opportunity. And whatever was about to happen, I knew I wouldn't be able to get out of it. Clearly thinking before I acted wasn't one of my strong suits.

"Oh, Michael, do you not believe in dragons? You are in for a surprise today, then. What we are hunting is very, very real and very, very dangerous."

I opened my mouth to respond, but the Corrupt Prince continued, "You know what, Michael? It's a break with tradition, but since we are celebrating your return to court, I believe we can make an exception. Why don't you go with the pikemen and lancers instead of with us nobility? We wouldn't want you to claim it was just a horse dressed up as a dragon, would we? It would also allow us to see what a Kingman is made of. What do you all think? Should Michael Kingman lead the hunt today?"

There was so much noise, it drowned out any rebuke I could have made. I could feel Domet's eyes on me from the other side of the circle.

"Sounds like we have a leader of the hunt!" the prince declared, clearly delighted.

Another round of cheers and clinking of glasses as I stood still after being completely and utterly played. I couldn't even claim he was sabotaging me, not when he'd conferred an *honor* on me after I snorted in front of everyone.

He knew me. My tendencies, my opinions, and my likely actions. I'd been a fool to ever think he might have forgotten about me after all these years and that he would sit idly by even after I had won our previous wager. But two could play this game, and there was a reason I talked while Sirash shot.

"My dear prince!" I shouted, jumping onto a nearby table as all eyes turned back to me. "I thank you from the bottom of my heart for offering me such an honor. But perhaps someone else deserves their shot at glory."

The Corrupt Prince quieted the crowds, his smile vanishing. "No, I think this is a perfect opportunity for you, Michael. View it as a chance to embrace your family's heroic side rather than the traitorous. Or do you want to reject this gift?"

"Never, my prince," I said as I slowly walked the length of the table. "I just worry that this may be a little . . . redundant for me. I am, after all, a Kingman. I have the blood of the Conqueror flowing through my veins. I was raised on stories about the Explorer and the Unnamed Kingman. Perhaps someone else would like a chance. Given the burden of my family's legacy, facing a dragon is nothing."

"The Kingman family was never credited with slaying a dragon."

I tapped my finger against my chin. "You're right. How could I forget? I suppose, if this truly is a dragon, then I could contribute something unique to my family's storied legacy."

"Assuming you succeed."

"Have no fear, my prince," I said with a smile. "I am a Kingman. I will lead this hunt and defeat this dragon and do something none of my ancestors have done. But I must ask: Do you think a Dragonslayer would be welcome at your father's birthday party? Or is that not enough?"

My mistake in Ryder Keep was our deal had been made in private. I had done something incredible—retrieving a piece of Celona with the entire city after it—but those who had been involved weren't going to change their opinions of me. This was different. If I got him to admit that a Dragonslayer would be welcome in Hollow Court, then I was guaranteed an invitation to the king's birthday celebration.

It helped I had always been better in front of a crowd than I was one-on-one. And, sadly, the Corrupt Prince had learned that the hard way. All eyes were on him, waiting for a response.

"Hollow has been without a Kingman for a decade. Do you really think you can take that place again? After what your father did?"

"I am not my father. I am better."

Whatever this dragon actually was, I was confident I could beat it. I wouldn't have done all this if I wasn't.

The Corrupt Prince cracked his neck. "My extremely well-trained pikemen and lancers would give you an unfair advan—"

"So long as I have more than a dozen able-bodied people who can hold a weapon, I can lead them to victory."

He wore a smile I didn't trust. "I believe I can scrounge up an appropriate force that would be more than willing to help restore the Kingman family to their honored place in Hollow."

"Thank you, my prince. But you never answered my question. Would a Dragonslayer be welcome in Hollow Court? Even if he was a Kingman?"

"Yes," he said slowly. "I think he would."

I jumped off the table with arms extended. "Well then, let's get this hunt started, shall we?"

The cheering was deafening. No one could ignore a good performance. Especially nobles. Even Domet, despite clenching his tankard hard enough to break it, knew this was the right move. Rather than hiding, I was acting like a Kingman, and refusing to be taken advantage of.

Let history remember this.

"I always wanted to ride with the vanguard. Father never let me," Kai said as he and the girl in red came to my side. "He said it was where good men and women died."

"You're joining me?" I asked. "You don't have to—"

"Too late," the girl in red said. "We already volunteered. Besides, you're going to need some experienced Fabricators."

In that moment I wanted to be a hero. Be like my ancestors, who charged their enemies alone like gods walking the earth to protect those they loved and the city they had sworn loyalty to. But—despite what I said in front of everyone—I knew I wasn't like my ancestors. I could barely keep my mother safe, let alone the city. If I was going to make it to the king's party, I was going to need allies.

"Thank you. I owe you both."

Kai patted me on the back. "It's the advantage of having friends."

"So, what do you think we'll actually be hunting?" I asked.

The girl in red and Kai both shook their heads, but instead of one of them answering, a Raven approached us and said, "It's a dragon, Kingman."

I looked at the Raven's hair and saw one feather. It was Chloe, though it was hard to tell at first glance, since she was wearing black plate mail. Her helmet was in her hand, and a short sword with a ruby in the pommel hung at her side.

"I'll believe it when I see it, Chloe," I said, remembering how hard she had fought in the Shattered Stones.

"You two know each other?" the girl in red asked.

"We've met," we said together. We exchanged a glance, and then there was silence.

"Chloe, why are you here?"

She didn't look pleased. "Prince Adreann has ordered me to fight with you in the vanguard."

"Did he send you to stab me in the back while we're fighting the horse dressed up as a dragon?"

"No," she said. "I'd only stab you if you threatened a Royal. And I'd do it through the front."

The girl in red crossed her arms as she said, "At least she's honest."

I suppose that was always an advantage. "Can you lead us to the rest of the vanguard?"

"This way," Chloe ordered, marching us over to a clearing amidst a grouping of pine trees where a large group of people had gathered. They all wore mismatched armor and carried weapons that had seen better days. The group was of all ages and genders, and the closer I got to them, the warier I became.

My stomach lurched when I saw the brands.

They were all Sacrifices. And, to be more specific, they were

Kingman Sacrifices, branded as such after the Kingman Keep riots. Every one of them was a former servant who had tried to kill us as an offering to the king.

I felt sick. The Corrupt Prince must have forced them to be the vanguard knowing they lacked the experience to lead a hunt and hoping for the opportunity to place me among them.

Shit. I had to get Kai and the girl in red out of—

"Michael, it's been years, hasn't it?"

It was *him*. Lothar Bryson, the man had who sworn to protect my family and instead abandoned us in the riots to die. The man who had been one of my father's closest friends. The man who only spoke of loyalty as I grew up, but forgot it when it no longer suited him.

I punched the oathbreaker in the face, hoping I broke his nose.

THE SACRIFICES

In the days following my father's execution, there were riots all over the city. Many called for his children to die next, arguing that every speck of treason had to be eradicated lest one of us rise up and destroy the country in our father's place.

Amidst all the confusion and anger and bloodlust and hate, me and my siblings had hidden in our keep, surrounded by everyone we had ever known that still had their head. The guards had seemed so brave, promising to stand by our side until everyone came to their senses. But they were the first to break, running away after a few of them had died. The servants were next, realizing the famous Kingman prowess was nowhere to be seen in us children. They looted what they could as they went. I'll never forget the woman with sharp nails who stole one of my mother's necklaces from Gwen's neck while she cried. After the servants, the knights left as well, without flair or dramatics. But they had never been heroes to begin with, just spoiled nobility who had wanted to ride my family's coattails. They were content with fading away into the night.

My father had once told us to never raise a sword in anger—even in war. That the calmer person always emerged victorious. We all ignored his advice that night, swinging our makeshift weapons at anyone who got close, fearful that they were after our heads after . . . after one had tried to stab me in the shoulder with a kitchen knife. He had been a friend. Someone I had played and shared secrets with.

Lyon had saved me, and killed him.

We should have died. The rioters had the keep surrounded, with their torches and sticks and stones and swords and knives, ready to spill High Noble blood for justice. But fate intervened. The Ravens and some sort of army arrived to stop them from killing us all. I suppose the king had no choice but to save us, if only to protect his own reputation from matching my father's. How they found us so easily, hiding in the pantry, I will never understand. It was the only time I ever thanked a higher power—well, right before I blacked out from blood loss and pain and shock. That night, in its entirety, is still foggy to me to this day.

I didn't care though. Some things weren't worth remembering.

In the months that followed, the king sent his Ravens after every person that had ever served my family and had them branded alongside me and my siblings. Not because they were traitors but because they had abandoned children to die. In his eyes they were as monstrous as our father, who had killed one with his own hands. But, unlike us, they hadn't been lucky enough to receive the treason brand. Instead, they were given the Sacrifice brand.

There are many stories parents tell their children to make them behave—about the once-great Kingman family, a reminder never to take anything for granted; about the gold-hoarding, children-stealing dragons and the titans who wiped them out—but they all paled in comparison to the Sacrifice brand.

At its best, it was like being an exile: a mark that showed you were not just unfit for pleasant society but barred from it. But that was at its best. At its worst, or usual, the name was literal for those that had it: sacrifice. And just like those sacrificed to dragons in stories, it meant they had no future. There was no meaning left to their lives except to die. There was no law, knight, noble, or king that could protect someone once they carried that brand. And every man, woman, and child who had served my household and fled during the riots had received it.

When I was younger, I had thought the punishment fit the crime. I wanted them all to suffer in the same way we had. I wanted them to know what it was like to watch their world burn down around them as they tried to catch the ashes of what they once held dear. All three of us had been scarred for life by those riots, as people we had lived with and cared for and loved either abandoned us or died trying to save us. At one point Lyon had been forced to kill the keep's baker after he had come at Gwen, all thin and wide-eyed at seven, with a knife. Gwen still had the scars on her stomach from it. And then there was what I had done during the riots that had caused me to black out from blood loss . . . But like most of my memories from that time, they only resurfaced in my nightmares.

Throughout the years, every time someone with the Sacrifice brand died, my desire for revenge slowly faded. At first my hatred blinded me, but eventually I understood they had gone through as much as we had. Some had wanted to protect their own children, and others had made a snap decision to run when a horde of angry citizens craving blood stormed the keep. I couldn't forgive them, but with the benefit of hindsight I could at least understand their actions. Although my compassion had its bounds. And my limit of understanding had a name: Lothar Bryson.

I stood over the oathbreaker as he held his bloody nose. He looked much like I remembered him: bright blond hair all over his body, sickly white skin, and a frame as solidly built as the Corrupt Prince's.

"Michael," Lothar said from the ground. There wasn't the normal iron in his voice but a lingering whimper. His age had caught up with him, the bright blond mixing with the white that was only found in those who lived too long. "I deserved that."

I squatted down so I could look into his eyes. "I should kill you here and end it."

"Sadly, you need me," he said. "I'm the only one here with any combat experience. It's not like any of the guards who were made Sacrifices survived this long. Just women and teenagers."

"How did the Corrupt Prince gather you so quickly?"

"We work for him. He enjoys the sight of us and thinks we're entertaining."

"What a waste of—"

There was a hand on my shoulder. I looked back at the girl in red. "Michael. Now is not the time."

I returned to my feet and didn't look at him anymore. Instead, I turned my attention to the other Sacrifices. "Anyone with combat experience, please raise your hand."

Out of the fifty, three raised their hands confidently and then four more did so with hesitation. Half of them visibly didn't know how to hold a spear correctly.

"That's not ideal," the girl in red declared.

"I'll think of something. Chloe, can you tell us what this beast really is? Knowing if it can fly or not is important to make sure we don't get . . ." I stopped myself from saying "slaughtered" and instead said "overwhelmed."

"I don't know," she said. "I wasn't privy to that information. All I know is that it's located near a cave to the north. I'm to sound this horn when we arrive, to signal the others."

"Are you allowed to help us fight it, or are you just here to blow that horn?"

Her silence was all the answer I needed.

"We need a plan, Michael," Kai said. "My Sound Fabrications will allow me to get a sense of its position, but unless it has very sensitive hearing, there's little I can do."

"I can use my Metal Fabrications to take the brunt of an attack," the girl in red said. "But I won't be able to move quickly if I use it on my entire body. If it's fast, it'll be able to outmaneuver me easily."

I put my hands behind my head. How was I going to do this? Without any definite idea about what we were facing, it was hard to make a plan that wouldn't collapse within minutes.

"I can lead the hunt," Lothar declared. "I have experience."

"I'm a Kingman. I don't need your help."

"You're a Kingman who never learned how to become one," he countered. "Your father had studied war and military strategy for nearly fifteen years before he led his first battle. You barely have five. You have the last name, but you're not yet a Kingman."

"You think you can do better than me?"

"I was your father's right-hand man through the Gunpowder War for a reason."

I held my tongue. I didn't want his help. Literally anyone else would be better. I didn't want to work with the man who had betrayed my family. But I needed to survive this if I was going to make it to the king's party. My future depended on it.

"What would you suggest, oathbreaker?"

He didn't gloat but picked up a stick off the ground and began to draw formations in the dirt. Everyone besides Chloe and the Sacrifices gathered around him. "We'll separate into ten groups of five, excluding you and your friends. Four of the groups will each form one line of a box formation, with another line directly behind them. Our goal will be to box the beast in with your Metal Fabricator friend so it can't escape. If she can hold it, then we'll have the numbers to overwhelm it. Even when half of them run away."

"And if it can fly?"

"Then we'll pray to every prophet that will listen that it has sensitive hearing and your Sound Fabricator friend can force it to land."

"It's not a bad plan. Especially when we don't know what we're about to face," Kai said.

I didn't want to admit it to him, but it was a good plan. So I didn't. Instead we began to prepare the Sacrifices, making sure they were aware of how they had to stand and how to hold their weapons, and understood that if they chose to flee, it was imperative not to knock others over. Once everyone had been briefed about the plan, we began our march toward where the beast would be found. All the Sacrifices followed me and Lothar, while Kai, Chloe, and the girl in red took up the rear.

While we walked, there was an itch in the back of my throat that wouldn't go away . . . a question I had to ask him . . . a question I needed answered in case he died fighting today. "Why did you leave us? Where were you that final night?"

Lothar didn't turn his head. "I didn't think you'd ask. I didn't think it would matter."

"Maybe it does."

He began to laugh, a sickening, twisted laugh that came from his belly and made those behind us whisper to each other. It stopped as quickly as it came, and he said, "My daughter. I saved her from the rioters instead of you. She resembles Gwen enough that I was concerned they would mistake her for your sister. Which they did. They nearly killed her that night, but she survived, albeit now with a scar that runs down from her eye to her neck. You remember her, don't you? Emelia Bryson. She used to make up stories with Gwen that they would re-create for everyone to watch. So when you ask where I was that night, understand that night I chose my daughter over duty. As your father would have done for any of you."

"Her life was more important than ours?" I asked, already knowing the answer.

Lothar met my eyes. His age disappeared for a moment, the younger man of confidence taking his place. "Always."

We continued to walk under the shade of trees, no words ever needing to be spoken between us again. At least I knew what he had exchanged his honor for. He made his choice, and that was that.

We marched for miles, until we ran out of water and were slick with sweat. Thankfully, we reached without too much complaint the small knoll where the beast was supposed to be located. There was a cave that the impostor was residing in, even if we couldn't see the Raven and Mercenary that were apparently watching over it. Chloe left to sound the horn to signal the others, and before we heard it, the Sacrifices were in position and charging the hill. They were acting braver than I imagined they would; maybe because they were finally getting the chance to relieve their pent-up anger after everything that had happened. Or maybe they thought bravery in the face of a beast would redeem them. Either way, they were brave.

Until a beast flew out of the cave with a roar that drowned out the bone horn Chloe was sounding.

It wasn't a dragon. Not in the way they appeared in stories at least. It clearly couldn't breathe fire or ice or lightning, or speak in a human tongue. Nor did it have hard metal scales covering its entire body—nothing to convince me that storybook dragons existed. But this thing was the closest anything ever could be to one. It had talons bigger than my hand and sharper than any sword among our group, and a barbed tail that seemed to act like a rudder as it flew. Rather than having its wings on its back, they were attached to the front legs like a bat's were. It lacked scales, but its smooth, slick skin allowed it to speed through the air, and it glided above us, blocking out the sun.

But despite being above me, I could tell it wasn't much larger than an elephant would be.

"Kai! Bring it down!" I shouted, eyes never leaving the thing above me.

"Where is it? At least give me a—"

Before we had a chance to attack, the beast landed on the other side of us.

"About-face!" Lothar shouted at the Sacrifices.

In that moment most of them did what I expected and dropped their weapons, then ran as far away as they possibly could. Those that didn't tightened their formation, raised their weapons, and advanced toward the beast.

The girl in red was already running toward the beast, slowing as her skin and muscles tightened into metal. Every step she took shook the earth. The beast swung its barbed tail at her and she deflected it with a flick of her wrist. She tried to grab one of the beast's wings to hold it down, but it was efficient at squirming away. It roared so loudly whenever she hit it, my ears rang. Slowly, and with Kai's help directing the Sacrifices, they soon surrounded the beast and boxed it in with their spears and pikes.

But no matter how hard the girl in red punched it or how it temporarily slowed, nothing seemed to be doing lasting damage. As the battle heated up and we were all drawn in, Lothar and Kai were shouting orders up and down the lines of Sacrifices or dragging away those that had been hit by the beast's barbed tail. As I shielded one Sacrifice from a strike, splinters of wood showering us both, the girl in red shouted, "Take cover! It's about to—"

She didn't have a chance to finish her sentence. The beast

leaned back on its hind legs and leapt over the line of Sacrifices in front of it. It landed with a heavy slam at the base of knoll and roared again.

"About—"

The beast leapt again, this time landing in the middle of the Sacrifices, snapping weapons and bones alike. The girl in red tackled its leg, dragging it to a halt before it attacked again, allowing some of the injured to get out of the way. But she couldn't stop its tail. It whipped at Lothar and Kai, the spikes hitting Lothar in the chest while the length swept Kai along. Both skidded across the ground like stones over water.

They both lay still, and I held my breath until I saw Kai struggle back to his feet. Lothar remained flat and unmoving. I felt nothing, and that was that.

I had to do something. It was increasingly clear we couldn't beat the beast in an outright brawl, but it had to have some weakness or vulnerability. Its eyes were likely to be one, and it was clearly vulnerable in the air—neither of which we could take of advantage of without a projectile weapon. I needed another idea. And, perhaps, I had one.

The Sacrifices were containing the beast in a circle with their spears. Its back was toward me while the girl in red held its attention, trading blows with it.

It was time to act like my ancestors and show this impostor why the legends about my family were real, while dragons were not.

I took a deep breath and sprinted toward it, picking up a fallen spear on my way. If I could vault onto its back, then I had a chance to get at the eyes. It wouldn't be enough to kill the beast outright, but if I could blind it, then it wouldn't be able to jump or whip its tail at us accurately. Of course—

My thoughts were cut off by the beast's tail hitting my chest.

The shield I had carefully strapped to my forearm and the spear in my hand were nowhere near me when I landed. I was in so much pain, I didn't even notice that I had hit the ground, my vision blurry and my head pounding. I groggily tried to evaluate my body, making sure I could move everything. Nothing was bleeding too badly.

As I tried to crawl back to my feet, I watched as the girl in red and Kai lead the Sacrifices against the beast. Kai was screaming, a high-pitched wail that sounded more animalistic than human, and the beast was hurting from it. It was cowering, retreating, as the Sacrifices stabbed it with their spears. The girl in red was deflecting all its attacks as if it were a fly she was swatting away.

By the time I got to my feet, it was bleeding, having been skewered by a dozen spears, with dozens more wounds slowing it down. There was no fight left in it as it whimpered and limped away from us. The Sacrifices surrounded it suspiciously, expecting it to swipe at them again. Instead, it just lay down on its stomach.

We had won, and I hadn't done anything to contribute. If I couldn't even defeat an impostor dragon, what kind of Kingman was I? Was I as much of an impostor as it was?

As the girl in red and Kai examined the beast, I made my way over to where I had last seen Lothar. If he was dead, I wanted to know. And if he wasn't, I wanted to know how he had been so lucky.

Lothar wasn't dead, but he was severely injured. He was standing, hand over his gut, to try to staunch the bleeding spike wounds. His shirt was soaked in blood. When he saw me approach, he said, "We won."

"No thanks to me," I said.

"I'd laugh," Lothar began, "but it hurts too much. You should be happy, Michael. All this does is prove that the Kingman family is no longer needed. Others can carry the burden your family has held since Adrian the Liberator took the throne over twelve generations ago. The age of Kingman and Royals is ending . . . and a new generation is being born."

"There must always be a Kingman in Hollow," I recited as we walked over to the beast.

"Maybe in the past. But no longer. Your father decided that when he killed the boy prince. We may never know why he did, but he decided that the Royals were no longer trustworthy or needed, and that the Kingman family didn't deserve to have absolute, unchecked power. He began a revolution, and I hope to see the end of it."

"Your opinion means as much to me as dog shit does on the bottom of my boots."

"One day you will see the truth, Michael," he said. "Then you'll decide which side you want to be on. One side will make Hollow prosperous, the other forgotten in the annals of time."

Ahead of us, the girl in red and Kai stood with their heads together beside the fallen dragon. I heard a stampede of horses approaching us from the south and a horde of riders emerged from the forest soon after, circling and surrounding us. The Corrupt Prince rode over and dismounted, Chloe at his side before his boots touched the ground.

"Well, look at this," he said, hand on the hilt of his sheathed sword. "You actually managed to wound it. I am both surprised and disappointed. I hoped it would still have a little more fight left in it."

The Corrupt Prince kicked the beast in the side, and it gave out a cry of pain.

"Adreann," Kai said. "You can't kill it."

"Oh, I can't? Why's that?"

The girl in red stepped forward. "High Noble Ryder and I believe it to be a Toothless Wyvern. Up until this moment, it was believed to be extinct. It's been drugged to make it more aggressive."

"I'm still waiting to hear a reason."

"Killing it would be genocide. It could be the last of its kind."

The Corrupt Prince tapped his hand against his chin. "It could be. High Noble Ryder, which is more valuable to me: to have its stuffed head mounted above my throne, or have it chained in my gardens for the rest of its life?"

Kai had no immediate reply. Both options were terrible in their own way, especially for someone whose family's symbol was a dragon. For him, this was a nightmare with no escape, not when he was in the Royal Garden and his adversary was the prince.

"What do you think, Michael?" the Corrupt Prince asked, turning toward Lothar and me. "Should I kill it or imprison it? As a child, I was always jealous of your Sacrifices. I have always wanted to have something I could kill if I wanted to. Having the closest thing to a dragon would be much better than your traitorous father's best friend."

"David Kingman was not a traitor," Lothar declared.

The Corrupt Prince made a show of being astonished, looking

around him before he said, "Excuse me, Sacrifice? What did you say to your prince?"

"David Kingman was a hero. And I will finish what he started."

It happened before I had a chance to move.

Lothar pulled a flintlock pistol out of his trousers and aimed at the prince. Before he could squeeze the trigger, Chloe's sword chopped into his wrist, slicing away his hand in one strike. He screamed as his dismembered hand hit the ground, and it was only then that I saw a tattoo of the rebel's red closed fist on the inside of his wrist, previously hidden by bandages.

My father's former best friend was a rebel, and an attempted royal assassin.

My mind reeled, seeing in one horrible moment how clearly I could be tied to the rebel cause, evidence or not. While I attempted to calculate the potential consequences, the Corrupt Prince laughed. He grabbed Lothar by his hair, twisted him around so he was in front of me, and then forced him to his knees with a dagger to his neck as the assembled nobility watched in silence.

"Can you believe the gall of this peasant, Michael? He tried to kill me! In front of my Ravens! In front of a horde of nobility in my own garden!"

I couldn't respond.

"What do you think I should do with him? Should I kill him right now? Or should I bring him to my dungeons and have him join the legion of other rebels that go there and never see the light of day again? My educator loves a bit of fresh skin."

Lothar was staring at me, teeth gritted in pain.

"Actually," he said. "I have a better idea. I want Michael to kill him. Chloe, give him your sword."

"My prince," she said softly. "I think—"

"Did I ask for your opinion? No, so keep it to yourself, Raven. But I suppose it would be unwise to hand a sword to the son of an infamous traitor just after a failed assassination. Thus, I have a better idea." The Corrupt Prince cleared his throat and continued, "Michael. I will let this man live if you say these exact words to me: 'Let this man live, my prince.' That's all you have to do."

My heart wouldn't stop pounding. Lothar's life was in my hands. I had no love for the man after he had betrayed my family . . . but could I be responsible for his death? It was one thing to hate someone and wish them dead; it was another to take a life. Even if he was a rebel. Even if he had abandoned us during the riots of Kingman Keep. Even if he was already dying.

Assuming the prince wouldn't kill him no matter what I said.

"What do you say, Michael? Will you condemn him with silence?" the prince taunted, tracing the muscles in Lothar's neck with his blade.

I mumbled to myself, uncertain what to say. My heart was being torn in two.

"Speak up, Michael! Say the words or his death will be on you!"

"He'll die no matter what I say," I said calmly. "The king would never let a rebel assassin live."

"Are you willing to wager this man's life on that belief? Are you unwilling to set aside your pride to save a life?"

Lothar wasn't family. Lothar wasn't even a friend of the family after what he had done to us as children. But I was the better man, and I would not have his death be on my—

"Too much hesitation. I'll decide for you, Michael."

The Corrupt Prince cut Lothar's neck with a single stroke from his dagger. Lothar's eyes went wide right before the Corrupt Prince shoved him to the ground so his blood wouldn't stain his clothes.

As the crowd around us cheered for the Corrupt Prince, I watched my father's best friend bleed out in front of me.

SHE WHO WOULD BE QUEEN

There was a party afterward, with the boar from the other hunt roasting on a spit over an open flame. It was nowhere near ready, but, judging by how much beer remained, I doubted the nobility cared. I had wanted to leave the party with Kai, who had been too distraught when the Corrupt Prince declared he would imprison the dragon in the King's Garden, but I knew Domet would never let me hear the end of it if I left. For now, I had to pretend to be the good moonstruck noble and let everyone praise me for my heroics during the hunt. If there was any comfort in the day, it was there was no doubt I would be invited to the king's birthday party and join the Hollow Court. Having heard I had captured a piece of Celona, defeated a Wyvern, and approved the death of an assassin, the nobles were too enthralled by their new Kingman to let me fade away so easily.

Any remaining fun in the party vanished when the Corrupt Prince began to hand out Lothar's fingers like trophies to his favorites, who carried them proudly in whichever hand wasn't holding their drink. The rest of Lothar's body, with the exception of his heart, was burned in the main bonfire, bringing a scorched-bacon scent to the party. The prince and his Throne Seekers were planning to roast the heart and eat it after Ambassador Zain said it would make them stronger Fabricators.

Just the sight of them all with butchered bits of a man made me feel sick, on top of Kai's distress. There was no chance I could enjoy the festivities, though the girl in red was making the best of it. When it was clear my mood wasn't going to improve, she'd gone off to dance with the first attractive person she saw. Domet hadn't bothered to congratulate me on what had happened, a sly smile from across the grounds the only interaction I expected until tomorrow. I wasn't looking forward to it, nor was I looking forward to another event with all these nobles or having to steal the king's memories.

All things considered, Angelo's offer to help me leave Hollow was becoming ever more appealing as I watched the pride of the nobility flirt and prance around, celebrating the successful hunt, the death of a desperate assassin, and the capture of the Rebel Emperor.

Naomi plopped down in the seat next to me, adjusting her dress. "Do you think this neckline shows enough cleavage?"

I didn't even look at her. "Depends who you're trying to impress."

"The Corrupt Prince, and it's a very fine line between lady and whore. Show too little, and men declare you a prude; show too much, and you're vulgar."

This time I looked at her. "It's good, then. You can always show a little more when you're with him. He'll definitely notice it then."

"Good idea."

"Where were you during the hunt?"

"Official Scales business. My commander wanted a full report on our latest assignment."

"What assignment?"

She gave me an overexaggerated wink. "I can't tell you. Official business, very secretive."

"Fine."

Naomi whacked me across the back of my head. "You're supposed to beg for more details. It's no fun if you give up so easily."

"If you're not here to return my ring, why are you even talking to me? There's nothing I can help you with right now."

"Oh, I don't know. You are the hero in residence. The Dragonslayer. For once, being seen with you is advantageous to me."

"It wasn't a dragon," I mumbled. "It was a Wyvern. There's a difference."

She rolled her eyes, still adjusting her dress. "Besides, wearing a mask for these fools is tiring. Sometimes I like being myself. And since I have leverage over you and don't care what you think about me, I view our time together as a slight reprieve."

"Why wear a mask at all? What can't you do as yourself?"

She plucked a random glass of wine from the table and finished it.

"I know you failed the Raven exam before you joined the Executioner Division. And how your mother actually died."

"You finally did some research. You'd have been stupid not to."

"What're you after, Naomi?"

"Isn't it obvious?" she asked, leaning back as she gazed out over the crowd. Her face grew dark, stern, and serious. "The Ravens said I lacked conviction, had no honor and no sense of duty. They claimed I only applied because my mother had wanted me to, which does not make a good Raven. It made me angry—angrier than I was at the monster who killed her. So I vowed that, if they wouldn't have me, I would make them serve me."

"Considering they only protect the Royal Family . . ." I stopped, suddenly very aware of what she wanted to do . . . and who she wanted to be.

The woman who planned to be Queen rose from her seat. "If you'll excuse me, Michael, I have a prince to seduce."

I watched her stride across the grounds toward the prince and his Throne Seekers and saw them welcome her with cheers and beer as she took a seat beside the prince and let him show off his trophies. She looked at me, winked again, and returned to whatever conversation she was in the middle of. It was clear that I was far too useful to her to let go.

I didn't want to be here anymore.

I didn't want to be involved in this noble society anymore, where cowards were rewarded for betrayal, selfish ambition, and kissing the ass of a parasitic Royal. I wanted out . . . I needed out . . . I needed to be somewhere else. So I left the party and headed toward the only place that wouldn't judge me for being myself. Somewhere where I could learn if the Kingman name was worth preserving, or if I should give it up and finally move on with my life.

THE MAN WITHOUT
HIS MEMORIES

A nurse at the asylum opened my mother's room for me. "I'll tell Gwen you're here."

"Don't bother her," I said. "I won't be long."

The nurse didn't question me. "I'll leave the door unlocked for you. Just let someone know so they can lock it when you leave."

"Thank you."

The nurse left after that, and I entered my mother's room. She was sitting up, knees against her chest as she stared at the portrait of herself and my father on their wedding day. From what Gwen said, she did this often, so I didn't interrupt, and simply sat on the bed next to her.

It wasn't long before she said, "I miss your father."

"I do, too." And I did, albeit for different reasons. I missed the days when life wasn't so complicated . . . the days when he was my hero instead of my shame.

"I'm sorry for what happened to me, Michael," she said. "Gwen tells me I don't have many good days . . . but today is one of them. I'm so sorry. I should have been taking care of you all . . . not the reverse."

I put my arm around her and she nestled her head against my chest. She was so cold, and I felt my warmth slither off my body and onto her. "It's not your fault, Ma. We never blamed you for what happened."

"That doesn't make it better," she said. "I wish I could remember . . . I wish . . . I wish . . . Every time I think I remember what happened I . . . I . . . ," and she trailed off, seemingly forgetting the words she'd been about to say.

"I know, Ma. I know."

She lifted her head and wiped her eyes with the back of her hand.

"Ma," I began, "can I ask you something?"

"Of course, Michael. Always."

I put my head down, avoiding her gaze to make this easier. "I don't think I want to be a Kingman anymore. I can't be a noble in this city. I can't do it. I tried. I can't."

My mother hugged me tightly. "Never feel bad about saying that, Michael." She made me look her in the eyes. "You are a Kingman, but that doesn't mean you have to live up to that legacy. Trying to almost killed your father when he was your age. He wanted nothing to do with it. He left Hollow for years rather than devote his life to war."

"But he came back."

"He did," she said. "But only after his parents, sister, and Queen were murdered. If they hadn't died then, I suspect he and I would still be . . . still be . . . ah. It doesn't matter. What matters is that neither of us wanted a life surrounded by politics. It drove us both away from our respective countries."

My voice was becoming more ragged, cracking like a boy's. "But there must always be a Kingman in Hollow. Everyone knows—"

"Fuck them," she snapped. "Fuck the nobility. Fuck the Royals. Fuck the city. You owe them nothing. You are my child, and if you need to leave, leave. Run as far away from Hollow as you can and take your brother and sister with you."

"Lyon might want to stay. He's . . . found a place here. But what about you? I've been trying to cure you, but . . . but nothing I've tried has worked."

She ran her fingers through my hair. "Don't worry about me, Michael. I'm your mother, knowing you're safe and happy is enough for me."

I didn't cry, but it was the closest I'd come in years. "Ma, I love you."

A smile. "I love you, too, David. Do we still have the war council with the king tonight? If so, I might have to reschedule a meeting with Edgar Naverre. He's concerned about one of his daughter's suitors, but it didn't seem urgent if you want me with you."

My momentary happiness shattered there and then, but the memory of my mother's words didn't. I rose from the bed, tucked her into it, and told her not to worry about the king's council. Then I went to find Gwen, deeper in the asylum.

My mother was right. My family didn't owe this city anything, and years of trying to preserve our legacy had done nothing for me. Well, except for the times it had nearly killed me. It was time to take Angelo up on his offer. Especially when he could guarantee me as much as Domet without having to deal with the nobility. I just had to convince Gwen. Whatever she thought about our father's innocence, I hoped she would be willing to leave it behind in exchange for a better life.

I didn't bother knocking on the door to the room she was in, pulling it open with ease, but because of my sudden intrusion, I heard the end of the conversation. "Your father had the gun in his hand when Davey Hollow was killed, but—"

"What?" I blurted out, confused.

Gwen jumped up from the floor. The man she had been talking to remained still and calm inside his ring of candles. As I stared at the man, I remembered Gwen calling him Blackwell. According to the notes I had found, Colton Blackwell had been an eyewitness to the murder of Davey Hollow . . . and here he was, talking about it.

"Michael," Gwen said, "you can't barge in like—"

"How long have you been interrogating him? Has he told you anything?"

"I don't know what you're—"

"Don't play the fool. Answer the question."

She hesitated. "How much do you know?"

"Enough to know who that is."

"I figured out who he was shortly after I started working here. He was having nightmares about our father coming to kill him."

"Why didn't you tell me?"

"Because it wasn't your business. Who cares if I talk to the witness who saw our father kill Davey?" Gwen turned her back on me.

"The king would, for starters. We could all be in trouble if the wrong person learned about this, Gwen." A pause. "Can we talk to him together?"

"It takes patience. His mind is so jumbled by Darkness Fabrications that he doesn't always make sense, and no one would believe anything he said. This is the best I've seen him in months. I just have to wade through his falsified memories to the truth of that day."

"Can you try again?"

I must have sounded eager, because Gwen nodded and made her way back to Blackwell's side. I took a deep breath to steady myself. I didn't know what I was hoping to hear, but if we were going to leave Hollow, I owed it to myself to make sure I was leaving a guilty father behind. Otherwise Gwen would never come with me.

"Blackwell," Gwen said, "this is my brother."

"Which one?" he asked. "Michael or Lyonardo?"

"Michael."

"I knew more of the Kingman children would come to talk to me eventually ever since . . ." Blackwell paused. ". . . ever since they put me here and Gwendolyn found me. Ever since it was discovered my mind had been muddled by Darkness Fabrications. Do you know what it's like? To know your mind has been corrupted? That everything you think you know could be fake? That your life could all be a lie?"

"Can't say I do," I lied, not wanting to tell Gwen I had been misremembering people lately. Now was not the time for that.

Blackwell stared at the wall behind me. "No. Not many know what it's like. Forgotten have it easier. Most think it's worse to not remember anything. But no . . . it's worse not to trust your memories. What is a lie and what is the truth? Nothing is real. Everything is imaginary."

This was going to be a long conversation. I slumped into a seat against the metal door.

"Could you go over that day again?" Gwen said.

"That day," he began tentatively, "Kendra had just got off a shift. We hadn't seen each other in what seemed like forever . . . We were young, wanted time alone, and couldn't wait to get home. No one was scheduled to be in the Star Chamber. David Kingman was expected to be at a meeting with the king and Davey with his sister . . . No one was supposed to be there. Yet, when we opened the door . . . we saw . . . we saw . . ."

"What did you see?" Gwen pressed.

Blackwell drew his knees closer to his chest, putting his hands on the sides of his head. "Haze. Darkness. A gunshot. The prince dying. David Kingman held the gun . . . Was his finger on the trigger? . . . I can't remember . . . He held the gun, though. I can still feel the heat of the room on my face. The smoke burned my lungs so badly, it hurt to swallow. Kendra arrested David Kingman, and then there was chaos. So much chaos."

My chest felt tight, and I asked, "Did you see my father shoot the prince?"

He shook his head back and forth quickly. "No! No . . . First memory I thought so, but after they put me here, things changed.

He had the gun in his hand, but the finger . . . his finger wasn't on the trigger. It was on the barrel. It was on the barrel!"

I held my hand out, imagining that I was holding a gun. It would be impossible for someone to fire a gun like that. And if the gun had somehow still been fired, the heat would have left burns behind. Which was the kind of detail that would have been mentioned in the murder report. Was Blackwell misremembering this? I asked him.

"No," he declared, voice rising in pitch. "No! The shadows tell me it was the trigger! But his finger was on the barrel! That's the truth!"

Shadows speaking to him? Not even Dark could make his Darkness Fabrications do that. What had happened to this man's mind? Even our mother, on her worst days, was in a better place than he was on his good ones. "If our father didn't pull the trigger, then who did? Where'd the gun come from?"

"The smoking gun fell into his hand."

This wasn't helping his story sound more credible.

"Is there anything else you remember?" Gwen asked.

Blackwell didn't respond, curling tighter into his body, wrapping his arms around his legs. Gwen had him rest his head on her shoulder as a mother might to comfort their child. She gave me a look, and I continued the questioning myself.

To gauge his sanity, I asked a question I already knew the answer to. "What about your Raven wife? What happened to her?"

"Dead. The shadows killed her in Naverre seven years ago. They said it was rebels, but I know the truth. Back then, the first memories were still in my head."

"The shadows?"

"They whisper lies," he explained. "They try to turn the truth into the first memories. They distort. Every time they come, they take more and more. They don't want me to remember I know about them, know what they're doing. That's why I keep these candles lit all day and night. They can't ever go out. Not ever. Never ever."

"How did you find out your memories were affected by Darkness Fabrications?"

He breathed in and out very slowly, rocking slightly, bringing himself back to reality. Gwen's attempts to comfort him were beginning to fail.

"Things changed," he said. "Hard to tell the difference between misremembering and not being able to remember. How many cups were on the table at dinner? Two or three. Small things at first, but then eventually they got bigger and bigger. Because they change things. And then they have to change other things, to make sense with the old memories. Unending cycle of change.

"They changed the color of Kendra's wedding dress. Then I knew. That memory was too bright for the shadows to change. Wasn't hard to figure out what had happened to my mind. It had to be Darkness Fabrications. People thought the stress of losing my wife in Naverre caught up to me and this was how my family showed me how much they cared . . . put me somewhere where they thought I could get better."

Although the asylum had been built to help people, nowadays it was closer to a prison for those whose families wanted to keep them out of sight.

"Do you know who did this to you?"

Colton Blackwell met my eyes, his own filled with longing and regret. "Do you think I'd be here if I did? Someone stole my life from me."

"Can't Light Fabrications reverse the process?"

He laughed. "Every day they use Light Fabrications to try and relieve what the Darkness Fabrications have done to me. All it does is create cracks in my mind before the shadows try to retake their lost ground. No one knows why, but I had to beg them to stop trying. The doctors here think my mind has been broken beyond repair. They're just waiting for me to die." He paused, drew in a long breath, and looked away from Gwen. "They don't think I listen."

I didn't know what to say or how to comfort him. I rose to my feet. The man was clearly mad, and he'd said nothing credible to support my sister's theories about our father's innocence—or Domet's that he had been set up. If anything, his words made me doubt there was anything to find, even if I could steal the king's memories.

I was more confident than before that leaving Hollow was the right thing to do. Gwen got Blackwell comfortable again and we both left the room, Gwen shutting the door securely behind her.

"Do you see? Our father was innocent! A Darkness Fabricator set him up!"

"Those were the ramblings of a madman, Gwen. A smoking gun fell into our father's hand? Nothing he said was proof of anything."

"Did you listen to the same conversation? Didn't you hear our father wasn't holding the gun correctly? Nothing is random. It means—"

I put my hands on her shoulders. "Gwen, Angelo has offered us a way out of Hollow. Our mother, too. If we want, we can be out of here and never have to worry about what the nobility thinks of us again. We don't have to live up to the Kingman legacy anymore."

Gwen knocked my hands away. "We don't have to? Of course we don't. You're the only one who ever thought we had to. Lyon and I accepted, the moment we were branded, that nothing would be expected from us again. The only reason I cared was because I knew it would affect my children—if I ever had any."

"I never knew you felt that way," I said.

"I was realistic about the future . . . You weren't."

Part of me thought I could continue the family legacy away from Hollow, rebuilding it slowly over the years. And then there was a part of me that understood that if I left Hollow, the Kingman legacy would end with me. But, like my mother said, I had to do what was best for me. No matter what kind of obligation I felt to the city for my father's betrayal. The city had survived without a Kingman for a decade; it could continue without one for as long as it had to.

"You're right. But I've grown up. We can leave Hollow, Gwen. We can have a normal life."

She started to pace. "I want that gun. I won't leave Hollow without finding it."

"What?"

"The gun that killed Davey. Bring me the gun and I'll leave Hollow with you."

There was a better chance of Celona repairing itself than that happening. All that finding the gun would do was aid her investigation. She would only leave Hollow when her hatred of the Royals was sated.

"You realize what you're asking from me, Gwen? If the gun

hasn't been destroyed, which it could have been, it will be held by the king himself. I'd have to break into the castle for a chance at finding it."

"Aren't you planning to already?" she questioned. "You're not participating in the Endless Waltz to hang out with nobles all day long. You're after something—probably with Domet's help—and since you've suddenly joined the Waltz, you must want something from the castle."

"How do you know the gun hasn't been destroyed already?"

Her expression grew serious. "If I were murdered, would you destroy the weapon that killed me? Or would you want to know everything: where it came from, who designed it, who built it, and how it ended up in the murderer's hands?"

"Maybe the king still has it."

"I know he does." She paused. "Help me. Prove our father was guilty beyond a shadow of a doubt, and then we can both put Hollow behind us for good."

We sealed the deal with a hug.

———

The moment I left the asylum, the shadows began to dance on the walls around me, and I knew my evening was far from over.

Dark was waiting outside on a bench, and once he saw me, he rose and walked over. The darkness seemed to distort him, elongating his features in the waning moonlight. "Michael, I don't think I need to threaten you or your sister in there to get you to come with me, do I?"

I shook my head. "I'm surprised it took you this long to find me."

"I'm patient." Dark turned his back to me. "Follow. We'll have a conversation somewhere more private."

I followed him further into the city. I couldn't make a mistake if I wanted to see the morning light. But I had more power than he realized, having hidden his documents.

That's what I told myself, anyway.

THE MERCENARY

I sat against the wall as Dark built and lit a fire in the hearth.

We hadn't spoken on the walk to Kingman Keep, maybe because there was nothing that needed to be said. He tended the first flickers of the flame, gently feeding wood into it until it could survive on its own, then stood and brushed off his hands on his shirt. He had changed a little since I had last seen him, more put together. His angular facial features were from Hollow, but his thick black hair wasn't. He'd trimmed his black beard and shaved the sides of his head to a thin stubble, while the rest of his hair was pulled back in a ponytail. His clothes showed proof of the athletic build I'd suspected he had when we first met, and his jacket was open enough that I could see the butt of his pistol in its holster.

"We're safe enough here. Give me my envelope."

"I don't have it here."

He looked at me. "I don't believe you."

"Give me some credit: I can be moonstruck sometimes, but I'm not an imbecile. Why would I risk losing your envelope by carrying it on me all the time when I could leave it somewhere safe?"

"Then where is it?" he said, a touch more anger in his voice.

"Somewhere you can't get to without my help."

"Doubtful."

"Since Tosburg Company couldn't, I doubt you could alone."

Dark went still. "How do you know about Tosburg Company?"

I hid my smile, realizing I had the upper hand for the first time. I'd still have to be careful if I was going to get out of here with my life intact. "Read about them in your notes."

"You opened my envelope? That was stupid of you."

"Would you be treating me any differently if I hadn't?"

Dark threw a piece of wood into the fire and watched it crackle. "Probably not," he admitted, and rubbed his chin. "I know that Tosburg Company attacked the Hollow Library seeking some specific information, and that their attack failed . . . so I'm assuming you've hidden my envelope there. That's annoying, and I'm not sure if I'd want to piss off the Archivists again. But I'll do what is needed." His hand curled around the pistol grip. "Your usefulness just came to an end."

"I can retrieve it for you, given a few assurances."

He looked at me with his grey eyes. "Michael, let me be clear. You stole from me. If you attempt to extort me for what is rightfully mine, I will kill you. That is a promise, not a threat."

I held up a hand to forestall him. "I didn't steal anything. You told me to hold on to that envelope, and I did. I had no way to contact you to return it, so I kept it safe until you found me. It's not as if I was trying to avoid you. It's yours in exchange for your word that this matter will be settled between us. And letting me know what happened to Sirash."

"Are you deaf? Didn't you hear what I just said?"

"I've made enough deals with people recently to know not to rely on their compassion once it's over."

"You realize what I am, right?" Dark asked, shadows darkening around him. "I am not a simple Waylayer or King. I am a Mercenary. Do you not understand what that means?"

"I'm known for my persistence, not my intelligence."

Dark laughed, a proper belly laugh, his head thrown back and the shadows retreating again. "I need answers about something in this keep. Give them to me as a show of good faith, and in exchange I'll promise you safety and tell you what happened to your friend."

What was another deal at this point? Soon the only person I wouldn't have made one with would be the king himself. "What do you want to know about?"

With a gesture, Dark led me into my old room in Kingman Keep. It was cold and dry, wind blowing leaves in through the broken window. Shattered glass covered the ground outside, glittering in the pale moonlight.

He stood in the center of it and asked, "Why is this room painted like this?"

There was a night sky painted across the walls and ceiling, dozens of constellations spread across them, from the Grey Dragon and

God's Left Eye to the seven major pieces of the shattered moon and the debris field around them. There was a painted sun setting into the tile floor where my bed had once stood. The paint had chipped slightly in the years it had been left unattended and uncared for, but it was still as wonderous a sight as it had been when I was a child.

"My father painted it for me. I was . . . maybe six at the time."

Dark was silent as he made his way around the room, examining it closely. "I didn't know your father was so skilled."

"He wasn't known for it," I said, "but he painted whenever he needed to relax. A lot of his work used to be displayed in the castle— portraits and landscapes, mostly—but all of it is gone now."

"It's rare to see someone from Hollow with this level of artistic talent." Dark paused and pointed toward the corner of the room where the seven major pieces of Celona were. "The brushwork there is amazing. Even masters have trouble blending colors like that. Where did your father learn to do this?"

I shrugged. "In another country, probably." It was just another mystery in a long line of things I didn't know about my father. Every- one spoke about David Kingman the traitor and little of anything else. I didn't even know how my parents had met. "I suspect he would've become a painter if the world hadn't needed him to be a Kingman."

Dark glided his fingers over the chipped paint. He did a lap around the room before he said, "Why did your father paint this for you?"

"I was afraid of the dark."

"The dark?"

"Yeah, I know, hard to believe," I said, rubbing the back of my head. "I thought the shadows that moved in the night were monsters coming to get me. It drove our servants insane. Sometimes I woke up screaming from my nightmares and lit candles to keep the shadows at bay, only to fall asleep again with open flames in my room . . . One night, after the drapes caught fire, my father took me outside and we stood in the dark together."

I cleared my throat and continued, "He told me that everything I was afraid of in the dark was also there in the light. The only difference was the way it looked. He made me touch the blue-and-grey flowers, walk across the wet grass, and watch the fish swim in the river's green water. Then he picked me up again and we looked at the stars. He told me that the greatest treasure this world offers us is only visible at night, and if we didn't go outside when it was dark, we would miss it. So, what was there to be afraid of? It was the first time I'd ever really looked at the stars and the moons before. They were gorgeous. We stayed up all night as he named every single constellation and told its story. The next day, he started painting this." I was quiet for a moment. "Back then, he was my hero."

"Fathers are like that," Dark said, almost as if he was talking to himself. "Always disappointing their children when they need them the most."

"Why do you care about this?"

"There's a room in the castle that's almost identical. I was trying to find out why."

Why did Dark care about a similarly painted room in the castle? I asked him that question.

"It doesn't concern you. But if you'd rather know why instead of what happened to your friend that night, I'll tell you."

"No, tell me about Sirash."

Dark took a seat on the edge of the windowsill, ignoring the broken glass. "He ran away shortly after you did. Didn't even stay behind to get paid. That's all I know."

"I don't believe you. How do I know you're not keeping him somewhere as a hostage?"

"If I had him, you would know."

"So you have no idea where he is or what happened to him?"

"None whatsoever. He could've made it out, or Scales could have him."

If Scales had him, his body could appear in the Hanging Gardens at any moment. And since he hadn't been paid, his family was in danger. Worse, it was another three days before we were due to meet up again, and if he'd been implicated and I went looking for him, I could easily be the one Scales executed. What could I do?

Dark's thoughts had already moved on.

"Tomorrow morning you're going to retrieve my envelope from the Hollow Library and then bring it to me after Lights Out. That's well after the third event of the Endless Waltz, so there shouldn't be any conflict."

"Tomorrow? You don't want it back tonight?"

He paused, as if thinking about what he was going to say before he opened his mouth. "No. If someone else is watching you, they'll get suspicious of why you're going to the library late at night. Especially when you're not supposed to be there. I could accompany you, but that might make it worse. Let it take longer rather than risk what is rightfully mine."

"If that's what—"

There was a crash in one of the rooms outside. Dark drew his gun and pointed for me to hide in one of the nearby rooms. I went without hesitation. The last thing I wanted to do was be seen with a Mercenary. Although, instead of breaking a window and jumping out, I closed the door to a sliver and watched to see who had found us.

It was Trey, and he was walking into the great hall with his hands up.

THE MERCENARY'S APPRENTICE

Trey stopped in the middle of the Great Hall before I could open the door and scream at Dark not to shoot him, and lifted his shirt to show he was unarmed.

Dark didn't lower his gun. "Who are you and what do want?"

"My name is Treyvon Wiccard," he said, hands still raised. "You're Dark, a Mercenary of Orbis Company, right? The one known as the Black Death?"

Dark was the Black Death? According to Angelo, the Black Death was credited with more than five hundred murders, all over the world. He was a daemon in human form. Only the Reaper was credited with more. What could Trey possibly want from him?

Dark must have shared my thoughts, as he asked the same thing.

"I want to join Orbis Company. I want to become a Mercenary."

It was hard to tell if I was alive after I heard that, because I was certain my heart had stopped.

Dark didn't share my shock and despair. He laughed, holstering his gun. "You want to be a Mercenary? Tell me, Treyvon, who exactly do you want to kill?"

That question caught Trey off guard, and with a stammer he said, "What? I don't want to—"

"Don't play me for a fool. People become Mercenaries for one of three reasons," Dark said. "Money. Those are usually your retired knights or corrupt members of Scales. Respect. But people who are seeking that don't stride up to a Mercenary with their hands up. So. You want to get away with murder."

"That was more obvious than I wanted it to be," Trey said, lowering his hands.

"Who do you want dead?"

I held my breath, hoping Trey wouldn't say my name.

"The rebel who killed my brother."

"And they are?"

"I don't know."

"Don't have a name? A description? Position in the army? Anything at all? Because if you haven't realized, there are thousands of rebels outside those walls right now."

"I don't have many specifics."

"Do you know anyone that does?" Dark asked.

"Yes," Trey snapped. "But I can't ask him."

"Why not?"

"It doesn't matter. I—"

"Do you even know what being a Mercenary's apprentice entails? How badly do you want to kill this person that you're willing to give up your freedom?"

"I thought Mercenaries could do whatever they wanted."

"Full-fledged Mercenaries can, not apprentices. You'd have to pass an examination by Orbis Company before you'd be allowed to leave my side. And we have high standards. Can't just have any random fool out there operating under our name."

Trey hesitated, fists clenched. "How long would it take until I was a proper Mercenary?"

"Ten years if you are lucky. A lifetime if you aren't."

That was a longer sentence of servitude than joining a High Noble Fabricator army.

"Would you help me kill my target before I became your apprentice?" he asked.

"Yes," Dark replied. "But I don't understand. You want to become my apprentice to kill the person who murdered your brother, yet you don't know who was responsible. It seems bizarre for you to be coming to me before knowing . . . oh, who do you blame for murdering your brother?"

Sometimes silence said more than words, so Trey didn't respond, staring into Dark's eyes instead.

"That's it, isn't it?" Dark said. "You don't want my help to kill the rebel responsible. You want to kill the Emperor and crush the rebellion as revenge. Am I right?"

"They took my brother's future away. It's only fair I take theirs."

"You're either extremely stupid or suicidal. Wait for the trial. I won't take on an apprentice who's just going to throw his life away to get revenge. I'd get nothing from you. You'd be worthless to me—"

A blinding light exploded from Trey's arms as he screamed, "I'm not worthless!" It was brighter than it had been in Margaux Keep. He'd been training . . . but how many memories had he sacrificed getting to this point?

Dark wasn't as impressed. "You're a Light Fabricator. A barely trained, unrefined one. Who taught you?"

Trey took a breath and the light evaporated from his arms like steam rising. "Self-taught. But I've been working with the Royal Fabricator Master for a few days."

"He's an imbecile," Dark said. "Has he even taught you how to identify when people are infected with Dark Fabrications? Or how to manifest your light into objects?"

"Not yet. But you could. Take me on as your apprentice. Teach me. I'm a Light Fabricator, a Throne Seeker, and could be engaged to a Low Noble by the end of the week if I wanted to be. I'm valuable."

Dark pointed upward. Black tendrils were hanging over Trey, close enough to brush against his cheek. They squirmed like worms in the dirt. "Your position in Hollow means nothing to me, and if you didn't even notice those Darkness Fabrications—which you have a natural advantage over—you're useless to me," Dark said as he turned away. "Leave."

"Not until you take me on as your apprentice."

"Fine," he said with a sigh. "I'll do it myself."

Black tendrils grabbed Trey's ankles, yanked him to the ground, and began to pull him away. He rolled onto his back, covered his hand in light, and punched anything within reach. They dispersed like spilled ink. But no matter how many he destroyed, more swarmed him.

"Name your price!" Trey shouted, holding his own.

Dark faced Trey, and the tendrils stopped dragging him away. "That's not something you should say to a Mercenary."

"Name. Your. Price."

The darkness seemed to dance around the Mercenary, a sickening smile on his face. "Would you kill anyone I chose if I promised to help you end the rebellion?"

Trey's restraints faded away and he climbed to his feet. "Yes."

"Even your mother?"

"She's dead."

"Father?"

"Left me when I was young. No idea who he is."

"I'm jealous. What I wouldn't do to be free of my own." A pause. "What about your best friend?"

"My brother was all I had."

"I don't believe you." Dark cracked his knuckles. "We all have bonds that tie us."

"Not me."

"Then maybe I have use for you after all. Have you ever killed someone?"

"I . . . I . . . It wasn't . . . There was no . . . ," he stammered. He closed his eyes and took a deep breath. "Yes."

Trey had killed someone?

"Do you regret it?" Dark asked. The shadows around him had

started to recede, and the moonlight was brighter than it was before.

"No," he whispered. "I did what was needed to survive."

"If I gave you a gun, would you hesitate to pull the trigger and kill a stranger?"

"Not if you promised to help me get revenge."

"Then let's make a deal," Dark declared with arms wide. "You lack refinement and potential for me to take you on as an apprentice right now, but I could use an assassin—one that can't be traced back to me. If you do what I ask, I'll kill the Emperor for you. And if you impress me, maybe I'll even take you on as my apprentice and welcome you into a family that will never leave you."

"Who do you want dead?"

Dark hesitated, glancing back toward me. "We'll meet again after the Emperor's trial. I'll tell you then. No point in me doing anything if Hollow goes through with the execution." Another pause. "And it'll give you time to reconsider. Because if you join me, you're with me for life. Is that truly what you want?"

"I won't reconsid—"

"I'll find you when it's time," Dark said as he snapped his fingers. "Now go away."

The black tendrils grabbed Trey's back and yanked him away from Dark. There was no time for him to fight back before he was out of sight, though his curses could be heard until they faded into distant echoes.

As soon as I knew Trey wasn't within earshot or could see me, I slammed the door open and screamed, "What the fuck was that, Dark? How—"

Dark put a finger gun to my forehead, his face expressionless. "Showing respect is clearly not one of your strengths, Michael."

"You're about to turn one of my friends into your personal assassin."

"Murderer. Assassin. Two sides of the same coin."

"Rescind your deal with him."

"Why?" he asked. "Do you want to take his place? Would you kill to save him?"

"I . . . I'm . . . Trey is . . . What are you truly after, Dark? Who are you scared of that you would create an assassin rather than kill them yourself?"

Dark put his finger gun down. "Does it matter? You know what I want from you. Get it done." He leaned closer to whisper in my ear. "Or if you continue this line of questioning, maybe when I meet Trey again, I'll put a bullet in his head. Thanks for giving me more leverage, Michael."

I fought back my temper and began to walk away, not wanting to provoke him and put anyone else in harm's way. I had learned more from him than I expected to, and walked away with my life. I didn't want to test my luck any further tonight, especially when it was clear that there was still so much I didn't know. Who would a Mercenary fear?

Before I left the room, Dark said calmly, "And, Michael, don't try to be clever. Do what I say."

I left him at that. On my way out of Kingman Keep, I wondered how I should feel about a Mercenary taking over my ancestral home . . . but I hadn't called it home for years, and it didn't truly matter if I was going to leave Hollow anyway. The thought that Trey might be so distraught he'd consider killing a stranger to get revenge was more concerning. How could I help someone that far gone—and would he even let me?

My heart ached over lost friends, and long-lost homes all the same.

THE REDEEMER

I stretched back in my seat, hands interlocked, until my back and knuckles cracked. Piles of open diaries were spread across the table. I had arrived at the library early that morning to make the most of my time. I needed to figure out why Dark wanted *The Journal of the Archmage*, why he wanted to know about a painting my father did years ago, and why he had taken an interest in my family before we had met. My search was futile thus far, and I'd have to leave soon to see Domet before the third event began so I would have an idea what to expect.

Gwen sat across from me, humming a lullaby to herself with her feet up on the table while she read a book about our ancestors. She had spotted me walking into the library and followed, choosing to read indoors instead of by the river as she usually did. I had tried to warn her that they wouldn't let her in, but they did without even a question. It made me fume a little that she could slide in on my deal. She winked at me and said if only I had a little charm I'd understand.

She'd been less smug back when all she did was cry.

The room was silent except for the creaks in the wooden floors and Gwen's humming. It was a peaceful serenity that I hadn't experienced in a long time as I turned back to the entry I was reading.

This war with New Dracon City has shown me how single-minded in medicine I was. No longer is it about sword wounds, missing limbs, or other easily treated injuries. No. Now they have bullets. Annoying little balls of iron that can kill people with a simple pull of a trigger. If they really wished to, they could arm every child in their city with these guns to repel us if we ever actually managed to get close. The way war is fought has changed, and we're on the losing side. We stick to our beliefs as David Kingman and King Isaac develop more strategies to outmaneuver the New Dracon City guns, but if—

"Where is the third event being held again?" Gwen asked.

I didn't look up. "Theater in the Upper Quarter. We're watching a performance or something. I'm not sure."

Gwen nodded thoughtfully and returned to her own reading. Every time she turned a page, it sounded as if she were ripping it.

—it weren't for the fact we had Fabricators and they don't—we would have already lost this war.

*Just this morning I treated a patient with a bullet lodged in
her intestines. A slow, deadly injury. One of the worst places
to get shot. We did what we could and removed the bullet, then
cleaned and closed the wound. But I fear blood rot will—*

"Do you think the princess hates you for what our father did?"
This time I looked up.

She had never asked that question before. If my memory was correct, she had never mentioned the princess once since our father had been executed. "I don't know. Your guess is as good as mine, it's not as if I've seen her more recently than you have. That probably answers your question. If she didn't hate me, she would've reached out."

Another nod, as if she were in her own little world. I waited for her to ask another question, but she returned to her book and so I followed suit, returning to the journals.

*—take her, swiftly. We still don't know what causes the
infection. All our surgery tools were cleaned, so it must have
been something else. Can it be the bullets themselves? There's
too much to learn and not enough time to do so amidst this war.
Her name is Amanda Trask and I fear I am responsible for her
death. Some days—*

"Do you think she might—"
I snapped my book shut and put it down on the table. I was going to throw it at her if she didn't get to her point already. "What do you really want to ask, Gwen?"

She closed her book and put it down on the table. "You won't like it."

"Try me."

Gwen didn't respond at first. "If you're serious about leaving Hollow, then we should talk about the Royals."

"What about them?"

"What I'm trying to say is," she mumbled, "we're Kingman. We should consider who we'd be leaving in charge. Whether they are fit for the role. And whether we should do something about it if they're not."

"Gwen, the whole point of leaving Hollow would be to get away from the Kingman legacy. You're talking about wading straight into it."

Gwen groaned, twirled her hair, and leaned back in her chair. It squeaked loudly. "Never mind."

After a sigh, I picked up another journal and flipped to a random page. Before I could read a word, Gwen continued: "But would you seriously be alright with leaving Hollow if there was a chance Adreann could sit on the throne? You've only seen a fraction of what he's capable of, and he was no better when we were younger. People just ignored it, myself included."

"You're right, I wouldn't be. But what could we do? The only way he wouldn't be second in line for the throne is if the princess marries and has a child and he abdicates or is proven to be illegitimate."

"And none of those scenarios are likely. No one has ever tried to court the Princess, Adreann's pride would never let him abdicate, and I doubt he's illegitimate. He has the hair of the Royals." She paused. "There is another option, but—"

"Are you suggesting we kill him?"

"Yes," she declared.

"Get that idea out of your head," I said. "We're Kingman, and we do not kill Royals regardless of how we feel about them or how unfit they are to rule."

"What if a Royal tried to kill me or Lyon?"

I took her hand across the table and looked into her eyes. "If anyone ever threatened our family, I would do whatever was necessary to protect us. And if that were a Royal, the Kingman legacy would end with me once and for all."

"Why do you get to choose when it ends?"

"Because," I said, releasing her hand, "I'm your older brother, and I will protect you. Even if it's from yourself."

Gwen cleared her throat, looked away from me, and then said, "So, uh, who was that woman Angelo saw you with?"

"What woman?"

"The one who brought you home a few nights ago."

"Naomi?" I asked.

A shrug. "I don't know her name. I just heard the gossip."

"That's Naomi. There's nothing romantic between us."

"There's never anything romantic between you and any women you meet. I may masquerade as a boy to work in the forge, but at least I interact with people I'm attracted to. You don't. And before you say Becca from the bakery, she doesn't count. You always say you're going to ask her father for permission to court her, but you never do."

Considering that women usually liked me before finding out I was a Kingman and then wanted nothing to do with me, my nonexistent love life wasn't entirely my fault.

"How about we support Lyon and his child before we worry about my love life?"

"Deal," Gwen said, a smile on her face and her attitude changed. "This means you'll have to apologize to Lyon. Last I heard, he had banned you from interacting with Kayleigh or his child."

"It's on my list of things to do before we leave Hollow. Along with getting the gun and finishing the Endless Waltz."

Gwen sat back down in her seat. "Good. Now, as much as I like talking to you, shouldn't you be off to see Domet? I'm enjoying not having him in the asylum, and I'd like to keep it that way."

"Shit. You're right," I said as I began to put the journals back on the shelves. "Do you want to come to the Emperor's trial with me after the Endless Waltz is over? I've barely seen you lately and I miss you. For some reason."

"I'd love to," she said. "I don't enjoy watching Lyon execute people, but I can make an exception for the Emperor. He's as wicked as the Royals."

With that, Gwen bid me farewell from the library as she returned to reading about our family. For once, Domet wasn't waiting for me on the steps of his house and I had to enter it. As I made my way in—Dark's envelope tucked into a journal I'd quietly borrowed from the library—and walked down the hallway, everything seemed to be too quiet. Something about the shadows seemed odd, a little reminiscent of how they looked around Dark.

Domet was in his main room, a bottle of vodka at his side as he stared into the roaring fire in his hearth. "Clothes are on the table," he said. "Respectable but a touch less formal this time. Gloves, too: it'll be cold tonight."

As I stepped behind a screen to change, I said, "What's the plan for tonight?"

"A concert arranged by the College of Music. Everyone will be separated into small groups to encourage conversation. I've secured you a spot with High Noble Alexander Ryder and his wife, Alecia. Naomi Dexter, Ambassador Zain, and his servants will also be there. It should be an easy night for you. Most of the nobility are in favor of your return after your performance in the garden. Me advocating for you only reinforced your position. All you have to do is not fuck it up."

"Don't sound so confident in me."

"I do have confidence in you, Michael. If I didn't, I'd never have hired you. And soon, through our combined efforts, we'll be one step closer to accomplishing our goal."

In the middle of buttoning up my trousers, I said, "Are you ever going to tell me what the plan is once we get to the king's party?"

"Once we've secured your spot, I'll tell you the plan. I don't want to tempt fate."

"Give me something. I won't keep stumbling into these events blind."

It was a half-truth. I needed more information if I was to find the gun that killed Davey Hollow as well—and I hoped the king might keep it in the same spot as his memories. Given that the Archmage stored a record of his life in the Hollow Library, it wasn't impossible to think the king might not keep everything in the same place.

Domet took a sip from his glass. "A record of his memories is most likely to be in his study in the Royal Tower, where he keeps everything that is precious to him. It'll be hard to get to, but we'll face that challenge once we're there."

That sounded promising. "Any idea how he might record his memories?"

"Most likely a journal. He may have used tattoos for the more intimate details, but no more. What kind of king wants to look in a mirror every morning and see the mistakes of his reign on his body?"

"A competent king wouldn't have many mistakes."

Domet finished his drink in a single gulp and rose from his seat. "There is no such thing as a competent king." He drew his jacket close to his body. "Are you ready, Michael? Tonight we secure your invitation, and tomorrow we steal the truth from the king. Redemption is close."

MUSICIANS

Shortly after arriving, Domet and I parted ways, each going to our respective parts of the theater to wait for the show to begin. We were late, which suited me fine, since I wouldn't have to listen to the nobles talk about the rebellion, the assassin who had attempted to kill the prince, or the emperor. I'd heard enough after the hunt. Especially since the nobility's primary concern was how they were going to divide up the city of Naverre and the land around it once the rebellion was over, and cared little of what had happened to the Militia Quarter or how many innocent people had been killed. They only cared about the noble deaths, and even then, only because it affected their precious lives.

Instead of waiting in the entrance to see Kai or the girl in red and risk becoming engrossed in noble bullshit, I went straight to Alexander Ryder's box, pulling at my collar and thinking what a waste formal wear was. People only ever wore these clothes to funerals, weddings, trials, or when they were pretending to be something they weren't. I was ashamed that this time it was the latter option for me.

Naomi plopped down in the plush seat next to me and smoothed her dress. I hated the way she snuck up on me, as if she could move soundlessly.

"Stop picking at your clothes," she said, feigning annoyance. "You look fine."

"I'd rather be able to breathe," I said, tugging again at my collar.

"You're complaining about a collar to someone in a corset?"

I stopped fidgeting and watched as other nobles filed into the seats below and gradually populated the other boxes. "How did seducing the prince go?"

"Quite excellently. He played the charming and attentive prince very well and only attempted to kiss my cheek after we had spent the party together. He probably found a whore for the night, but I don't care."

"That doesn't bother you?"

"Whores? No, never. Whores don't sit on thrones and bastards don't inherit."

"What about love?"

"What about it?" she asked sincerely. "No one with power marries for love. Not sure I'd want to be in love anyway. I've seen what it can do to people."

"That's depressing."

"So is a broken heart."

Our conversation ended there as Ambassador Zain and his friends entered the box. As usual, Zain was the only one of the three who talked. They took their seats in the row behind us. Zain massaged my shoulders playfully as he said, "Michael! My friend, how have you been? I heard of your exploits in the hunt and wish I had been at your side. I've always wanted to see the legendary Kingman family in action."

"I'm afraid it wasn't very glamorous, Ambassador."

"Death is rarely glamorous, my friend," Zain said. "That's why we have events like these: to balance out our bloodlust. Have you seen the star performer, Red, before?"

"No," I said. "I've never even heard of her before. Everyone seems to be excited, though. Who is she?"

Naomi said, "No one knows. She wears a gorgeous mask during all her performances and brings her own staff to wait on her. There are endless rumors about her identity. And the name? Well, that's kind of obvious once you see her."

Ambassador Zain leaned toward us, elbows resting on the backs of the seats. "My favorite theory is that she's a bastard born from the Hewitt Clan on the Gold Coast who defied her clan and ran away to Hollow in search of a better life. Now she wears a mask for her own safety in case one of the Hewitts ever wants to eliminate the blight on their holy clan."

"I heard a better one," Naomi began. "Some say she grew up in Naverre, surviving the rebellion and the war that plagued the city. The rumors claim she was found, her hair stained with blood, singing 'The Angels of Naverre' until her throat was raw . . . years before the song was officially composed. The trauma left her unable to sing, but the moment she overcame her fears, she was reborn, and the song became her crowning achievement. Her mask is worn in memory of all those who died."

"Those all sound ridiculous," I said. They were too romantic to be anything but lies.

Zain laughed and slapped my back. "My friend! What is life without some humor and fun? I'd rather enjoy a harmless lie than live a boring truth. She's probably an ordinary woman who fears showing her face and being dragged into the light. There are many people who don't seek power."

"Many fools, that is," Naomi muttered.

"Few need it, and not everyone can have it, Savaii," Zain declared, his golden eyes fixed on Naomi. Even his Skeleton and Azilian friend were staring at her. "But if you ever want more than this place can offer, let me know. You could be the most beautiful wife in Goldono and the envy of all my colleagues."

Excessive flattery was clearly the quickest way to Naomi's heart. She looked steadily at the Ambassador, then said, "I'm honored, Ambassador, but regretfully I have my eyes on another."

"I understand, Savaii. If circumstances change, please do let me know."

Before Alexander Ryder and his wife joined us in the box, the flames in the lanterns around the theater were lowered, except for a few on the stage, as performers set up chairs and instruments toward the back of the stage. Two men, dressed in all black, took positions at either side of the stage, and after a flurry of preparations everyone else, bar the musicians, left the stage. A hush fell in the auditorium then as a woman in a flowing black dress and small white gloves stepped onto it. There was a ripple of delight and the audience broke into spontaneous applause. Upon her face was a scarlet mask, which flickered and glowed in the lantern light. Her auburn hair was carefully arranged to spill over the left side of her mask. Her shadow seemed to inhabit the stage as if she had been born on it. She held up a hand, and the applause died away.

Who knew walking could excite everyone so much.

"Welcome, distinguished members of Hollow Court and participants of the Endless Waltz," she said, her soft voice carrying clearly throughout the theater. The men on both sides of her were mouthing words to themselves. "Thank you all for attending this performance tonight. Without all of you, this wouldn't be possible. But enough tedious pleasantries: Let's get to the reason you're all here tonight." She exhaled and it sent shivers up my spine. "'The Angels of Naverre.'"

She hit the first note and it was over for me. Mesmerized. She controlled the stage and held her audience absolutely rapt, counterpointing every rise and fall of the melody, sharing the pain that lingered in her voice. It wasn't sweet or soft; rather, her voice was layered with suffering, and instead of shying away from that, she would highlight it and let us hear the roughness in her voice. She wasn't trying to hide the imperfections; her talent lay in letting everyone hear her flaws and embrace them.

Red drew us all into her song of love and hopelessness, her voice the needle that wove emotions into the tapestry of history. The audience was ensnared in her dream as Lyra, the hero of the song, found herself in her own personal nightmare, Red's vibrato underlining her desolation as the city of Naverre crumbled around her. Capturing children who screamed, trying to shake their parents awake, and the innocent hiding underground, waiting for the explosions to end, more frightened of the silence than the noise. She belted out the chorus, oblivious to the pitch of her own voice, focusing solely on Lyra's pain.

As she neared the end of the song, her tone changed, becoming as limitless as the stars in the sky and as deep as darkness could be without moonlight. She sang without restraint, her passion and the roughness of her voice combining perfectly with the lyrics' beauty and the musicians' nimble fingers. Her auburn hair was coming unbound, strands of reddish brown escaping their careful arrangement. As she sang of the angels descending to cast their judgment on Naverre, her tone changed again, Lyra's story began to unravel, and the audience was caught in the full awe and tragedy of the moment and Red's soaring, astonishing finale.

Then it was over. Red stood onstage, out of breath, her hair unbound. At some point in the finale she must have pulled out the clip. I didn't even see it happen, lost within the world her voice created. The audience remained silent for a moment, many of them in tears. Then, as one, they came to life and surged to their feet, cheering and filling the theater with thunderous applause and sharp whistles.

Ambassador Zain was on his feet behind me. "Bravo! Bravo! Encore! Encore!"

Naomi wasn't as impressed, but nonetheless she clapped for her. Slow and steady. "I'm surprised. After all that praise, I found her voice amateurish. The boy with the troupers lute I saw perform last month with my division was much better." To no one's surprise, the Skeleton and Azilian didn't share their opinions, so she turned to me. "What did you think?"

"It was fine."

I'm not sure why I chose to lie. Maybe my pride prevented me from admitting I'd been both transfixed and moved by her song. Maybe it was a desire to conform. Or maybe it was because the only person in the box who seemed to enjoy it as much as I did was the guy who cut out his servant's tongue. It wasn't the best company to have.

"Thank you. You're all so generous," Red declared, a bouquet of Moon's Tears in her hands. "I will return, but for now please enjoy the other performers from the college. They're all remarkable individuals that I'm lucky to share a stage with."

As she took a final bow, the crowd overwhelmed her with one more wave of applause. Only when she was out of sight did Zain return to his seat. My skin felt hot and flushed and I tugged at the collar of my shirt. There seemed to be a haze of heat lingering over the audience.

"I hope I enjoy the next performance more," Naomi said.

I had to get some air; the box was suffocating me. Or maybe it was the people in it. "I'll be back in a few minutes," I said, leaning toward Naomi. "I'm just going to get some fresh air."

After a pause, she said, "Enjoy."

I scooched past Naomi and out of the box, heading for an exit. The moment I stepped through the curtained doorway, I exhaled in relief. It was considerably more pleasant outside. Leaning against the stair railing, I stared up at the stars and seven major pieces of the shattered moon in the sky.

I couldn't help but think of my father . . . and of the days when he had been my hero.

"Michael? Is that you?"

I turned around and dread overcame me.

Jean Lorenzo, Sirash's dark-haired girlfriend, stood in front of me.

THOSE WHO REMAIN

There are these fleeting moments. Where even though I was eighteen years old, my mind regressed to that of a child, right before I was scolded by my mother. It was almost magical how certain people could do that to others. Lyon used to be a master of it, too.

Jean Lorenzo was dressed simply, in a loose white dress that fell past her knees and simple copper studs in her ears, carrying a piccolo. "Michael? What're you doing—"

"It's not what it looks like," I stammered out.

"What do you think it looks like?" she questioned. "Because I didn't accuse you of anything. Where's Sirash?"

I felt cold. "You don't know where he is?"

"No," she said. "I saw him after the Militia attack. Came to me saying he had to get him and Arjay out of there that night. Said he had a job that could get him the money he needed, but he'd need your help to do it. So, what happened, Michael? Where is he?"

Dead. Alive. Missing. In prison. In hiding. I didn't know which.

All I knew was what a failure I was. I couldn't protect anyone.

"I have no idea," I eventually told her when the silence became unbearable.

"Were you not with him that night?" she asked, voice wavering.

"I was. But Advocators found us, and I ran."

"You left him? What happened to the family looks after family nonsense you've been spouting ever since I met you?"

"I didn't have any other choice," I muttered. I could feel the gaze of hundreds of eyes on me, as if my ancestors were all wondering how a child like me could ever take their place.

Would I ever be anything but an impostor?

Jean narrowed her eyes with one hand around her flute and another brushing against her side, ready to move if needed. "Why are you here, Michael? You came out of the Ryder family box, and the way you're dressed . . ."

"I'm a participant in the Endless Waltz."

"How'd that happen?"

"It's a really long story."

"I've got time. I'm the last performer before Red sings again."

But I didn't. Last thing I needed was someone in that box to come out and overhear anything. If the wrong—or right—thing was overheard, it could expose what I was doing with Domet. Or, worse, give Scales a reason to try me for collaborating with the rebels.

"What if we meet up after this? I'll tell you everything from the beginning. And we can come up with a plan to save—"

"I get it," Jean said with an exaggerated smile. "You only want to hang out with me when it's convenient for you. I thought we were better friends than that."

I glanced at the curtain that led to the box and then took a step closer to her. "That's not what I meant. This is just a very sensitive situation and—"

Her voice got louder. "Really? And Sirash going missing isn't?"

"Of course it is! Sirash is family, and fam—"

That's when she moved, hiked up her dress, and pulled out a knife hidden along her thigh. She pushed it against my neck and I could feel the steel tickle against my throat. "Tell me where he is, Michael, or I'll cut your throat and watch the blood spill out."

I gritted my teeth. I knew she'd never liked me. "I don't know. I didn't even know he was missing. We agreed not to meet for a few days if we got separated."

"I doubt that," she declared. "You stabbed Sirash in the back for a place in the Endless Waltz. Did you tell them he was a runaway Skeleton or lie that he was a rebel? I never trusted you, Michael. Once a noble, always a noble. But what did you get for turning over Arjay? A big feather bed? A gold ring? I hope it was worth your life."

"What're you talking about? What happened to Arjay?"

"He's missing, too," she hissed. "I haven't seen him since that night either. Was he a little bonus for your Scales friends?"

"Jean," I said, "I didn't know he was missing. I didn't even know that Sirash was missing! If I had, I would have been at your side, helping you look for him."

"Why weren't you checking up on him, Michael? Sirash would have if you were the one missing. Sirash disappearing shouldn't have stopped you from being a friend to me or his brother."

"Jean, it's what we agreed. I'm on probation," I pleaded. "We agreed to wait before contacting each other if something went wrong. Six days. I had no idea what happened to him. I kept checking bakeries he worked at, hoping he'd left me a message. You have to believe me."

Jean shook her head, pulled the blade away from my neck, and wiped her eyes with the back of her hand. She wouldn't meet my gaze. "At this point I'm just waiting for his body to appear so I can have a funeral. If I'm lucky, they died together. Neither of them had anyone else."

The heartbeat in my throat returned, but it was my turn to avoid her eyes. My one night of cowardice and selfishness had messed up three people's lives. I had to make it right before anyone else died. Jamal's death was enough guilt for a lifetime.

"I'll find him," I said. "I'll find him and Arjay and bring them back. I promise."

She looked over her shoulder at me, her face sour. "Don't make promises you can't keep, Michael."

"Michael?" Naomi said, pulling back the curtain. "Is everything alright?"

Jean glanced at Naomi and then at me. "I should be going. Knives to sharpen and instruments to tune. Good to see you again, Michael."

I watched her go in silence, vowing to make it right by both of them. Wherever Arjay was, I would find him and keep my promise. Once Jean was gone, Naomi came over to me and ran a finger over the thin red line on my neck left by the knife. It didn't hurt as much anymore. In a whisper she asked, "What happened?"

Knowing her sympathy was just another way to manipulate me, I moved her hand away. "I have to go."

"What? Why?"

"Family issues."

"Michael," she said, "you can't walk out of—"

"Let me know how the rest of the performances go."

I bounded down the stairs taking two at a time and hit the ground at a run. I wouldn't fail Jean, Sirash, or Arjay again.

While Jean lived at the College of Music, Sirash and Arjay lived on the east side of Hollow in the Rainbow District, famously known for its high density of tweekers and Blackberries, close proximity to the dye pits, and bright patchwork coloring on all the buildings. It was the poorest area of the city, most of the inhabitants struggling to get enough to eat each day. Every other building in the district was abandoned and boarded up . . . though people still lived in them, they just did so quietly. Desperately. Sirash and his brother among them.

The abandoned house Sirash lived in was on the outskirts of the district and bright pink in color, a rarity even in the Rainbow District. As I approached the house, I ignored the boarded-up front door and headed for the window they used instead. I found it easily, completely covered in dust, except around the edges where hands had forced it up and squeezed through.

It had been ransacked.

ROCK

Tables had been broken in half, moldy bread covered the counters, the fireplace had collapsed in on itself, and dried blood was splattered across the walls and floors. Something terrible had happened here, and I had no idea what.

I began to search the house. Sirash always left Arjay an emergency plan, in case something ever went wrong, but no matter where I looked, I couldn't find any sign of it. Though I did discover a sharp piece of flint, a rusty dagger, a flintlock pistol with a single iron ball, and all the fixings to make it fire. I took it all with me. I didn't know what I was going to run into while trying to find Arjay, and everything helped.

I left the house through the same window, flintlock pistol hidden in my waistband, with no real idea how to find Arjay. But I had to keep my promise to Jean, so I would find him. Somehow.

"Not much to steal when you break into an abandoned house," a boy said, leaning against the house next door. He was about ten, dangerously thin, with dark skin and finely braided hair. The boy was surrounded by piles of rocks. "Especially that one. It's been really abandoned recently."

I thumbed toward Sirash's house. "Do you know what happened to the people that lived there?"

The boy picked up a few rocks and skipped them across the street. "One disappeared, other got taken. Why do you care?"

"Because I do. Where was the other taken?"

The boy looked me up and down. "Why should I tell you? You're not from here. Too clean to be."

I had no reason to trust anything the boy said, especially since he was alone at night in the most dangerous district in the city. Either he was overconfident or stupid. And what was with the rocks? They were piled up around him with care, too precise to be random.

"How do I even know your information is reliable?"

The boy extended his hands, showing off all his piles of rocks. "What would I get from lying to you? You're not a tweeker or dimmer, and you're probably not stupid enough to buy my miracle cure-your-addiction rocks. I gain nothing."

I saw his logic, but it still didn't mean he'd tell me the truth. "Name your price."

There was a pause as the boy calculated in his head. "Your gloves look warm."

"Done." The black leather gloves Domet had given me were off my hands before the boy knew it. He put them on, slowly, and then rubbed his face against the leather, showing me his crooked smile. "What happened to the other? Where did he go and who took him?"

The thin boy left his rock piles. "We walk. Talk on the way. No point in waiting."

So we did. The boy whose name I didn't know walked with me through the Rainbow District down the alleyways and through derelict buildings left open, questioning what I knew about snake oil. We tracked mud and watered-down shit everywhere we went, the gutter overflowing from a recent rain shower. Only the roads were stone here—everything else fields of dandelions, but even they were rife with bumps and cracks.

We stayed off the streets to make sure we didn't run into tweekers, since they lingered on the main roads late at night. Usually they were passed out, enjoying their high, but not always, and that was when they were the most dangerous, between highs. Unless necessary, the boy never talked or asked my name, and in return I never asked his. I simply addressed him as Rock, and he called me Blunder, and we let this anonymity between us remain. After a long walk, we reached a long, flat stone building painted red and grey, with tattered flags flying on the roof. All the windows had been boarded up with grey-painted wood, and a black crown had been painted on the front door. Something about the place made me feel more nervous than any High Noble keep ever could.

"What is this place?" I asked, watching from a distance. There didn't seem to be any movement or life in the building. It was late, but too early for most to retire for the night.

"Tweeker Keep," Rock stated. "Stranger than the other tweeker dens, run by a metal man who demands to be called Sir. The Sir takes boys sometimes. Only boys around ten, though. Once they enter, they're gone for good."

"Sir?" I spat. "Who does he think he is?"

"A knight," he said. "The Last Knight, or the last one with honor."

I bit down on my tongue. There weren't any knights left in Hollow. The Gunpowder War had killed most of them, and those that survived either joined Scales, retired, or took their ill-gotten money and lived out their lives in luxury in lavender fields. Few, if any, continued to serve after the war, only because they had no other option.

Now, thirty years later, I imagined that they were all gone. If there was one thing guns had done, it was make knights who wore plate mail and rode horses into battle utterly obsolete. If this man who claimed to be the Last Knight truly was one and he had hurt Arjay . . . well, then the Age of Chivalry would end with him.

"If this asshole is taking boys, and multiple ones at that, why haven't I heard of him before?"

Rock looked at me, emotionless. "Where d'you live?"

"The Narrows."

"That's why. He don't steal boys from the West Side, so why would the people care? It's not like we care about the Rebel Emperor. Our place doesn't depend on which sir or ma'am sits on the throne."

Rock was right. To the people on the East Side, those who lived on the West must've looked like nobility; our homes weren't rundown or forsaken, our grain wasn't mixed with maggots for protein, and we lacked their noticeable tweeker population. I could only imagine how the High Nobles and Royals looked from this side of the river.

Before the awkward silence could take over, I asked a different question: "What did you mean? That the tweekers were organized?"

"The tweekers follow the Last Knight. They patrol the house, defend it, and steal boys for him. He rewards them with Blackberries. And any tweeker that doesn't follow his orders are thrown out or killed."

"Killing tweekers is hard," I muttered, still crouching behind a stone wall.

"Telling them what to do is harder," Rock replied.

I nodded and examined the house again. I couldn't see any other way in but the front door. Unlike every other building we'd passed, the woodwork here was new and strong and would create a lot of noise if we tried to rip it off. The stone walls weren't any weaker. But the flags flying from the top of the house reminded me of something. They were unique—almost forgotten fragments, just beyond my recall. And then I did, and understood what I had to do.

I took out the flintlock pistol and the ingredients to load it properly. Rock didn't say anything, silently watching. Once the gun was ready, I slid it into my waistband. There was a bulge, but unless someone was looking, no one would notice it in the dark.

"What you doing?" the boy asked.

I hopped over the stone wall we were hiding behind. "I'm going to lie. C'mon."

"Not a chance. I did what you paid me for. There's no—"

I pulled a sun from my pocket. "Act as my support, and it's yours."

Rock held out his hand.

"After."

"If you die?"

"Then loot my body for all it's worth."

I'd been in his position. I knew he wasn't going to turn me down. A gold sun could change his life, and as a smart child he could do a lot with it.

Rock stalled in place before joining my side, frantically.

I rapped my knuckles against the door to Tweeker Keep and waited. My answer came quicker than an intake of breath. The door swung open and, in the frame, stood a tweeker, sickly pale, with red eyes, every tooth showing and as sharp as canines. He wore red-and-grey rags, confirming the suspicion that I had outside: that whoever this knight was, he thought he was my family's servant. Red and grey were my family's colors.

If they were stupid enough to display those colors, they must've been stuck in the past.

"Take me to my knight," I demanded. "His lord, David Kingman, wishes to see him."

The tweeker looked me in the eyes and then fell to one knee. Of all my siblings, I looked the most like my father and like a Kingman in general. My plan relied on the hope that this tweeker had been too obsessed with drugs to know my father had been executed ten years ago. And from this reaction, my hope was a reality. "M'lord. It's an honor. Follow me."

The tweeker shambled into the house, and Rock and I followed into the darkness. Bar the occasional candle, surrounded by three or more bodies, there was no light. Beds of blankets were spread out across the floors, wet scraps of cloth hung from the ceiling, and a sickly-sweet smell permeated the den. And it was cold, dreadfully cold—the kind that lingered on the skin and in the throat like needle pinpricks. This place was chaotic but controlled in a way that made sense. To an addict, at least.

"Lord? I didn't sign up to work with any lord," Rock said as his eyes darted toward every creak and crack we heard. "What did I get myself into?"

"Take a deep breath."

"If we die, I'ma curse you, Blunder."

"We'll be fine. Calm down," I said quietly.

"Calm down, he says. Face your death with pride, he says. Don't worry, death is only forever, he says."

"Are you done? Or are you trying to get more money out of me?"

"Money won't help me if I'm dead."

I didn't respond to Rock after that. I needed him calm and silent, which was becoming less and less likely the more time passed, and talking to him only achieved the opposite.

The tweeker led us into a wide-open room filled with candles and with a skylight that let the moonlight in. With every step there were multiple crunches from wax breaking beneath our feet, and at the far end of the room a man in metal knelt in prayer before a makeshift altar. There was a small body hidden in the shadowy corner of the room. It wriggled, and muffled sounds could be heard when we got closer to it.

"Sir," the tweeker squeaked. "Our lord is here to see you."

The man in front of the altar didn't move. "Our lord?" He rose after that. "Our lord? Who dares insult the memory of our late lord?

Our lord gave his life to save this city and—" He turned, seeing me for the first time. He dropped to one knee, the anger disappearing.

"My lord! You have returned! I knew our enemies spread lies about you, but I never imagined they spread lies about your death, too. I thought . . . I thought I saw you die on the steps. How did you survive, my lord? Was it the Ryders? The Solarins or the Dawnstars? Did they remember the Old Words? Oh, my lord, I'm so happy you have returned once more."

The knight was groveling in front of me, holding back his tears and on to my leg at the same time. He had been plagued by war and age, leaving their mark in wrinkles on his face and the grey in his beard and hair. He was missing the lower half of his red plate mail armor, wearing a pair of leather trousers instead. What armor he wore was polished so it shone, even in the dim light. The knight kept sobbing at my feet, repeating nonsense to himself over and over.

I had no recollection of the man at all.

Before my father died, the last knight we had was D'Arcy Wolf-hard, a fat, jolly man who lived in Kingman Keep with his young son and daughter. But he had died protecting me and my siblings from rioters. His children were probably long gone from Hollow, escaping someplace where the name Kingman meant nothing. Whoever this knight was, he hadn't been one of my father's. He was an impostor, just like me.

"Rise, my knight," I commanded. He did as he was told, standing straighter than I'd have believed he could. The palm of his hand was on the pommel of his sword, more out of habit than a show of strength. "One of my allies swapped with me at the last moment. He took the ax instead. Tell me, what you have been doing since we last spoke?"

"My lord," he began, "I've been continuing the work you gave me before your death. I have brought your youngest son here, where he's safe from our enemies. We have been waiting for an opportunity to move him out of Hollow. I was considering the Warring States, but I will do as you command. I confess, my lord . . . the crown persecuted us at every turn and it's forced me to employ," and he lowered his voice, "not quite honorable men. Tweekers, they are called. Loyal to little except their high. But so long as I keep them supplied, they will follow us to the end of the world."

I glanced at the boy in the corner again. It must've been Arjay. He was tiny, and few other boys were close to him in size.

Rock was at my side the entire time, eyes always glancing at the tweekers behind us, only their red eyes visible.

"I will never be able to thank you for the loyalty you have shown my family," I said as I clapped my hand on the knight's shoulder. "But I'll be taking my son home. I have a place for him until it's safe to be in the public again. The king will not get his revenge by killing my children."

The knight showed me his yellow smile. "Of course, my lord. I understand completely. It has been my honor to watch over him for you."

I motioned for Rock to free Arjay from his bonds. He did so silently, and as he did, the knight stood nearby, proud of himself. "I have waited for the day when you or one of your blood would return and we could reclaim what was lost when Davey Hollow was murdered by our enemies, my lord. The Kingman family will rise again. I am certain of it."

I nodded. "It will, my knight. The Kingman family will not be forgotten. I'll make sure my ancestors acknowledge me."

Arjay was almost completely unbound, only the rope around his feet remaining.

"My lord," the knight said softly, his hand tightening around the pommel. "What is my name?"

I paused. "What's wrong, my knight?"

He unsheathed his sword slightly. "What is my name?"

"Take a deep breath, my knight. There's no need to unsheathe your sword. Let us—"

His brown—almost black—eyes narrowed. "What is my name . . . my lord?"

I pulled out the gun from my waistband, but I was too slow, and he knocked it away with his sword. The gun skittered across the ground toward the boys, and with no other weapon I went low and tackled the knight to the ground. Much like the gun, his sword skittered across the floor to the other side of the room. I punched him twice in the face before his metal gauntlet found my jaw and sent me spinning off him, the edge of my vision blurry. He kicked me in the chest, sharp pain overwhelming me as I tried to take a breath, and then rolled me onto my back and began to choke me. One of my hands scrabbled at his while the other tried to claw at his face, just slightly out of reach.

"I knew you were a pretender!" he screamed, face red. "How dare you impersonate my lord? How dare you mock me, Sir Tristin Harbour, his Last Knight? Do you know my name now, pretender?" His grip around my neck tightened, my breath shorter and shallower than before. I couldn't even gasp. "Die in the name of the Kingman family! Die for my lord and his children! Die! Die! Die!"

I didn't want to die like this, choked out on the floor by a madman who thought he worked for my father. I kept reaching for some skin to grab onto to get him to stop, but . . . nothing I could reach . . . I had to do some—

And that was when the gun went off.

Blood splattered across my face.

The knight's eyes went wide and he released my neck, grabbing his own instead. Blood was seeping through his fingers, drops landing on my face. I gasped for air, half wheeze and half shriek. With one hand around my own throbbing neck, I pushed the knight off me and he complied easily, falling onto his back. Blood was beginning to pool in, on, and around his armor, the puddle around him growing wider and wider with each second. One hand to his neck, the knight reached up toward the shattered moon with the other, as if trying to seize something that wasn't there. He was wheezing, trying to get the words out.

"My . . . lord . . . I'm sorry . . . I have . . . I have failed you and your children. I couldn't . . . I couldn't protect them. Forgive . . . forgive . . . "

His hand fell less dramatically than it should have, almost silently to the floor. I expected more noise when it hit the ground, a grand declaration of his death. But it didn't change anything. The Last Knight was dead from a gunshot wound to the neck.

As I started to get my breath back, I realized we were in a house full of tweekers and that one of us had just killed their leader. I looked toward the shooter and saw Arjay on the ground, the pistol still pointed at where the Last Knight had been.

His small hand wouldn't stop shaking. He was barely a decade old and now a murderer—for me. Had I saved him at all? How could I possibly tell Sirash?

"I . . . ," he started. "I . . . I was aiming for his knee. I thought . . . I thought . . ."

I didn't let him finish, moving toward where he was and taking the gun from him. Once it was back in my hand, I wrapped my arm around Arjay. "Rock, we need to get out of here."

We traveled out of the keep silently and quickly. Red eyes stared at us from all angles and corners in the darkness. I waited for them to strike, but they never did. Perhaps they didn't realize what had happened yet—or maybe those who had were already searching the Tweeker Keep for the supply of Blackberries. Or maybe they were making sure the Last Knight didn't go to waste. From what I had heard, they weren't picky about their food. I would've felt worse if I had known the man, but I didn't. We were both con artists, and those in our profession rarely got happy endings. Tragedies were the standard.

When we finally got out of the house, the door to the keep shut behind us instantly, making sure we knew we were no longer welcome. It was well into the night when we exited, the stars bright against the black curtain. The wind blew through the streets and against my skin, prickling it. Arjay didn't stop shaking as I held him, and I knew it wasn't because of the cold.

After hesitating and gagging, Rock bent and puked against the stone wall we had hidden behind earlier. And this time I couldn't say he was being dramatic. One child had just murdered a man, with the other his accomplice. Then there was me, the fool who had caused both. A villain masquerading as a hero.

After he spat out what remained, Rock gave me a look, different from the one he had earlier. "Well, I've had enough fun for the night. We both got what we wanted, and I think I'll have some fresh customers tomorrow. Please never come see me again, unless you want some miracle-cure rocks. You make a dimmer look sane."

I gave him his sun, and Rock left us.

It was a long, slow walk in the darkness to Jean's home, and neither of us initiated a conversation. As we crossed one of the bridges, I threw the flintlock pistol into the river on the off chance it could be traced back to Arjay, Sirash, Jean, Rock, or me. And I doubted Arjay would want a souvenir of what he had done. I didn't even know what to say to him . . . thanks didn't seem appropriate anymore, especially not when I could still taste the blood on my lips, long after I had scrubbed it off with my sleeve.

When we finally got there, I gave Arjay a wordless hug, promising nothing this time. He returned the hug and then said, quietly, "Bring Sirash home, Michael. I need him."

He knocked on the door and it opened shortly after, a blinding light coming from the house. Jean ushered him in, seizing him with a tight hug as she glared at me, noticing the blood that covered us both. I gave her a nod and then walked away. My promise to her was fulfilled, even if the friendship was likely over.

I'd save Sirash, too . . . somehow . . .

TINDER

I washed the Last Knight's blood off with river water before I went to Domet's. My body was cold and wet, and my mind was dull and hazy, but I knew I had to meet with him tonight or risk letting his anger grow. He must've known I'd left the theater by now, and no doubt there would be repercussions. I could have jeopardized everything we had been working toward.

Upon entering, I knew something was incredibly wrong. It was hot inside: a blistering sweltering heat that reminded me of a blacksmith. Paintings were crooked, broken pottery strewn across the floor, and there was a steady *thump-thump-thump* that echoed throughout the house. When I reached the main room, I saw Domet sprawled out facedown on the floor, empty bottles around him.

"Domet," I said.

No response.

"Domet?" I said more cautiously.

No response.

I reached down and shook him. When he didn't move, I flipped him over and checked his pulse. There was something there, but it was faint. He probably had alcohol poisoning. I had seen it in others, but some naïve part of me had assumed alcoholics couldn't get it. Clearly, I was wrong. I'd have to wake him up and make sure he didn't die in his sleep.

I began to search his house for anything with a strong odor I could use as smelling salts. There was little in his kitchen cabinets besides bottles of alcohol, a few fruits and vegetables, and slabs of meat from a butcher—until I opened a cupboard to find more spices than I had ever seen before. They'd have to do. I grabbed a few hot peppers and peppercorns, then ground them all together in a mortar. It produced an eye-watering smell that I doubted any living human being would be able to ignore.

But he was already waiting for me in his chair when I returned, another bottle of vodka in his hand. How had he recovered so quickly? It wasn't natural. He shouldn't have been able to stand, let alone be coherent. "Michael."

I put the mortar with my concoction down. "Domet, you're awake . . . You should go to—"

"Do you realize what you've done?" he growled. "Do you realize what you've endangered? You snubbed High Noble Alexander Ryder tonight. You've alienated someone who was on our side. Without his support, your invitation to the king's birthday party is no longer guaranteed."

"I'll fix it. I had something more important to deal with that forced me to leave."

"More important? What was more important than our deal?"

"My friend's brother went missing. I had to save him, and now I know my friend is missing, too. They're family."

"Family?" Domet mocked. "Is there another Kingman I didn't know of? Your friend Sirash is not a Kingman. His life is not important in the grand scheme of things. I knew you would get distracted if you knew he was in trouble."

"You knew he was in trouble?"

"Of course I knew," Domet said. "You mentioned him the night we met, so I made sure I knew who he was. I received word from my contacts that he'd been arrested the next day, but he wasn't important, so I never mentioned the predicament he was in. You'd be distracted trying to save him and ignore the Endless Waltz."

"The entire time . . . you knew?"

"Did I stutter, Michael? His life was expendable, and your participation in the Endless Waltz was more important."

I wished I hadn't thrown the flintlock pistol into the river. "Where is he?"

"Why would I tell you? You betrayed me, Michael."

"I betrayed you? You betrayed me," I said through gritted teeth. "You swore that you would take care of my friends if something happened to me."

"And did something happen to you, Michael? Can you not

breathe? Can you not walk? Are you in danger? Explain to me what happened that compels me to care for your friends."

My face felt hot and everything seemed hazy. This was the world I had returned to by choice. This corrupt world where the nobility only looked out for themselves and let those they deemed unimportant die in the streets like rats. I hated them. I hated all of them. Maybe the rebels were right. Maybe it was time for others to rule in their place.

"Our deal is over, Domet."

Domet threw back his head and laughed dramatically as he rose from his seat. "No it's not. You will do as I say, Michael. You will steal the king's memories and let me have my redemption or—"

"Threaten my family, and you won't survive the night."

Domet continued to laugh as he moved toward the hearth and picked up the poker. "I don't think you quite understand who I am, Michael. I didn't lie to you. I need redemption. I have to know what truly happened to your father. If I don't get the redemption I seek, then I can't die. Literally."

That was when he took the poker and stabbed himself in the stomach. Maintaining eye contact with me the entire time, he dragged the poker up and to the right across his body, tearing flesh and organs and letting blood spill over the floor. To emphasize his point, he removed the poker and then stabbed himself in the chest, this time tearing all the flesh on the left side of his body. Through the hole I could see the wall behind him.

Dragging it back out again, he ripped his shirt off and made me watch as his body repaired itself. Skin and flesh stitched seamlessly back together. I felt sick as I watched it happen. It defied every rule of nature and made me realize how ignorant I was about the world that someone like him could exist without me being aware . . . without everyone being aware.

Blood trickled from his mouth as he said, "I can't die, Michael. I'm immortal, bound to live until I correct all the mistakes I've made in life. You will not take away my chance at death. Do you understand me?"

"How?"

"How am I immortal? You don't need to know, since it doesn't concern you."

"No, how have you been able to hide your immortality for so long without someone noticing?"

"Michael, should I give you a list of those I bribed and those that had accidents? Should I tell you about the kings, queens, and Kingman that helped me remain hidden and those that saw me as a threat? No, I will not. All that concerns you is what you're going to do for me."

"If I refuse?"

"Being the enemy of a Mercenary or king is one thing . . . but do you really want to be the enemy of a rich, bored immortal man with an endless amount of time to plan his revenge? I was there when the First Kingman emerged hundreds of years ago, and unless you aid me, I will be alive when your children and their descendants take your place. Think about this carefully, Michael."

I didn't respond, unable to find the words to confirm or reject what Domet had said. What had I become involved in? Who had I been working with this entire time?

Silently, Domet cleaned the poker with his shirt before returning it to its proper place. "I'll fix your horrendous miscalculation tonight and make sure you get an invitation to the king's party. But after this I hope you understand how serious I am about getting what I want. Be grateful that I'll keep up my end of our original deal."

"What about Sirash?"

A shrug. "Don't annoy me further and maybe I'll help him out. You can leave. Take what money I owe you from my purse on the table."

I did as I was told.

Domet returned to his seat in front of the empty hearth to drink. The conversation was over, and so was our business relationship.

I had always thought it was Lyon, but in the end I was the real dog of the nobility.

I left his house and stood in the cold, thoughtless. I pulled my jacket tight around me. It wouldn't be much longer before it started snowing. Maybe a week or two if we were all lucky. I exhaled and saw my breath, clear as anything, and wondered where Sirash was. If he was alone and scared, too. I felt so guilty and had no idea how to help without incurring the wrath of Charles Domet for focusing on anything other than the Endless Waltz.

Domet was wealthy beyond compare and . . . and immortal. I couldn't hurt him. Not in the traditional sense. But maybe I could distract him by taking something away from him. Something he cared about as much as I did Sirash. Get his focus off me and the Endless Waltz so I had an opportunity to help my friend.

I stared around, senseless, at the recently extinguished lantern streetlights, and the flickering wick barely holding on in one gave me an idea. I'd show Domet he had tried to manipulate the wrong person.

SPARK

Striding into the Shrine of Patron Victoria in the Upper Quarter, two bottles of grain alcohol in my hands, I paused before crossing the shrine threshold, but nothing struck me as I entered with my boots still on—not that I had thought something or someone would. I uncorked the first bottle, holding it between my teeth as I choked out the liquid, pouring it over the stones until it flooded the cracks. The wood was soaked until the top was wet and black. I drew a wet circle around the shrine and then splattered the walls. It sounded as if someone was drowning, gurgling and sputtering water from cold lips.

Once the exterior reeked of alcohol, I went to the inner shrine. It was plain and simple. Patron Victoria stood in the center, a chiseled memory in marble. She was carefully posed, arms extended as if singing for a long-lost love. Her windswept hair framed her face, a portrait of beauty.

I placed the bouquets of morning glories and Moon's Tears that decorated the shrine against the statue and soaked it all in alcohol until droplets streamed down her face. I had my pyre. I used the rest of the bottle to draw a steady line from the base to the perimeter. Then there was only one thing left to do.

I took out Sirash's piece of flint and a knife and stood over the trail of alcohol. Was I going to do this?

Yeah.

Yeah, I was.

I struck the flint against the knife until the alcohol ignited. The flames spread and swirled down the path until the shrine was engulfed and the smaller timbers cracked and fell. Heat lashed across my face and stung, until it was all ashes and embers.

EMBERS

The devout were out in full force this morning. Scorchers and Eternal Sisters wandered toward the Church of the Eternal Flame, performing tricks for the children and asking for donations from their parents along the way. An average day with a typical service. My neck and back cracked, stiff from a night sleeping against a stone barrier in the cold on a rooftop overlooking the remains of the shrine.

It was amazing, really.

Not a single person stopped to take note of the shrine of ash down the alleyway. The Advocators were too busy watching the crowds with their controlled eyes as the Scorchers guided the devout to church. All those who weren't going walked with their heads down to avoid the guilt. It was easy to see from high above the streets. Only

Charles Domet was different—carrying a bouquet of Moon's Tears and morning glories, actively meeting the Scorchers' gazes, guilt-free. His clothes were formal and pristine as always, unblemished despite his state last night. It was probably one of the benefits of being immortal.

It was only after he reached the alleyway that anything changed.

Domet screamed, falling to his knees, cane bouncing to the ground at his side, and bouquet landing in the gutter. Petals scattered, painting the grey concrete in purple and white splotches. The devout watched as Advocators rushed to his side.

I hoped this hurt enough that Domet drank himself to sleep for the rest of his endless life.

No one used my family against me to accomplish their own goals.

Not even God or an Immortal.

ASHES

Since I was already awake, I decided to fulfill my promise to Angelo and make breakfast for my family that morning.

Gwen was the first to find me in front of the stove after coming home from her night shift at the asylum. She was barely awake, mumbling and yawning at me instead of speaking in complete sentences. She gave me a hug, then took a piece of toast with raspberry jam on it back to her room. I could hear her snoring moments later.

Angelo was next, stumbling into the house in his full Scales uniform. He took a seat at the kitchen table, rubbing his eyes. "Breakfast?" he questioned.

"Breakfast," I answered as I put a plate of eggs, toast, and mushrooms in front of him and poured myself a cup of tea. I would have offered Angelo one, but he hated tea, and sometimes, if the smell was strong enough, it would make him gag. Thankfully, this blend didn't cause that reaction.

"I appreciate this, Michael. It's been a terrible morning and I doubt the day will be much better."

"Why? What happened?"

"The rebels infiltrated the city and attacked last night. No one noticed it until this morning. Half the nobility is enraged with King Isaac and the other half with Scales for not stopping it. Or even realizing it happened."

"What did they attack?" I asked. I could smell the sulfur from the Militia Quarter again.

"The Shrine of Patron Victoria in the Upper Quarter. They burned it to the ground."

No matter how good a liar I was, nothing could have hidden the shock from my face. The rebels were being blamed for something I had done. Something I had done to spite Charles Domet. It wasn't supposed to affect anyone except him.

"W-What? Why?" I stammered.

With a mouthful of mushrooms, he said, "No idea. It doesn't match their previous attacks, but the nobility is convinced of it. They've been looking for the final nail in the Emperor's coffin, and this, combined with the attack on the colosseum, will force a quick trial and execution. Although, for all we know, it could have been a power play from one of the nobles. I have to change and then head straight back to headquarters to find out what really happened."

"Were there witnesses?"

"Yeah, and a suspect. Advocators are bringing in the man who found it burned down, while others are hunting for someone seen in the area last night. There's an entire division of Advocators searching. Even the Whisperer for the Church of the Eternal Flame is lending his Church's followers to help, despite the fact they're only supposed to aid in government trials. It all leaves a bitter taste in my mouth."

"Who found it burned down?" I asked, hands on the back of a chair.

Angelo's plate was empty but for a slice of toast. "High Noble Charles Domet. Can't say I'm very excited to interact with him. He's an irrational, pretentious, elitist asshole who'll want blood spilled—and I'll have to supply it, one way or another, if I value my position in Scales."

"Good luck," I said in little more than a whimper.

Angelo rose and wiped his mouth with the back of his hand. "Don't worry, Michael. I've survived worse. High Noble Charles Domet will not be the end of me." He paused and glanced down at the Archmage's journals that I had stolen from the library, with Dark's envelope still tucked into it. Cautiously, he picked it up and twirled it in his hand. "Since when have you had access to the Hollow Library?"

"Recently. Traded an Archivist some information for access," I said. "How do you know about them?"

His finger ran over the edges of the journal as if ready to flip it open to read. "I read a lot of these journals after my wife was murdered. Before I took all of you in. They comforted me. Gave me something to focus on and progress through as I grieved, even if most of them are just the ramblings of a Forgotten."

I didn't know how to respond. Angelo never talked about his late wife much. All I knew was that he'd loved her immensely and that she had been taken from him too soon. I didn't even know her name. "How many did you read?"

"Enough to last a lifetime," Angelo said with a laugh. He put the journal back on the table, ignoring the envelope I'd failed to return last night. I knew I'd have to do something about that soon. But what that was, I didn't know yet.

"Speaking of lifetimes, have you thought about my offer?"

"Yes. I think I want to do it. I just have to convince Gwen to come with me."

"Let me know when you do. It'll take a few days to set up, but doable whenever you want."

"Thank you, Angelo."

He tapped the side of the doorframe and said, "Don't. I am nothing without my family."

Angelo went to his room after that and left me alone in the kitchen with more food than I could finish on my own. I took a seat at the table, tea in hand, and drank it slowly, trying to piece together the repercussions of my actions.

My thoughts were interrupted by someone coming down the stairs. I was poised to tease Gwen about being so hungry, when Lyon entered the kitchen. Wordlessly, he put together a plate and took a seat across the table.

Aside from the sound of him eating and his utensils scraping against the plate, it was silent, neither of us wanting to talk after our last meeting. And despite the fact I had told Gwen I would apologize, I didn't know how to. Finally, when he finished eating, Lyon folded his hands together and said, "I think we should talk."

"If you're going to yell at me, I won't sit here and take it quietly."

"I'm not going to yell at you. Why do you always think I'm going to yell at you?"

"Because you always yell at me and judge whatever decisions I make."

"Only because you make stupid decisions."

"This is what I'm talking about!" I said, voice becoming louder. "Unless you have something new to say, I think—"

"I'm proud of you," he interrupted.

Nothing had ever silenced me so quickly. I cocked my head and looked at him. I had never heard him say the word "proud" before, and especially not directed toward me.

Lyon let out a sigh and leaned back in his seat. "I'm proud of you, Michael. Angelo told me you were participating in the Endless Waltz and I was ready to kill you. Especially after all the hassle you've given me over the years for what I was forced to do by the king. Then he said you almost drowned one night, and . . . I don't know . . . it changed things. All I could think of was how our father never got the chance to teach you how to swim, and how I should've. It made me feel like I failed as your older brother."

I opened my mouth to respond, but Lyon continued: "Let me finish. If I don't do it now, I'll never get the chance." He took a deep breath. "I don't know why you decided to participate in the Endless Waltz or how you were even able to. I don't know why you've lied to me so much over the past few years. But I don't care anymore. I'm your brother. I don't want to constantly be at odds with you. I want to talk to you about your life, about my life . . . Have you realized that I've never told you how I met Kayleigh? You're both such huge parts of my life, and neither of you know each other. I want that to change."

"Lyon, I—"

"I'm almost finished, I promise." Lyon reached into his jacket pocket and slid an envelope across the table to me. He motioned for me to open it. As I tore it open, Lyon began to smile sheepishly. The heavy-paper-stock invitation inside read:

Michael Kingman,
    You are formally invited to King Isaac's fiftieth birthday celebration at Hollow Castle tonight, at three bells before Lights Out.
    Entry into Hollow Castle will require you to present this invitation to the guards at the doors.
    Gifts are at the guest's discretion.
    Welcome back to the Hollow Court, Michael Kingman.

The king's signature was at the bottom of the invitation along with his crest.

I had survived the Endless Waltz.

After all these years, I was going to return to the Hollow Court.

I would be in the presence of the Royals and the Ravens.

And I was going to have to steal from the king.

Fuck.

"I found it on the door this morning when I came back from my patrols," Lyon said. "We haven't been friendly lately, and I know that it's as much my fault as it is yours, but Kayleigh and I are going to attend together, since we're betrothed. I was hesitant because of my last name and the fact that our child will be considered a mistake and a scandal, but I'd have more confidence if you'll be there. I suppose it's time our family began to restore the legacy our father ruined, isn't it?"

I slid the invitation back into the envelope and put it on the table. I didn't know how to handle this side of him. It was easier when he yelled at me . . . and just when I was ready to walk away from the Kingman legacy, he wanted to be a part of it again. What was I supposed to do?

"I was able to convince Kayleigh to get Gwen an invitation as a guest of the Ryder Family, so we could do this as a family . . ." Lyon trailed off. "It took some bartering, and Gwen wants to attend dressed as a man so the Corrupt Prince doesn't recognize her, but she'll be with us, too."

I could only imagine what he had offered to convince Gwen. Her stubbornness put mine to shame, and she had vowed to never enter the castle until our father was proven innocent or the king was dead.

"But we'll be there together," he said. "The three Kingman children."

"We will." I hesitated. "Lyon?"

"Yes, Michael?"

"I'm sorry I'm an asshole sometimes. You're family, and I love you, and I don't want you to forget that."

Before he could reply, I made up an excuse and left him. He didn't stop me; he was relaxed and smiling, content with the progress we had made in improving our relationship. I was glad at the steps we had taken, too, but my own thoughts were focused on everything that could go wrong as I attempted to steal the gun that killed Davey Hollow, and the king's memories of the event, with my nobler-than-thou brother in attendance. My greatest fear was what he would do if my actions put his unborn child in danger. The answer was obvious, but I didn't want to admit it to myself unless I had to.

————————

I started my errands with a visit to Kingman Keep with Dark's envelope, hoping he could forgive me for not meeting him the night before. But there was nothing there but the cold stone and musky smell that had inhabited this place in the ten years since my family abandoned it. There wasn't any trace that the Mercenary had ever been there, not even ash in the hearth. With no further idea what to do or how to find him, I left before the shadows began to dance on the walls again. Hopefully he'd be back there tonight, after the king's party.

With that task a failure, I went to the Upper Quarter in search of Charles Domet to see if he had any idea I'd burned down the shrine, only to get sidetracked by a crier in Refugee Plaza trying to rally the citizens in support of the rebellion. Few stopped to listen before Advocators chased him away. He would've had more luck in the Narrows or the Fisheries. Refugee Plaza wasn't the place to gauge a common citizen's opinion. They avoided it like a plague.

If only he had gone to a bakery instead. With the price of bread and salt rising, he would undoubtedly find a few people willing to risk everything for a chance at a better life.

When I finally reached the Upper Quarter, I found a seat on a fountain near Domet's house and watched large groups of Advocators patrol the area while I waited for him to return from my foster father's questioning, paying attention to my body and what it was trying to tell me about Fabrications while I waited. For some reason, no one questioned me about why I was in the Upper Quarter when I clearly didn't belong. I attributed that luck to my charm. Or the fact they had more important things to worry about.

For a long time there was no sign of Domet, and when the sun began to set, I was forced to return home to prepare for the king's party. If Domet made an appearance tonight, I'd get the information I needed from him then. If he didn't, well, I would steal from the king, in his castle, on my own.

Tonight, I would earn my freedom and escape Hollow with my mother and sister.

NOBILITY

Gwen and I walked toward Hollow Castle among a horde of nobles on a pathway of multicolored leaves, the trees they had fallen from bare. I was dressed as I had been in Ryder Keep, and Gwen had borrowed similar clothes from Lyon, even going as far as to tie her hair in a bun and don a formal hat to complete her masquerade. Even in disguise she still wore our mother's scarf, albeit around her waist as a belt instead of around her neck.

It was cold outside, and snow was very, very close, a few days away at most. I wasn't excited about it, since there was more slush than snow in cities, but it was one of the few things in Hollow that only mildly infuriated me.

I could tell Gwen was nervous. She had barely said more than a few dozen words, too focused on every big man that passed us and grateful when it wasn't the Royal she was bound to. It was like talking to a tweeker, and I gave up when the only responses I got were grunts and nods. I focused on what I would have to do tonight instead.

I barely had any memories of Hollow Castle from my youth, just snippets of experiences. No matter how hard I tried, I could never remember all the details. Climbing a broken tree with the princess, staring at a starry night with Davey, playing hide-and-seek with Lyon and Gwen, and practice fighting with Adreann. But after we showed the guards our invitations and entered the main area, I realized memories couldn't have done it justice anyway.

Blue-and-gold banners hung from the ceiling, the wooden floors were so polished that it was like walking on glass, and small circular tables ran along the sides of the room with nobles crowded around each one. Castle guards were positioned throughout the room, standing as still as statues, while servants in the Royal Family's colors circulated with trays of drinks. And the best part? None of them were Skeletons. In the past, despite slavery being outlawed, there always seemed to be a few present.

Domet's book had included notes about how royal celebrations operated nowadays. This part, if I was correct, was known as the Welcoming.

It was the only point at which bodyguards could be in the same room as the nobles they were protecting, and was naturally used by the nobility to show what they had at their disposal. Some even went so far as to hire Mercenaries as bodyguards. It wasn't common, but it was possible. Usually they used their house guards or a knight, before they had gone extinct.

Looking the part was also essential: cut, color, fabric, all made a difference, and getting it wrong meant instant social ostracism. Wearing solely the Royals' colors would make someone look spineless, while not paying any respect to them led to others questioning their loyalty. If the style was too extravagant it was gaudy, unless it was a High Noble. Showing up in nothing but nightwear would probably get one a standing ovation. And the fabric—it had to be purposeful and beautiful. Wearing silk handspun by blind monks might look incredible, but if it left the wearer cold, they'd be ridiculed.

Luckily for me, I could be soberly dressed: I was just trying not to agitate anyone, and there were only a few people who might try to start something with me tonight.

"We're meeting up with Kai, right?" Gwen asked, inching closer to me.

I glanced around the room. Kai's blond hair caught my eye in the corner of the room, and we wove through the crowd to join him. He was with his younger brother, who was sitting on the table wearing loose-fitting gold-and-black-trimmed clothes.

"Kai, pleasure to see you. And Joey! How are you tonight?" I said as I ruffled his messy blond hair. He gave me a wide smile and looked at me with his bright-blue eyes. "Enjoying the evening?"

Joey nodded.

"Would you happen to know where my brother and your sister are?"

Joey frowned, shook his head, and then tugged at Kai's shirt for help.

"They were talking with my parents and some other High Nobles," he said. "They'll wander over eventually. We'll certainly see

Lyon once we split. And, Michael, my father wants to talk to you about what happened at the theater."

I didn't pursue that subject. If Kai's father was annoyed with me, that was a problem for later. Hopefully he wouldn't be too angry at me for insulting him and his entire family at the theater . . . Well, maybe he wouldn't be as angry as Domet had been, if I was lucky.

Which I rarely was when it mattered.

"Excuse my bluntness, but, Michael, who is with you?"

Before I could lie, my sister said, "I'm Gwen Kingman, High Noble Ryder. I wanted to attend, but I've done so dressed as a man. Perhaps you can understand why I've chosen to be here discreetly?"

I hadn't expected her to tell Kai the truth. Why did she trust him so much? I'd have to ask her when we were alone.

"Gwen," Kai declared. "I'm sure you look wonderful tonight."

Gwen had her hands in her trousers pockets. "I appreciate it, High Noble Ryder."

"You may call me Kai."

A hand ran down my back, a sweet fragrance accompanying it. "Michael," Naomi said. "I wasn't expecting to see you here after you left the theater abruptly. I thought they would have kicked you out of the Endless Waltz."

"My father isn't a cruel man," Kai said. "He wouldn't have done that to Michael. Or the Kingman family. But excuse me, who are you?"

Naomi held out her hand for Kai or Gwen to kiss, her disguise working better than I expected. When neither of them did, she drew it back, hiding her sour expression. "I'm simply Michael's friend, High Noble Ryder. And who might you be?" she asked Gwen. "My apologies for not recognizing you all by sight alone."

"I'm Dolyn Woodsman, a Low Noble under the Ryder family," Gwen said quietly.

"Low Noble Dolyn, excuse my bluntness, but what brings you here? You weren't a participant in the Endless Waltz, and the territory the Woodsman family oversees is quite far away."

Kai interjected for my sister. "Low Noble Dolyn is a childhood friend, here at my request. My father advises me to know those who pledge allegiance to the family, so I try to."

"That's very—"

"Excuse me for interrupting, but you didn't give your own name," a voice from behind said. We all turned toward it and I saw her. The girl in red was not in red but in a full-length gold dress with purple trim and matching lace gloves. Her hair was pinned up in an elaborate spiral with a few strands over her forehead. She looked like a princess, only missing a crown nestled over her brow.

"I'm Naomi Dexter. Pleased to meet you, High Noble Margaux."

The girl in red was a High Noble? How had I not realized that sooner?

And why did that name sound so familiar?

"I am as well," she declared. "I've heard a great deal about you, Sergeant Dexter."

"Oh, you have?" Naomi said, curious. I could see that she was still wearing my father's ring. "All good things, I trust?"

High Noble Margaux gave her a look I could only describe as pity. "Many have noticed how friendly you are with Prince Adreann."

"Becoming friendly with one's peers is, I believe, the purpose of the Endless Waltz."

"It is," she said, stepping closer to me. "But are you sure you want to be friendly with him? I know you're a newcomer to noble society, and I—"

Naomi's nostrils flared, but she took a breath, smiled, and then said, "I'm fully aware of who he is and of his reputation. I'm not daft."

"I didn't think you were. But I wanted to be sure."

"How very kind of you," she said. "Michael, save me a dance."

With that, Naomi left, disappearing into the crowd of nobility. The room was getting busier by the moment. Out of the corner of my eyes, I saw Kai whisper something to my sister that caused her eyes to widen at High Noble Margaux.

"That was uncomfortable," Kai said.

High Noble Margaux folded her arms and looked in the direction where Naomi had gone off in. "I'm concerned about her. She's not the first to attempt to seduce the prince, and I doubt she'll be the last. How well do you know her, Michael?"

"I wouldn't call her a friend," I said. "Accomplice" was the better term for it, but only if being blackmailed counted as a relationship.

"Still, I hope she knows what she's doing."

Before Gwen could introduce herself or I could tease High Noble Margaux about finally learning who she was, a thunderous orchestra marching in armor announced a royal arrival. Everyone turned toward the ornate wooden doors that went to the ceiling. They opened, musicians began to play, and in strode King Isaac and Efyra Mason, his new right-hand woman, with all the Ravens standing behind them.

Everyone bowed or curtsied to him, Gwen and me included, albeit shallowly and reluctantly.

I hadn't seen the king in nearly eight years, but his likeness had been ingrained and perfected in my mind with such clarity that it was almost impossible to comprehend that I was seeing him. No part of me recognized him. He was tall and thin, and the trademark red hair of the Royal Family was dulled to a muted auburn in his age. His skin wasn't perfect compared to other nobles, instead plagued with wispy silver scars. A gold crown with a sapphire the size of an eye was nestled among the tangles of his hair.

Childishly, I couldn't stop thinking of my father and how he had been murdered by the woman at the king's right side, where a member of my family had stood for years. It felt wrong to have someone else there, and I wondered if Lyon and Gwen found it as uncomfortable as I did.

"Welcome, distinguished members of Hollow Court and participants of the Endless Waltz. I would like to welcome all of you to my home and thank you all for gracing me with your presence tonight to help me celebrate my fiftieth birthday," King Isaac declared, his voice a booming baritone. "While I am greatly saddened my daughter and wife could not be here tonight, I am honored to have my youngest son and so many friends in attendance. Your endless support makes being King of Hollow easier. Ladies, canapés await you in the Grand Ballroom; gentlemen, you will be served in the Entrance Hall. All the bodyguards are welcome to enjoy the balcony over the Grand Ballroom. Please enjoy the night. Eat to your hearts' content, drink so much your bellies burst, and be daring . . . like it is the last night of your lives."

The Entrance Hall applauded as the raven-haired woman at his side whispered to him and the king nodded. The ladies began making their way out of the hall. Most, if not all, curtsied to their king before leaving. High Noble Margaux left after a quick goodbye to us all, smiling to herself as she did. Soon after, Joey tugged at Kai's jacket and then tapped him on the shoulder. Kai carried him off in search of a bathroom and left me with my sister.

"It feels bizarre to be here without our father," I said.

Gwen was leaning on the table, frowning. I knew her eyes were on the king as he left the Entrance Hall. "Efyra Mason looks too comfortable beside the king," she said.

"I don't enjoy it any more than you do. But she's been there for a decade—it's not surprising she acts like she belongs there."

Gwen smoothed her hands over the table. "I've always thought it was her. That she was the one who framed our father. That she was a little too infatuated with the king. I remember a particular look that she—"

"Michael Kingman, I wasn't expecting to see you here. What a pleasant surprise!"

Charles Domet put his hand on my shoulder and winked at Gwen.

Knowing he was immortal only made it creepier.

GOODHEARTED

My skin crawled as Domet put his nearly empty glass of red wine down on the table. "What brings you here tonight? I'm so sorry, excuse my manners: I don't think we've met before, young man. I'm High Noble Charles Domet."

Gwen glanced at me as she introduced herself as her persona and shook Domet's hand. Why was Domet pretending not to know her? What did he gain from interacting with us? Especially after all the other times he had made sure we weren't seen in public together. Did he not care what happened to me tonight? Had he given up on stealing the king's memories? Or worse . . . did he know I'd burned down the Shrine of Patron Victoria?

"Young man," Domet said to Gwen. "Could you do me a favor

and get me another glass of wine? Specifically white. I don't really like red—it's too tart for me. Be my hero and bring me another?"

Gwen nodded and left the table without a word. When she was out of earshot, I said, "Are you kidding me, Domet?"

"Of course I am. I drink barrels of red wine. As much as I adore your sister's presence, it was just an excuse to get us alone. Albeit a very bad one."

"I was talking about how you blurred the lines between my personal and professional life. After last night, you have no right to talk to her like we're friends."

Domet laughed and finished his drink. "Michael, that's perfectly impractical, if you think about it. We're not strangers. Anyone could learn you've been employed to aid in my recovery outside the asylum. So why should we pretend that we don't know each other? It's impractical. Anyway, who cares? I don't."

"I do, because after I steal the king's memories, we'll never have to see each other ever again." And I would be free of him, and Hollow, forever. I didn't even care about the money, or learning how to use Fabrications anymore. After tonight he'd have nothing to hold over me and I'd have my freedom again.

Domet seemed amused. "Are you planning on doing it without my help? Because you never came—"

"I did. You weren't home. I waited as long as I could. Unless you wanted me to be late."

"Fair. I have been dealing with something else today," he said, voice slightly higher than normal. "Speaking of which, I'd like to make an adjustment to our deal."

He was delusional if he thought I would agree to that. "No."

"I thought you'd say that. But hear me out: we have a good partnership, Michael. I will offer you Sirash's freedom in exchange for identifying whoever burned down the Shrine of Patron Victoria."

I felt pale. This was too good to be true. "You want me to find the person that burned down the Shrine of Patron Victoria? You don't trust the Evokers to do it?"

"The Evokers," he began, the words coming out of his mouth like poison, "are convinced it was the rebels, because some spineless nobles couldn't tell the difference between a rebel attack and a personal one. The rebels are delighted: if they can prove the Emperor's innocence of this crime, they can cast doubt on his involvement in the attack on the colosseum as well. The nobility's determination to pin it on the Emperor will destroy the case against him, and they're too stupid to realize it."

We paused, watching as two low nobles strolled past us—close enough to hear our conversation if they wanted to. They looked lost, glancing around the room with glasses of wine in their hands. Once they saw someone they knew and walked away, we continued.

"How are you so confident they didn't do it?" I asked.

"The Shrine of Patron Victoria isn't a symbol in our city. Destroying it won't undermine the king or help the rebels gain power. There are only a few people that even visit it, myself being the primary one." He ran his free hand over his mouth. "This was an attack against me. I don't know why, but someone wanted me to suffer. They knew *exactly* what would hurt me the most."

"Why can't you find out whoever did it yourself? You clearly have access to information I don't."

"Don't be clever with me, Michael," Domet growled. "They

knew how to hurt me. I suspect they know about my condition, too . . . otherwise they would have attempted to take my life instead of breaking my heart. They wanted me broken, but I will not break so easily. Not after everything I've been through."

"How do you expect me to help you find out who was responsible? It could be anyone."

"Doubtful. Only two mortals know of my condition." Domet reached into his jacket pocket and handed me a crumpled piece of paper. Sure enough, there were only two names written on it: Efyra Mason, the Captain of the Ravens, and King Isaac.

"What about me? I know about it."

That seemed to bring some of the life back to him that years of wine had weathered away. "Michael, bluntly, you have neither the guts nor the imagination."

If only he knew the truth. "So you want me to find proof that they attacked the shrine?"

"Yes. And the motive. Tonight."

"That's impossible."

"No it's not. If my suspicions are right, then the king's memories will hold the proof. Neither would strike against me without consulting the other first."

"If that's true, then everything I'd need would be in the same spot."

"Exactly."

This was too good a deal to ignore. Not only would Sirash go free, but Domet would never suspect me of attacking the shrine. And the fact that the king and the woman who executed my father would take the blame? All the better.

"It's a deal."

"Excellent. Leave the Grand Ballroom when the first dance begins. Go through the bodyguard balcony. I'll have the guards distracted. Take the third door on the right to get to the Royal Tower—not the first or the second, both of those lead to the Star Chamber. Once you're in the Royal Tower, search his desk and bookshelves for hidden alcoves. Understand?"

"How am I supposed to get up to the bodyguard balcony?"

"Alas, not my concern. Figure it out."

I almost had the perfect comeback when Gwen returned to the table, a full glass of white wine in her hand and Lyon by her side. Domet took the wine, thanked her, and then took a sip from it. My brother didn't look pleased.

"High Noble Domet," Lyon began, "I'm pleased to see you this evening. I apologize for being direct, but I didn't know you knew my brother."

"Pleased to see you, too, Lyonardo. And, yes, I know Michael. He oversees my progress as an outpatient from the asylum for a month. Michael is quite the charming young man, and he's more entertaining company than stuffy nobles. As you could imagine."

Lyon nodded after a slight hesitation. "I can only imagine."

After another sip of his wine, Domet said, "I should mingle. No doubt there's someone looking for me or my money around here. Enjoy the rest of the evening." He left slowly, looking all three of us in the eyes before he did. Soon after, he was snapping his fingers toward the servants to get him more wine.

"Why was Domet talking to you, Michael?" Lyon growled. "What did you do to get *his* attention of all the people here tonight?"

"I work for him."

"Domet doesn't approach people out of nowhere for no reason, even if they work for him. He stalks people, learns everything about their lives, and then destroys them. He has more money than the entire government and no one knows how. Be honest with me: Has he ever offered you a deal? Anything, even if it was trivial."

"No," I lied, "he hasn't."

My brother exhaled in relief. "Thank God. You should be fine if you avoid him from now on. Never be alone with him and never accept anything from him. Promise me. Promise as a Kingman you'll never accept a deal from him."

My chest tightened. He had never asked me to swear on our heritage before. He was serious about this. "From now on, I promise I'll never accept anything from him."

"Good," he said. "Good. I need to return to High Noble Ryder and the others. Thank you for getting me, Gwen. I'll catch up with you all later."

For the umpteenth time that night, another person left our little table. When it was just me and Gwen again, she asked, "Are you angry that I got Lyon?"

"No," I said. I was angry that I just promised as a Kingman to never make another deal with Domet . . . and I wouldn't. But it wasn't my fault we'd agreed to a deal moments before. It was just good manners to finish it—another lie I told myself. They only grew in number these days. "I'm not. You were trying to help. It's not your fault Domet came over to me. Or that he was acting strangely."

Gwen rubbed the back of her neck. "I didn't want you to be alone with him. I was concerned what he might want, approaching you here. Something seemed off about Domet tonight, and it made me uncomfortable. I thought I'd seen the worst of him, but I've never seen him like that before. I looked for Kai first and only asked Lyon when I couldn't see him."

"Lyon and I have been on better terms lately, and once he's with Kayleigh he'll forget about it."

"Lyon really loves her, doesn't he?"

I nodded, seeing Kai headed back to our table with Joey in his arms. The young boy was resting his blond head on his older brother's shoulder. "Never seen him happier. This world suits him."

"I have also never known my sister happier." Kai had caught the end of our conversation. "Even when they were childhood friends, she was always more energetic when he was around. I'm happy they were able to reconnect."

"How is Joey?" Gwen asked. "He looks pretty exhausted."

"He is," Kai said. He ran his hands down Joey's back. The young boy trembled a little in his arms and then was still again. "I'll probably take him home when the dancing starts. My father is staying; the High Nobles are all discussing the Rebel Emperor's trial."

"Do you think they'll find him guilty?" I asked.

"Only God knows," Kai said. "If you had asked me two days ago, I would have said yes without hesitation. Everything is more complicated since some fanatic burned down the Shrine of Patron Victoria. I would have more confidence if the Emperor were not on trial for every terrorist attack in recent memory against the citizens of Hollow. But since he is . . ."

The implication was enough.

"We'll find out tomorrow," I said.

A dinner gong had begun to sound, and the nobles were being drawn toward the Grand Ballroom. We followed the crowds and the shuffle of feet against the tiled floor, hearing an announcer calling out names as the various nobles entered the Grand Ballroom.

I didn't hear much as I approached the door to the ballroom, only the pounding of my own heart in my chest from nerves. Tonight was the night I either sank or swam to freedom. I didn't plan on drowning, but then, few rarely did.

Without asking for my name, the announcer shouted, voice amplified into the ballroom, "Presenting Michael Kingman to King Isaac and the Hollow Court."

EXPOSURE

Ever since I was little, I had always thought the rhubarb pie the nobility served after their fancy dinners tasted like hardened snot. No, it was more like rancid butter with fly guts sprinkled over it.

The only reason the nobility said it was delicious, and demanded it, was because the ingredients were rare and poisonous if prepared incorrectly. In reality, it was an expensive hassle for the chefs to bake the dozens of pies needed for an event like this. My opinion was only reinforced years later as I nibbled on the end of one and was met with a taste more bitter than pure vinegar.

I may have been alone in this belief, and I watched everyone else at my table devour it.

"I don't think I can eat another bite," Kai declared, leaning back in his seat. As he did, a servant dressed in blue and gold cleared away the remains of the lettuce wraps and the Gold Coast marinated meat and firestone we had cooked it on. Moments after he was gone, another filled our glasses with crisp white wine. Everything was in excess tonight, our scenery included.

The Grand Ballroom was something straight out of tall tales. It was a massive room with tables all around the edges and a slightly sunken dance floor in the middle. Above us was a large balcony where all the bodyguards were eating and relaxing. During the lulls in the music it was possible to hear them drinking and laughing together. It sounded like a merry time. At the end, as far away as possible from the door, was the king's table, where the most important people sat. King Isaac was in the center with Efyra Mason in my family's seat. Domet was at the closest table nearby—not that I expected any less of him.

The Corrupt Prince was at a separate table as well, off to the side with his Throne Seekers. Naomi and Trey were with him, drinking and eating and laughing—well, Trey wasn't laughing, but that didn't seem out of the ordinary. In all the years I had known him, I had only ever seen him laugh once: when a High Noble tripped and fell face-first into horseshit. As I stared at Trey, I saw that there was another member of the Throne Seekers tonight, but I couldn't see their face from my seat. Only his big frame.

Regardless, neither the prince nor the king nor the Raven nor Naomi mattered to me tonight so long as they didn't bother me. I had a job to do and I couldn't get distracted. With the feast conclud-ing, the dancing would soon begin, and I still had to get to the body-guard balcony above the Grand Ballroom. I thought there might be a way up via the lower balcony, near the king's table. Not that it would be easy. Ravens stood guard at all exits, and there was nowhere they wouldn't see.

As the servants cleared away the last few plates, King Isaac stood and tapped his glass with a knife. "My fellow citizens of Hollow, I would like to take your attention away from each other for a brief moment." He paused and glanced at three empty seats at his table, one covered with a black cloth. "As we celebrate, we must always remember those who couldn't be here with us today. While my wife and daughter are merely indisposed, I would like to observe a moment of silence for my eldest son."

Without another word, he laced his fingers together and bowed his head. Silence overtook the entire ballroom and the bodyguard balcony. Even the Corrupt Prince's entourage stopped what they were doing to pay respects for the late prince. I lowered my head and did my best not to look in the king's direction.

"May the Wanderer watch over his journey into the beyond as the Eternal Flame lights his path," the king intoned before he raised his head. "As much as I would love to take the first dance with my wife to celebrate my birthday, she is sadly unavailable. Thus, I would like to extend the invitation to start to High Noble Morales and his husband."

An elegant, obsidian-skinned couple near the king rose from their seats and walked toward the dance floor together as a crowd began to gather and the musicians prepared for a change of pace.

"How much do you think they paid for the honor?" Kai asked, leaning closer to all of us at the table.

"They sponsored a memorial on the Gold Coast for Davey," High

Noble Margaux said. "My parents were telling me about it last night. Apparently it's going to be massive. Any idea where they acquired that much money, Kai?"

"No," he said. "They're not an old High Noble family, so all their money is new and undocumented. The Andels claim it's drug money and that they're the ones poisoning the East Side with Blackberries. But you know how much the Andels like to besmirch anyone who doesn't look like them or the Royal Family. Their claims are ridiculous."

"Especially when everyone knows the Ryders are the only true High Nobles that hand out drugs willingly," Gwen quipped.

Kai chuckled and smiled. "I think my father prefers to call it medicine, but we do what we must."

Noble gossip. My favorite. As stimulating as it was to listen to, I had other things I needed to do. Out of the corner of my eye, I saw Naomi get up from her table and move toward the lower balcony.

"I'll be right back. Need to use the bathroom before I dance," I reassured Gwen. The last thing I needed was for her to question where I was going—or follow me—but their conversation continued seamlessly, and I crept away toward the lower balcony.

As I walked out onto it, into the cool night air, Naomi was leaning against the railing, a glass of wine in one hand as she gazed at the black horizon. It was early still, and neither the stars nor moons had emerged yet. She drank silently as I approached.

"Is your company not as stimulating tonight?" I asked.

She shook her head. "Just needed a breath of fresh air." A pause. "Why are you here, Michael?"

"The same reason. There are only so many times I can listen to noble conversations about how this family got their money or what that family's most recent scandals are."

"If you dislike it, why did you return? I never understood why you would when you clearly hate everything about noble society. And it's not just because I was blackmailing you . . . You were already a participant when I caught you outside Kingman Keep."

"It was what I wanted at the time."

"Was it really?" she asked, sipping some of her wine. "I don't believe you, but it's not my place to question. We're not friends or anything. Though I wouldn't judge you if you told me the truth."

"If I did, that would make us friends."

Naomi puckered her lips and looked away from me. "Better not, then. I wouldn't want to ruin a good thing. Oh, and before you ask, I'm not returning your ring this evening."

I didn't expect her to, but I still asked the question she wanted to hear. "Why not? Tonight marks the end of the Endless Waltz. After this, it's pointless to blackmail me."

Naomi played with my father's ring, her back to the railing. "Would it really be pointless? I'll visit you tomorrow morning and return it then. When the Endless Waltz is officially over."

That was oddly nice of her. Which meant it probably wasn't happening. In fact, if everything went according to plan, I'd probably end up leaving Hollow without my father's ring. I suppose it made some sense to leave it behind, if I was abandoning the Kingman legacy.

"Thank you," I said.

Naomi walked away, dismissing me with a wave of her hand. "No thanks needed. If you'll excuse me, I'm going to go talk to my

Raven friend over there before I return to my future beloved's side. I'll see you . . . I'll see you tomorrow, Michael. Enjoy the rest of your night."

Before I had a chance to respond, Naomi initiated a conversation with the guard on the balcony. I don't know if she had intended to give me a distraction, but there was no time to ponder it. I had to get to the upper balcony, and this was the best opportunity I'd have. I stepped onto the railing and looked up the wall, parts of which were broken off or chipped away. There was no need for me to look down; I was already fully aware a sheer drop awaited me if I fell.

I began my climb, gripping an old brick where the mortar had eroded away, and pulled myself upward, trying to remain as straight as possible. With every new handhold I found, my foot slid into an old one, and I crawled upward. My forearms tightened and my fingertips went a little more numb with each new hold, and by the time I neared the upper balcony, I was covered in sweat and all my muscles burned. Worse, the remaining distance between me and the lip of the balcony was perfectly smooth. I couldn't see any handholds.

I would have to jump for it.

I took a breath and launched myself up into the air. My grip left the indentation I had been using, and for a moment I was weightless, floating upward. My hands slapped against the bottom of the railings and I hit them hard, my body falling forward and my fingers nearly slipping. I tightened my grip on the bar and hung there, breathing deeply. I couldn't stop shaking as I pulled myself up and over.

Everything hurt, but I had made it. I exhaled toward the sky. Something, for once, hadn't gone wrong. It was a good feeling, and as my breathing returned to normal, I gathered myself and entered the bodyguard balcony.

It was a whole new world.

Within seconds of stepping into this place, despite obviously not belonging, two different people pressed tankards into my hands and told me to drink. They were both filled with the sweetest liquid I had ever tried, and it was significantly better than the wine the nobles were drinking. I finished one quickly and put the empty tankard on a table as I continued to wander around the balcony. Despite the fact everyone seemed to be indulging excessively, none of them seemed to be drunk.

There were bodyguards playing Three Brothers in a corner as others looked on, betting knickknacks, small vials of exotic spices, and whatever else caught their fancy. I snagged a delicious roast chicken leg from a plate as I passed, seeing heaps of buttery mashed potatoes and glazed green beans up for grabs as well. I ate with relish, far preferring this hearty fare to the fancy dining and foul rhubarb pie I had left behind. It was such a contrast to the world down there.

But it couldn't be all good. There were Mercenaries from three of the biggest companies up here.

They were having fun together, swapping stories and showing off different currencies. Mercenaries from Machina Company, the Black Company, and Regal Company all mingled together without a care for name or rank or fashion. They were playful in their antics and words, taking nothing seriously. Yet, they made sure everyone around them knew what company they were in and what their position in it was. As if it were more important than their own names.

As I clanked glasses with a Machina Company Mercenary, others began to gather near the ledge over the Grand Ballroom. A few of the bodyguards were leaning over, laughing together. I joined them as I drank and saw the dancing was beginning in earnest now, the ceremonial first dance having finished a long time ago. From up here they looked like little spinning puppets. All that was missing was the strings.

Domet was nowhere to be seen.

I finished my second drink and reluctantly headed toward the exit. I would have stayed there if someone put another drink in my hand. No one did, though, and the door slammed behind me, cutting off the laughter from the balcony. I was alone and unseen, and as I walked down the lavish hallway headed toward the staircase and the Royal Tower, I felt a little bit lighter on my feet than I normally did. Domet had kept his end of the deal: there wasn't a single guard in the hallway.

The third door on the right had been left slightly ajar. As I made my way up the staircase, I tried to come up with a name—any name that would make sense to Domet as the shrine arsonist. Ideally someone linked to the Rebel Emperor. Needless to say, I didn't have an answer by the time I entered the royal living quarters.

Compared to the rest of the castle, which was elegant beyond reason, this area was plain—bland, even. The walls in the circular entrance chamber were unadorned, and the hardwood floor was dull and scratched, with well-worn paths to each of the seven doors. The first was marked *Dining Room* and the second *Conference Room*, followed by the rooms that belonged to the Corrupt Prince and the princess—both locked. Then there was the fifth door without any marking to indicate what it was, but I had a nagging feeling that it had been Davey's. The last room was the king and queen's quarters. And, for whatever reason, it was unlocked.

I stepped into the king's personal chamber. Like the entrance, it was plainly decorated aside from an intricate tapestry showing the various stages of a red-haired man's life, from birth to the moment a heavy crown was placed upon his head. I glanced at the details, seeing the same man married, celebrating the birth of his three children . . . mourning the death of his son. The only king who fit the tale was Isaac Hollow. Did the king use this tapestry to record his—

Someone put the barrel of a gun against the back of my head and interrupted my thoughts.

"Michael, how many times do I have to warn you not to fuck with me?"

It was Dark. He had come for me. Inside Hollow Castle no less.

"I searched for you in Kingman Keep this morning," I said, unable to move my head at all.

"If you had been there last night, you wouldn't have had to."

"Something came up. There was an emergency and—"

Dark grabbed me by the neck and slammed me against the wall. I could turn my head and see his face now, and it was too calm for someone who was being so hostile. "Do you think I care why you didn't show up? Do you not take me seriously enough, Michael? Have I been too generous? Have I been too lenient? Should I have killed your brother the first time you fucked with me and your sister the second time?"

He was choking me, so I couldn't respond; nothing came out but wheezes and gurgles.

"Where is my envelope?"

He released the pressure on my neck and I collapsed to the floor on my ass. When I could, I said, "Home."

"Your home?"

I nodded as I tried to get my breath back.

Dark put his gun back in the holster. "Inconvenient, but . . . but I can deal with the consequences if we're seen together. How did you think you were going to get away with this?"

"Didn't. Planned on giving it back. Accidents happened. Wasn't intentional."

"Imbecile," Dark said as he hauled me back up to my feet. "Come with me. We're getting it now. I'm not waiting any longer for you to do it on your own."

"I can't, I—"

Dark punched me in the jaw and I was back on the ground, everything blurry. In hindsight, it wasn't a good idea to say no to a Mercenary. He probably hadn't heard the word before.

"Willing to try that again?" he asked.

"I need to find something in the king's study first."

"And?"

"Let me search it before we go."

"Not a chance."

"If I don't—"

Dark's face was expressionless as he held a finger gun to my forehead. "I don't care. You're coming with me."

There was nothing I could do but follow Dark. I hated it. I hated that my decision to save Arjay meant I had forgotten my meeting with Dark, and now he was ruining everything. Without the gun that killed Davey Hollow, Gwen wouldn't come with me to the Gold Coast. And without the king's memories, I was making a lifelong enemy of an Immortal and relinquishing any hope of clearing my family's name. At least I could still give Domet a name. Maybe he'd understand if I explained what happened. It was doubtful, given how desperate he was to die.

Every step we took away from the king's bedroom made my heart sink further into my stomach, and by the time we made it back to the Grand Ballroom, I was in despair. The king and most of the Ravens were nowhere to be seen. Only two remained, both guarding the Corrupt Prince. The bodyguard balcony had cleared out, the once-lively affair only containing a faint memory of what was once there. The noble's party, however, was still going strong, with drunk patrons enjoying a performance from Azilian fire dancers.

"Say goodbye to your friends," Dark said at the exit. "I don't want them to be suspicious."

I did as I was told, trying to formulate a plan in my head. Kai and his brother were nowhere to be seen, and as I walked past the lower balcony, I paused, hearing a conversation I could barely make out. My sister and High Noble Margaux were drinking wine and laughing together. I couldn't even remember the last time Gwen had laughed. Months? Years? I wasn't sure.

I didn't linger. It was clear they were having a good time and they didn't need me to ruin it. They probably hadn't noticed I'd been gone—and they were the only people likely to. All the same, I did one last lap around the ballroom just to make sure. As I passed by the Corrupt Prince's table, I saw who his new friend was: a brutish man with a broken nose that whistled every time he breathed.

I froze mid-stride, recognizing him instantly. He was talking to Trey with a huge grin on his face and a glass of wine in his hand, and though he'd somehow concealed the rebel tattoo on his neck, there was no mistaking him. Trey was talking to the man who had killed his brother. I had no idea how a rebel got himself invited to the king's birthday party as a guest of the prince, or if he would recognize me.

Dark was waiting for me, and I knew what could happen if I disobeyed him again . . . but I didn't have a gun to my head right now, and I wasn't about to let the rebel who had murdered Jamal go unpunished.

The only problem was how.

There were dinner knives on the tables that hadn't been cleaned up yet. I could sprint toward the Corrupt Prince's group, jump the table, and stab the rebel in the throat with one of them. But with a weapon in my hands, at that table, the Ravens would cut me down. I wouldn't escape with all my limbs attached.

There had to be another way. Something that didn't put me in as much risk.

The Mercenary was at the exit to the Grand Ballroom and still had a gun. If I could steal it from him, I could take a shot across the room and . . . No, that wasn't any better. If by divine intervention I could steal Dark's gun, I'd need another miracle for the bullet to hit the rebel and not one of the dozens of innocents in the way.

I had to do something. I couldn't stand by and do nothing while Jamal's murderer drank and ate and laughed with Trey, and my legs were carrying me toward the rebel before my brain understood what I was doing. Rage drove me forward with my fists clenched tightly.

The Ravens didn't have a chance to stop me, and by the time

they noticed I had crossed the distance to the Corrupt Prince's table, I was already on top of it. I brought my leg back and aimed for the rebel's jaw—only for Trey to catch my leg before it connected with the rebel. He slammed me down with his open fist, and my back seized up as it hit the table.

Trey must've assumed I was coming for him.

Shit.

The Corrupt Prince couldn't stop laughing. Naomi looked shocked, eyes wide. The other two Throne Seekers were in a similar state to her, while the Ravens were watching me carefully, hands on their sword hilts.

"Michael," Trey growled. "Was my brother not enough for you? Do you want to take everything from me? Am I not allowed to be happy as long as you aren't?"

My head was spinning, my back was aching, and I couldn't find the right words. The brutish rebel wouldn't stop laughing, and laughing, and laughing.

I didn't see Trey move, but the next thing I knew, I was on my back and he was punching me relentlessly. I did my best to block his blows, but more got through than I would have liked, and one of the Ravens finally pulled him off after he hit me in the eye. The other dragged me down off the table.

Flushed, Trey said, "Savor your breath, Michael. You're dead. All of you Kingman are dead."

A crowd had formed around us, and the Corrupt Prince, never one to miss a good fight, suddenly took more of an interest. "Oh, Trey, Michael Kingman was responsible for your brother's death? You never told me that. Only that it was someone very, very important. As much as I would love to watch you stab Michael in the heart and quench your thirst for revenge, I think I have a better idea. A more entertaining idea."

We both looked at him, neither understanding.

Prince Adreann clapped his hands together and smiled. "Ladies and gentlemen! I hope you're ready for a show! Michael Kingman swore an oath to protect a child. Which he broke, that child died— and now his brother seeks vengeance! I, Prince of Hollow, declare that these two will duel to the death, right here, to settle the matter!"

The Corrupt Prince turned to Trey. "As the avenger, you may choose the weapon."

"Duel?" Trey snapped. "I don't want to duel him, I want to destroy his family—"

The prince squished Trey's cheeks so he couldn't talk. "And I will not stop you. But I am the prince, and I have declared you two will duel. You will not deny me this. Understand?"

Trey nodded slowly. "Guns. I want guns. I won't duel Michael Kingman otherwise. He has too much experience in everything else, since he grew up as a High Noble."

"Guns?" the Corrupt Prince said, amused. "Well, my father isn't here, so why not? Does anyone here have a brace of pistols?"

No one in the crowd responded. After all, who would? Owning a gun in Hollow was still illegal.

"No one? Well, maybe . . . ," the prince trailed off, eyes falling on Dark. "You! Mercenary! There's no law against you and your kind carrying a gun in Hollow. Would you indulge a prince? I will repay your generosity in this matter tenfold."

Oh, no.

Dark stepped forward from the crowd and drew two guns from his jacket. One was a flintlock pistol and the other was a more advanced model, able to fire more than one bullet before reloading. I had never seen something like it before. Even New Dracon City—which was much more advanced in gun technology—didn't have anything like that.

"Yours for the event, for a small fee," Dark said. Even though he wasn't looking at me, I knew what Dark was thinking. This was what I deserved for treating him like a fool. My life didn't matter to him now, since he knew where his envelope was. Sure, it would be annoying to get, but he would get it. He was a Mercenary, after all. Who could stop him? Maybe Angelo, but not my siblings.

"So you know, one is more advanced than the other," Dark said. "It's more accurate, can hold more than one bullet, and doesn't need to be loaded like the guns you're used to."

"Minor differences," the prince said. "What matters is that both can shoot once without reloading. Ladies and gentlemen, we have a duel!"

There were cheers within the crowd, but to me it was white noise as I stared at Trey and he stared back, both of us knowing only one of us would survive what came next.

LAWFUL

Obviously, I was given the flintlock pistol.

The Corrupt Prince set Trey and me up on the dance floor as he lounged in his father's chair, Chloe and the three-feathered Raven, Rowan Kerr, at his side. Everyone else—including High Noble Margaux, Gwen, Naomi, Ambassador Zain, his Skeleton, the Azilian, and the brutish rebel—were watching from the railing above me, all of them unable to talk to me since the prince had announced the duel was going to take place.

The only one that could—not that he wanted to—was Trey. Instead of us sharing our deepest fears with each other, asking to be remembered after one of us died, he spun the cylinder that held his bullets, eyes focused on the shot he was about to take at me.

I didn't know what I was going to do. We had one shot each, and the Corrupt Prince had been clear that if we both missed, the duel would be over and we could walk away unscathed. But . . . that relied on Trey missing me, not taking his revenge for my failure to protect Jamal. If I could explain what happened, tell him that the brute at the prince's table was a rebel, then maybe this could end without violence. But the odds were against me. I was going to have to decide whether to miss or take a real shot at my friend.

"Trey," I said quietly, hoping the prince couldn't hear me. "I was attacking that brute beside you, not you. He's the rebel who killed Jamal. There's a mark—"

Trey leveled his gun at me in silence, the action speaking for him. So much for both of us throwing away our shots and living. Someone was going to die here tonight. And even if I survived, it would only be because I killed my friend. Could I live with myself if I did that?

The Corrupt Prince bellowed from above, "I think our duelists are ready! No more waiting around or last words! Let us begin!"

Trey lowered his gun and said, "Hold on. I want your word that I won't be prosecuted for killing the man who murdered my brother."

Everyone in the Grand Ballroom awaited the prince's response.

"Of course you have it!" he said with a smile. "Nor will the Kingman be prosecuted for killing in self-defense, despite being responsible for the death of your brother. Unless you have another stipulation, the duel will begin on my mark!"

Trey and I stood back-to-back, then began to take our steps away from each other.

One step, and my heart was pounding. Every noise turned to scratches in my ear.

Two steps, and my palm was sweaty and shaking, barely able to hold the gun.

Three steps, and I could see High Noble Margaux holding my sister back from jumping over the railing to protect me.

Four steps, and I could see the brutish rebel in front of me, leaning over the railing, hollering to see someone die.

Five steps, and the lights from the lanterns above seemed to blind me. Would they obscure my vision when I shot?

Six steps, and I was panicking. Would my family see me differently if I killed Trey to survive? Or would they rather have me alive and a murderer than dead and honorable?

Seven steps, and I was remembering my father, my forgotten hero. He had been everything to me at one point . . . and I missed him so much. I just wanted him to be proud of me.

Eight steps, and I wondered where Domet was. Was he watching from above? Was he stealing the king's memories himself when he realized I had failed? Was he going to watch me die? Here, of all places?

Nine steps, and I was breathing, listening to my body. If there was any time for me to figure out what kind of Fabricator I was, it would be now. Could a Metal Fabricator stop a bullet? I didn't know.

Ten steps, and I stopped, facing the crowd, the air still. Whenever the prince said "Fire," I would turn and shoot, but I still didn't know what I was going to—

"Fire!"

I turned and threw my gun aside and watched it slide across the floor to a collective gasp. If I was going to die, I might as well die honorably and be remembered as a Kingman who failed instead of letting one brother die and killing the other myself. Trey was family, and family didn't hurt family.

Trey wasn't as heroic. I watched him raise his gun toward me and take a breath, steadying his aim. Killing the Emperor must've been more important to him than my lousy life.

I closed my eyes and waited.

The shot might not kill me. And if it did, hopefully my family would remember me as a man who had tried his best.

Trey shot as I took a breath. The air seemed to crack in two at the sound, and I took an involuntary step back. Without opening my eyes, I felt for blood in case I was shot and in shock. But I found nothing.

Had Trey missed on purpose?

I opened my eyes. The gun was smoking in Trey's hand, sweat dripping down his face as his eyes were locked on me . . . No, his eyes were locked on something beyond me. Looking over my shoulder, I saw what had happened. The brutish rebel had collapsed against the railing, a shattered wineglass on the dance floor below him. There was a red mark on his upper chest, and blood was beginning to drip down from it.

No one in the crowd of nobles, even the Corrupt Prince, found any words to question what had just happened.

Trey walked past me and toward the dead rebel. He licked his thumb, then ran it over the rebel's neck to expose the bright red tattoo of a closed fist concealed beneath.

"This man was the rebel who murdered my brother during the attack on the Militia Quarter," Trey declared. "I didn't realize who he was until I saw a hint of the tattoo on his neck while I was on the dance floor before the duel. Thus I withdrew my right to take Michael Kingman's life despite the fact he was partially responsible for my brother's death. Instead, I took the life of this rebel. Just as the prince promised me, in front of you all."

Someone in the crowd shouted, "How can you be certain this man was the one who murdered your brother?"

"He's a rebel who matches the description I had," Trey said. "And if I'm wrong, who cares? Who knows what he had planned to do here tonight, with access to the prince? We should all be thankful the prince's food is always tasted beforehand and that this rebel never had the chance to poison him. Perhaps another assassin failed here tonight."

Nobles whispered to each other as they waited for the Corrupt Prince's response. By all technicalities and laws, Trey was in the right. It just wasn't what the Corrupt Prince had wanted.

The prince rose silently from his seat and made his way down to the dance floor. Both Ravens were at his side, and Naomi, for some reason, was close behind.

"You should have told your prince before you shot him," he said as he brushed off a speck of dirt from Trey's clothes. "I would have let you kill him. I would have even let you borrow the castle's torture rooms. Our educator could have made him regret killing your brother. It saddens me a child-murdering rebel died so easily."

"My prince, as I said, I wasn't certain until the last moment."

The prince held his empty palm out. "Give me the gun."

Hesitantly, Trey gave the prince the loaded gun.

The prince walked past him and toward me, only stopping once he was within arm's length. "You put me in a difficult situation,

Treyvon. On one hand, you have relinquished your right to take Michael Kingman's life tonight. And on the other hand"—the prince aimed the gun at me—"he's a Kingman who couldn't even protect a child from rebels. Is his life worth preserving? Like his father, he's a disgrace to the name."

"My prince," Chloe said. "I think you've had too much—"

He looked over his shoulder. "Did I ask for your opinion, Raven? Have I ever asked for your opinion?"

Chloe shook her head and backed away from him.

"Regretfully, Prince Adreann, in the past week—before your nobility—Michael Kingman has shown himself to be a better man than his father ever was. We have all seen what Michael is capable of," Ambassador Zain said from above. A smile was on his face. "I, and I suspect others here, would attest to this. He is a worthy Kingman."

Many more than I would have expected called out in support, with Gwen, of course, the loudest of them all. The prince was expressionless as he watched and listened but never lowered the gun he had aimed at my chest.

"I can also speak for the Kingman child," Domet declared, voice booming. He pushed his way through the crowd to make himself visible. "He has begun to redeem his family, and even if it's a long path . . . this city was built by the Kingman family and has been without one for too long."

Even more sounded their agreements. Gwen didn't even need to yell this time.

And yet, the Corrupt Prince still aimed the gun at me. Without moving, I tried to spot Dark in the crowd and see if he was going to let a prince murder a Kingman with his gun. Sadly for me, he probably didn't care one way or another.

"Prince Adreann," Naomi said quietly, approaching from behind him. She ran her hand down his back, and the prince lowered the gun slightly. "Let the Kingman go. He's not even worth the price of the metal used to make the bullet. Who cares what he does? You're the Prince of Hollow, and nothing will change that. Not even him."

"You are correct," he said, finally lowering the gun. I let out a breath I hadn't realized I'd been holding in. "You are all correct! And I did give my word not to stand against you during the Endless Waltz, Michael. But I cannot stand by and let your treacherous, scheming plots go unpunished. Blood must be spilled."

I froze.

"At first I found it humorous," he said. "But to be so brazen. Here. Of all places."

I looked to Domet. Even he was uncertain. How had the Corrupt Prince figured out we were planning to steal the king's memories?

"Do you have anything to say for yourself?"

I stood straighter.

"Pity. I would have liked to hear you beg."

The prince turned, faced Naomi, and then shot her in the stomach.

I didn't run to her side to help, my legs shaking too hard, forcing me to watch instead. The three-feathered Raven caught Naomi as she began to fall, while Chloe put pressure on her stomach, her blood already flowing freely. They were shouting to each other and to others in the crowd. I couldn't hear a single thing they said, my focus on the laughing prince in front of me.

"Do you think me a fool, Michael? I knew she was meeting with us both. Did you think it would go unnoticed? I am the Prince of Hollow, and I will not be played by a Kingman and a whore!"

The Corrupt Prince turned toward the silent crowd of nobles. "Any who aid her will have their titles and lands stripped away the moment I take power from my senile father and absent sister. Whether you like it or not . . . I will be your king."

I could feel Gwen's anger from where I was.

But, to my surprise, no noble in the room challenged his claim. Even Domet stood still as a statue, refusing to look at the girl bleeding to death in front of him. The only one who moved was Dark, who calmly came forward and reclaimed his guns.

"Mercenary," Chloe said, hands dyed red, "help us. Please. You must have experience with gunshot wounds."

The Corrupt Prince found her pleas interesting and listened intently.

Dark didn't respond to Chloe's plea, only staring at Naomi's unnaturally still body.

"I'll give you whatever you want—just save her, please."

"Unrestricted access to the king's archives?"

"Done."

"Raven!" the Corrupt Prince shouted. "Are you disobeying my orders?"

"No," she said, stepping out of the way as Dark moved to Naomi's side. "I'm hiring a Mercenary to do something I cannot. Punish me for insubordination if you must, but I have no lands or titles for you to take. Only a life I have already pledged to sacrifice to protect yours."

"So be it." He looked down at Chloe. "But I want to hear you beg me to let you use the Mercenary to save her life. Or . . . ," he said, trailing off. The Corrupt Prince took a dagger off his belt and held it over Naomi's eye.

"Please, my prince. Please let the Mercenary save Nao—"

"Use her title," he ordered.

"Please let the Mercenary save . . . save the whore's life."

"All you had to do was ask, my Raven," he said. "Do not forget that in the future. But do get the whore out of my sight quickly, will you? I worry her blood will never come out of the tile."

The two Ravens picked Naomi up gently, according to Dark's instructions. Before they left, Dark said to me, "Tomorrow. Same place and time, understand?"

I nodded as they made their way through the silent nobility, watching as the unstoppable prince cemented his power and truly began his reign of terror, with only a Mercenary and the Ravens brave enough to defy him.

All these nobles were cowards, complicit with the antics of this prince so long as it didn't hurt them or what they had. They were as much to blame for the downfall of this country as the Royals were. But curing a symptom does nothing while the disease remains. As a Kingman, I had a duty to do what was necessary to protect this country, regardless of what happened to my life. Or what I had to do. Maybe my father thought similarly at one point.

"You will never take the throne," I said.

The Corrupt Prince turned to me. "What was that, Kingman?"

"Did I stutter?"

No one laughed, but the Corrupt Prince snarled either way. "Are you threatening your prince?"

"It's not a threat. It's a promise."

Then I was floating through the air backwards, staring at the golden ceiling. My ears were ringing, my breath was nowhere to be found, my head pounded, and I slowly clawed at the grooves between the tiles with my nails. The prince stood over me, every muscle in his body more defined and visible, all the fat seemingly trimmed away with a scalpel. He was a Metal Fabricator—and a powerful one at that. I hadn't had any time to react before he hit me.

"Adreann! Stop it!" Gwen screamed.

The Corrupt Prince squatted down in front of me, his face close so only I could hear his words. His eyes were focused on my sister, fully aware of her presence. "Your whore is going to die tonight, Kingman. Then, once she's in the ground, I can focus my attention on your sister. What a pleasant surprise to see her here tonight. I'll have to find out if she's still pure. I wouldn't want to be gentle the first time, if she's already been passed around the entire city."

I snapped.

I screamed and threw back my fist, the warmth welling up in my body, ignoring the consequences of what I was about to do. The warmth was overflowing within me, and I *repelled* it out of my body and across the Grand Ballroom, then punched the Corrupt Prince in the jaw, expecting to find metal but discovering soft, pink flesh instead.

The Corrupt Prince fell back on his butt, shocked. He was staring at his body, eyes darting between me and his own hands. "My Fabrications . . . didn't work? They should have stopped you . . . but they didn't . . . Why . . . Why . . . Oh, oh, I underestimated you . . . How pathetic of me . . . ," he trailed off, noticing no one was paying attention to him.

Some nobles were staring at their hands as if a finger was missing. High Noble Margaux was being held up by a servant, her legs no longer able to hold her own weight. There were whispers of horror within the crowd, but no one seemed to be focused on the Corrupt Prince. Only themselves.

"It seems, my prince," Domet said, stepping toward him, "that you just picked a fight with a Nullify Fabricator. Your Metal Fabrications won't protect you from him."

Nullify. I closed my fist and watched the muscles twitch. I steadied my breath and felt the warmth in my body again. With a little focus I could make the sense of warmth go wherever I wanted it to, covering my body like a second skin. I twisted my hand slowly, observing the warmth I had directed there. Nothing was out of the ordinary, and it didn't look any different. No wonder I hadn't been able to figure out what kind of Fabricator I was: it was only visible in its effects. I wondered how many times I had used it without knowing . . . and how many memories I had sacrificed. It could have been dozens or hundreds of times, and as many memories lost.

But this was my power, and this was a power I could protect everyone with. Well, everyone except myself. The Corrupt Prince hadn't backed down, getting a sword from one of his servants instead. I had never seen him smile so broadly before. From how he was acting . . . I . . . I couldn't help but think he was enjoying himself. As if he were a performer on his stage.

"Thankfully, High Noble Domet, I am not dependent on my Fabrications," the Corrupt Prince said. "I am more than that. But what about you, Michael? Could you beat me in a duel? When was the last time you held a sword?"

Gwen stepped between us, calm and with a slender sword in her hand. "Enough, Adreann."

The Corrupt Prince looked at me. "Have you always let your baby sister fight your battles for you, Michael?"

I glanced at Gwen. The small, fragile, tear-stained girl I had seen for years was missing. In her place was a woman facing down a monster twice her size. And since she was bound to protect and serve and guide the Corrupt Prince from birth onward, I knew this wasn't my fight anymore.

It was hers.

OVATION

"Adreann," Gwen said as she stepped in front of me. "Do you know why Kingman and Royals are bound together?"

"Save me the history lesson, Gwennie, and get out of my way so I can kill your brother," the Corrupt Prince said.

"You never did pay attention to the tutors, so let me explain. The Kingman family was designed as a counterbalance to the Royal Family. We don't aspire to hold power but to serve our country and the Royal we've been bound to protect. And sometimes protecting someone means doing things they don't appreciate."

"Oh, Gwennie, if you want to serve me, I can think of a few things I would appreciate. How much experience do you have on your back?"

"Do you truly not understand what I'm saying, Adreann?" she said as they began to pace back and forth, maintaining a small distance from each other—just out of reach of their swords. "Think about it carefully."

"Gwen, as nice as it is to see how much you've grown, I don't give a—"

Gwen closed the distance between them and attacked. As she lunged, the Corrupt Prince caught her blade and, with a smile, pulled her so close to him they shared a breath. "Too slow, Gwennie. Try again."

He pushed her away and Gwen nearly stumbled to the ground. Eternally arrogant, the Corrupt Prince put his sword down on the ground and then kicked it away. "I wanted to embarrass your brother with a sword because he was once renowned for his skill. But you, Gwennie . . . I don't think I'll need it. I wouldn't want to scar your lovely skin."

"You'd underestimate God if They stood in front of you, Adreann," Gwen said.

"How else would God learn what perfection is?"

"As we all do. With practice."

Gwen attacked again. But this time she spun right before he caught her blade and then kicked the prince in the backs of his knees. He toppled, his size and weight working against him for the first time in his life, and crunched to the tiles, the tip of Gwen's sword against his throat. She was tenser than I had ever seen her, and her hand was shaking. I knew what she was considering, and I hoped she didn't do it.

Not with every noble in Hollow watching.

Punching the prince had been foolish of me and would only create problems in the future. What Gwen was doing . . . it was as if a true Kingman from the stories had returned to put her Royal in his rightful place. It was a feat no one had seen in a decade.

How long had I been underestimating her for?

"Adreann, I am bound to serve you by law, which includes calling you out for your monstrous behavior."

"Clearly I underestimated you, Gwen. That won't happen again. But do you truly think a dated law will save you? My father will hear of what you two Kingman did tonight."

"Given how you turned out," she began, "I don't imagine he'll care. If he did, you would have become a better person. But do tell him what happened here. Explain how you instigated a gun duel at his birthday celebrations, shot one woman out of jealousy, and how another half your size put you on your ass in front of the nobility. I'm sure he'll find that befits a man who wants to be king."

The prince's face was as red as his hair, and he was breathing short and shallowly, eyes focused on my sister. He pushed the blade away from his neck and rose to his feet, scraping Naomi's blood off his soles once he was standing. "I'll remember this, Gwen."

"As you should."

Without another word, the Corrupt Prince stormed away. Whatever Throne Seekers remained at the party trailed behind him. It was only after he was out of sight that the nobility finally began to disperse, eager to get away from the Kingman children.

I wanted to get to Gwen. But, because my life was an endless joke, Domet intercepted me before I could. "You and your sister both assaulted the prince—incredibly stupid, both times, and there will likely be consequences—but—"

"I didn't find the king's memories, Domet. Someone interfered before I could, and then all this happened."

"Maybe there will be another chance to—"

"No," I said. "No more deals with you or any of the nobility. I'll tell you who burned down the shrine, you'll free Sirash, and that'll be the end of our relationship. I don't care about your money or your help with my mother. I'll do it on my own."

"That's not what—"

"What's more important to you, dying or revenge?"

There was no hesitation. "Who was it? And why?"

At least I knew what he valued over everything else. "Dark, the Mercenary. He was hired by King Isaac, who worried you might make a play for the throne."

Dark might be trying to save Naomi now, but I couldn't be sure what he would do once he had his documents. Giving his name to Domet was a countermeasure, in case he came after my friends and family. Because if anyone stood a chance against a Mercenary, it was an immortal High Noble.

Screwing the king over in the process was more personal: a decade's worth of anger finally getting an outlet.

"Well, Michael, thank you. Your friend will be released tomorrow after the Emperor's trial."

"Thank you." I left Domet after that, no longer interested in speaking to him anymore and uncertain why I had been in the first place. He had promised so much—Fabrication training, a place at court, answers about my father, and a cure for my mother—and delivered none of it. My head was beginning to ache and my lips felt cracked as I joined Gwen and High Noble Margaux sitting at a table together. High Noble Margaux was clearly in pain as she sat down, and I didn't know why, but that didn't feel odd. "What happened?"

Gwen was drinking wine, the slender sword in front of her on the table. "I'm not sure. She was fine and then the next moment she fell. A servant caught her, but I think I heard something break—"

"I'm fine, it happens," she said through gritted teeth. Obviously, she wasn't, but neither of us knew why. "More importantly, are both of you well?"

"I don't know," I said. And I didn't.

"Not surprising. You did punch the prince in front of dozens of nobles," Gwen said.

"You put a blade to his neck."

"I'm not scared of him. I know him too well to be."

"I'm aware. But it was still stupid. What if the king does retaliate?"

Gwen continued to drink her wine. "I don't know. But I had to do it, Michael. I couldn't stay silent any longer. Someone had to stop him, and I'm the only one that could. I just hope I did enough."

"You definitely did—"

Yet another interruption. This time it was a blond-haired man carrying a bottle of whiskey and two empty glasses. He was dressed in yellow and black and had an ugly scar over the bridge of his nose. Age hadn't been kind to him, but it rarely was for anyone. "Michael, join me. We should talk. And drink."

Gwen spoke for me. "No. I don't care who you are or why you would think otherwise, but we're going home."

High Noble Margaux put a hand on her shoulder. "Gwen, let me introduce Kai's father, High Noble Alexander Ryder. He's a Kingman sympathizer. No harm will come to Michael, and after punching the prince, Michael is going to need all the help he can get. He doesn't have the protection of being bound to him, as you do."

"Oh," Gwen said. "High Noble Alexander, I'm so—"

Alexander Ryder seemed amused. "Do not fear, Gwendolyn. Your father would have been proud to see you defending your brother and standing up to the prince."

"Thank you, sir." For Gwen, there was no greater compliment.

Alexander Ryder bowed slightly. "You are welcome. But I do ask that you allow me to talk to Michael. We have a lot to discuss."

"I apologize, sir. I do need to escort my sister home after—"

"She will stay with me tonight as a guest," High Noble Margaux declared. "Prince Adreann will not disturb us. That I can promise you."

I looked to Gwen and she nodded in approval, and that was that.

I said my goodbyes, then followed Alexander Ryder to an empty table in the corner of the room. Once we were seated, he slid me an empty glass and poured some whiskey into it. "Cheers."

"Cheers," I said, and drank. I had never relished that burn in my throat more than in that moment. The first sip was always the worst, but then it was like lemon water.

"Long night?" he asked. His coat was unbuttoned, and he looked comfortably disheveled. Leaning back in his seat, he looked less like a High Noble and more like a soldier who had finished a night shift.

"Long night," I agreed. "Longer night than I've had in a long time."

"I'd imagine so. Despite punching the prince, I don't think you have much to be worried about . . . so long as you don't go around boasting about it."

We drank to that.

"That girl the prince shot . . . was she your friend?"

"No, she was a . . . ," but I didn't know how to finish the sentence anymore. Neither "acquaintance" nor "friend" felt right, and I couldn't think of a word that did. Because even if she had been playing both sides, I was still partly responsible for her getting shot.

"Complicated, then," he said. "I get it. Your father used to talk to me about your mother. The man was madly in love with her—never so much as looked at another. He would talk, and I would drink, and sometimes I would even talk back. It was a good relationship. I miss that man every day." He paused. "Your father was one of my best friends, and now one of his sons will marry my daughter. God has an interesting sense of humor."

"You knew my father well?"

"I did. We grew up together, and we fought together most of our lives from the Day of Crowning to the Gunpowder War."

"The Day of Crowning?"

"Yes," he said, swirling his drink in its glass. "You've probably heard of it before. It was the first major battle your father ever led. We were Hollow Academy students when Tosburg Mercenary Company attacked and killed all the teachers. We were forced to lead the students against them, and your father led us to victory himself. Of course, it changed him. It changed all of us. You don't know what conflict is like until you're trying to put pressure on your friends' wounds as they're bleeding out and screaming for help. I killed three people that day—all Mercenaries." He stared into his glass. "I still remember their faces."

Alexander Ryder paused and took a deeper drink. "The entire country praised your father for his actions . . . for his heroics and tactical brilliance. He got scared that war would be his business for the rest of his life and ran away. Disappeared without a trace for . . . five years, I think. Then, when he came back to Hollow with your mother, he discovered his parents, his older sister, and his queen had been murdered and a war had broken out. Not a single person blinked when he took his father's seat as the right hand of the king and the rest, well . . . there's enough history about that."

The Day of Crowning. He was right, I had heard of it but had never heard the details. If Alexander Ryder was telling the truth, then the account I had read in Dark's envelope had been written by my father.

He had been worried he would be forgotten, and now . . .

"Why are you telling me all of this?"

"Because I miss my friend," he said. "He ruined everything by dying young . . . and stuck me with a lot of his civic duties. I cannot say that I enjoy them, either, no matter how much they aid the country. Your father was supposed to be the one who talked, and I was the one who drank. Instead, I've been forced to do both. My family is wise enough to not ask me any questions once I start doing either."

"You're the only person I've ever heard talk about my father in a favorable light since his execution."

"That is because I know he did not murder Davey Hollow."

What? I must've heard that wrong.

"He had no reason to. People said he was grief-stricken about your mother. Yes, he was bitter about it. And, yes, it changed him drastically. But he loved you, Lyon, and Gwen more than anything in the entire world. He would never have risked your lives—not for revenge, justice, money, or power. He wasn't that kind of man. He was the best of us."

My heart started beating rapidly. This wasn't happening. No. No. No. It was one thing for Domet—crazy, immortal Domet—to make that claim, but if someone else was, too, then there was a chance Domet was right. Was my father truly innocent? With a lump in my throat, I asked, "What was the official motive, then?"

"David Kingman's motive was never revealed," he said. "No one knows but the king, the judge, and the members of the council who decided his fate. I always suspected it was done to protect someone else and that he pleaded guilty so the truth was never revealed."

I felt nauseous as I held my glass. "Do you . . . Do you think someone might have . . . framed him for the murder?"

"There's no doubt in my mind. Hollow executed an innocent man."

"Then why did—"

"Didn't I say anything? I ask the king for the truth every chance I get."

I took a deep breath. There was too much information for me to process at once. I had to ask the right questions. I didn't know if an opportunity like this would come up again.

"Who would have wanted to frame him? And how would you narrow the suspects down? If he disappeared for five years, could he have made an enemy abroad? Countries have fallen in less time."

"In my opinion, there are three options. First, it was someone from Hollow," Alexander Ryder said. He reached for the bottle and refilled his glass with amber liquid. "The prince was killed and the king's best friend was blamed. As both the Royals and the Kingman family struggled to remain a family, others began rising in power, unchecked. Ten years later the ideals that our country was founded on have been forgotten or desecrated. What happened back then was more than a royal assassination: it was the assassination of our country from within."

He continued, "The second option is that it was a Cobbler trying to destabilize the country so New Dracon City could have a bigger role on the world stage. I find that less likely, since New Dracon City would've made a move against us if they were responsible."

That all made sense to me. Before my family fell, it was hard for upstarts to rise in Hollow. The old families never wanted to relinquish power, a tentative balance between all of them for generations. But now new families sprang up regularly, and some of the High Noble families I had grown up with had fallen. The Endless Waltz itself was completely different.

"Who could've done it, then?" I asked.

He chuckled to himself. "Probably someone ambitious who's gained a lot of power recently."

Power. It always came back to power. Who wanted power and had enough patience to wait years to get it? Domet didn't want power—he already had more than enough—so that eliminated him. Adreann wanted more power, but patience wasn't one of his strongest qualities. And he had been a child at the time of Davey's death.

The only person I knew who was that dedicated and reeked of new power was Dark. He had hounded me for his documents and he would have come after me for years if I had continued to evade him. Had the same thing happened to my father? Wait . . . Was it that obvious? Could my father and I have had similar problems?

"What about the Day of Crowning?" I asked. "The leader of Tosburg Company got away, right?"

"I have no idea. Your father was the only one who saw his face when they met during negotiations. After, he claimed the leader's body wasn't among the dead. We never heard from Tosburg Company again, so we never pursued it. There was always something more important to deal with."

"Could they have framed him?"

Alexander Ryder leaned back in his seat. He seemed so old sitting there. His blond hair thin and wispy. Dark circles under his eyes from not sleeping well and wrinkles etched into his face. I wondered how he'd looked when he was my age. Like Kai? After a few moments he said, "There's no information on Tosburg Company besides the few mentions of it in the history books. I can barely even remember their symbol. What was it . . . ?"

I rubbed my eyes and shook my head. This was just another wild hunt for a truth that didn't exist. Why was I listening to another drunk? Especially after the last one. Maybe because he claimed he was my father's friend and believed in his innocence. Domet did, too, but Domet had other priorities.

"It was in direct opposition to the Kingman symbol."

I looked up at Alexander Ryder with a start. "What?"

"Tosburg Company's symbol was in direct opposition to the Kingman symbol. I can't remember anything else. Just that thought from when I saw it for the first time. Right before the vanguard charged."

That wasn't anything tangible. "If you were such good friends with my father, and you even thought he was innocent . . . where were you when we were kicked out of Kingman Keep, alone and scared? Why didn't you take us in?"

He breathed in through his nose and closed his eyes for a moment. "Because I had a family to protect. In those early days, directly after your father's trial, anyone who questioned the king might as well have been a traitor, too. I hope your father would've forgiven me. He loved you three more than his own life, and I feel the same toward my children. I'd burn down the city to protect them."

"So, what is this, then? Having made it this far on my own, you're going to—"

"I've always looked out for you and your siblings, Michael. Even if it didn't appear so. Your foster father chose to isolate you from the court, but I was there whenever I could be. Did you really think it was luck that your foster father would happen upon new clothes when you were young and growing? Or wonder how your sister got a job in an asylum and your brother got a glowing recommendation to join Scales? Or how you got a private room for your mother in the asylum so easily? A traitor's family would never be that fortunate."

I stared at him for a moment, gulped, and then said, "How . . . how long did you . . . ?"

"Only when it was needed, Michael. I only guided, misdirected, and schemed when I was concerned for one of my closest friend's children. Just because the king, his Ravens, and most of the nobility have forgotten the Old Words doesn't mean my family has. We remember where our loyalties lie, Michael. And always will."

I nodded and watched as he raised his glass to his mouth, fully aware I had no way to thank him for protecting my family in the past.

"You said there was a third option. What was it?"

Alexander Ryder filled my glass to the brim. "Your father. He could have framed himself, taking the blame for an accident."

"An accident? Why would my father take the blame for an—"

"He would have if it was caused by one of his children."

It was one of those world-shattering moments when time slows down and nothing seems real. If Alexander Ryder was implying what I thought . . .

"Does the king think one of us killed his son? Is that why the motive was never revealed to the public? Is that why there are inconsistencies in his trial and the witnesses' memories were altered? Did my father trade his life for one of ours?"

Alexander Ryder didn't speak until his glass was empty. "Enough with the questions. We need to drink. We've been lacking on that part."

Kai's father never answered my last questions as we finished the bottle together. Instead he told me stories of my father from his earliest days to some of his last. I barely spoke the entire time, as I began to see my father as my hero again. Eventually, when we were both drunk and alone in the Grand Ballroom, two guardsmen took High Noble Ryder home. I sat by myself at that table for a while, staring through the windows at the stars, wondering what my father had endured, what choices he'd had to make, and whether he had known the same dull pain I felt in my heart.

Did I kill Davey Hollow?

STANDSTILL

I hated hospitals.

I had hated them ever since my first visits to my mother, shortly after her mind began to slip, when no one knew for certain why. I had spent days in them and their sharp sour smell still made me gag. I hated how plain and drab they all were, more like prison cells for the dying than a place for recovery. But, despite my hatred, there was someone I needed to see after what had happened last night.

Naomi's room was near the end of the hall, the last door on the left. I knocked before I slowly opened the door, peering in before I entered, and saw a man sitting next to her bed as she slept.

He didn't turn as I entered, and it was only when I was standing next to him that I saw his face. It was Bryan Dexter, Naomi's father, and the leader of the Evoker Division of Scales. He was a muscular middle-aged man with a permanent shadow of a beard, and his eyes were red and glassy from a lack of sleep.

"How is she doing?" I asked. Naomi was sleeping more peacefully than I thought someone who had just been shot might be. She didn't look like she was in much pain, though sleep was where the mind went to escape.

There was no response from her father at first, but after clearing his throat he said, "Stable. Sleeping. Lost a lot of blood. And there's still a high risk of infection. We won't know the full extent of the damage until much later, but she's alive. That Mercenary saved her life."

"I'm glad that he helped her."

"Me too." He paused to breathe deeply. "You're Michael Kingman, aren't you?"

"I am."

"I heard the prince shot her because he thought you two were in a relationship . . . Are you?"

"No," I said. "Not in a romantic way, at least."

He played with something in his hand. "Then why was she wearing your ring? I recognized it instantly, your father wore it . . . as did you for most of your young life. Don't try to lie and say it wasn't yours."

Despite standing over his injured daughter, I wasn't about to tell him how Naomi and I had begun our agreement to work together. Not unless I wanted to confess to violating my probation. "She was holding it as collateral. I owed her a favor and she was keeping it until the Endless Waltz ended."

Bryan Dexter made a clicking noise with his tongue. "My daughter probably wanted both the prince and a Kingman under her control," he said softly. "She was stupid to think that would work."

I didn't respond, unable to think of anything that wouldn't imply that I agreed with him.

Bryan returned my ring to me. "Take it. She has no need of it, and this will make sure you two can't be connected. Otherwise her reputation has no chance of recovery . . . Some of the prince's inner circle are already calling her the Kingman Whore."

"I'm sorry this happened to her."

"Me too, but she did this to herself," he said before tossing something to me. "Oh, and, Michael: Catch."

I caught a spent bullet. Likely the one that had nearly killed Naomi.

"If I ever see you with my daughter again, I'll put a bullet like that in your gut. I know my daughter was likely to blame for what happened, but I'm still her father. And I will protect her from anyone. Even if they're a Royal or a Kingman. Understand?"

"Understood, sir," I said as I pocketed the spent bullet.

"Leave us."

I did as I was told, eager to get away from Naomi's father before he lost some of his logic. On my way out, I slipped my father's ring back onto my middle finger, the familiar weight a relief after a long week.

LUNACY

The sun was already setting by the time me and my friends crossed over the western bridge to the Isle to see the verdict of the trial of the Emperor.

It had been going on since sunrise with the king, the Whisperer of the Church of the Eternal Flame, and High Noble Ata Morales presiding. A trial for treason was one of the few areas the Royals didn't have complete control over; King George the Paranoid had executed more than fifty people during his reign after making false accusations of treason, and the Kingman family had subsequently insisted any trial for treason required three judges, and so it had been.

The courthouse doors were barred, as no one was allowed to

leave until a decision was made, but we had decided to wait for the verdict with hundreds of others. We could see the crowds from the bridge, chanting or yelling for the Emperor's head. If the verdict was guilty, the Rebel Emperor would be taken straight to the execution block. He was too valuable a target to wait around in a jail cell and give the rebellion a chance to rescue him. They wanted to cut off the head of the rebellion with his death, hoping it would implode without him. Whether that would really happen remained to be seen.

Most of the people huddled outside were from the west side of Hollow, the jangle of coins in their pockets audible whenever they moved. Kingman Keep was visible to the south, the glow from the Moon's Tears beginning to emerge in the dwindling light. I didn't want to look at or even think about that place until I had time to clear my head and figure out what had happened, fearful I'd lose more if I didn't. Because if I continued to pursue the truth . . . would I discover I was the traitor instead of my father? Until last night, finding the truth simply meant absolving my father. Now it could mean implicating myself or one of my siblings instead. Was that worth it anymore? I didn't know.

Gwen found us a place to wait on the outskirts of the crowd. It was close enough to hear the verdict but far enough away that we weren't pressing our bodies against sweaty citizens who had been baking in the sun all day. There were dozens of armed Advocators patrolling the area. I wondered if they expected a riot or feared rebel sleeper agents in the crowd, waiting for a signal to attack. After the Militia Quarter was bombed, another attack of that magnitude wasn't improbable, and that fear explained why there weren't any nobles around—well, not that I could see, at least. Who knew who might be hiding in the courthouse? I was certain Lyon was in there.

Gwen and Kai were discussing something a bit away, so High Noble Margaux took a seat next to me, crossed her legs, and then said, "I'm worried about the verdict. I thought we would have it by midday."

"It'll be fine," I said, double-checking that Dark's envelope was in my inner jacket pocket. "Maybe they've spent the day recounting all of the crimes the Emperor has committed against the crown."

She nodded, eyes fixed on the courthouse.

"But you'd know how these trials go better than I would," I said. "The only trial I've ever had an active role in was my father's."

"I remember that one vividly." She pushed a few strands of hair behind her ear. "My father was on the jury, and he went prepared for a long, drawn-out affair that would divide the High Nobles between supporting the Kingman and Hollow families."

"I think everyone expected that. Then he shocked them all and pleaded guilty."

"'Shocked' is an understatement. It changed everything—and might have averted a civil war. But that's the past. How is Naomi doing? You saw her this morning, correct?"

High Noble Margaux had a knack for bringing up topics I didn't want to talk about.

"She's stable," I said. "It'll be hard to tell the extent of her injuries until much later though."

"Any infection?"

I shook my head. "Not at this moment, but there's still a high risk."

"Does she still have full range of mobility?"

"Not sure. Her father didn't say otherwise, so I assume so."

High Noble Margaux put her hand to her chin. "It might be hard to establish the damage until she's fully conscious and stable. Hopefully the bullet didn't hit her spine. She doesn't deserve to be paralyzed for the rest of her life because of the prince and a misunderstanding."

"How do you know so much about gunshot wounds?"

Her mouth was a straight line. "I spent more of my life in hospitals than in my own keep. I listened and learned a lot."

"Why were you in hospitals so much? Does it have something to do with why you fell at the king's party when I nullified everything?"

She opened her mouth slightly, prepared to respond, but instead closed her eyes and sighed. "It is a long story. And one I shouldn't tell you until you remember who I am. No matter what you say, you would see me differently, and I don't want to stop pretending yet."

"But I do know who you are. You're High Noble Margaux."

"Shit," she said with a laugh. "I completely forgot Naomi said my name in front of you. What a pain." A pause. "Maybe I should continue this until you remember my familiar name."

"Isn't the point of not telling me your name already ruined?"

She lay down on the stone with an arm extended, as if trying to hold the sky in her palm. "It is, but I like having someone who doesn't care about my title. Kai would tell you the same, but as High Nobles we don't have many people we can consider close friends. Everyone around us only wants more power or more money or more land and will do whatever they can to get it. It makes one true friend more valuable than all the gold in the treasury."

"Is that why you two were so nice to me? You wanted me to be your friend?"

"Obviously."

"We haven't talked in a decade. What makes you think I'm still the person I was when we were children?"

"Because you're Michael Kingman," she said, meeting my eyes. "You've always been fiercely protective of those you view as family. And all we want is to be considered your family again."

After a pause I said, "Here I was thinking you wanted to court me."

High Noble Margaux started laughing. And laughing. And laughing long past when I began to blush and feel uncomfortable sitting next to her.

When she found her breath again, she said, "Oh, Michael, never. Not even when we were young and I was in awe of you and the stories you'd tell me. You were always a friend to me. Nothing more. If for some reason I did find you mildly attractive, you were always meant for another."

"Another?"

She chuckled to herself. "She'll tell you when she wants you to know. We should join Gwen and Kai before you get me into trouble."

Frustrated, but knowing she wouldn't say anything more, we walked over to Gwen and Kai. Both were watching the courthouse with their arms folded.

The executioner's block had been placed there, giving off a dull shine even in the low light. Despite its modest size, it loomed over the crowds like a lighthouse in a storm. Someone had clearly decided that the Rebel Emperor should die like a noble, not swing like a commoner, if he was found guilty. I suppose any man who called himself an emperor and led an army against Hollow deserved as much. I noticed that the Wardens, the metal monsters of Scales, were positioned at the bottom of the stairs, holding back the crowds. They almost never came out in public.

"Wasn't expecting Wardens here today," I said. "What do you think they got for being here?"

"I'm unsure," Kai said. "They're not trying to hide the fact that there might be riots after the verdict, are they?"

"No. They are not," High Noble Margaux said.

"We should be ready to leave quickly if fighting breaks out. I don't want to get stuck on the Isle."

"We could always take refuge in Kingman Keep," I said.

My sister stifled a laugh as they looked at me.

"It was a joke."

Some people had no sense of humor these—

The courthouse doors swung open and the crowd went silent. Even the Wardens and other Scales operatives looked toward the door as a stunning woman strode out. It was the Emperor, unchained and unbound, flanked by two rebels with a closed red fist on their clothes.

It was her.

The woman who had knelt in front of my father's grave. I should have realized she was the Emperor, not the lemon-smelling man; they had all been listening to her, after all.

The shockingly young woman, covered in fresh bruises and shallow open wounds, walked like a conquering hero instead of a terrorist, dressed in a plain flowing dress of red and grey, my family's colors. If the choice hadn't been intentional before, it was now. No one walked out of a trial for treason in Kingman colors without knowing they were making a statement.

And then I saw the Sacrifice brand on her neck.

It finally clicked.

The Rebel Emperor was Emelia Bryson, daughter of Lothar Bryson, former guard captain at Kingman Keep and attempted assassin of the Corrupt Prince. Seeing her in my family's colors with the Sacrifice brand on her neck, I remembered her, a forgotten memory stowed away. She had been Gwen's friend and, at one point, the subject of Lyon's admiration. She had grown up alongside us and dreamed with us, and she was as much a member of the Kingman family as any of my siblings. Only she had risen from Sacrifice to become the leader of the rebellion against those who had unjustly branded her—and those who had said nothing as they did.

The king had created her. And because of his orders, she had started a rebellion that had killed thousands. A rebellion to right a wrong. Based on what Lothar had said, how the rebels seemed to idolize my father—and what she had said in the graveyard—she probably thought she was acting as my father's successor.

I felt sick. Would she contribute to my family's legacy?

The Kingman is a traitor. Cut off his head.

"Oh my God," High Noble Margaux said, covering her hand with her mouth. "The Emperor's a woman. And so young at that . . . She can't be much older than we are. A few years at most."

"All of us High Nobles were told something completely different. Why did they keep the truth hidden?" Kai muttered. "Was it because she was a Sacrifice? Michael, Gwen, do either of you recognize her?"

Gwen stood perfectly straight, gripping my arm, her attention fully focused on the Emperor. I didn't respond due to cowardice and the childish belief that if I didn't acknowledge her, she would disappear.

It didn't work.

The Emperor stopped at the top of the stairs and shouted, "Today is a historic day for the free states of Hollow! Your government has blamed me for everything these past seven years, but today they have failed to convict me! Two of my three judges have declined to convict me, the leader of an open rebellion against your king! Ask yourselves what else they have falsely been blaming the rebels for! The attack on the colosseum? The fall of Naverre? The burning of the Shrine of the Patron Victoria? The Farmlands Massacre? What other lies have they spread to advance their own ill-gotten delusions of grandeur? Seek the truth! Reject the lies they've fed to you!"

There were growing murmurs throughout the crowd as my friends and sister seethed next to me. I put my hands behind my head. Was I to blame for this? Had burning down the shrine destroyed the case against the Rebel Emperor? Or was she speaking the truth?

King Isaac stood in the doorway of the courthouse with his Ravens around him. He ran his hands through his frizzy red hair and then approached the Emperor as she continued to denounce other offenses she had been blamed for. The crowd had fallen silent, in awe of the scarred woman who seemed anything but a rebel mastermind.

"—lies and more lies! Don't listen to what they say! Find the truth for yourself! The truth that David Kingman died for!" She paused as King Isaac walked past her and down the steps of the courthouse. The crowd remained silent, the only noise around was the sound of the king and his Ravens walking down the steps. *Clap. Clap. Clap.*

"This is the man you call your king! A coward who can't even face the woman he longed to execute mere moments ago! A man who sends the young to die for a meaningless cause! Yet lets his only daughter lounge around her mother's walled city on the Gold Coast and allows his remaining son to act like the city is his personal brothel! Is this the man we want to represent us? A man who can't even control his own children? A man who branded children for the crimes of their fathers? A man who has brought nothing but war to Hollow? And a man who has banned a new military weapon because he doesn't like it? Can you not see this pathetic excuse for a man? Think about how much better we would do without him! There is no hope for Hollow with him in charge!"

King Isaac never stopped to address the Emperor. The Wardens parted for him and he, along with his Ravens, hopped into a waiting carriage. No one did anything to stop him. Not even the Emperor said anything else. King Isaac just left. He didn't even have the courage to say anything in response . . . or maybe it was an act of bravery to walk away. I didn't know.

Once King Isaac was out of sight, the Emperor continued her tirade. "I ask you to question everything! Don't blindly follow the lies of this pathetic king that you all swear fealty to! Find the truth! The days of the Royals and the other High Noble families are over! This is our city! Our country! Our rebellion! Let's take back what is ours!"

Kai tapped me on the shoulder. "We should go—we don't want to be here if a riot starts."

He was right. As much as I expected nothing to happen, it was hard to—

A gunshot rang out throughout the crowd.

Screams followed soon after as pandemonium came from the courthouse.

I looked toward the Emperor. She stood smiling at the top of the courthouse, watching all the citizens below her flee in terror. There was a rebel at the bottom of the steps with a bright red dot in the middle of his chest. Within moments Wardens had beheaded whoever had shot him.

How was she allowed to speak freely in front of the crowd? Why hadn't they stopped her? What had happened in that courtroom that two people found her innocent of treason? And what was she after? If her target was the king, wouldn't she have taken a shot at him when he passed? Had I misinterpreted her—

"Michael!" Kai said. "We need to leave!"

We did. On our way out of the Isle, we walked in silence and took as many alleyways as possible to avoid the crowds. As the others crossed the bridge to western Hollow, I paused to look back. There was still a big crowd outside the courthouse struggling to get away, Advocators forcing everyone into single file to check for guns before they could.

I don't know why that bothered me so much. But it did.

We kept looking back toward the Isle, expecting the crowds to catch up to us, but they never did. By the time we reached my house in the Narrows, it was clear that Scales wouldn't let the riots spread beyond the Isle. It was a relief for all of us.

Gwen's hand was shaking as she put it on the doorknob. "They should have killed her."

None of us said anything.

"Does that make me a bad person?" she asked. "That I wish they had killed her, even if two of them found her innocent? My father had less evidence against him than she did, so I don't get why she gets to live when he didn't. Her head should be rolling down those steps."

High Noble Margaux ran her fingers down her arm. "Gwen, we should go inside. It'll be easier to talk in there."

"No," she said, taking her hand off the doorknob. "I'm not going to stand by and let the Emperor get away with mass murder. I'm going to deal with her myself. As I should have with the Corrupt Prince last night."

"That's murder, Gwen," Kai declared. "And watch your tongue. It's treason to threaten the prince, no matter if everyone agrees with you."

"So?"

"So they'd execute you for touching either of them! I doubt you'll get off because of her Sacrifice brand—not after they recognized her as a citizen of Hollow by putting her on trial."

"I don't care," she seethed. "If she's dead, then I can stop her from killing others and using my father's name as a rallying cry for rebellion. I'm already marked as a traitor, so who cares about my life if I can save—"

High Noble Margaux slapped Gwen, silencing her mid-sentence.

Gwen was so shocked at the slap, she didn't even move her hand to the red mark that was beginning to appear on her cheek.

"Your life," she began, voice rising, "is important. All our lives are important—from the guards in my keep to the dye pit workers on the East Side. Don't throw it away just because you're angry at some bitch in red and grey. What would your father think of that? If you want to stop her, change the country. Ensure that we never see another rebellion like this again. If you're angry with the Corrupt Prince, aid the princess so he never sees the throne. You are a Kingman, and sacrificing your life would be pointless and cowardly. Do you understand me? Or should I explain it again?"

No one responded at first, all three of us glancing at each other instead.

"Do you understand me?" she repeated, staring at Gwen.

Gwen nodded, the anger that had its hold on her long gone.

"Say it."

"I understand. I won't throw my life away trying to get revenge against the Emperor or the Corrupt Prince."

"Good. Now let's go inside, get a drink, and . . ." She trailed off, noticing a letter stuck between the door and the frame. She pulled it out, saw my name, and then handed it to me, wordlessly.

It was written in a scratchy short script I wasn't familiar with. I opened the envelope and pulled out the letter. In black ink it read:

I have your friend.
Don't miss our appointment tonight or
he'll get a bullet in the back of his head before
I throw him in the river.

I didn't hear myself scream, but, judging from how everyone re-acted, it was clear I had.

My friends and sister were at my side in an instant, asking me what had happened and what was wrong. I couldn't speak. I pulled at my hair hard enough to rip some out. Dark had Sirash. There was no one else it could be. Dark had found Sirash and taken him hostage. This was my nightmare.

High Noble Margaux grabbed me and forced me to look her in the eyes. "Michael, what happened?"

I slammed the note against her chest and walked away. I couldn't breathe as she read it aloud. It felt so hot out here.

"Michael, who is that note from? Who do they have?" Kai asked.

"It's from a Mercenary," I said, my breath ragged. "He hired Sirash and me to steal some documents. There was an ambush and I escaped with them, and he's been hounding me for them ever since. I was going to return them last night, but . . . Naomi and ev-erything with the prince happened and he accepted a deal with a Raven and . . . and . . . and he has my friend."

It was High Noble Margaux's turn to scream. "Michael! You stole from a Mercenary? What did you think was going to happen? Are you insane?"

"As unlikely as it sounds, it was an accident."

"How?" she questioned.

"Who does he have?" my sister said.

"Sirash."

"Shit. Are Arjay and Jean safe?"

"Not really."

"Wait," High Noble Margaux said. "This Mercenary is holding one of your friends hostage?"

Another nod. "He must've taken him after Domet had him released from jail."

"Jail? Why was he in jail?"

"Domet? What does he have to do with this?"

Everyone was asking their questions at the same time. My head was pounding. I couldn't focus and held up a hand for them all to stop.

"I made a deal with Domet to free him. It was one of the conditions of me participating in the Endless Waltz."

"Domet wanted you to participate in the Endless Waltz?" Kai said.

High Noble Margaux was shaking her head. "Michael, we can't help you unless you tell us everything."

I steadied my breath and looked at them. She was right. It was like they were participating in the Endless Waltz without understanding who belonged to the Royal Family. It wasn't fair to expect them to know or understand everything when they were playing at a disadvantage. If I wanted their help, they needed to know everything. Maybe if I had trusted any of them earlier, one of them could have helped before it reached this point.

I did the only thing I could do. I told them the truth about everything.

I didn't skip a single detail.

I began at the beginning, as all stories should, with how I had met Domet and the deal we had formed out of a mutual interest instead of a friendship. From there I went on to detail how I had met Dark and accidentally stolen his documents, and lost Sirash in the process. After that it was Naomi and how she had begun to black-mail me during the Endless Waltz to suit her own agenda. With an idea of what I had been dealing with during the Endless Waltz, I explained all the minor interactions I had dealt with that they might not have been aware of. I spoke without pause and told them every-thing. Even how I had watched Trey's brother die in front of me and how I had given Dark's name as the culprit who had burned down the shrine.

The only things I withheld were the burning of the shrine and Domet's immortality. Both were my burdens to bear, not theirs, and, given how much I had to share, it wasn't hard to omit those details. They bought it. Maybe they suspected I was hiding something, but none of them questioned my story. There was too much else to focus on instead.

They sat in silence afterward. The only sound around us was the flickering of the fire burning in the lights and a gentle wind whistling through the spaces between the buildings.

Gwen spoke first. "Michael, that's . . . a lot."

I kicked at the ground, wondering if they saw me differently. I wasn't a traitor before I had told them the story, but I might be one now, considering I had wanted to steal from the king and help Domet prove my father had been framed for the murder of Davey Hollow.

"Is that everything?" Kai asked.

I nodded. "That's everything."

There was more silence. I couldn't keep still, kicking at the ground and pacing back and forth. I wanted someone to say some-thing. Anything.

"None of that explains why the Mercenary went after Sirash if you two were supposed to meet tonight," Gwen said.

"Maybe Dark knows Domet believes he burned down the shrine?" Kai asked. "This could be his revenge."

I shook my head. "Domet wouldn't have acted that quickly."

"What else could it be?"

"I don't know," my sister said, "but it doesn't make sense. Domet's too calculating to rush something. He wouldn't have—"

"The ring."

We all turned to High Noble Margaux. It was the first time she had spoken since hearing my story.

"The ring you said was in the envelope? It's about that. Someone else must want it; that's why Dark is so determined to get it tonight. Whoever else is after it must have figured out he doesn't have it."

"What're you talking about?" Kai asked. "It's a ring. Why would a Mercenary care about a ring more than dozens of incriminating documents?"

"Most of them were about my family, too," I added.

"How do you hide something you don't want people to find? Put it in plain sight. What's better to hide something in than a bunch of documents about the traitorous Kingman family?"

It couldn't have been that simple. She had to be wrong.

"Think about it," High Noble Margaux continued. "You said something was off about him after he found out who you really were the night you met. He was probably running through the variables of bringing a Kingman to an exchange of documents about the Kingman family. He killed the person who knew the contents but let the one who saw a Kingman and Mercenary together live.

"Anyone who investigated the contents would assume you were the one looking for information about Davey Hollow's murder and that you hired the Mercenary to facilitate the deal. They'd have to investigate you. The king might even order them to devote an entire division of Scales to it . . . but no one would think twice about the Mercenary who was there that night. Even if they were initially there for him, you'd become the focus and he'd get away with his ring. Unnoticed."

"He couldn't have planned for that," Kai said.

"He didn't. He got lucky and stumbled upon Michael, then took advantage of it."

"You think he did all of that for a ring?"

High Noble Margaux nodded. "Unless he's secretly a member of your family, I doubt anyone else would kill for a page of the investigation into Davey Hollow's murder or for a handwritten account of the Day of Crowning. Do you have the ring with you, Michael?"

I reached into my pocket, took the ring from the envelope, and handed it to her.

She held it up to the light and gasped as the light passed straight through it. All the colors in the rainbow radiated from it. "You are so dense, Michael. Do you realize what this is?"

It was a glass ring. What was important about that? I asked as much.

"A glass ring is popular as an engagement ring in the Warring States and on the Gold Coast," she said. "It's been gaining some traction in the Hollow Court, though most still use the memory tattoo. How did you miss this inscription around the inside? Did you even look at it, Michael?"

"What does it say?" I asked.

"*To the light of my life, forever will I be yours.*"

"So this ring is his?"

"No," she said. "Women wear glass rings. I'd wager this is for someone he loves. That's why he did so much to get it—and why he's still after you."

"But you suggested someone else might be after it, too. Who else would want it?"

"Maybe it was his mother's ring," High Noble Margaux offered. "I don't know."

Suddenly I saw Dark's comment about his father in a different light. If it was his mother's ring, and his father wanted it back, it would explain why he had been so cautious about retrieving it at first, and how determined he was now that so much time had passed. I wondered how powerful his father must be to make a Mercenary nervous.

Whether High Noble Margaux was right or not, I still had to bring Sirash home. No Mercenary was getting in my way.

I had tried to play according to everyone else's rules and failed.

Now everyone was going to play by mine.

"I need to get to Kingman Keep before Lights Out."

"Well," Gwen said, rising to her feet and clapping her hands, "we'd better be off, then. Who knows what has happened on the Isle since we left."

"Scales has probably blocked the bridges off," Kai said.

High Noble Margaux gave the ring back to me. "We'll find a way. But, more importantly, we have the upper hand now," she said. "We know what he really wants."

I felt the weight of the glass ring in my palm, amazed at how much effort Dark had gone through for something so small. "You don't have to come with me. This isn't your problem."

Kai laughed at me. "You can't use your Fabrications reliably and you'll need all of us if it gets ugly. Especially if he can use two types of Fabrications. Anyway, I gave up my eyes to save a friend once; I'm not scared to help save someone else. I know the risks of using Fabrications better than most."

"And stop being so dramatic," my sister said with a wide smile. "Sirash is family, and family is there for family."

Maybe my burdens weren't mine to carry alone.

It was time to bring Sirash home.

YEARNING

I clung to the edges of the rowboat, splinters digging into my hands as we floated down the gentle river toward Kingman Keep.

This wasn't my idea, but we had exhausted every other option. The bridge to the Isle was blocked off by Advocators, we didn't have the time to walk around to the other one, and neither High Noble Margaux nor Kai could use their status to help—they'd risk being escorted home for their own safety. So we had traded a dimmer four bottles of wine from our house for his rotting old boat, some rope, and a lantern. It was the only viable way to get to Kingman Keep in time. It helped that it would give us an element of surprise, as Dark would expect me to come through the servants' entrance. Coming by boat, we would be able to enter through the waterway, creep up through the basement, and catch him off guard. That was our plan, at least.

Hopefully I wouldn't drown before we got there.

I had almost drowned too many times recently for my own liking.

As I clung to the sides, my friends navigated down the river without light, the mist enveloping us. High Noble Margaux was working the rudder while Gwen rowed. Kai was sitting across from me, holding the unlit lantern close to his chest, breathing steadily. It was cold and dark out on the water, and none of us were really dressed for it, but we weren't willing to risk using the light in case we were seen. We went slowly, navigating carefully. So long as we didn't go too far and hit the rocks, we would be fine.

Hopefully.

As we neared Kingman Keep, it struck me how much more intimidating it was from the water than from the land. From here it looked like a decrepit pillar of stone extending far into the sky, the top hidden by the mist and clouds. Even the Moon's Tears did little to soften its appearance. High Noble Margaux turned to me. "Michael, Gwen, do either of you remember where the water entrance is?"

I pointed to the bend in the river, upstream from pointed rocks that could shred flesh from bone faster than a butcher. "Stay by the bank close to the Isle. It's just past the bend." I took the rope in my hands. "Once I get this around the post, we'll be fine."

No one responded. They were all concentrating. If I didn't get this right . . . well, we would all be taking a dip in the water tonight.

Hopefully they were better swimmers than me and Gwen.

I was hoping for a lot of things tonight.

That probably wasn't a good sign of my chances.

The water crashed against the rocks ahead of us as High Noble Margaux and Gwen maneuvered the boat to the edge of the river, struggling against the increasing current. Kai held the other end of the rope, fumbling and cursing as he tied it to the boat. Moments after it was tethered, it rocked violently. Gwen and High Noble Margaux cursed and adjusted as Kai and I grabbed the sides for support. The current was getting stronger, propelling us faster as more and more water splashed over the sides. Kai bailed the boat out with his hands as I went to the side, waiting for us to turn the corner toward the water entrance.

That's when the waves hit the boat full on the side and I went over. It felt like a gunshot when my face hit. Water went up my nose and down my throat and burned like coals and I gripped the rope for dear life and sank back into the darkness of the water. I kicked for the surface as shadows nipped at my ankles, trying to force me down, and felt a pocket of warmth spread from the center of my chest and down to my legs. Someone was pulling on the rope as I struggled upward until my head broke the surface. Such a bittersweet breath came when it did. Right before my shoulder slammed hard against the boat, sharp pain tingling through it.

"We're going to hit the rocks!" High Noble Margaux shouted as she steered the boat to the left. "Throw the rope!"

My head bobbed up and down in the current. I couldn't get an accurate throw from the water. I had to try something else. As I wrapped the rope around my wrist and hand, I grabbed the side of the boat and then pushed myself off it toward the entrance. I went under again, but this time I didn't feel cold or scared, the pleasant warmth on my body giving me courage despite the current dragging the boat—and me—further down the river. I couldn't see anything underwater, in the dark, but I felt it when my back hit the dock and I grabbed the edge of it and pulled myself up. I was just in time: the rope went taut, yanking me back toward the boat. Pain ran through my tongue as I bit down on it, planted my feet on the dock, and pulled, head down and screaming. The rope burned my hands as the current tried to pull it away.

I looked up, expecting to see the boat. Instead, High Noble Margaux broke the surface of the water and climbed onto the dock moments later. She helped me pull Gwen and Kai out of the water. When they were on the dock, I let the rope go and it flew out of my hands, leaving a bright red, snaking burn behind.

I collapsed onto the dock laughing as my friends composed themselves. Kai coughed up water as High Noble Margaux patted him on the back. We were all alive, and I was grateful, and the river seemed calmer now that we weren't on it. The rough waves that had crashed against the nearby rocks seemed like a gentle sway from here. Everything had changed so fast, but it turned out it was man-ageable when I wasn't alone.

"Where's the boat?" I asked, standing up. The dock creaked be-neath me.

High Noble Margaux pounded her fist against her chest and then pointed to the nearby rocks. "Hit the rocks when you were under. Blasted to bits . . . we all grabbed the rope and hoped you got to land. When did you learn how to swim?"

"I didn't." I coughed. "Learned not to drown."

Kai chuckled from his prone position, leaning over the dock. "I'm never going near the water again."

I started to inspect the metal grate blocking the entrance, shaking the bars. They were sturdy, and there wasn't much rust. It wasn't old enough that it would break from just my hands alone. "How are we supposed to—"

High Noble Margaux waved me out of the way. She rolled back her sleeves, and then punched through the metal lock holding the door in place. It was more brittle than I thought, or she was much stronger. It was hard to know for certain. Things were always muddled around her. She swung the door open and looked back at us. "You three coming?"

We entered the keep through the basement, a steady stream of water lapping gently against the bricks of the walkway. Moss covered the brick above the waterline and everything smelled damp as we crept toward the upper floors. Nothing was locked, but just as I was about to head upstairs to the main hall, Kai grabbed my shoulder and said, "Hold on, Michael."

"What?"

"We need a plan in case everything goes wrong up there."

I paused. "If someone gets shot, hit the Mercenary until he falls down and doesn't get up again."

Kai shook his head and we continued up the stairs until I could open the door a crack. Beyond, there was a fire in the hearth that was out of control. Dark sat in front of it, prodding it with a poker as shadows danced all over the walls. There was a still body next to the hearth. I couldn't see his face, but I knew it was Sirash . . . it had to be him. If only I could see his chest rise to know he was well.

The moment I stepped into the main hall, Dark shouted, "You're early, Michael. You must've received my letter."

I signaled for everyone to wait behind the door, and they backed away while I took a breath and advanced further into the main hall. "Didn't want to be late! There's a blockade on the Isle. Something about a trial. Not sure if you heard about it while you were busy kidnapping my friend."

The fire crackled. "The first time we were here you made a mistake: you took something that belonged to me. I gave you multiple opportunities to return it, so this time I ensured you couldn't run unless you were willing to lose a friend."

"I was always going to return it."

"Then your friend has nothing to worry about," he said. "So long as you give me what's mine."

"I have it," I said, heart racing, "but you wanted to frame me, didn't you? You wanted me to take the fall for what was in the envelope, so let's stop the runaround and all the games. Lay your cards bare and tell me what's so important about this ring."

Dark didn't stop looking at the fire despite lowering the poker to his side. "Lay your cards bare? You've never been this confident before, Michael. I wonder what's changed . . . but don't flatter yourself. Any fool could have seen that the ring was what I wanted, although it took you longer to figure that out, so what . . . ah, tell your companions to come out and say hello. The Ryder, Margaux, and the other. Have some manners, Michael."

I cursed under my breath as they all emerged, and we stood in a ragged line.

Dark still hadn't turned around yet. For a moment the only sound in the keep was the crackling fire and our footsteps, and then slowly, and with a groan, he slapped his hands against his thighs and rose to his feet. He cracked his knuckles and then stretched his arms.

"I'll take my ring back."

"How do I know you won't hurt Sirash once you have it?"

"Because I would have killed him already if I didn't plan to let him live. Just saying I had him was enough to make you come running."

He wasn't wrong. "How do you want to do this?"

Dark extended an empty palm toward me. "Hand it to me, and you can have your friend back."

I felt the warmth slither over my skin again, nullifying my body on reflex. I didn't quite know how it worked, but it seemed like the right thing to do. After nodding to Gwen, I walked toward Dark, the distance between us seemingly vast. I'd seen what he could do; I'd seen the sheer carnage he wrought on a brigade of Scales. But I wasn't going to put my head down as I walked toward him. I had to be brave—if not for myself then for Sirash. I wouldn't let him see my fear, those days were behind me. I was a Kingman, and I had people to protect.

I put the glass ring in the center of his palm.

Dark closed his hand slowly around it. He closed his eyes, muttered something to himself, and then said, "Well, that's that, then. Your friend is all yours and our business is concluded. If you had only done this days ago, I wouldn't have been forced to kidnap your friend and threaten your family. Apologize to your siblings for me."

I didn't care what Dark had to say; I was already kneeling by Sirash.

He was still leaning against the stone next to the hearth. His eyes were closed but his breathing was steady. That was the only thing that looked right about him, though. Half-healed, jagged scars covered his body and his right cheek was badly burned, the scab still red and flaky. His copper skin was pale and he seemed leaner, all skin and bone and muscle.

I ran my hand over his good cheek, and he inhaled sharply, winced, and turned away from me. He looked mangled, malnourished, and broken. If only I'd gotten to him sooner.

The warmth remained on my body as I rose to meet Dark again. "Did you do this to him?"

Dark shook his head. "Found him like that when they were transporting him out of the dungeons. The Executioner Division must've grabbed him when he tried to escape that night. Unfortunate, since they were most likely torturing him for information about me, which, clearly, he didn't have. On the bright side, he's probably the first person to ever make it out of the castle dungeons alive."

"Why would someone in the castle care about a Mercenary like you? It's not as if they can arrest you for crimes against the country."

"They can still kill me. Or attempt to. You've seen what happens when they try." Dark held his hands over the fire. My friends were beginning to cross the distance between us now that it was clear he wasn't looking for a fight.

"That doesn't answer my question."

"Nor was it supposed to."

"It's your father, isn't it? You want to keep your mother's ring from him; he's the one you wanted Trey to kill. Is your father scared you could be traced back to him? Is that why Scales sent a squad after you? Did someone pull some strings to try and take you out?"

Dark didn't respond, still staring into the fire.

As the flames danced across his face, I realized that, despite his dark hair and his grey eyes, he spoke and carried himself a little like a High Noble from Hollow. It could be something he'd learned from a young age . . . and it wasn't impossible that Dark was a bastard son of one of the High Noble families. There were always rumors, and if hundreds were speculated upon, the odds were one had to be true. If Dark was illegitimate, it would explain why his father was after him and the ring: a bastard son, a Mercenary no less, would be shameful in their civilized society. It might compel the father to destroy any trace of their connection.

"Who is your father?" I asked.

For the second time he didn't respond, offering only a slight upward curl of a lip to indicate he had heard me.

My friends had reached us. High Noble Margaux and Gwen went to check on Sirash, both knowing more about medicine than I did. Kai stayed with me. Dark had begun to pack up his things, seemingly uninterested in anything that would happen from here on out. He had what he had come for; nothing else mattered.

There was little I could do but watch both scenes unfold in front of me, unable to contribute to either. Anxious, I played with the spent bullet Naomi's father had given me. It still amazed me that this stupid little metal thing had caused so much damage. It barely seemed significant in a world populated by children who could summon hurricanes and adults who could spin lies that eclipsed the truth. And yet bullets and guns and gunpowder had been hailed as the great equalizer of our world, reducing those who used magic to the same page as everyone else.

It was no wonder they had been outlawed in Hollow. The nobility wanted to retain power and gunpowder diminished them to humans masquerading as gods instead of the forces of nature they had seemed before. It amazed me that people had the audacity to mark them. It was as if they wanted people to know who had created them and who was responsible for the devastation they caused. Even this one was marked, with a crown being ripped apart at the side by a pair of hands.

My heart stopped.

A crown being ripped apart . . . the same etching that was on the bullet that killed Davey Hollow. I'd read about it. And this bullet had to have been custom-made for the gun; it wouldn't fit any other. But it was impossible. The gun that killed Davey was a one-of-a-kind. How could Dark have one that could shoot the same bullet? Either his gun had killed Davey or it had a twin . . . a twin that could be connected back to the person who had the gun, or guns, before they had been used to kill Davey.

This entire time Dark had exactly what I was looking for. A gun that I had seen repeatedly while being unaware of its significance, though it had nearly killed me and had wounded Naomi. A gun of unknown origin that might belong to a High Noble's bastard son . . . and which might have been used to kill—

I pushed those thoughts aside, unable to deal with them.

All I knew for certain was that Dark had a connection to my father and Davey Hollow's murder. If I could get his gun, I could convince Gwen it was the one that had murdered Davey and finally give her some peace. We could leave Hollow . . .

. . . but, after all this, would I be able to leave Hollow without knowing for certain my father was guilty? It wasn't just the ramblings of a drunk Immortal anymore. Respectable members of noble society believed it, too, and didn't I have a duty to find the truth . . . as a Kingman and as a son?

Sadly, there was only one way to learn it.

"Dark. Hold on. I need your help."

The Mercenary turned to me, as did the others.

"I want to hire you to break me into the Royal Tower of Hollow Castle."

My family may have been at war with God for generations, and I distrusted organized religion, but it still felt like making a deal with a daemon when Dark smiled and said, "Tell me more."

IMPASSE

Needless to say, everyone thought I was batshit crazy.

Gwen was the loudest. "Michael, what the fuck? You want to break into the castle with a Mercenary?"

"He kidnapped your friend!" Kai added.

"I'm just as surprised as you are," Dark said. "But I won't turn him down if he wants to hire me. They can't charge me the same way they can him." He had a dagger in hand.

High Noble Margaux was quiet, still examining Sirash as she listened to the conversation.

"I don't have any other option," I said. "I have to break into the castle and I need his help to do it."

"It's treason, Michael," Kai said. "If you get caught, you'll be executed before first light."

"Maybe. But I punched the Corrupt Prince last night, and nothing has happened to me yet."

"Yet," Kai declared. "No doubt he's planning something to get back at you and Gwen."

"What do you want in the castle so much that you're considering hiring a Mercenary to help you get it?" Dark asked.

"The truth about what happened to my father. The reason he confessed and pleaded guilty was never released to the public, and if it was recorded anywhere, it'll be in the king's memories. I'm tired of being ashamed of my last name. I need to know what really happened," I explained.

"As interesting as that sounds, I—"

"And I want to know more about your gun."

"My gun?"

"It's either the gun that killed Davey Hollow—which was supposed to be one-of-a-kind—or its twin," I said. "Anything you can tell me about it could lead back to the person who framed my father. If someone did."

"What?" I heard my sister whisper.

The Mercenary ignored her. "Why would I tell you anything about my gun? What's in it for me?"

"Consider it part of our deal."

Everyone was silent.

"Walk with me and we'll talk. Alone."

I was astonished as I followed Dark into my former room. That had worked? Holy shit, that had worked! How had that worked?

"You don't think it was me? Have you considered that I might be responsible for your father's and Davey Hollow's death?"

I looked him up and down. He was a Mercenary, an enigma, and a nightmare. But I knew it wasn't him. He was too young—only a few years older than I was. Why would a child murder a prince and frame my father for it? I was looking for someone like him, for sure. Only older.

"No, I don't."

"Why n—"

"I'm not looking to manipulate someone. I just want the truth. Is that the gun that killed Davey Hollow, or its twin?"

Dark reached under his jacket and pulled out the gun. After a slight pause, he flipped the butt toward me. "Consider this an apology for not taking the gun away from the prince sooner. This gun is the twin."

I took the pistol from him. It was a single-action long-barreled pistol with a bone grip. It was nicked and marked but felt smooth to the touch. It could hold six bullets in a cylinder compartment and was a little weightier than I expected, and the bullets in it were different. It didn't need black powder as the others did. It was special. And its twin had killed Davey Hollow.

"Why is this gun so much more advanced than any of the others I've seen before?"

"It's called a revolver, and it's a prototype. There's only one other like it."

"How did you get it?"

"I stole it from a nobody who claimed to have made it."

"To have made both of them?"

"Yes. But he was lying."

"How do you know? Who was it?"

Dark held out his hand for the gun. Once he had it again, he said, "Someone long since dead."

"Tell me."

"What're you going to do, Michael? Dig up his grave? Track down his next of kin? Try to find some clue in his life that may or may not advance your agenda? That's not how it works. There's no proof he made them, he can't admit it, and, like I said, he probably lied about it anyway. There's no one left alive who knows who made them."

"Someone must."

Dark shook his head as he holstered his revolver. "Go home, Michael. Kiss a girl, laugh with your friends, and hug whatever family you have left. Grow up and act like you're worthy of the life you keep trying to throw away."

He began to walk away, uninterested in the job I had proposed to him. Only I couldn't let him leave, not when I was so close. One more clue. That's all it would take. Just one more. So, instead of relying on logic, I took a chance and said, "All I want is to get into the Royal Tower. Name your price."

He turned, and his cold eyes stared straight into mine . . . cold, and yet there was a life behind them. A look I couldn't quite explain, like why that ring was so important to him. "Are you certain you want to say those words to me?"

"Yes," I said. I had never said a word so quickly or confidently before. It was like striking iron and commanding thunder in one word. It felt good.

"Imbecile. You know it will never be as simple as you think it will be."

"I didn't ask for a lecture," I said. "Name your price or go. I'll do it on my own if I have to."

Which was a complete and utter lie, but he didn't know that.

Dark crossed his arms and looked at me silently. Maybe he was judging me or assessing how serious I was. Breaking into the castle wasn't going to be easy. Even if we got in and out without trouble, someone would come after us. And with the entire city under curfew and security tightened after the riots on the Isle, it was a terrible night to try it. It would be impossible to get to the castle without being spotted. By all logic, it would be the worst night to do so. But I had to. I had to know the truth if I was going to leave Hollow.

"Besides storming through the front door, I don't know any other way into the castle," he said slowly. "Would your friend know?"

"Who?"

"Whatever his name is. Burn boy. The one who was tortured."

Sirash? Was he talking about Sirash? "How would he know a way in?"

"He wouldn't—not intentionally," Dark said. "But he was being held in the dungeons beneath the castle, and I've heard rumors of secret pathways all over that monstrosity. I wouldn't be surprised if there was a water entrance just like the one in this keep. But without knowing where it emerges, it's suicide. We'd be walking in blind."

"What makes you think Sirash would know where this waterway leads? Or want to help us? He's been through enough. I don't want to put him into any more danger."

"It's his life," Dark said. "He can choose for himself."

"If Sirash knew there was a way into the castle . . . would it be feasible?"

He crossed his arms. "The king's memories are most likely in the Royal Tower. And with the riots, King Isaac has probably been evacuated somewhere safe and private that the rebels wouldn't know of. So it's possible you could get in there and find the information without being caught."

"You know the way to it?"

"I have a good guess."

"What do you want in exchange?"

"A sample of your blood."

A sample of my blood? I opened my mouth to question why, but it wouldn't matter, I would agree no matter what.

"Done," I said. "I'll talk to Sirash. But before I do, I've seen you use both Ice and Darkness. How do you have two Fabrication specializations?"

He chuckled. "For a Kingman, you really are ignorant of how the world works."

"No I'm not."

"Oh, really?" he mocked. "Can you tell the difference between Gold Coast clans' masks? Can you distinguish between a gun made in New Dracon City and one made in Eham? What about the difference between someone in the Warring States that identifies as a Winter man compared to a Summer man? Can you answer any of my questions?"

"It's been a long—"

"Michael, I'll tell you this much: if you think Fabricators are the only thing the Royalty and Emperor fear, you're mistaken. If they were the only source of magic in the world, Hollow would be an empire, not a kingdom. But now isn't the time for me to explain myself, no matter what you may think. Go get your friend. You're wasting time."

Frustrated, I left the Mercenary and joined the others. Besides Sirash, everyone else was huddled together and talking quietly, most likely discussing whether I was still sane and what they should do about me if I wasn't.

Sirash, on the other hand, was sitting in a chair, staring into the fire. I took a seat on the floor next to him with no real idea what to say. Or even how to convey how sorry I was. Or how to tell him what had happened with his brother, someone I should have been protecting. I couldn't express any of it in words.

"You got away," he said, still staring at the fire. It crackled in front of us.

"I'm sorry."

"I'm not angry," he said. "Maybe I was at some point, but not anymore. You got me out of there. That's thanks enough."

"How did you—"

"Know you were responsible?" he said. He shifted in his seat. "The castle educator told me I was going to be released at High Noble Domet's request. Domet the Deranged isn't known for his mercy. Why would he care about a Skeleton like me? I'm a nobody . . . and it's not like I have any other friends who could have influenced Scales to release me, so it had to be you. I don't know what you did to get me out of there and I don't care. We're good. Always will be."

"Sirash, I—"

"It's weird: I was so sure I was going to die in there, I gave up on my future. Now I have a life I don't know what to do with, and I'm fucking it up just sitting here, and yet I have no idea what to do."

"Jean misses you."

He nodded solemnly. "I haven't figured out how to face her yet. Part of me wants to hug her so tight and never let her go. Another part . . ." He took a breath, "Maybe it would be better if she and Arjay think I died."

"Sirash."

I was standing over him, glaring. He looked at me, expression-less, eyes lost in a daze.

"She would be better off without me. Without my problems. All I do is drag her down. She deserves better than that. That's why I was so proud when she finally joined the College of Musicians."

"Jean loves you Sirash. She always has."

He cupped his face in his hands. "She'll be better off without me."

"What about Arjay? Are you just going to abandon him, too?"

"He survived without me before."

I put my hands behind my head. Sirash was broken. He couldn't even face his own fears, and I wanted him to lead us back to the site of his torture. I didn't think it would be this bad, but he was in no state to help. I would have to come up with another plan. Maybe there was someone else who knew how to get into the castle. Or something. There had to be another angle.

"Do you remember the old days?" Sirash asked. "Back when we used to run jobs every night together. All that time we spent just talking in the darkness? I thought about those conversations a lot when I was there. My memories of you, and Jean, and Arjay kept me alive."

There was a lump in my throat that wouldn't go away.

"I don't think I can keep conning nobles after this. I need a stable life. Far away from anyone with power or delusions of it."

A life without delusions of grandeur. I had wanted that once, and some part of me still did. Back before Domet had intervened in my life. Back when my only concern was to protect my family, while living month to month. I'd had simple goals: cure my mother and figure out why my father had given me a useless, rusted ring before he had died.

"Do you remember when we daydreamed about robbing King Isaac?" Sirash chuckled to himself. "It was a child's dream of hidden passages and secret ways . . . They turned it against me, you know? While they tortured me. The educators said there was a way from the dungeons to the river; I just had to find it. I think they enjoyed watching me run through the labyrinth—their own personal hunt. I almost found it, too . . . I'd been searching in a pattern, and one day they were almost frantic when they dragged me back to my cell. They never let me out again."

This was that moment. The one that could plague my nightmares for years to come, depending on what I said next. I had thought Jamal's death would haunt me, but in the end I had only been a witness to his death. Everyone can watch someone get hurt and still sleep at night. But only monsters lie to and manipulate their friends when they're down. If I truly cared about Sirash, I would tell him what had happened to his brother and take him to Arjay tonight, let them walk down the road toward recovery together.

I am not proud of what I did, but I couldn't stop it. Not this close to the truth.

"The man who did that to your face . . . what if I said we could get revenge against him?"

Sirash's eyes lit up, and just like that, we had a plan.

———————

I wasn't expecting them to handle it well. My sister especially.

They didn't.

"I'm not letting you go alone," Gwen declared.

"Neither am I. That Mercenary could kill you and we would be unable to do anything to stop him," Kai said. "Or he could betray you inside the castle. I doubt the king would be merciful."

"I'm not asking for help," I said. "I'm going and you three are staying here."

"We're not asking to come with you, Michael. We're planning to," Gwen said.

"If you're caught, you could be charged with treason. No one is being executed because of me."

Gwen turned to Kai. "Can you give us a moment?"

He hesitated but nodded and walked away. High Noble Margaux was watching from a distance away, leaning against a wall with her arms crossed.

"So," Gwen said, "we're just supposed to wait around here and see if they're going to cut off your head in the morning? Is stealing the king's memories worth the risk? What will you gain?"

"It's about our father, Gwen. What if he's been innocent all these years? What if—"

"Michael," she said, "I've always known he was innocent. We don't need a document in that castle to prove it. What if there's another way?"

"There isn't. Everything I've learned about our father and that trial leads back to the king. If we want the truth, this is the way to get it."

"Do you swear this is the only option?" she said, eyes intent. "That this is worth the risk?"

There was no hesitation. "Yes."

"I'll stand with you if you want to do this," she said. "But you're risking everything you gained during the Endless Waltz. If you're caught, nothing can or will save you. But if you don't go through with this asinine plan, we can rebuild the Kingman legacy as a family. We can find the princess and work with her to ensure the Corrupt Prince never leads Hollow."

"Isn't this what you wanted? A week ago, wouldn't you have killed for this opportunity?"

"A week ago I would have burned this city down at the chance to redeem our father," she clarified. "But now I've had a taste of it . . . and I don't want revenge to be my life. I don't want to fight war after war like our ancestors did. If there's a way we can help this country without killing others, I'd like to try and find it. And the only way that can begin is if I abandon the hatred I have for the Royals. Please, Michael. Stay with me."

"I have to go," I said, more meekly than I expected. "I have to know if our father was innocent."

Gwen didn't look at me with anger or sadness in her eyes. No. Her eyes simply seemed faded and cloudy as if she was too exhausted to pay me any more attention. I wondered how she shouldered the burden of believing in our father's innocence alone for all these years, and now that I believed it, too, the anger that had ruled her for years was beginning to calm.

No wonder she seemed so tired.

"Do what you have to do," she sighed. "Good luck, Michael. Promise me you'll be careful."

"I will, Gwen. I promise."

"I love you, Michael. Don't forget that."

"I love you, too, Gwen. And I won't."

My sister joined Kai, to plan their night while waiting for the blockades to rise. I knew that should have been me. That I should be next to her, planning our next move together. But I wasn't, and what happened next would be on me . . . and me alone.

High Noble Margaux was waiting for me by the exit.

"If Gwen couldn't convince me to stay, you have no chance," I said.

"I have no intention of stopping you, Michael. I just wanted to say goodbye."

"Goodbye for now," I clarified. "I'll be back."

She stopped leaning against the wall and smiled as she put a hand on my shoulder. "Thanks for not judging me. I appreciated it. More than you can imagine."

"I'm not dying," I said as she walked away.

"You're not. But sometimes it's important to remember that you are mortal and that some goodbyes are forever. Even if they weren't meant to be."

There was nothing else to say, so she went to the side of the others. As much as it hurt, I pushed open the door to the waterway and went to meet Sirash and Dark down there.

Sirash was waiting on the docks next to Dark. As I approached, Sirash asked, "What was that about? Why were you arguing with your sister?"

"I'll tell you on the walk over. Now, let's go break into Hollow Castle."

NUANCES

Slowly, we walked on ice up the river. With every step the Mercenary took, the water beneath him froze instantly with an orchestra of crackles. We followed him carefully, the water rushing past us on both sides of the narrow ice bridge he was making. I had no intention of swimming again tonight. The wind was cold enough against my skin already, and the later it got, the more and more I wanted to be away from this river.

None of us talked. Dark was too focused on the ice pathway he was creating, and Sirash was struggling to walk on the slippery surface, still feeling the abuse he had endured. With every exhale a white wisp escaped his lips as if all the heat was leaving his body. I did what I could to help him. It was my fault he was here. I never should have let him come.

"Tired? We can rest if you need to," I said.

Sirash shook his head. "No. Sooner we get there, the better."

He was shivering, wobbling back and forth on the ice as if daring the water to take him. I took off my jacket and bundled him into it despite his resistance. I could deal with the prickly skin from the cold if it meant he was better.

"You didn't need to give me your coat."

I shrugged. "I'm too hot. I wanted to feel the cold air against my skin. You're doing me a favor by wearing it."

"Liar. Now, you going to tell me what happened with Gwen back there, or are we going to pretend that didn't happen?"

"It was nothing."

"I've seen you two argue before. That was different."

I stopped on the ice, the wind blowing my ragged brown hair. My body didn't shiver, though, comfortable in the cold air. "What's wrong with different?"

"She walked away from you. Gwen's never done that before," he said. "Don't just stand there. Walk and talk. Or don't. Your choice."

Sirash followed Dark as I stood there silently. After running my hands up and down my forearms, I continued, eventually walking side by side with him again. "My sister and I had an argument about what I'm doing. She's finally starting to move on from what happened to our father. But . . . I . . . I . . ."

"Can't?"

"No, not yet."

"Why not?"

"Because what if my father was innocent? What if I can prove he was framed?"

"Do you want to know if he was innocent, or do you want everyone to know that he was?"

"Both."

"Why?"

"Because we're Kingman, and Kingman—"

"Michael," he said, "you're too obsessed with your family legacy, and one day it will kill you."

"It's only because it's what I've had to do to make sure my family—"

"If it was always about your family, you wouldn't care so much about how you're seen, even by people you hate. You wouldn't care about the nobility that insult you after we've conned them, or about all the people unjustly hung by Scales. But you do. You've always been mindful of how everyone views you."

"I hate the nobility. I don't care—"

"Do you want me to give examples? Because I can do that. I've known you long enough to be able to."

I held my tongue.

"You don't know how to deal with what happened to your father. I get that. You remember him as a hero, so none of it makes sense for you. But you can remember him like that without caring what others think. No parent is perfect, and growing up is realizing that. If you're determined to make the world remember him fondly, but treat it like it's your family against the world, you'll drive away anyone who cares about you."

"I'm a Kingman, I have to—"

Sirash paused as if about to drive the final nail into my heart.

"Michael, your father didn't destroy the Kingman legacy . . . the king did. He banished you and your siblings from Hollow Court and branded you as traitors because of your blood. That is not you or your father's fault, so stop acting like the world is watching you. Maybe it will one day, but it isn't yet."

"Sirash, I—"

He stopped on the ice and turned to me. "Omari Torda. That's my real name. You never asked, and I never told you. But I have my own family legacy to live up to, so we might as well work on them together."

"Why didn't you tell me your real name sooner?"

"Because I was scared. Because when I was forced into slavery as a child, I was made to believe I was worthless. That my life wasn't as important as those I served. That I was the other. Even though I got out of that life, those lessons are hard to unlearn. Some part of me thought you'd turn your back on me eventually." A pause. "I don't think that anymore."

I didn't know how to respond. The pain in my chest had turned to a steady heat running through my veins. It wasn't my Nullify Fabrications. No, it was something else. Acceptance, maybe? I couldn't tell. Only that I felt relief. Then guilt. Deep, penetrating, overflowing guilt that made my head spin and my breath race. Guilt over how selfish I'd been.

Whether I had accepted it or not, my father was dead, and the truth I kept chasing after wasn't for him or Gwen. It was for me, so I could have faith in the man I had once thought of as my hero. But Sirash—Omari—was right: it wasn't worth it anymore.

Heh, and truthfully . . . my family's legacy would probably be my downfall at some point.

I was aware of that. But it wouldn't be tonight.

It was time I followed my mother's advice: Fuck 'em all.

This was a mistake; I had to get us out of here.

"Omari, how about—"

"Do you two like being cold, or can we hurry this up already?" Dark bellowed. He had stopped walking when we had, standing in front of a wall alongside the river. I looked up and trembled.

Hollow Castle was towering over us. We had arrived.

Omari Torda smiled, patted me on the back, and walked as fast as he could over to Dark.

Dark was waiting for me by a slim, triangular metal door in the wall with a rust line at the river's high-tide mark. Omari knelt, rummaging with the lock.

"Where does this door come out to?" Dark asked.

"Dungeons," Omari said. "Not too far from the torture room. I can lead you into the basement of the castle, and from there we can get to the tower."

"Can we do it without being seen?" I asked. "We aren't exactly dressed as nobles."

Dark stared at me and called me an imbecile with his grey eyes.

"That's why we're going in as Advocators," Omari said. "There should be some spare uniforms in the dungeon or the basement. If not, we'll knock some guards out and take theirs. Shouldn't be a problem to find a few empty cells for them to nap in." The lock clicked and inched open. "And that's our way in."

Dark grabbed the door and pulled it open.

The wind howled down the empty tunnel, and chains rattled somewhere within. "First stop is the torturer's room for uniforms. Then we'll work our way through the castle to King Isaac's study. Don't use anyone's real name while we're in there. If it all goes to shit, well, I won't be around to see it. Any questions?"

Before I could protest about his plan, Dark shoved me through the door as he said, "Good. You're leading, Michael. Be quiet."

Once we were all in, Dark closed the door and then iced it over with his Fabrications. A thin, translucent layer covered it. If I wanted to get out of here without him, it would be through another door.

We walked down the tunnels in silence except for the sloshing of our boots through the water. As it began to dry up, we came to a fork in the corridor with lit torches going off in three directions, a symbol over each path. No sound came from any of them. Only deafening silence.

"Which way?" Dark asked.

"I'm not sure," Omari said. "I knew the way from my cell to the waterway, but . . . I didn't realize there were three ways to the main dungeon."

"Of course it couldn't be easy," Dark muttered. "If we come out in the wrong place, it would mess our plan all up. Who knows where these paths go."

"We didn't plan for this. Maybe we should leave and come back with a better plan. We don't have to do this tonight," I said.

Both looked at me and then turned to each other. Dark was the first to speak. "We have two options: explore as a group, or each take a path and meet up again inside."

"We can cover more ground if we split up—" Omari began.

"But we'll be alone if something goes wrong," I said.

"So don't let anything go wrong," Dark said. "We'll each take a path and meet up inside the castle. It might be better, anyway. One person can blend into the crowds easier."

"I don't like this plan."

Omari put his hand on my shoulder. "It's the best option we have. Don't worry, we can all take care of ourselves for a bit."

"Where are we going to meet up?"

"The Star Chamber. It's right next to the Royal Staircase, so we'll have plenty of warning if there's a patrol coming."

Omari answered without consulting me. "That works for us."

"Then let's go."

Dark went down the middle path and disappeared into the darkness without a goodbye. I paused before taking the left one. "Are you sure you'll be fine on your own?"

Omari was standing straighter at this point, chest pushed out. He wasn't shaking anymore and his eyes were newly determined. "Trust me. I'll meet you at the Star Chamber once I'm finished with my business."

I held my open palm out. "See you on the other side?"

He clasped my hand and held it longer than normal. "See you under the stars."

Though I had promised him revenge, I couldn't stand by and watch him become a murderer as I had his brother.

When Omari let go of my hand, I waited in place until I couldn't hear his footsteps anymore. Once it was silent, I began to follow him down a corridor that seemed to stretch away forever. I didn't even know how long I'd walked until eventually the air grew hot and humid, forcing me to pull at the collar of my shirt for a moment of relief from my sweat-stained clothes. The door at the end of the hallway was warped from the wet air and heat, the lock so rusted that it broke open with a simple twist. As I forced the door open, it made a loud *crack* and the wood splintered, and I was greeted with a face full of steam and the realization that I must have missed a turn Omari had taken at some point.

I coughed loudly into my forearm, eyes watering.

"Hello?" a woman called.

I held my breath and moved further into the steam before ducking behind a column. My throat was burning, but I suppressed my cough. Everything smelled like oranges and lemongrass.

The voice called out again, "Is anyone there? Karin . . . Rowan . . . Efyra . . . Chloe? Was that one of you?"

All I could hear was my heart beating in my chest.

The voice sighed. Quieter, she said, "I must've been hearing things. Not that you can blame yourself. The rebels have essentially declared open war, the Emperor is a free woman, the city is in lockdown, and you're under house arrest, instead of out there with the other Evokers, and . . . now you're talking to yourself. Great."

There was a splash as she slapped the water in frustration.

As my eyes got adjusted to the steam, I realized where my path had led me: the baths in the basement of Hollow Castle. With an unknown Evoker. If she caught me, she'd probably drown me first, then ask questions.

Just my luck.

The woman began to hum to herself while easing into the water. A slow, steady tune almost like a lullaby. It was so familiar that, without thinking, my body began to ease and relax. My eyes felt heavy, and I had to use all my strength to stifle a yawn. It was almost like magic. How was she able to do that? Who was she? And why did it sound so familiar? I knew that tune somehow. But how? It didn't sound like any of the classics.

"Princess! We have an emergency!" a voice shouted as the door to the baths was thrown open. Someone walked in, armor clanking with every step.

No, it had to be someone else. It couldn't be *her*.

She cursed and lifted herself out of the baths. "Give me a report. And hand me my towel."

"We're under attack. Guards found the torturer, hanging by his mandibles, in a cell. His throat was cut and his tongue was missing."

"Rebels?"

"No signs of them, Princess. Nor did he seem like their kind of target."

"He wasn't. Who else knows?"

"Myself, his apprentice who found him, and you. I wanted to get you before informing your father. He had one of his incidents earlier today."

Omari. It had to be. I hadn't been able to stop him.

"Put the castle on lockdown and gather the rest of the Ravens. Put two on the door to my father's suite, one guarding the main entrance, send another to watch my brother, wherever he is, and the rest will be with me. If my father or Efyra asks why, tell them we're running a training exercise. I can handle this on my own. Besides, whoever it was, they haven't escaped the castle yet. We'll hunt them down in no time. Understand?"

"Yes, Princess. We'll be ready to search the castle by the time you're done changing."

"Thank you, Karin. You're . . . Wait, Karin, do these baths connect to the rest of the dungeons?"

"I think so, Princess. Why? Do you worry the intruder might try to escape through them?"

"No . . . no, I don't think so. It was just simple curiosity. You're excused."

The Raven left the baths in a hurry, slamming the door behind her. Shortly after, the woman walked around the bath, muttering to herself. Dark would've called me an imbecile and I knew I shouldn't . . . but I peeked around the corner. I had to know for sure if it was *her*.

Amidst the steam, I saw the Princess of Hollow wrapped up in a short towel, her lightly tanned skin contrasting with the sharp white, braiding her auburn hair to the side. My face flushed and I hid behind the column again, heart pounding. It felt like it was about to burst. I hadn't seen *her* in years, and to see the Royal my life was bound to . . .

"I know you're in here."

My heart stopped.

"I'll be honest," she said. "I had no love for the torturer we had. He was the worst of men, and only lasted this long because my father thought he was necessary. I was going to get rid of him when I could."

I couldn't help but wonder how long I could survive without a beating heart.

"I don't know why you killed him, and I don't really care. If you leave the way you came in, no one else will be harmed tonight. We have bigger problems to deal with. If you haven't noticed, there's a rebellion outside our walls. But if you take even one step out of these baths, I will show you Hollow's justice myself. Do you understand?"

I closed my eyes and put my head against the column.

"So be—"

"It was a mistake coming here," I croaked. "But I think my friend killed the torturer. I need to find and protect him."

"Are they worth the risks?"

"Family looks after family."

"Any fool can say those words, but few follow through."

"I'm here, aren't I? Your criminal brands don't scare me, but losing him does."

"Wise men fear more than just the ax." She hesitated, taking a deep breath, then letting it out. "I wish you luck in finding your friend and hope we don't meet again in these honored halls tonight." She rubbed her left wrist. "Whoever you may be."

I waited until I heard the door close again, wondering if our conversation would've ended differently if she knew who I was. When the Princess of Hollow was gone from the baths, I emerged from my hiding spot. There were two doors out of there: one for the men and one for the women. I left through the male one, passed through a small changing room—grabbing a dirty Advocator's uniform as I did—and then ran up the stairs toward the Star Chamber, trying to recall as much as I could about the Princess of Hollow and trying not to think about what would happen if we ran into each other again.

GONE

Dressed as an Advocator, no one gave me a second glance.

The servants avoided the eyes of anyone dressed more formally than they were, staring at the ground as they walked to and fro. The nobles were talking in groups and paid little attention to anyone else, as if declaring that if they didn't know you, you weren't worth talking to. Even the guards stared straight ahead in their places, perhaps assuming that anyone in here deserved to be. I walked confidently, and it wasn't long before I was back in the right hallway, looking for the door to the Star Chamber again.

When I found it, I swung it open without care. Dark, also in uniform, was sitting at the head of the table with a familiar night sky painted on the walls around him. "Took you long enough."

"Where's Omari?"

"Close the door. Do you want someone to see us?"

As I did, I repeated my question.

"Clearly not here."

"Enough," I growled. "I didn't like this plan to begin with, and now the castle is on lockdown and they're searching for intruders. We need to find Omari first."

"Calm yourself. They're only watching the exits. So long as he found a uniform and doesn't try to leave, he'll be fine," Dark said. "Let's go to the Royal Tower. This is our best chance—"

"We're waiting for him."

"He'll be fine, and it's the perfect distraction. No one will be watching the Royal Tower since they evacuate somewhere else during a lockdown. It's now or never."

"Then it's never. There's no choice between a chance at getting information about my dead father and saving the life of my friend."

Dark clicked his tongue, leaned on the table, and said, "This was your plan, Michael. You had to convince us to come with you. Now, after we've done the impossible and broken into the castle, you want to turn around and go home? What is wrong with you?"

"My priorities changed."

"Oh, really? What are they now?"

"Find Sir—I mean Omari—and get out of here without being arrested."

"I don't have time for this," he declared, rising from his seat. "All I've ever seen you do is make a stupid choice, complain about it, feel bad about it until whatever you want gets dangled in your face, and then go after it again to repeat the cycle."

"That won't happen anymore."

"It'll happen again and again because you keep acting like a child. For once in your life, make a decision and stick to it. Wavering back and forth like this is useless. All you're doing is ruining the lives of everyone around you."

"Says the murdering, torturing, maiming Mercenary."

Dark laughed, grabbed my hand, and then sliced my forearm with his dagger. Blood covered a side of the blade. Before I had a chance to yelp in pain, he was already filling a vial with my blood. After he was done, Dark ripped my sleeve and then used it to cover my wound as he said, "And you haven't done a thing to stop me. You're as bad as I am. If not worse. I'm not hurting the people I call my friends and family—you are. Now, are you coming?"

"I'm waiting for Omari."

"Then I'm leaving. I wasn't hired to babysit, and I have no desire to run into—"

"Your father?" I ventured, one last time.

Dark stared ahead. "Yes, and if you were smart, you would fear his eyes, too. They're everywhere. Goodbye, Michael. Let's not do this again."

He left the Star Chamber without a backwards glance. This wasn't my fault; it was Domet's . . . No, it was mine. I had to admit that. Just as I had to admit I was obsessed with my legacy. Domet may have given me the information that started it all, but I had gone to him seeking a job. I had done enough to hurt him anyway. I had taken away the only thing that man had left to cherish.

All of this was because of me. The sooner I admitted that, everything would begin to improve. I would get Omari to safety, tell Domet what I had done, and then live with the consequences.

With nothing else to do but wait, I took a seat at the table in front of the rising sun painted on one of the walls. I had never been in this room before, and yet it felt so familiar. Stars and constellations had been painted all over the walls with delicate care. I felt at ease with a night sky around me, relaxing as I sat there in silence.

Until someone came in, boots stomping against the floor.

"Omari?" I asked, turning toward the door.

Trey Wiccard met my eyes, mouth agape and eyes wide. In unison we said, "What're you doing here?"

We had spoken at the same time, but only Trey laughed. He sat next to me. "I suppose neither of us truly belongs here, and it doesn't make sense why we are . . . but we prevailed when others did not. That's a feat in and of itself."

"Trey, about Jamal . . . I'm so sorry. I wish I could have protected him."

Trey's fingers traced the grain of the wooden table. "I wanted you dead. No, I'm lying: I wanted to kill your family in front of you so you could feel a fraction of my pain. But Jamal wouldn't have wanted me to go down that path. So, once I got my head clear, I investigated on my own. You told me a rebel killed him, and I discovered you were telling the truth."

"You believed me."

"No. But I found evidence that proved your story, that you were just a witness, although I lacked a description of the man. So I resigned myself to hunting every one of them down until I found the

Emperor and killed him—I mean her—myself. I almost made a deal I would've regretted. But your actions at the king's party made me reconsider."

"That made you believe me?"

"You were my friend . . . but, no, not completely," he said. "Jamal made me believe. He had faith in your family and the heroics and honor they were once known for. I trusted his judgment and took the shot . . . though it helped when you threw aside your gun."

"It wasn't planned. Just felt right."

Trey nodded then scooched his chair closer to mine.

"So where does this leave us? Can we go back to being friends?"

"I don't know," he stated. "On one hand, you're all I have left and you did everything you could have to protect my brother. Even though he died, I'm thankful for that . . . only . . . every time I look at you, I think of Jamal and get angry that he died so young when others should have instead. So, where do we stand? I don't know. And I doubt I'll know today, or tomorrow, or the week after."

All things considered, his reaction was understandable. Trey hadn't had much time to grieve for his brother, and his death would haunt him for a long time. It would be months before he would even begin to feel like he had before, albeit with a cut on his heart that would never heal. Maybe one day we could be friends again, but, for now, I would give him his space and be there for him if he needed me.

"Michael, why are you here, anyway? In an Advocator's uniform no less."

"I'm waiting for a friend. Are you here to kill someone for Dark?"

"What? How did you . . . No, I turned the Mercenary down. In the end, my freedom was more important than revenge. I'm here because a man named Shadom gave me access to the castle and was supposed to meet me here . . . He claimed he knew the identity of my noble father."

"Shadom?" I said. "Did you meet them? Do you know what they look like?"

Trey eyed me curiously. "No to both. I was sent a letter with instructions to follow if I wanted the information. Why do you care so much?"

"Shadom knew my father." I groaned and leaned back in my seat. "I'm a little surprised you trusted a mysteriously sent letter."

He smiled slightly and opened his jacket so I could see that there was a flintlock pistol hidden there. "I didn't. But what do I have left to lose? I brought this in case it was a trap set by my pathetic father. I doubt Shadom will show, now that the castle is on lockdown. Maybe it's for the best."

"Are you insane?" I said loudly. "You brought a gun into the castle? All for what? Revenge? I thought you were over finding your father."

"I was, but now he's the only person I share blood with. I want to know who he is and why he left us."

"Trey . . ."

"Don't pity me, Michael. I should go . . . but before I do, have you ever noticed that there's something odd about your shadow? It's twisted and distorted for some reason. I've seen others whose shadows are similar, but yours . . . yours is different. It's adapted and hidden in plain sight more than the others. For years I thought my eyes were tricking me, but I've been learning more about Fabrications, and I understand what it is."

That was an odd turn in the conversation. "What're you talking about?"

Trey put his hands flat on the table. "This is going to hurt."

Trey put his hand over my face, a blinding light accompanying it. Everything went white and then gradually returned in a splotchy haze. I felt as if my shadow had been ripped out of my body and splattered against the wall behind me. My entire body shook, wobbled, and then I collapsed to the floor on one knee, struggling to breathe.

Everything was fuzzy as Trey stood over me, saying something I couldn't comprehend. The words disappeared before they reached my ears, and then Trey squeezed my shoulder and was gone. I hadn't even seen him open the door. As I continued to struggle, I put my back to the painted sun on the wall, breathing shallowly and watching the slow rise and fall of my chest.

When I was certain my heart would keep beating and I could still breathe, I stared off into the room of stars, the flush on my face melting away as I wondered what Trey had done to me.

Looking at it from below, I saw that this room was a near-perfect replica of my own back in the keep. Mine must've been his practice attempt, because everything here was perfect, down to the seven major pieces of the shattered moon Celona . . . but something was off with it. There was an eighth piece in the center of the others. It was wrong. I had studied the night sky enough to know that, and so had my father. I made my unsteady way over to it, running the tips of my fingers over each painted star. Soft, delicate strokes of paint covered everything. The flat of the brush had been smashed against the night blue to create the twinkling stars and constellations. My thumb stopped over the piece of Celona that didn't belong.

There was a small, circular crevice around a raised section carved into the wall, disguised by the painting. Instantly I knew the value of the ring my father had given me. That there was something he had wanted me to find. Something he couldn't tell me in words before his death. But something he had left behind in my scattered childhood memories. And there was only one thing it could be: the truth.

I took my father's ring off my middle finger and slid it into the indentation. It fit perfectly. With the key in place, I pressed against the extra piece of Celona and it went into the wall with a click.

The wall to my left rumbled and moved away, revealing a staircase wrapping around the room, spiraling upward. I climbed it, though I made sure I grabbed the ring before I did. There were hundreds of tiny little holes in the walls, invisible unless you were walking up the stairs. A thousand openings for a spy or the barrel of a gun to hide among the stars on the walls. There was no better place for an assassination.

I would love to say I knew why I followed the staircase, but I didn't.

I was climbing into the unknown, following the clues my father had left me, hoping for another clue at the top . . . and that Omari would be waiting for me in the Star Chamber when I returned. When I reached the end of the staircase, I pulled down on a metal chain that hung from the ceiling. The wall moved once again and opened onto a pristine hallway with a bland blue carpet.

There was a large tapestry hanging on the wall, each part of it showing a different scene. One scene was of an auburn-haired boy and girl playing together. Another of a young man with bright red hair having a crown placed atop his head. Then the same young red-haired man kissing a frowning woman on the cheek as he held her tightly. Three children ran around the couple in the next one, and then, finally, the man stood alone in front of a memorial, crying. A headless man knelt next to him.

I knew these people . . . and I knew where the stairs had led me.

"Who are you?" a voice from behind me demanded.

I put my hands up, my father's ring visible, and turned to face King Isaac, crossbow in his hands. The brand on my neck felt as fresh as when I first got it, ten years earlier. "My name is Michael King-man. You may remember me."

KINGMAKER

There were a lot of people who might hold grudges against me because of choices I had made: Domet, Naomi, and Dark. But King Isaac was the only person I was confident might simply wish to kill me because of my last name.

His finger never left the trigger, and when no one came to see where the king was, I was certain we were alone in his suite. No one would mourn me. Least of all him. Would he see it as justice? A son for a son? Did he still bear that resentment toward my father, or had it died with him? And why had my father left me a trail to King Isaac that few, if any, would know about? Did he . . . Was I . . . Was there something he wanted me to finish? Was a different Royal supposed to die that day? One who might have been harming the country more than helping it? As I held my sweaty palms in the air, I waited and hoped I would live long enough to find the answers.

"How did you get in here?"

I nudged my head toward the secret entrance.

"There are only two people alive who know of that entrance, and they're myself and the captain of my Royal Guard. How did you discover it?"

"My father painted my room exactly the same way. All that was different in the Star Chamber was a piece of Celona, and—combined with the ring he left me before he died—it opened. I didn't know where it led, though."

King Isaac fidgeted with the crossbow. "Even to this day, ten years later, your father continues to be an incurable disease in my city." A pause. "So why are you here?"

"Looking for evidence."

He looked at me, taking his eyes slightly off his aim. "Evidence of what, exactly?"

"Evidence that my father was framed and that you executed an innocent man."

King Isaac lowered the crossbow so it was pointed at the floor. "You do know who you are addressing, correct?"

"I can prove it."

A crossbow bolt thumped into the side of a bookcase near me. My skin prickled. I hadn't even seen him pull the trigger. King Isaac turned away and beckoned me to follow. "Then do so. Prove a king wrong."

My hands fell to my knees as I hunched over, trying to regain my breath. I wasn't in a position of power here. Maybe I could run away through the secret entrance . . . No. If he wanted to find me, he would be able to. I would have to do this. I would have to convince the king that my father had been innocent.

I followed Isaac further into his suite, gathering my thoughts as he took a seat on a leather chair in front of a fireplace. There was a long, rectangular, red wooden box on the table in front of him with a simple iron lock. I sat across from him and waited as he fidgeted with the lock. It sounded like he was scratching at the walls with his nails. "Are you going to explain yourself? Or was what you said back there a ploy to get me to lower my guard?"

"No," I declared. "I meant what I said. I just need to figure out where to begin."

"Begin at the beginning."

Considering I didn't know the end, I'd have to.

"What made you think my father shot your son?"

King Isaac stopped fumbling with the lock, met my eyes, and said, "He was caught holding the smoking gun by a Raven and her partner. There was no one else in the room, and no reason for Davey to be there but at your father's invitation. That's how I know."

I took a deep breath and then exhaled. If I could prove that those points were wrong, I could show that my father had been set up. I could put the pieces together. Start at the beginning.

"How do you know he was the one who pulled the trigger on the gun? There didn't need to be someone in the room. They could have fired from the secret passage and then dropped the gun to my father before he noticed what happened."

"Impossible. That would mean me, my captain, or the builder . . . If the passage was used, that damns your father further. Especially since it can only be opened with a ring like the one you're wearing. And before you ask, the person who built it is long since dead, before either of us were born, and all the other rings are accounted for. I wondered where your father's went. I never would have suspected you had it . . . and in such poor condition."

"What about the Captain of your Ravens?"

King Isaac laughed. "A ridiculous thought. Efyra would sooner fall on her blade than betray me."

"I bet you would have said the same about my father."

"Yes," he said. "Then he murdered my son."

"Listen. He was found inside the room, holding the gun, but Blackwell's memories could have been altered by a Darkness Fabrication. He's in the asylum now, terrified of the shadows that falsified his memories . . . but he said that my father's finger was on the barrel—not on the trigger. There's no way he could have fired it like that. But the gun could have been thrown to him from above."

King Isaac lifted the lid of the box. I couldn't see what was inside from where I was sitting. He ran his fingers down the side of the box, staring into it as he spoke. "To your own credit, I thought you would be less versed with the case. I expected a child, whining about what I had done. Trying to make me feel remorseful for the choice I made. That's not the situation, and I'll treat you as such.

"To answer your question: while it wasn't made known to the public, we did use Light Fabrications on Low Noble Blackwell after he saw the scene. His memories did not change, nor did he show any signs he was under the influence of Darkness Fabrications. I'll admit that we did not use Light Fabrications on my Raven, since she was a Light Fabricator herself. Only after she died in Naverre did Blackwell begin to show signs of madness and change his account. That's grief, not proof. Losing a loved one can change a man drastically, and not all can fully recover from it. Most barely survive. All that remains in Blackwell is regret, grief, and a desire to do something worthwhile. Do not fault him for it."

"But his story changed! Even if it was sparked by grief, you can't ignore that the story changed!"

"You're a Fabricator yourself, correct?"

I nodded.

"Most of us are terrified of losing our memories whenever we use Fabrications. We're taught the price of power and always expected to know what we might have to give up to attain it. But the problem is, the older you become, the more you discover that memories change on their own. Some fade away, some stories change slightly, and some memories are so drastically different a decade after they occurred that no one can be quite sure what the truth is . . . So when a man changes a key piece of evidence years later, after losing the love of his life, I'm hesitant to believe it. Because at that point it's not the truth he desires but some personal satisfaction he believes he can get out of telling others. You're not the first person he's spun that tale to, nor will you be the last. You'll just be the one that it hurts the most."

I closed my hands into fists. "But his story changed. That has to mean something."

"No," King Isaac said. "It does not. The man has been in an asylum for years. He's no longer a credible witness."

"What about you? Were you a neutral judge for my father when you decided to execute him?"

"I was not. I never could be. That's why the Captain of my Ravens served in my place during the trial."

"What about the timing? A Raven just happened to walk in and witness a murder? Don't you find that a little too perfect?"

"Are you suggesting I would rather have my son's murder unsolved?"

I opened my mouth to object, but the king continued, "But, yes, we examined that possibility, too. The Raven was on her second half-day shift in a row after switching with one of her sisters at the last minute. That was impossible to predict. And, as I have been told . . . it was not where they usually went for some privacy."

My face was hot as he sliced through all the evidence I had gathered like it was the ramblings of a child. I kept going. "The gun and the markings on the bullets that only it can use . . . the markings on the bullets belong to a Mercenary Company called Tosburg Company. They were the ones that fought against my father on the Day of Crowning. That day the leader of the company was never caught or killed. He got away. What if the leader got his revenge on my father after all those years? It could be—"

King Isaac reached into the box in front of him and pulled out a revolver. A perfect replica of Dark's. This gun had killed Davey Hollow. There couldn't be a third.

This gun had killed a future king.

He put the revolver between us on the table before laying out two bullets. Both were engraved with hands ripping apart a crown. At least now I knew he had kept it after all these years.

"This is the gun that killed my son," he said. "I have spent every single moment since that day trying to learn who made it. I am aware that Tosburg Company once used this emblem. I also know they have never reappeared since the Day of Crowning. And I know of the other half a dozen ways this emblem is used in the Gold Coast, the Warring States, and in New Dracon City, because I have tracked every instance down . . . and still never uncovered where this gun and its bullets came from. So don't sit there and try to spin me a tale about the escaped leader of a Mercenary company who might have held a grudge for over two decades, just to return to Hollow to kill my son and frame your father. Don't. You. Dare."

I swallowed. "What about Shadom? They were mentioned in the reports. Who are they?"

"It's not a name; it's a code. Used whenever someone wanted to have an off-the-record meeting. It tells everyone to avoid the room. Except this time."

And just like that, there was nothing left to ask. All my questions had answers. After everything I had done to uncover the truth, all I had to show for it was embarrassment and shame.

"Can I ask you one last question?" I said softly. "Why did he plead guilty?"

King Isaac reached for the revolver and loaded a bullet into the chamber. He did it quickly, almost as if it was a habit, and put the gun back down between us. "Your father loved you three. In the end he pleaded guilty for his family."

"Really? Because it seems we were worth much less to him than power was! His own damn children!"

"He pleaded guilty after I branded each of you in front of him while he screamed for mercy. I told him that if he confessed, I would let you three live. Else, I planned to hang you, Lyon, and Gwen over my balcony."

My ears rang. I blinked to regain focus on the king sitting in front of me. Dark lines seemed to move around him. "Excuse me?"

He looked me in the eyes. Without any emotion he said, "I told him that if he said a single word in his own defense, having been caught with the smoking gun in his hand, I would kill his children as he did my son."

"You killed him."

"I did. After he killed my son. What I did saved everyone from further pain. The Kingman family against the Hollow Family. It would have caused a civil war, and it would have destroyed this country."

"You said the trial was impartial. That's why you had the Captain of your Ravens serve in your place."

"The trial was impartial. I was not. I wanted revenge; I wanted him dead."

"He could've been innocent. You stopped him from defending himself."

"He was guilty."

"How do you know? You never gave him the chance to defend himself! He was your best friend and you killed him! And this brand you gave me and my siblings—what was that for? To share some of your son's pain?"

Silence.

King Isaac didn't respond. He looked at me. No emotion. Nearly a statue. He had threatened me and my siblings because he was angry. He had abused his power and murdered my father. This coward. What kind of king was he? A useless king for a useless city. I had met so many nobles who proved I'd been wrong about them, but I had been right about him. He was no better than his useless son.

"Do you want to continue the cycle and kill me in retaliation?" he asked. "For all I have done to you and your family?"

I was standing in front of him, breathing hard. My mind was blank and my brand was throbbing in pain. I couldn't focus on anything but the king before me. And what he had done.

"If you do not, you should refrain from pointing that gun at my head."

I blinked, focus returning. The gun that had killed Davey Hollow was in my right hand, pointed at the king. I hadn't realized I had picked it up, but my finger was firm on the trigger. Nothing shook.

"Do you, Michael?" He paused. "You should understand that this is what happens when people think justice has failed and try to take it into their own hands. Do this and all you will be remembered as is your father's son. No one will care about the truth you think you discovered. You will destroy the Kingman legacy that your father already ruined."

"Who are you to lecture me? Are you any better? After what you did?"

"No," he said, "but my morals died with my son. Since then, I have merely tried to keep this city alive. My reign as king will be remembered for little more than death and war. I have accepted that. . . . Do you know what that is like? My grandfather brought education to Hollow, almost eradicating illiteracy, and after him my father brought medicine to this city, saving hundreds from the plague. I suspect historians will compare me to the king during the War for the Bloodline, since I am responsible for depleting a generation of its best and brightest . . . just like he was."

"You killed my father," I repeated, eyes itchy.

"That is the least of my crimes. I made us fight the Gunpowder War because I refused to kneel to the foreigners who murdered my older sister. I'm responsible for the Bloodbath of Vurano, and it is my fault Naverre fell to the rebels and all those innocent people died. The rebel leader is still out there because my justice system was inadequate enough to convict her. And I destroyed my best friend's family to avenge my son. Even that is merely what I remember in my old age. I have done more. Much more."

I steadied the gun, my free hand cupping the other. "I hate you."

"You and so many others. The nobles think I am either useless or a Forgotten unless I throw a feast every week telling them that everything is as expected. Most, if not all of them, are waiting for me to die so another can rule in my place. They all want the power they think I have. Then there are the citizens of this city who think I am a glutton who sits in his palace surrounded by walls and that my guards laugh at them while they starve and work to death in the dye pits or farms on the East Side. Even my own children hate me, and my wife thinks I'm worth less than the barnacles she scrapes off her ships. This country and everyone in it despises me. The only one who did not was your father. Look what I did to him."

"We'd be better off without you," I whispered.

"You are correct. Who am I to rule, when I could not even protect my own son?"

"Maybe the wrong Royal died that day in the Star Chamber.

Maybe my father was trying to put an end to your incompetent stint as king."

"I have had that thought many times."

Silence.

"Do what you must, Michael Kingman."

I looked down the barrel of the gun, with King Isaac at the end of it, my finger gently resting against the trigger.

I had done a lot of things that I regretted recently. Things I wished I could tweak or change slightly for the better, in my endless pursuit of the man I wanted to be and the man I thought I had to be. But, either way . . . I knew I wasn't a king killer.

I was a Kingman, and I would not let my descendants be ashamed of me.

Gwen had said it herself: Kingman don't kill Royals, no matter how wicked they were and no matter what a piece of the moon had declared. I wondered what she would think of this. Maybe she would be proud of me for doing what she had done: walk away from a Royal without killing him.

I put the gun on the table, sat down, and lowered my head into my arms. I was unable to cry. It was like my tear ducts were broken from lack of use. Everything I had sacrificed for the truth had led me to aim a gun at the king. I was a child playing at being a detective. Who was I trying to fool?

King Isaac moved closer to me, ran his hand down my back once, and then gently pulled me up by my shirt, motioning for me to follow him to the balcony. I did as instructed, watching the entire time as he held the gun gently in his other hand. Once we were outside, he put his hands on the railing and looked at the view.

The entire city was visible from up here, from the Isle with the Church of the Wanderer and Kingman Keep to the dye pits on the East Side. The sun was rising and its light shone through the gaps between the buildings, covering the entire city in a warm orange glow. It was morning, and nothing had changed. The rebels hadn't started a grand revolution overnight, and the guards were not massing to save their king. A few citizens were walking below, bundled up like it was any other winter morning. I didn't understand then . . . why, to me, it felt like the world had changed.

"We all make our choices in life, Michael," he said. "Some good. Some for the worse. Your father made his a long time ago."

"I miss him."

King Isaac nodded. "I miss my son. And the family I once took for granted . . . I was a terrible husband . . . Then there is your father. He was my best friend, my confidant, and my trusted advisor. I lost everything the day he died."

"Me too. Can I still love him even if I'm ashamed of what the world says he did?"

"We love despite a person's flaws, not for their lack thereof."

We stood in silence for a moment watching the sun rise further into the sky. The stars could still be faintly seen. The moon Tenere was whole and wide, a perfect bluish-orange marble. My brand didn't even itch. It seemed the world was at peace.

"Did you know that no King or Queen of Hollow has ever reached their fiftieth birthday before? They have all died before it."

"Congratulations on being the first."

He shook his head as he leaned further over the rails toward the rising sun, a small smile on his face.

"No," the king said. "My actual birthday is still a few days away. It's always the case: we Royals have official birthdays and private birthdays. Very few people know that. Your father did and always made sure we celebrated the right day together. Even if some years it was just the two of us." He rubbed his eyes. "I suspect your father would have made a better king than me. Everyone loved and respected him, from the High Nobles to the roustabouts. It's why our laws stipulate there must always be a Kingman beside the throne—to keep the Royal Family in check and be someone the common people can trust. It can never be the king. It is too much of an occupational hazard."

"Kingman stand beside the throne," I said softly. My family's motto.

King Isaac stood straight. "They do. I hope you and your siblings will protect the princess when she sits on the throne. Do not judge her too harshly when you meet her again. She had a rough childhood without her family to support her. But she will be a good queen. A smart and just queen. Much better than her worthless father. She reminds me of my sister."

He took a breath in through his nose. "I was never meant to be king. The crown was an inheritance I had to accept, as your father had to inherit your family's legacy. We both had older sisters who were taken from us too soon and left us with a duty neither of us wanted. I wanted to step away, once we had our revenge against New Dracon City, but, alas, there was always something more important. Citizens to protect from rebels, nobles to court favor with so no one starved in the winter, a political marriage meant to bring two countries together, children to keep happy, and so much more. The only good thing I have ever done was bring my children into this world. Can you do me a favor, Michael?"

I nodded. If I was going to truly be a Kingman and not a pretender, I'd have to serve the king. Regardless of my opinions of him or his son. I would not let our legacy end in ruin.

"Tell my family I love them. That what I do, I do for Hollow. This country will flourish without me. I hope they will understand when they are older."

I looked at him. He was facing the rising sun, standing straight, a small smile on his face. What was he saying? I didn't understand at all.

"Davey," he muttered. "I will be at your side soon. Goodbye, Michael. I am glad I was able to greet this morning with you."

King Isaac smiled as he lifted the gun and put it under his chin.

There was a *bang*, my ears rang, and blood sprayed across my face.

The gun clattered to the ground as his body fell against the rail and then slid over it.

My body moved on its own, snatching the gun off the floor. It was still warm and reeked of black powder. With shaking hands, I grabbed the rails and looked over. Maybe it hadn't happened. Maybe he wasn't—

King Isaac's body was spread out on the ground below, staining the stone around it red.

My hearing returned in a rush and I heard the screaming as pedestrians began to rush toward him. There was a Raven at his side, checking for any signs of life as another pounded on his chest, demanding he stand up as she cried. Advocators, Scorchers, and other nobles gathered around them, silent, hands over their mouths.

Then one of the Ravens saw me from below, gun in my hand and blood splattered over my clothes and face.

"KING KILLER!" she screamed, pointing at me. "HE KILLED THE KING! GET THE KING KILLER!"

48

Deep breath in. Deep breath out.

My first instinct was to throw myself off the balcony and land next to Isaac Hollow. It would be a clean and easy way to go. A moment of fear in exchange for it all to be over. It would be a better death than any traitor or king killer would be given.

Yet my body wouldn't move, as my mind had escaped to a place beyond madness once faced with the realization that I had let my ancestors down. The Kingman legacy would end with me. And it hadn't even been my choice.

I don't remember moving back into his chamber or how long I sat in his chair, but eventually someone came for me as the pounding on the suite door intensified. With a gentle hand, they guided me through a hole in the wall, down a set of steep stairs in the dark, and through hallways of gold and blue. The gentle hand told me when to follow, when to stop, and when to remain silent as monsters with metal hands patrolled the hallways.

It wasn't until we were outside that I felt anything. My face felt warm under the new sun. It only lasted for a second before a strong wind blew against me and I was cold again. So cold that my teeth chattered and my knees buckled. And then: nothing. The gentle hand drew a cloak around me as they took my hand in their own and led me through the falling snow. It crunched under my boots like shards of glass until we entered a house and I was settled on a divan. Time continued to elude me as I drifted off to sleep soon after lying down. When I awoke, there was odorless and bland food waiting for me along with mild water.

That routine continued for as long as it could. I slept without dreaming, ate without pleasure, drank to survive, and visited the bathroom without conscious thought. As if I were kept in a prison in my mind. My eternal punishment for the consequences of my actions that had brought me here. Those actions that had caused me to watch King Isaac kill himself instead of having the courage to face the city that had stolen his family from him. I understood him better than I wanted to admit.

I almost wished I had followed him. No Royal in Hollow's history had ever taken their own life. And after the world had seen me on the balcony with the revolver in my hand, my chances of convincing it he had were nonexistent.

My only solace, I suppose, was that I felt closer to my father than ever.

As I lived under an endless night in a sea of darkness, the only respite I had was the few moments when I ate before returning to sleep. This pattern continued and continued and I thought I would be trapped in this state forever. A slave to my own mind and body. Once, when I slept, I awoke surrounded by white. A stark, blinding white that was like looking directly at the sun. It burned my eyes and awoke me from my dream, so, afterward, I ate and drank some more. When I went back to sleep, I returned to the strange white place and found it didn't bother my eyes as it previously had. It was the only possible escape from this broken life I lived.

At first the desert of white seemed to be similar to the sea of darkness I had been a resident in for so long. Yet, it was different. In this desert of white, I could see my hands and feet. They were light white things, the skin as soft as a baby's. My calluses and bruises and cuts were gone, as if the slate had been wiped clean. My only thought was that I was dead and I had gone on to whatever afterlife would have me.

"You're not dead," I heard. "You're just having a hard time remembering."

My ears rang as if another gunshot had gone off. I turned to the voice. Most of her features were indistinguishable in this sea of white, except for her brown hair. But I felt warm for the first time in a long time.

I opened my mouth to speak but found no words. Not even a grunt or murmur.

She spoke for me. "It will hurt at first. But that's what happens when you're healing. There's always pain before you fully recover. Take it slowly. Focus on me."

I tried. Brown hair tied back in a ponytail, a few strands hanging over her forehead. A pair of front teeth that were slightly too large. A smile that made me feel warm. And not the same warmth that I felt when I nullified things. It was more soothing than that. More comforting. Motherly, even. Familiar.

"Don't strain yourself," she said. She took my hands in her own and then slowly brought them up to her lips and kissed them. "All better."

I swallowed. "Who are you?" I said in little more than a croak. But they were my words. Bought and paid for with my pain and suffering.

"Don't try to skip steps, Michael," she said as she swung my arms back and forth.

It was childlike. So innocent. I couldn't help but smile, as if I was reliving my childhood with her.

"Now," she said, her voice growing more serious. "I want you to tell me a story."

"A story?"

"A story," she declared. "Tell me a good story."

I did.

We sat down together in the white, holding hands as I told her my tale of a man who had become a hero by killing a dragon. I stretched the truth as far as I could to fit the majestic scope of this story, filling in the details of the dragon's scales, metallic grey with freckled green that had dulled with age.

I described the heat of the dragon's breath perfectly so she could feel the prickle of it on her skin and how it was so pungently sour and rancid that people fainted from smelling it. I made it whole and real and perfect. The description of the battle between the hero and dragon was as painstakingly detailed. From the notches on the swords to how he had to oil his sword behind a boulder as the dragon tried to melt it. It was all about the small details in stories, the ones that no one paid attention to but made everything feel whole. The story was perfect, and it was the greatest story I had ever told.

When I was finished, she simply shook her head and said, "No. I asked for a good story, not an exaggerated one."

I took a deep breath. Half of storytelling was finding the right tale for the audience. Maybe the exaggeration hadn't been for her. But I would find her story eventually. All it took was time. So I told another, one about a man who did anything for the love of his life, until she died tragically in a starless night. The man yearned for a second chance to see her, and was willing to do anything to see her face one more time . . . so he made a deal with a trickster god to etch her face into the moon and make him its keeper, bound for eternity.

Every day he pulled her across the sky by hauling on a long chain attached to a massive anchor on the sea floor. I described his torment and pain and how his hands would rip until they were raw and bleeding in the first few weeks of his torment. And how they soon became callused and hard as diamonds.

Then I told her about every time he saw the moon in his underwater cave for those brief moments before he released his love back into the sky again. I described the pain that stabbed at his back with every pull of the chain. That sorrow as he dragged the moon and its light down into the darkness of the water. That anguish that can make a heart numb and cold, and the shame of his selfishness that he had done all of this because he couldn't let her go. Then the release and joy when she was bright in the dark sky, giving the world her light.

But once again, when my story was finished, she shook her head and said, "That's not what I asked for either."

I told story after story. All the tales I knew about my ancestors and every tale I had created myself. But she always shook her head at the end and said, "That's not what I asked for."

It wasn't long before my confidence was as drained as my treasure trove of stories, unable to even make her smile. Yet, there was nothing. She was hidden behind a mist I couldn't pierce through as I tried to tell her a good story.

"I don't have any more," I said. "I've run out of stories for you."

I felt that warmth from her smile again. "Then tell me a different kind of story. Something that you haven't told someone before."

"I don't know what that means."

She pondered for a second as the silence settled between us.

"Tell me a true story."

A true story.

"I can do that," I said.

And I did. My story began with a keep on the murky river's edge that dozens of people walked in and out of each day. How it was almost its own city nestled within a much larger one. I described the windows and the stained glass and how it shined vibrantly like a lighthouse when it was first light and last light, and everything else I had ever known of this keep down to the minor details of which stair boards creaked where and how the wind howled through the hallways on spring days.

I saw my parents' bedroom with their massive feather bed

draped in red and grey. Only the right side of the bed was disturbed, the left side still and flat. I explained how the carpet was soft and fluffy and how toes would cling to it. I described how the glass doors to the balcony were always without a speck of dirt on them. And how the Moon's Tears sprawled over the balcony like vines with their pale white glow. I told her how my father always sat outside on warm nights to work. How the night sky always seemed to calm him even though he carried the weight of a country's future. Whenever he was stressed, he would just sit outside with a glass of wine and—

"No," she interrupted, "that's not the truth."

I blinked. "Yeah," I muttered. "You're right. My father never drank after what happened to my mother. He wouldn't sit outside with wine. Just water."

I held my head as a low, dull growl filled my ears. The lines in the room seemed to grow darker, too.

"Why were there glasses of wine out there, though?" she asked.

My story became real again, and we stood in the room together, staring out onto the balcony. On the small side table were two glasses of wine: one empty and the other half-full. Why was there wine out there when my father stopped drinking years ago? That was wrong.

"I don't know," I said. "One of the last memories of my father involves him outside with two glasses of wine. Something is wrong."

The darkness opened and swallowed me whole. It surrounded me instantly, dulling my senses and mind. It pulled at my limbs and scraped at my skin. It left no marks and yet kept trying to take everything else. I felt my mind drifting away, just as it had before the sea of white appeared. My memories were lucid in that moment. Everything was going blank except for the fact there had been two glasses of wine on that table and that my father stopped drinking.

I held on to those memories like a scared child clutching a lantern as the darkness tried to peck away his eyes. I repeated the memories to myself. Two glasses of wine when my father didn't drink. Two glasses of wine when my father didn't drink. With every repetition, I felt the warmth of my power swell inside of me. Two glasses of wine when my father didn't drink. The warmth soon covered my entire body and I knew peace. Two glasses of wine when my father didn't drink. It wasn't long before the warmth was everywhere, overwhelming me. I wasn't the child I had been. I could protect people. I had my own power.

I *repelled* the warmth in my body as I screamed.

The darkness dispersed around me, a blinding light replacing it. I stood in my parents' room, screaming as I watched the darkness fizzle out around me. I didn't stop until there wasn't even a shadow in the room, only the blinding light I was radiating. I had never felt better . . . like I was finally whole.

"Welcome back, Michael," she said.

Finally, I saw the girl in red for who she was. High Noble Danielle Margaux, known as Dawn to her friends and family, stood in front of me, smiling. That smile she always had since we were children. The first time I had seen it, I was in her room, trying to make her laugh as she lay in bed all day because of her legs. In that moment, staring at Dawn in my parents' room, reminiscing about our childhood, my memories returned to me, and I remembered.

I remembered Dawn lying in bed as I told her stories of the adventures I had gone on, and the smile she always gave me when I came to visit, and how much it meant to her when I did. In her youth, her legs were frail and the bones would break easily, and only learning how to use Fabrications gave her freedom to move without worry. But always at a price: one day she'd be forced to choose between her freedom and her memories. Her distinct smile was born in those days of sickness and would remain with her for the rest of her life.

I remembered Kai, shy and clumsy, always running after his big sisters. How I had been there to pick him up when he fell, and knew how much I had hurt him when I didn't remember him after all those years of friendship. Then I remembered the real reason of how he had gone blind, using his Sound Fabrications to cover the entire city to find me and my siblings during the riots following my father's execution. His sacrifice had saved my life, and then I forgot him so easily. Even after I had hurt him so much, he stayed true to me, always at my side whenever I needed him.

I remembered Kingman Keep in its splendor and grandeur.

The cooks who would give me pastries when I came lurking for them in the morning as the bread came out of the ovens. The guardsmen's dogs, who jumped in the river and made the keep smell like wet fur, and the parties we used to hold, and the stuffy clothes that I was made to wear for them. My brother who always talked to the knights, ready to become a leader in his own right. My crybaby sister and how she used to cling to our mother's legs. The princess and her voice that stole my heart as a boy, and King Isaac ruffling my hair and saying he couldn't wait to see the man I would become as my father looked on, a smile on his face.

Lastly, I remembered Davey Hollow, not in words or images, but by the tears that came when I thought of him. The day he died, Lyon, Gwen, and I lost our brother.

Dawn wrapped her arms around me and hugged me. I wiped my eyes on my forearm and let my focus return to the balcony, watching the scene unfold with a newfound warmth. It was time for the truth I had been hunting for.

My eight-year-old self pushed open the balcony's doors. "Da?"

My father looked at him with his eyes red and puffy. "Michael?" He sniffed and wiped the tears away from his eyes. "Michael, what are you doing up so late?"

My younger self yawned. "I heard you yelling at someone."

"Oh, Michael, I'm sorry about that. I didn't mean to disturb you. I was just talking to my friend here. Shadom—I mean . . . Domet, apologize for bothering him."

Charles Domet sipped on his glass of wine, glaring at my father. "I apologize, Michael. I didn't think we could be heard up here." He looked the same as the last time I had seen him. He hadn't aged a single day. But of course he hadn't: He was immortal.

"My window was open."

"Ah, that explains it. All right, Michael, since we're being loud, here's the plan: you're going to stay with the Margauxs tonight while we work. I'm sure Dawn would love the company."

"Yeah!"

"I'm glad," he said, ruffling my hair. "Domet, could you get Sir Tristin Harbour to take Michael over to Margaux Keep? He should be downstairs. Before you ask, I trust him with my life. He won't question his orders, and he won't mention seeing you here tonight. He'd sooner die for me and my family than betray us."

Domet rose from his seat, leaving his wolf's-head cane behind. "I trust your judgment. I wouldn't be here if I didn't. But I will bring back another bottle of wine. I'm still rather thirsty."

My father scoffed at him as he walked away and mussed up my messy brown hair.

"Da? What's going on?"

"It's nothing to worry about, Michael. High Noble Domet was just warning me that evil men might try to hurt Davey tomorrow."

"You're going to stop them, right? You're going to save Davey?" my younger self asked, bright-eyed and innocent.

"Of course," he said. "I always have. And always will. It's what our family does."

My younger self hugged my father's chest, content. "Do you think I'll be a good Kingman?"

"You will, Michael. There will be some days you hate it and other days when you can't imagine your life any other way, but either way you'll see all the good our family does for the world and smile. Even if you spend a lot of time negotiating marriages and territory claims with High Nobles, reminding the Royal you're bound to who they're addressing, or listening to merchants bicker about taxes. It's a lot of responsibility, and our legacy doesn't exactly allow room for mistakes. Eyes are always watching us."

"I don't care!" my younger self declared confidently. "I'll be the best Kingman there ever was! Better than the Conqueror or the First Kingman! Don't worry, Da. My name will go down in history as a hero. Just like you."

My father laughed at me. "I've long since stopped caring about my legacy, Michael. You and your siblings and mother are the only things I care about. I'd sacrifice everything to protect you. One day you'll understand there is more to life than the Kingman legacy. It'll probably take a woman and a child to teach you that, but one day you'll understand."

My younger self didn't exactly agree, but he didn't protest either. I knew what was in my head back then: dreams of fighting wars and dying heroically as my ancestors had done before me. Kingman rarely lived long, but history always remembered us, and as a child that had seemed more important than anything else.

"Michael, can you get me that cane over there?"

I did as I was told and brought Domet's cane to my father. He held it in front of me so the wolf's black eyes were level with my own. As my younger self was focused on the eyes, my father formed a pitch-black ball in his own palm. A Darkness Fabrication. "I'm sorry, Michael. This is just a precaution," he said to himself. "I can't have you going around talking about what you overheard in case the assassin gets wind of it and changes their plan. I'll reverse it tomorrow, but, for tonight, a part of your memories will be sealed away."

He put it behind my ear and I watched it seep into my head. Once the Darkness Fabrication was gone, the wolf's eyes turned red. "Magic! Impressive, right?"

My younger self was astonished. "How'd you do that?"

My father ruffled my hair and put me back on his lap. "I'll tell you when you're older."

I held out my hand and then closed it. The scene stopped, frozen in time in my mind.

I was crying, and I hadn't even realized. "He was innocent," I said. "He used a Darkness Fabrication on me to protect me and planned to reverse it the next day. But because he never did, I couldn't remember Dawn, who was named at this event. The Darkness Fabrication must've taken away any connection to this memory that it could find. Maybe that was why I couldn't remember Kai, either, since he was another one of my childhood friends. The Darkness Fabrication kept taking and taking anything that might lead me back to this memory. All of that pain in my life . . . all the pain I caused because I couldn't remember . . . all because my father was trying to protect me from someone trying to assassinate Davey."

I howled with laughter. "And Domet knew. He knew about the plot against Davey Hollow and sent my father to deal with it. But . . . something must've gone wrong. The assassin succeeded and ended up getting my father in addition to the prince. Or maybe it was all a part of his scheme. Maybe Domet was in on it. Or maybe the assassin used him to get to my father."

"But now you remember," Dawn said behind me. She hadn't let go of me the entire time we had been watching the scene on the balcony. "All it took was for the truth to come out."

My truth. Every lie I had told had clouded my mind to the truth. But now I remembered.

I closed my eyes, took a breath, and then let it out slowly. There wasn't any darkness or light waiting for me this time. Just a new view on life.

My life was finally my own again.

THE LAST ACT OF MICHAEL KINGMAN

I awoke to the smell of pepper and oil frying in a pan and then heard the sizzle that came when meat was added. I swung my legs over the edge of the divan and rubbed my eyes. My body was tight and everything cracked when I moved. Half-eaten plates and half-full glasses of water were piled up on the table in front of me. Everything around me looked opulent. It wasn't a jail cell. But there weren't always bars in a prison. Some cells were less obvious.

Someone off in the kitchen began to sing. They were terrible, hitting every note in a shriek. I didn't recognize the voice, which was a relief. No one I knew would sing like that in public. I paused. How had I escaped from the king's suite without being arrested or killed?

Had someone else known about the secret entrance through the Star Chamber after all?

Footsteps moved toward me. I lowered my head and tried to zone out my focus. I didn't want whoever had me to think I was back to normal yet. No, not until I knew what was going on.

Someone sat in the chair opposite me. I could only see their scuffed shoes and the plate of peppered pork and toast placed in front of me. "Good morning, Michael!" Charles Domet exclaimed. "I prepared another amazing meal for you. I hope you enjoy it more than the others. I'm positive that this will be the one that you fall in love with and demand I make it for you for every meal."

I was in Charles Domet's house. Of course I was. It was always him.

I raised my eyes to look at him as he lifted a glass of wine to his lips and knew he would take a sip from it. Typical. I needed to find out why and how he had saved me. That had to have been him leading me out of the castle. Why had he done that? And how had he found me? There were so many questions I still needed the answer to.

"Well? Do you like it?" Domet asked.

I took a bite out of the pork and then swallowed. He was on the edge of his seat, waiting for an answer.

"If I don't," I began, "are you just going to continue to lie to me about my father and what happened with Davey?"

"Michael? What are you talking about? I—"

"I remember the night on the balcony with my father. I remember you, Domet." I spat out his name. "Why bother lying to me? You knew my father was innocent because you were Shadom. You told him about the assassination attempt."

Domet put his glass down on the table. "I did what I thought was right at the time."

"Why am I here? How did you get me here? The last thing I remember is . . ." I paused, thinking of Isaac and the gun and the bang it made. ". . . what happened on the balcony."

"Aren't you interested to hear what happened to your father? I thought—"

I looked up from the plate of food. "Nothing you tell me is going to bring Davey or my father or the king back to life. All I want is to make sure my friends and family are safe. The truth won't protect them. Tell me what happened after the shot."

Domet traced his finger around the rim of his glass. "They've been looking for you everywhere. Advocators are knocking down doors, the Ravens are interrogating people, the Corrupt Prince is making moves to claim the throne, and the princess is out for your blood. You are the most wanted criminal this country has seen since your father."

"Are my friends and family well?"

"The nobles are protected by their families. Scales has Angelo, who knows nothing. The only ones who are in any real danger are Lyon and Gwen."

"Are they going to come after them?"

Domet paused, hand shaking as he tried to hold the glass. "Only if they can't find you."

I nodded and began to eat slowly, cherishing the crunch of the buttered bread and the salt from the meat. Even the water was wonderfully cold and crisp. I couldn't help but wonder about Naomi. Even on the terms we were on, would she be blamed for being associated with me? Would she be safe? Would she still have her job? It was strange: I worried about her, even knowing how she had manipulated me. And then there was Omari. I asked Domet about him.

"Sirash?" he asked, repeating the name. "No, he's not under arrest. Why would he be?"

I sighed in relief. He must've escaped, and maybe, if I was lucky, they would blame me for that murder, too. If they even cared to bring it up in the trial. They might have learned from their mistakes with the Emperor's trial. But if he was safe—if they all were—nothing else mattered.

"Don't worry about them," Domet said. "They'll be safe. After I get you out of Hollow, I can get them, too. I'll send all of you somewhere else. Somewhere far away from Hollow and all its politics. Somewhere you'll be safe from the princess, the Corrupt Prince, the Ravens, and all of the High Nobles."

"They would still come after us. If I run, they'll just find others to blame. This has to end with me."

"I'll protect you."

I looked up at him. His hands were laid out on the table, shaking slightly. The glass of wine was untouched. He hadn't taken a single sip yet.

"Why haven't you asked me if I killed the king?"

"I know you didn't. As I knew your father didn't kill Davey Hollow."

"You know that for certain? King Isaac sounded quite confident of his guilt."

"He had to, to live with sentencing his best friend and right-hand man to death."

Maybe it was my fault that the king killed himself. All he needed was that little bit of doubt. Leaning back on the couch, I said, "Why do you care what happens to me and my family? You've done nothing but make my life worse. You made me think my father was innocent, hid my friend's imprisonment, and damned me from east to west in this city. Now you want to help me? Give me one good reason why I should believe anything you say. For all I know, this is just another one of your tricks."

"I'm the reason your father died," Domet said without pause. "I'm responsible for him being in the Star Chamber when Davey was murdered, and I'm the one who told him not to warn the king or Ravens about it." He gulped, looking down at the table. "I learned that Davey was in danger from some . . . one I created accidentally, generations ago. I warned your father; I thought it was the smartest way to deal with it—to warn the man to protect the Royals. That's why I was there that evening. Telling him what I had done. Apologizing. But I underestimated the assassin: he took advantage of what changed in his plans. Ended up getting a Royal and a Kingman as well. He was smarter than I ever imagined."

"If you knew who did it, why did you need me?" I asked. "Why drag me in?"

"After your father, I tried something different. I had to create someone who would be able to stop him. I needed you or one of your siblings to be smarter, stronger, and a harder worker than anyone else around you. So I acted indirectly, trying to assess you all. Did you really think someone could put me in the asylum against my will? Or wonder why the wards were always pressing you for more money? It was a trick to get close to you and your family. I thought Gwen would be the one, initially, but she had already been claimed by another, and Lyon was already deeply ensnared in Hollow politics, so I focused on you, Michael. Everything I've done has been to ensure you have a chance—"

"What do you mean, you created him?" I interrupted.

Domet gulped again. "A long time ago I met a man and his son. I had been drinking and I thought they were harmless. The father figured himself an amateur historian and asked me questions about the secrets of the city—things that people usually attribute to long-forgotten myths. No one had ever wanted to talk about them before, so I told him everything. But he didn't talk of them like they were just stories. He believed they were real and asked me about immortality, how to bring someone back from the dead . . . and I told him what I knew.

"At the end of the night, the father used a Darkness Fabrication on me—one stronger than I had ever seen before—to erase his face from my mind. All I remember is his eyes . . . those damn grey eyes. He left the conversation intact, though. As a twisted joke. He wanted me to remember everything I'd told him. And no matter what I do with Fabrications or drink, that conversation won't leave my mind, and I relive it every night while I sleep. It's like he wanted me to know how I had damned and twisted the rules of God again. I know he's the one who planned the assassination. How many others could have conned me so easily?"

"What was the man's name?"

"I don't remember."

Domet met my eyes. His were faded, weak, begging for forgiveness for what he had done. I couldn't quite determine whether it was for the knowledge he had given away or what he had accidentally done to my family and its legacy. I had been overestimating him. Drinking didn't make him careless; it was his strength. He was nothing without it.

How pathetic.

I couldn't believe that I thought he had been in league with the person who had murdered Davey Hollow.

"I was just a drunk old man who has lived too long. I didn't see what I was really dealing with. I knew the first King of Hollow, and the First Kingman who stood by him against the Kings Who Came Before. I knew your father's father, and his father's father. I saw your family rise and I've witnessed every action they've ever taken to defend the crown and the Hollow Family. My arrogance blinded me. I hadn't met someone I've feared like that since the Brothers. If I hadn't indulged in drink so often, I could've—"

"Shut up," I said.

Domet did, his eyes pink and puffy.

"Enough excuses. We're all responsible for our actions. Running away from them won't help anyone. Complaining won't change anything." I laughed at myself as I rose to my feet, every bone in my body cracking and stiff. I was such a hypocrite, a series of contradictions.

I began to walk away from Domet.

Despite everything that had happened between us, I felt bad for the man. He was a chronicler of the world, never gathering anything of his own. No friends. No family. No legacy. Only empty bottles and regrets. Why had I feared this broken man holding on to what little he had? No wonder he wanted to die.

Eternity must be awfully boring without anyone to share it with.

"Where are you going?" he asked, leaning forward in his seat.

I kept going. There was still so much to do before.

Domet grabbed my wrist. "Wait! Stop! If you leave this house, they'll find and arrest you!"

"That's the point."

"They'll kill you! The trial will be a formality; your innocence won't even be considered. I've made mistakes in the past but I won't with you! Give me some time and I'll—"

"If you want to help," I said, "protect my friends and family. That's all I've ever cared about."

"No. I won't let you die like this. All your potential will be wasted! I've been an observer for too long! I won't let another Kingman—"

"I did it," I said. I looked straight into his golden eyes. "It wasn't Dark. It wasn't some rival spy, or king, or noble, or military genius striking against you—it was me. I hated you for threatening my family and keeping Sirash's imprisonment from me, so I burned down the Shrine of Patron Victoria to hurt you. So don't think I'm as good as my ancestors. I've had this coming. I deserve this. If you want to do something for me despite that, protect my friends and family from the Corrupt Prince as you promised to do, back when all this began. They don't deserve to suffer because of my actions. Do that if you must help. But I don't need you anymore."

Domet let go of my wrist, hand limp. His mouth was slightly open and his eyes were staring beyond me. I left him in his living room, the fire sizzling out.

———

It was bitterly cold outside. I dug my hands into my pockets and watched my breath mist in the air.

In the little time I had as a free man, there were a great many things I wish I could have done. I wish I could have walked around in the snow, listening to the crunch it made under my boots while basking in the sun's glow. Or wandered the city one last time, seeing everything from the dye pits to Kingman Keep. Or even to have one last meal of freshly baked bread and butter.

There were people I wished I could speak to one last time: Omari, Jean, Arjay, Gwen, Lyon, Angelo, and Trey. But if I was caught with any of them, they would suffer with me. I doubted the princess or the Corrupt Prince would be merciful to anyone until my head was separated from my neck.

But I did have one last selfish act left.

I was thankful that the path I had taken from the Upper Quarter the morning after I had burned down the Shrine of Patron Victoria wasn't commonly known. It allowed me to traverse a heavily patrolled area easily, and by the time I had to step onto a crowded street, I was already close to my destination.

Once I could smell smoke and musk and saw the abandoned buildings that had once been used by Hollow Academy, the Hollow Library was in sight. From there it was even easier. The Archivists were so preoccupied with their own work, they didn't notice me sneak past them and into the depths of the library. And since I knew its layout so well, I was able to avoid most of the Archivists on my way to the Archmage Room.

The Recorder jumped to his feet as I entered the room, knocking his chair to the floor. His eyes widened and his mouth opened on instinct to ask me his final question.

I cut him off before he could. "Before you ask your question, I'll offer you something better. Why have a yes or no when you could have the entire story? Everything that led to me being labeled a king killer. And all I ask from you, in return for the greatest story ever told, is a small favor and to let me live long enough to tell it."

Symon tapped his fingers against the table. "You'll tell me? Everything? You do realize what you'd be giving me, correct? There will be no one to refute what I write once you are gone. You are placing yourself, and your family's legacy, in my hands to preserve or destroy if I wish."

"I'm aware."

"What is this small favor you'd ask of me?"

"I need your Light Fabrications to help me cure my mother. She's been in the asylum for a decade with all the symptoms of a Forgotten. I've tried everything to help her except magic, and before I die, I need to know I did everything I could."

"Close the door," he said. "Juliet Kingman has been alive this entire time? I feel like a fool. And you should, too. Forgotten can't be cured."

"She can't be a Forgotten, she's not a Fabricator. It has to be caused by a Darkness Fabrication."

Symon righted his chair and sat back down in it. Reaching into his bag, he pulled out a pair of red robes—the same as the ones he wore—and then slid them across the table to me. "Put this on and pull the hood up. It's not much of a disguise, but it'll buy us time while you tell your story and get us to the asylum."

As I changed, I said, "No, you'll get half now and half once you've treated my mother."

"That's absurd," he said. "It'll take you a long time to tell me the entire thing, and I have everything I need to record it here. If you don't trust me to keep up my end of the bargain, you can hold on to this."

Symon handed me a small book that showed years of use. Softly he said, "That's my diary. I write in it every day. If something were to happen to me, it's the only way for me to remember anything about my life. If I break my word, destroy it."

I flipped through it. Symon wasn't lying: there were diary entries in there that dated back to his eighth year. It was his lifeline as a Fabricator, and while it was not nearly as valuable as the story I was about to tell him, it would do. With insurance in case he betrayed me, I took a seat.

Symon already had a quill in hand and a stack of parchment next to him. "Begin whenever you're ready."

I took a deep breath. "You will hear this story as I have lived it."

THE LAST TESTIMONY
OF MICHAEL KINGMAN

". . . And that's how I ended up here. With you. Bartering my story in exchange for a chance at saving my mother."

Symon set his quill down on the table. "I should have realized you nullified my Light Fabrication when I used it on you. I was a fool to think I had seen your shadow wrong when you had been here."

"My shadow?"

"Yes," he said. "When someone is affected by Darkness Fabrications, their shadow usually looks distorted to Light Fabricators. Yours was subtle—it flickered in and out—but it manifests differently for each individual."

"How did I not know that?"

"How many trained Light Fabricators do you run into daily?

Untrained ones wouldn't understand what they're seeing. It's a trade secret, and one we keep very well hidden."

I didn't respond, suddenly seeing Trey's words in a different light. Even as I told my story to the Recorder, I wondered how much I still didn't understand. How much I had missed.

"You must know," Symon said, "no one will believe that the king killed himself."

"I'm just satisfied that someone knows the truth."

"If you say so," he said as he placed all his papers and books into his bag. "Pull your hood further forward: we're heading to the asylum."

Traveling through the city with Symon was the most pleasant stroll I'd ever had, even before my father had been executed. We were ignored in our red robes, and people moved out of our way. At the asylum Symon had the nurses lead us to my mother's cell with just a few words, and once they left, I sat down on my mother's bed as she slept while Symon rolled up his sleeves.

"Is her shadow distorted?" I asked as I gently ran my fingers through her hair.

"With no natural light in here, it's hard to tell. I'll try using a Light Fabrication, anyway."

He put his hand to my mother's forehead and a blinding light came from it to cover her like a veil. Symon let the light bathe my mother for considerably longer than he had when he had used it on me in the library, and when he was finished, he stepped away from the bed and attempted to catch his breath.

"Did it work?" I asked.

"Unsure," he said. "But I used more magic on her than I

needed to lift twenty-year-old Darkness Fabrications from an elderly gentleman's mind. If it didn't work, there's nothing I can do to help her."

"How long will it take before I know?"

"Hours? Days? Weeks? It's hard to be precise. Certainly within a month."

"I don't have a month."

"Then you'll just have to hope."

I kissed my mother on her forehead and let my warmth flow over my body and onto her like a blanket, to protect her from what was about to come. With any luck it would also nullify any trace of the magic Symon's Light Fabrication had missed. If it had worked, I hoped Gwen and Lyon would get their mother back. And if not, I hoped that whatever afflicted her mind would allow her to forget me, too, rather than grieve for her dead son.

"It's time for me to go," I said. "Can you stay with her until Gwen arrives? If it works, I don't want her to wake up alone."

Symon hesitated for a few heartbeats, then said, "Fine. I can go over your story again while I wait."

"Thank you," I said as I returned his diary.

"Don't. I wouldn't if the position were reversed."

"Do you think they'll remember me?"

"The world will know your name." Symon held out his hand and I shook it without hesitation. It was a small comfort that someone knew the truth. Maybe he'd tell Gwen and Lyon some of it, too. Then they'd know what I was about to do had been to protect them.

I bid farewell to the self-proclaimed King of Stories and left the asylum in no rush for what was about to come.

———————

Dressed as I was, it would have been simple for me to walk away from the city and disappear, to start a new life somewhere on the Gold Coast or find out wherever my father had gone in those years he walked away from Hollow. I'd never figured that part of his life out. Or heard how he met my mother. I guess I never would. It didn't matter: where I was going was no place for the truth. I walked the same path he had taken a decade ago, if for different reasons. I had known since I left Domet's house how I wanted this to end, and who I wanted at my side when it did.

I waited outside Naomi's house, bundled in the Archivist's robe. There was only one light on in the house, but it felt alive, albeit only slightly more than I did. I waited until Lights Out before I approached. I used the metal knocker on the door and watched as the light moved through the windows and down to where I was waiting. Naomi opened the door, lantern in one hand and cane in the other, and didn't say a word when she saw my face. She was paler than I remembered, but that was to be expected after taking a bullet to the gut. She took a step out into the street with me, and we stood together as the snow fell around us.

I pulled back my hood. "Naomi."

Her electric-blue eyes were as fierce as when I first met her.

I held out my wrists to her, palms up. "I surrender."

Naomi looked at my wrists and then my face. "Did you actually do it?"

"Would you even believe me if I said no?"

"Why are you doing this?"

"I'm done lying and running away."

"And why come to me for this?" she said, voice rising. "Why not just walk into the castle, or Scales headquarters? I don't want your charity."

"I don't want to be alone when it happens. I trust you."

That much was true. She was cunning and ambitious, but she was honest. There wouldn't be many honest people where I was about to go.

Naomi wiped away an unexpected tear, the first genuine emotion of hers I had seen.

"Then on behalf of the Executioner Division of Scales, Michael Kingman, I'm arresting you for the murder of King Isaac Hollow."

THE LIFE AND DEATH
OF MICHAEL KINGMAN

They tortured me.

Not systematically. But once I was in my cell, various people took turns beating me until I was coughing up blood and my chest was as colorful as a painting. The Ravens were the worst; they truly wanted me to suffer. The others were simply joining the mob. Like father like son, some of them said to me as they cleaned my blood off their knuckles. I had no doubt my father had gone through the same thing a decade ago. And I'm sure we both got the same special treatment from the Ravens. One would hold me while another cut into my skin: long, shallow slices. They didn't want me to bleed too much; it was about the pain. The worst was when they cut down my fingers from the base of my nail, over my knuckles, and across my palm.

Whenever I opened or closed my hands, they would burn in pain, more so after grain alcohol was poured onto them. As soon as the cuts closed over, they would do it again, a fresh slice beside the old one. For variety they would bring out a pair of pliers and threaten to rip out my nails one by one until I wanted to rip my own throat out—but couldn't. One wanted to rip out my tongue. Another wanted to castrate me and make me eat it. A third wanted to mix broken glass with my food to shred my insides. I was thankful that Efyra needed me presentable and whole for my trial, or else I suspected the Ravens would've done much worse to me.

Neither Chloe nor Kai's elder sister were among the Ravens that came for my flesh. Perhaps because it wouldn't quench their thirst for revenge as it did the others. Or perhaps they didn't have a high enough rank to torture me. I didn't know. But it was among the millions of questions I asked myself while in that cell. And although the torture was relentless, I never said a word to them. I wouldn't give them the pleasure of anything but my screams.

They saved something special for the night before the trial. After starving me and leaving me in a completely dark cell devoid of windows, I was taken out and pampered like a prince. The Ravens who had subjected me to all that pain proceeded to clean my entire body with lavender soap and scrubs. They cleaned and dressed my wounds, cut my hair, and brought a barber to shave me. Then they dressed me in one of the fine outfits Domet had given me and said how handsome I looked. How proud my father would've been of the man I had become.

I wasn't angered by the torture. But for them to treat me like that afterward wasn't human. It scared me. So much so that I couldn't look any of them in the eyes after what they had done. I felt like a pig being presented to a butcher before slaughter, with fresh rosy cheeks and a bow on my head.

When the trial finally came, it was a relief. Domet was on the council that would decide my fate—a small benefit of keeping our connection a secret, though I was sure anyone who was determined to could have discovered it. But I doubted anyone cared, since Domet wasn't trying to protect me in this trial, just my friends and family.

The prosecution didn't have any real evidence against me, just the testimonies of witnesses who saw King Isaac hit the ground. Most, if not all of them, claimed they had seen me pull the trigger of the gun right before he fell over the ledge. A bunch of liars.

But who was I to judge?

After their stimulating testimonies, the prosecution reconstructed the timeline while speculating about my motives.

Some scared guard with freshly shined boots was their first major witness against me. He told a wild story of how I had climbed over the walls and snuck into the Royal Tower through a window. No one could back up his testimony, but neither could he be discredited. Of the two true witnesses, Dark couldn't be found, and Domet had protected Omari.

Trey wasn't called, either, despite having seen me in the Star Chamber. Toward the end of the trial, he did appear in the back of the courtroom, dressed as an Advocator, watching me. Deep down he might have had a thought about where my secret passage was, but I could only guess that he remained silent because of everything we had done together.

Over the course of the trial, I heard people damn me with every misstep I had ever made, to prove that I had been slowly blooming into my father's successor—a true king killer—and the council and audience ate it up like slop in a trough.

Naomi didn't give a testimony. Perhaps she didn't want to, or possibly her superiors or her father had prevented it. So the nickname of Kingman Whore could die with me.

But, more surprisingly, the princess was absent, too, despite talking to me in the baths. Perhaps out of shame or anger at having a chance to stop me but failing to, she remained silent and out of sight.

Every so often, between bouts of berating and dehumanizing me, the judge would ask me two questions: Do you have anything to say in your defense; and do you plead to be a Forgotten? Both questions were ridiculous. If I said anything in my defense, I would risk making the Royals angrier and more likely to lash out against my family once I was gone. Their strongest defense was that I said nothing. And, no, I wasn't a Forgotten. I remembered everything. Now more than ever. My only regret was that I would never be able to make amends with my family and friends in person. Maybe one day they would understand what I was doing was for them—as I had with my father.

The verdict came quickly: I was guilty. I would be executed. No big surprise. The only thing I hadn't expected was that the judge declared that I would be executed in the same vein my father had been. He must've been a romantic at heart. Two Kingman traitors having their heads cut off at the top of the steps to the Church of the Wanderer. Maybe someone would write a ballad or song about it. Maybe then my name would be known to the world and I wouldn't be forgotten.

I didn't want to be forgotten.

But so long as my friends remembered me, I wouldn't be completely gone. Maybe, if I was lucky, they would tell their children about me. Back when my biggest worry was where I was getting money to pay for my mother to remain in the asylum. Back when I was a fool who couldn't see all the good that was in front of me.

In the days that followed my guilty verdict—and I use "days" lightly, as who truly knows how long I was in that dark cell?—I thought about my life. All the anger I had used as fuel for years eventually soothed into sorrow as I thought of everything I would miss: seeing my friends, attending Lyon's wedding and holding his child, teasing Gwen, falling in love with the perfect person, having children, staring at the stars, and so much more. I finally understood what it was like to live a life full of regrets. It made me cry at first. But eventually I cried so much to myself in the darkness that I simply couldn't anymore. I would sit there numb, knowing I was doing the right thing.

I didn't want to. More than anything, I wanted to feel the light against my skin, its warmth. Or see a whole moon with a sky full of stars around it. Something simple. It would never happen, though. The only light I saw was when the guards would come and give me enough food and water to sustain my life long enough to die for them. Yet, I cherished seeing that brief sliver of light that shone from behind the metal door as if it were the sun, and hoped its glow would nourish me. It never did, but it was something tangible that let me know a world still existed beyond this cell. The world that had shunned me.

Only once was there ever any more light. It appeared out of nowhere, a dull, low, breathing flame contained in a lantern. It kept coming closer and closer to me, enticing me with its back-and-forth dance. I was so entranced by it that I didn't notice Angelo until he was in front of me, with the lantern in one hand and a slim book in the other.

His voice was the first I had heard in a seemingly endless amount of time. I don't even know if I understood his words at first. "Michael, it's Angelo. I'm here to see you. Are you well? Can I come in?"

I nodded slowly. I wasn't positive he wasn't a figment of my imagination yet. The darkness had tricked me before, but if I was hallucinating someone, Lyon would have made more sense. Gwen even more.

Angelo fumbled with the locks, opened the cell door, and then took a seat on the floor directly across from me, setting the lantern between us. A coarse black beard had grown in; I'd never seen him with one before.

"How're you doing, Michael? Are they looking after you?"

I nodded slowly as I rubbed the itchy skin beneath my shackles.

"That's good." He paused. "I'm here to tell you the execution will be tomorrow at midday. I've been entrusted to hear your final statements. Lyon fought for me rather than a Scorcher or a Reclaimer to witness your last wishes, and I hope you're fine with that. Is there anything you want me to tell anyone before . . . it happens?"

My last wishes. My last words. The way I would be remembered. Words that could be twisted and mistaken for another's need. No, it might be harder for them in the long run, but my silence would protect them all. I would die without saying a word. They would forgive me one day.

I curled my legs up to my chest and remained silent.

Angelo sighed. "I suspected as much, honestly," he said. "It's why I brought this book. It's one of the volumes of *The Journal of the Archmage*. It's one of my favorite sections, and I don't think you've read it, so I wanted to read it to you. I know you enjoyed them, son."

I nodded. It would take a lifetime to read all of them. There wasn't enough time for me to anymore. It was a shame I'd never identified what the Mercenaries had been looking for all those years ago. Or why a piece of Celona had claimed that the Kingman was a traitor when I knew my father was far from it. Maybe neither detail was important. At this point, neither mattered.

Angelo cleared his throat and began the tale:

I don't think I'll ever understand what power is. Even after all these years of research and studying Fabrications, I still feel like an apprentice on the subject. Truthfully, I feel further from the answers I pursue than ever. Have I just been spinning in place, blind to how the world is changing around me? How can I even begin to understand the nature of power when no one shares a common definition of it?

Is power the ability to protect our friends and family? Is it an ever-burning desire to shape the world as we see fit? Is it love? Or is it something else? Is it something that we can't collectively define because we're all so different? Can a man who takes power after losing his wife be faulted for taking action to protect his children? I don't know. And it concerns me. How am I supposed to make amends for this immortal life if I can't even figure out how to best use it? I feel like a child. Maybe I've lived so long I've forgotten what it's like to fear death. Maybe my atonement should be finding a way to kill immortals. Certainly, if I have reached this state, others have, too, and humans are not supposed to live forever. We live our lives to their fullest and then die, hoping we did something memorable in our brief time alive.

Even after all this time, it was still always about power.

Angelo closed the book gently, laying his right hand against it. "This passage always comforted me after my wife died. I hope it's brought a little comfort to you before you go, son."

I exhaled deeply, my focus returning to the flickering fire in the lantern, throwing its light into the corners and over the stone, memorizing it so that when Angelo left, I would still be able to picture it in my mind. Then I wouldn't be in the darkness anymore. There was just enough light to see the ring on his right hand, which he was always knocking against things: I could just make out the sigil.

An iron ring with the crest of a crown being pulled apart by two hands engraved on it.

It was the same symbol on the bullets that killed Davey and Isaac Hollow.

A nearly exact opposite rendition of the Kingman family crest.

Which Alexander Ryder claimed was the Tosburg Mercenary Company's sigil.

A Mercenary company that had attacked Hollow, trying to obtain *The Journal of the Archmage* from the library.

Which would have failed no matter what, as it would have taken a lifetime to read all the Archmage's journals in there.

A lifetime of peace and solitude that a Mercenary could never have had.

A life that only a noble, Royal, or highly privileged person would have.

A life that would have led to a marriage and children. Or even adopted children.

I looked into Angelo Shade's grey, smoky eyes.

Eyes so distinct yet nearly perfect replicas of Dark's.

Eyes that Domet had claimed a boy and his father had. People he had told the secrets of achieving immortality to.

Eyes he had never forgotten. And now eyes that had been passed down throughout their family.

Along with their profession.

It was in that moment I knew, more than I knew anything in my entire life, that the man who was responsible for framing my father was sitting in my cell, reading me a story before I was sent to the gallows. And he had called me *son*.

"It was your company all along," I mumbled, a twinge in my throat from disuse. "The gun, the assassination, the journals—all of it. You raised and mentored me and said I was the son you wished you had . . . Was it one last insult to my father? Did you want to take his children from him after taking his life?"

Angelo shifted, leaning closer to me. "I'm sorry, I didn't hear what you said. Could you repeat it?"

"Tosburg Company. All those years ago on the Day of Crowning. It was yours, wasn't it?"

Silence.

I stared into his eyes. I knew. And he knew it. He couldn't hide in the darkness anymore. I knew who he was. I knew what he did. I knew everything now. A simple slip of the tongue and a little arrogance was all it took. He shouldn't have been brazen enough to wear the ring. Not in front of me. And all those times I hadn't paid attention, and my answer had been right there. If I had been a better man, King Isaac would still be alive. Because of me, Angelo had two Royals and two Kingman as notches in his gun.

No, I was wrong. He didn't have me yet.

Angelo knocked his ring against the stone and the clang of it echoed through the cell, heating my skin. All those times he had done that. The answer had been so close. But my blood didn't boil in anger; it just focused on him as if I were taking aim.

"I think I should leave, Michael," he said. "I don't want to aggravate you. It was never my intention to, *honestly*. I hope you've enjoyed our time together and understand that . . . I was trying to help you. Nothing more. I took you in because I was the only one who saw the potential you had, to be something greater than your father ever was. I suppose, in a way, being a king killer is a step up from murdering a prince."

"Why? That's all I want to know."

"Michael, I don't know what you've come up with in your head while you've been in this maddening darkness for so long. But I would advise you not to make accusations that you have no evidence to support. The law can be a cruel mistress that destroys families in its unrelenting pursuit of the truth. It would be a shame if something happened to Lyon, his unborn child, or Gwen in their sleep, wouldn't it?"

I bit down on my tongue as Angelo left without another word. I watched the flame in his lantern vanish up the staircase. But as the light faded, the cold stayed at bay and I was left with a sharp focus on the truth. Since my last attempt to find the truth had brought me here, alone and about to be executed, I had to be careful. Going after it again could cost others dearly.

I was at a crossroad. I knew it was Angelo, and he wore the evidence. His son carried the twin of the gun that had killed Davey and Isaac Hollow. But he was threatening my family and friends, and Domet was no protection against him. After all this, I couldn't go after him using the law.

The warmth returned, slithering over my skin. It felt like an insult, reminding me of who I was and what I could have been if I hadn't been obsessed with my family's legacy.

I took a deep breath, exhaled, and waited.

THE EXECUTION OF
MICHAEL KINGMAN

Every move from dungeon to nondescript house to nondescript house on the day of my execution was so strategic and planned out, I thought I was going to die from the boredom of the routine rather than on the executioner's block. I almost wished someone would just shoot me in the streets mid-transport to end my suffering. At least we were only a few hundred yards from the Church of the Wanderer now. Advocators were hustling and bustling around me, making sure everything was perfect. Only the Ravens that guarded me looked calm. Only they seemed to know this was an execution, not a festival.

A squad leader, his clothes recently laundered, his black shoes shined, and decorated in medals, approached us. This was his day as much as mine. He saluted Rowan Kerr, the three-feathered Raven, and said, "Raven, we're ready to move to the execution block. The Warden is waiting for me to transfer the chains to him. Are you ready to proceed?"

Three Feathers nodded. "I'll take the front and Chloe the rear. You may unlock and transfer the chains."

"Yes, Raven." The commander knelt as he took a key from his pocket and unlocked the chain that bound me to the floor. He held it firmly, the key back in his inner jacket pocket. "Rise, king killer."

My legs had just enough strength in them to stand on cue, wavering back and forth to the find balance. Only a little longer left. Soon my body would be able to rest.

"Move, king killer!" the commander howled, yanking on my shackles. My knees buckled, and I collapsed under my own weight, falling against him. He shoved me off him, and I hit the floor with a loud crash.

The commander kicked me in the torso and pain spiked through my body. Everything went fuzzy and white as I stared at the ground, hands closed tightly.

Chloe grabbed me by the neck and hauled me back to my feet. "Commander, watch yourself. He has to be able to walk to his execution and look unharmed before the people. Do I make myself clear?"

The commander hesitated and then bowed to her. "Yes, Raven." He took my chains again and led me more gently toward the exit.

My senses were overwhelmed when he opened the door.

I could smell everything, from the rotten vegetables ready to be thrown at me to the hot metal smell that lingered in the air. There was a bitter twinge on my tongue when the Warden took my chains from the squad leader and wrapped them around his gauntlet. The roar of the crowd all merged together into white noise. I wasn't even lucky enough to die with blue skies above me. Grey clouds shrouded the sun instead. Such was my luck.

The Warden, encased in armor, lead me down a narrow path through the crowds of people toward the Church of the Wanderer. Three Feathers was in front of him as Chloe watched me from behind. Advocators created a barrier between my escort and everyone else. No doubt there were Evokers watching for anyone suspicious in the crowds. They weren't going to take any chances. Not with me. Not today. Not after what had happened in the courtroom.

The executioner's block was waiting for me at the top of the stairs. The great stone church was behind it, glowing a pale white with all the Moon's Tears that covered it. All the major players in Hollow were waiting at the top of the stairs behind it for me—except for the princess, which made no sense when she was in Hollow. Captain Efyra and the Corrupt Prince stood on the sides of it, the prince with a big grin on his face and an executioner's ax in his hands. Clearly, he had decided he'd rather kill me himself than force my brother to do it.

My bodyguards dropped me off at the block, locking my chains so I was kneeling in front of it. They took their place behind me. My knuckles rested against the wood so I could feel something before the ax came down on my neck.

To the left, Captain Efyra raised her hand to silence the crowd and then shouted, "We are gathered here today to witness the execution of Michael Kingman for the crime of regicide. May this day serve as a reminder to all that the enemies of Hollow will be caught and prosecuted to the fullest extent of the law. Hollow will always have justice, and this is what happens to traitors of Hollow. No longer will they be able to—"

She was such a performer. It wasn't even worth listening to her. She was just telling the crowd what they wanted to hear, to restore some of the confidence that the commoners had in their government—especially after the Emperor had escaped justice—and I was the sacrifice to do it. Out of the corner of my eye, I watched as Angelo entered the Church of the Wanderer. I guess he wasn't going to watch the show unfold. Didn't he want to see his handiwork in person?

I must've missed the end of her speech, because the crowd was cheering as Efyra swapped places with the Corrupt Prince. It was time for the main event.

"Enough!" shouted a voice from behind me.

I couldn't turn my head fully, but I caught a glimpse of the Reclaimer—and all the monks—filing out of the church.

"I won't let you kill him," the Reclaimer proclaimed. "I watched his father die on these steps and I won't let another Kingman die like this. I do not give permission—"

The Corrupt Prince strode over, grabbed the Reclaimer, and slammed his head against the side of the church. There were popping sounds as brittle old bones snapped and collapsed, and then it was over. A few people gasped and looked away, but most had watched, unmoving.

I felt sick as his blood began to trickle over the stones. I had tricked and stolen from him, and the old man had still defended me—and had died for nothing . . . Foolish old man . . . I hoped he found peace in whatever afterlife there was for his following.

"Interfering with an execution is punishable by death," the Corrupt Prince said. "Does anyone else wish to speak up, or do we have the Church's permission to continue?"

No one moved as the prince returned to his spot, and the hairs prickled on the back of my neck as the ax hovered over it.

This was it.

For everything I was or had been, I had never really come to terms with what I was. I wasn't a noble, not even before my family had been disgraced and abandoned to wolves. This past week had taught me that: I would never be able to conform to their lives or play the games of nobility. Even at my best I had been tricked and manipulated. I wouldn't have liked the person I would've become if I had remained a High Noble, but I had learned what they stood for and made myself better in the process.

I hadn't accepted that until I had been thrown in a dungeon, deprived of light, with nothing to occupy my mind. I wasn't a noble, or a thief, or a con man, but I wasn't some common citizen either. I was Michael . . . Michael Kingman. And how I would be remembered didn't matter in the end, so long as my family and friends knew I loved them.

The Corrupt Prince began to lift the ax high into the air above my neck.

Although I did know how to pickpocket.

And it had been easier to steal from a cocky commander in the streets than from a king in his castle.

The key to my irons slipped out under my sleeve and fell into the keyhole as if drawn to it. I unlocked it with my deft fingers as the ax began to fall. The ax slammed against the block and, having found nothing, shook as if lightning had struck it. I whipped the irons at the Corrupt Prince. He screamed, dropped the executioner's ax, and held his face, blood gushing everywhere.

As if I were going to go quietly. There was still one last thing to do.

The crowds didn't have time to react, and before anyone had a crossbow drawn, my body was nullified and I had my chains wrapped around Chloe's throat, taking her hostage in front of her mother. My other hand, the one that wasn't choking her, drew her sword to keep back those closest to me. Waving it frantically, I backed away from everyone, the entrance to the Church of the Wanderer behind me.

Efyra, Captain of the Ravens, pointed her sword at me but raised her hand to everyone around us. "No one fire! Not while my daughter is in the way! Let her go, Kingman! I swear to God, I won't let you take another!"

I continued to back away from everyone toward the doors of the church. Angelo was somewhere in there, and I had to get to him alive. Just a little longer.

"You're a sick monster, Kingman. Just like your pathetic father," Efyra snarled. "Do you get some perverted pleasure out of killing people? You little bastard. I should've snuffed the life out of you after your father's execution like I wanted to."

I said nothing, continuing to back away into the church. As soon as I crossed the church's threshold, I shouted, "Close the doors! Do it, or I'll kill her!"

Efyra snapped at two Advocators. "Do it. Close the doors. Lock the son of a bastard in there. He can beg for forgiveness to God before I rip out his entrails. Do it!"

The Advocators looked at Efyra multiple times before grabbing the edges of the massive wooden doors and closing them. Efyra stood directly in the center, watching me through the gap until the doors were fully closed with a thunderous crash. I dropped the sword and then pulled the wooden bar down as the pounding on the door began.

"I'm sorry," I said to Chloe as I wrapped her wrists up in my chains. "I'm sorry it had to be you. There was no one else. You were the only one I thought your mother wouldn't risk."

"Are you deranged? How do you plan on escaping here with your life?" she said.

"I don't." I tightened the chains and then pushed her to the ground, her armor clashing against the stone. I took up the sword and walked down the aisle toward the man waiting for me behind the podium.

THE LEGACY OF
MICHAEL KINGMAN

Angelo Shade leaned against the podium, staring straight at me with those grey eyes of his. His military jacket was pristine, his black hair tidy, and the beard he had in the dungeons was gone. There wasn't even a flush across his face. "I'll be honest . . . ," he said. "I didn't expect this, Michael."

"Isn't this what you wanted? Why else walk in here during my execution but to give us some private time once I escaped?"

He rolled his eyes, muttering something to himself. "Turn your-self in, and maybe Efyra will show some mercy and only behead you."

"Why did you frame my father? Was it really because he defeated you on the Day of Crowning?"

Angelo glanced toward Chloe on the floor. "I don't know what you're talking about, Michael."

"Don't lie to me! Why did you frame my father for Davey's murder?"

"You're delusional, Michael. I didn't do anything to your father. I never knew him. I didn't migrate to Hollow until long after he was dead."

I tapped the tip of the sword against the stone. "Stop lying to me. Tell me the truth about the assassination of Davey Hollow. I know it was your gun that killed him. The symbol on the bullets matches the one on your ring!"

He held up his hands. The ring with the hands ripping apart the crown was missing. "What ring, Michael? You've lost your mind. Put the sword down. There's no need for further bloodshed."

I cursed. "I should've expected you to take the ring off. There's still the—"

Sharp pain splintered through me and I screamed, then collapsed to the floor, shaking in pain. The sword fell to my side. I tried to spread the warmth over my body but . . . I was so cold, I could barely hold on to it, let alone spread it over my entire body.

"Commander Shade," Chloe called from the back of the church. Her hands were electrified and the chains had been cut in half. "Are you well?"

"Yes. Be wary! He's a Nullify Fabricator. He may not be as weak as he appears."

Chloe shot me in the chest again with lightning and I screamed, convulsing on the floor. She kept me pinned with a steady stream of lightning until my body went so numb that the pain stopped. I closed my eyes and focused on the small warmth in my chest. I still had a chance so long as it didn't go out.

When I stopped moving, Chloe stepped over my body to pick up her sword and then walked over to Angelo. "Commander Shade, we should open the doors and let the captain deal with him. It's my priority to get you to safety."

No, not yet. I grunted and pushed myself off the ground, wobbling to my knees. I couldn't give up. I couldn't let Angelo win. I had to stand. For Davey. For Gwen. For Lyon. For my father, and for everyone else I had hurt in my pursuit to restore my family's legacy. I couldn't let it go to waste. Every muscle was shaking, but I continued to rise steadily until I was standing and looking them in the eyes. The small warmth in my chest steadied me like a lone star in a cloudy sky.

"I warned you he was resilient," Angelo declared.

"Not for long," she said, electrifying her hand. "Stand back, Commander. I'll end this once and for all." Chloe wound up and threw a bolt of lightning at me.

I put my hand out, remembering the stories from my youth about my ancestors and the legendary feats they had accomplished. I let all my warmth cover it and plucked the lightning out of the air. I held it, snapping and crackling in my hand, steadier on my feet while I looked at the lightning I held.

Perhaps I could stand side by side with my ancestors after all.

Jamal would be proud of me.

With all my remaining strength, I threw the lightning back at Chloe. She didn't move or dodge it, eyes wide as the lightning hit her straight in the chest.

The Raven crumpled to the ground like a bird with clipped wings.

I fell to my knees, breathing heavily. All my strength was gone. I had nothing left. And yet Angelo was perfectly fine.

Angelo kicked at Chloe. She didn't move. I couldn't even tell if she was breathing.

"Interesting," he said. "You learned how to use your Defensive Fabrication as a weapon. I'd be impressed if I wasn't so annoyed. Why did you have to go digging into the long-buried past, Michael? You could have been at my side instead of trying to oppose me."

"Why did you frame my father?"

He laughed and took the sword from Chloe's hand. "Do you know how I've achieved so much in my life, Michael? I wasn't born into the noble lifestyle. A single father raised me and taught me that power was the worth of a man. I was born with nothing and had to earn everything, without even an inkling of power to protect myself . . . I'm not even a Fabricator. Did you know that?"

"Answer my question."

"Aren't I?" he asked, extending his arms out as he walked toward me. "I don't know how your father figured out what I had planned that day, but he showed up at the right spot at the right time and was about to ruin everything. He nearly caught the assassin and saved the prince. I did the only thing I could: I bet on the unrelenting love a parent feels for his child and ordered the murder of the prince in front of your father. Honestly, I couldn't believe it worked. The king instantly accepted that his best friend had murdered his son. I didn't even need to give your father a motive: the king assumed it was a power play for the throne. I love when people put emotions over logic. It makes them easier to manipulate."

"I don't understand."

"Don't understand what? That I took advantage of your father's love of his family and duty to his country to destroy him? I knew that if King Isaac threatened you and your siblings, your father would crumble under the pressure and admit he murdered the prince to protect you all. King Isaac simply believed the lie that was fabricated for him that day, and the days that followed. Not that I can fault him . . . grief is a terrible burden to carry. Better men than him have been destroyed by it. I'm honestly surprised he lasted as long as he did before he killed himself."

I opened my mouth to respond, but Angelo cut me off.

"How do I know you didn't do it? Simple. The king has been a broken man for a very long time; he's been a puppet for years, and ideally would have been until his daughter was old enough to rule, and then, well . . . I won't ruin the surprise, but I suppose you've moved up my timeline a little bit. It's better this way. I couldn't distract you from your crazy idea of restoring your family honor; thankfully Gwen and Lyon never aspired to do that, only you . . . but I imagine it'll be easier to destroy them now if they do. Your death will haunt them for the rest of their lives. The last members of the Kingman family. What a title to hold."

Angelo raised the tip of the sword over my heart and prodded me with it. I fell over onto my back like a dying animal. It hurt to breathe. I had nothing left, and Angelo stood over me, the sword pointed at my heart.

"Why take us in? Why take care of us?"

"Because you were malleable children that I could shape and direct any way I wanted. Did you think I loved you? Or that I made so little money I couldn't afford decent food or nice clothes? I hope not.

Else you'd be stupider than I thought you were. Michael, let me be clear: you were nothing more than pawns I planned to turn against Hollow one day. It was my dream to watch the Kingman family destroy the country they had been bound to protect—and I was so close. What sweet irony it would have been."

"But why?" I asked one last time.

"Because you're a High Noble. I have a blood debt to repay to all of you for what you did to the love of my life and unborn daughter. Don't worry, the rest of your kind will face the same fate soon enough. I don't discriminate."

Angelo pushed the tip of the sword through my shirt and cut into my skin until it dug ever so slightly into my chest. I couldn't even scream, just gasp for air and claw at the edges of the sword. My cut palms didn't do anything but dye the blade red as I tried to pull it out. I was useless and powerless once again. "Don't make this harder than it has to be. This was never your story, Michael. *It was mine.*"

Angelo pushed the sword further into my chest, wiggling it back and forth with a smile. Wood snapped and cracked behind me as my vision began to blur.

So this was how it was going to end. I didn't feel any warmth, as I had under the river. There was nothing. Nothing except for a set of very . . . very . . . heavy . . . eyelids.

My search was over . . . my legacy written . . . now it was time for me to see my father and tell him I did my—

"Get the fuck away from my son!"

"And would you kindly take that sword out of my apprentice's chest?"

Ma? Dark? What . . . ? How . . . ?

I gasped for air as the sword left my chest. I convulsed, covering the wound, bleeding profusely. As I tried to put pressure on it, I rolled my eyes back to the entrance. My mother, Dark, Lyon, Gwen, Charles Domet, the Whisperer for the Church of the Eternal Flame, and the Captain of the Ravens, along with every Raven in Hollow, were walking toward us. The Ravens surrounded me and Angelo, then stood still as statues. Behind the Ravens were others, all smiling and standing as tall as titans.

"Captain Efyra," Angelo stated. "I was dealing with the king killer. He attacked me in a delusional rage. Luckily, I was able to disarm him after your daughter distracted him. I—"

"Where is she?" Efyra said.

Angelo pointed behind the podium.

The captain walked past me, stepping on my wrist as she made her way to her daughter's side. She removed the chest plate and put her fingers on Chloe's neck. "Breathing. Thank God. The Wanderer has guided God to watch over her today, it seems."

My mother beckoned Gwen and Lyon forward as she stood between Angelo and me. I had never felt safer in my life, and was suddenly very aware of what the Kingman family had once been like. She was in charge, everyone following her directions without complaint, even if she was a traitor's wife.

Lyon knelt at my side and put one of his hands over the wound as he ran the other through my hair. Gwen was hugging me, crying, and getting covered in blood.

"We're all here, Michael," Lyon said, staring at our mother. "You'll be fine. Just hold on a little longer. Breathe deeply and slowly.

We have you. She's back, Michael. She's back. Ma's back to normal and I have no idea how or why, but she's back to normal."

"I don't understand," Angelo said, looking around. "What is going on?"

Efyra had her daughter's head in her lap, running her hands through her frizzy black hair.

Instead my mother said, "There was a mistake."

"A mistake?"

"Yes," Charles Domet said. He didn't look anywhere near me. "A mistake, Commander Shade. We almost executed a Mercenary of Orbis Company on false grounds. We almost started a war. Luckily, this Mercenary and his company came forward in time to stop it."

"What? Explain."

Dark stood straight and looked his father in the eyes, a big smile on his face. "I thought I explained when I walked in. He's my apprentice. And you almost killed him. At least, if these imbeciles had done it, they could've hidden behind politics, but you . . . I wonder what it would have been like to be the person who started a war with Mercenaries."

There was a round of hollering from behind the Ravens.

"Him? A Mercenary? Are you all blind? How can he be a Mercenary? I've been his father for—"

"Foster father," my mother corrected icily.

"Foster father," Angelo said with disdain, "for ten years, and never once has Michael come anywhere close to fulfilling the necessary trials, let alone the documentation—"

Dark pulled a rolled sheaf of paper out of his pocket. He faked being shocked once it was visible to everyone in the room. "Oh, goodness me, is this what I think it is? A Mercenary contract signed in Michael's own blood? Don't bother worrying about whether it's really his blood or not. It is. There were witnesses. Even one or two respectable ones. Like it or not, Michael Kingman is a Mercenary, ready to serve his company. He's *mine*."

"When did he sign the papers?" Angelo inquired.

Dark tapped his chin. "Not positive. Must've been before the king died, but I can't remember when. Maybe I lost the memory when I used a Fabrication. It happens; no catastrophe, since we have the paperwork."

From the back of the church, Efyra said, "Until we can prove beyond doubt that Michael Kingman killed King Isaac, we're forced to release him into Dark's custody." She had one hand tenderly on Chloe's face.

"A king killer walks free? First the rebel leader and now the king killer? What has this country come to if we can't even prosecute those two?" some obnoxious religious figure asked.

"As I said," Dark said, "do you want to be the one who starts a war with every Mercenary company on this continent? You all know the rules: Prove it beyond a shadow of a doubt and my company will send you his head on a silver platter. But it must be us who do it. Only Mercenaries try other Mercenaries."

"As it should be," voices bellowed from behind the Ravens.

"Michael Kingman can't leave this city until we know the absolute truth of what happened on that balcony," Efyra stated. "That's the condition. These Mercenaries want proof? We'll give them so much evidence, they'll choke on it. Every Evoker, noble, bounty hunter, Tweeker, Royal, and Scales operative will be after him. This is merely a delay. Nothing more. Justice will come for him. Be it in the street or at the end of an executioner's ax, our king will be avenged and our country will have its revenge."

"Or maybe," Domet said, with a glance at me, "we've just saved ourselves from executing another innocent Kingman." Everyone looked at him except my mother, who smiled at me instead. "Ignore me: I'm still drunk from yesterday."

"Efyra is right. He can't escape justice forever," Angelo declared. "Michael Kingman will die before we crown another. I have faith in our city to purge this evil. Hollow has not survived by being weak and powerless."

"No," my mother said with iron in her voice. "Hollow has survived because of my family, and now we're back to avert a war. You can thank us later."

I stared at the colored light streaming through the stained glass windows. I was free—well, as free as I could be after being tried for regicide. And although the government was still coming after me, I could feel the warmth on my skin again. It was a brilliant-light warmth, like lying on the grass in the sunshine. Something I'd thought I'd never feel again.

The bells tolled above me as I drifted away with my brother at my side and my sister whispering comforting things in my ear.

I had my truth, my freedom, and my life.

Angelo Shade would die by my hand another day.

EPILOGUE

DAWN OF A NEW DAY

"Hey, Da."

My father's grave was overrun with weeds, the three-tier head-stone was discolored, and a blanket of frozen snow covered it. The spot for candles and incense was completely empty, and it hadn't been maintained in years. Nature had been allowed to run wild with the space no one wanted to care about. His headstone didn't even have his name on it. Instead, the words *May Happiness Find Him in Death* had been engraved on it in plain bold lettering.

It was nowhere near any of my other ancestors' resting places—almost half a city away from the water crypts below Kingman Keep. It was Isaac's last act of revenge against my father, or maybe it was his only act of mercy. Maybe I would have been buried next to him, in this empty place on the outskirts of the city, full of dead trees and cold, rocky ground.

I wondered if my grave would have looked like this. Probably, since people don't visit convicted king killers. I hadn't, and he was my father . . . but it didn't matter. I knelt in front of his grave and began to pull the weeds. It would take a while, but we had a lot to catch up on.

"It's been years since I visited last. I . . . uh . . . I meant to come back more. I'm sorry I didn't."

I yanked a pocket of weeds out of the ground. The bristles dug into my palms, numbing them. Or maybe it was the cold. Winter was in full swing, even though most of the snow had melted. Only the bitterness and a memory of spring remained.

"It's been five years, I think," I said. "I never meant to stop visiting, I just . . . I felt . . . I stopped coming because . . . I was ashamed of you. I tried not to believe the charges against you, and for a while I was strong—I denied them for a long time—until the last time I came to visit. You probably saw what those children did to me that day. I gave up after that. It was easier to hate you than to keep fighting. I wasn't strong enough to defend you. Or smart enough to see that you were selfless enough to put your pride aside for us. Everything you did was for us."

I swallowed hard. All the weeds were gone. The next step was to sweep off the snow that covered his headstone. He deserved as much after all these years.

"I hope you can forgive me. It was just so . . . hard. But that's not an excuse, is it? Not a good one, anyway. I'm a terrible son, aren't I? I don't know what to say besides I'm sorry. And that I'll try to be a better son.

"I'm doing better. As good as I can be, I guess. Angelo is still out there, and he'll retaliate, now that I know his secret. I'll have to get evidence and make sure I know the whole story of what happened before I do anything. Domet hasn't contacted me yet, though I'm sure he will eventually. With Ma back to normal . . . and she is back to normal, Da. The Light Fabrications, or the Nullify Fabrications, worked, and she's back. We don't know why, and we don't really care.

"We're all living together now, and Lyon, Gwen, and Ma have been amazing. Gwen says I'm the first Mercenary Kingman in written history. Which she claims is a big deal, since our family has done everything, so I've found my legacy by accident . . . and it was all Lyon's idea . . . He saved my life.

"Then there's Dark . . . I'll have to start working with him soon. I don't know why he agreed to save me. I don't know what he has planned for me. I don't know anything . . . Da, I don't know if I can do this. I've made so many mistakes, where do I even begin to make amends? I feel so overwhelmed."

My father's tombstone was silent and still as it always was and always would be. He couldn't give me any answers. But he had shown me what love and courage were with his final actions, and through his example I knew who I wanted to become. Step by small step.

"It looks better," Lyon declared, with Gwen at his side as they joined me at the grave. She was holding a bouquet of Moon's Tears, while Lyon carried a bucket of soapy water. Our Mother was behind them, a chicken leg in her hand as she tried to regain some of the muscle and fat she had lost over the years.

"It does, doesn't it?" Gwen said. "We brought Moon's Tears for Father."

Lyon knelt next to me, dipped his brush in the water, and began to clean the gravestone. We had divided the tasks for this. I cleared it, Lyon cleaned it, and Gwen provided the finishing touches. Family is family, no matter what. It had just taken us a while to figure that out.

"Your father should be in the crypt below Kingman Keep with the rest of the family," my mother said. "We'll have to arrange that—soon."

"That requires us to have Kingman Keep again," I said. "Which isn't likely."

"Why not?" my mother asked. "It's our home, and I'd love to see who stops me from returning."

"We're not High Nobles anymore, Ma."

"So?"

"We can't live there, it's—"

"It's our home. Always has been and always will be. Let them tell me otherwise."

I didn't know how to respond; she gave me butterflies in my stomach. If my siblings heard us, they didn't respond. Lyon was too busy cleaning the headstone, muttering to himself as he did. Gwen sat on the cold ground behind him, Moon's Tears in her lap. I suppose, after all these years, waiting a few more minutes to put flowers on my father's grave was nothing.

She had been right after all. Our father was an innocent man.

He may have left me with nothing but a beating heart, a tainted name, and the belief that family was the most important thing in the world. But he had given me the opportunity to become the man I wanted to be. Everything the Kingman family would be known for from now on would be because of us and what we chose to do . . . or what we chose not to do. The world would not be kind to us. But, together, I knew anything was possible. The Kingman legacy was not mine to bear alone anymore.

"Ma," I said as I went to my feet. "I'm going to go—"

My mother kissed my forehead. "Go. Don't worry about us. We'll be at home; bring your friends for dinner if you see them, and don't be late?"

I lingered in front of my father's grave for a moment, playing with his ring. I didn't cry. I didn't have a reason to anymore . . . and even as I thought that, tears found their way down my face anyway. I walked through the cemetery with my head down, watching my breath float away whenever it left my mouth.

Trey was pacing back and forth at the entrance of the cemetery. I slowed, trying to find something to say to him, and he stopped when he saw me. We stood in mutual silence.

"Trey," I said finally.

"Michael."

We looked at anything but each other.

"Why are you here?" he asked.

"Visiting my father. Are you seeing your mother and Jamal?"

Trey nodded. "I haven't been here since . . . since Jamal died, and I wanted to see where they buried him. He's supposed to be next to my mother. Not that either of them have headstones . . . or plaques . . . or anything that identifies them."

"Well, I'll let you—"

"I don't remember."

I paused. "What?"

Trey stared at the ground. What was he so ashamed of?

"I don't remember where my mother was buried," he said. "I've been here for a while, trying to remember, but I can't. I can't remember where she is, which means I can't find Jamal's grave and . . . and . . . and I want to say goodbye to him."

Had he lost that memory in the castle when he used the Light Fabrication on me? I put my hand on his shoulder and smiled as best as I could. "I remember. I'll take you there."

He nodded like a child. Together we went to their graves, silent the entire way. When we arrived, he collapsed to his knees in front of two freshly dug mounds. One of them was much more recent and smaller than the other. "Thank you."

"You would've done the same for me."

"Maybe." A pause. "I never told you how my ma died."

"No, you didn't."

"If I tell you . . . will you tell me whether you actually killed the king or not?"

"Of course," I said. And I meant it.

Trey watched the cold-snap sparrows fly through the sky. "I killed her. She came at me, eyes burning red, and I stabbed her. In the stomach, and in the heart, and then in the shoulder before she stopped moving."

I didn't respond, letting him talk.

"I couldn't bear how she treated us. Like we were her bank," he continued. "I snapped. I thought I could live with killing her if it meant our lives would be better . . . only, as she died . . . she said she was sorry. She asked me to forgive her, said that the Blackberries fucked up her head. She said she still loved me. Even if I had killed her."

"Trey, you—"

"I don't blame anyone except her for what happened. She was the one who chose to indulge in Blackberries," he growled. "It was the right choice. She was a parasite on my life. But I could never bring myself to tell Jamal. I just didn't want him to leave me. And now he has."

"Trey," I said softly, "what do you plan to do when you find your father?"

"I'm not going to kill him," he said slowly. "I need answers first, and then I'm going to make him regret leaving me. I'm going to rise above the East Side and rewrite all the useless rules this country was founded on, to make sure my life can never happen to another. My brother deserved more. In his memory, I'll make sure others like him get it."

"Why do you want to know if I killed the king?"

"Can't you tell? I'm the villain, Michael, and I want to know if you'll be in my way or by my side. Rewriting the rules of this country means tearing everything down . . . and, well, you are a Kingman. So, did you kill the king?"

"No, he killed himself," I said. "Though I came close. My father didn't kill Davey Hollow, either. He was set up by someone and I found out who."

Without hesitation, he asked, "Who was it?"

"Angelo Shade."

Birds chirped from the branches above.

"Your foster father? Why?"

"I'm not completely sure. But the High Nobles did something to him and his family and he's wanted revenge against them ever since."

Trey shook his head and climbed back to his feet. "What happens now? Are you just going to find Angelo and then shoot him in the head to get revenge?"

I shook my head. "No, I'm not going to throw away my life like that. My father wouldn't have wanted me to."

"You're going to give up on getting revenge? That doesn't—"

"Oh, I'm going to get it. I'm going to take everything from him, piece by piece, until he wishes I'd killed him in that church. Then I'll get the Rebel Emperor, for what she's done to my father's memory and for everyone else those rebels have hurt—Jamal included. They might be able to escape Hollow's justice but not mine."

"How do you plan on doing that?"

"With my family back, I'm going to make myself a king. A Mercenary King."

"Michael," he said, staring me in the eyes so there was no confusion, "if you rise to become a king or even remain at the side of the princess, I will tear you down. No more kings. No more queens. No more nobility. Because if they exist, so will people like me and Jamal. Do you understand what I'm saying?"

"I do. But I don't have any other solution right now, so I'll do what I must. If you come up with one that doesn't involve killing every noble there is, I'll listen."

"But not before."

"Not before."

And under the cold winter sun we stood together in front of two graves, enjoying each other's company before we went down separate paths, breathing and alive and together for now.

ACKNOWLEDGMENTS

I'd like to thank all the wonderful people at JABberwocky Literary Agency, John Berlyne, and my agent, Joshua Bilmes. I was lucky enough to find someone who believed in me and has been my biggest advocate every step of the way. Words cannot express how much it has meant to me.

Next, thank you to everyone at Saga Press, Gollancz, and my editors, Joe Monti and Gillian Redfearn. Joe was willing to listen to me rant about the nitty gritty of what I was trying to do in this book, showing me that someone might want to discover all the secrets within it. Gillian's surgical editing pen cut away all the nonessential bits and constantly questioned what I was doing and why. Without them, all the good parts might not have made it in.

Thank you to my copyeditors, Stephen Breslin and David Chesanow. Also, thank you to my proofreaders, Christopher Milea and Katie Rizzo.

Thank you to Lauren Jackson, Madison Penico, Stevie Finegan, and Brendan Durkin for all their hard work.

Thank you to my cover artists, Richard Anderson and Bastien Lecouffe-Deharme, for their breathtaking art.

So much effort goes into taking a book from conception to print that it makes writing look like the easy part. All of you helped the book in my head become the book in print, and I will always be grateful.

Thank you to my mother, my family, my grandparents, the Church of the Overlord, the Aikens Group and that Graham kid, Jamie Nelson, Joshua Palmatier, Elise Salada Hazlett, Kyle Van Larr, Erin McKeown, and everyone else who helped me get here.

Lastly, thank you to my dad. He once asked me, back when I was in the eighth grade, if I was serious about this writing thing. And said that if I was, he would support me every step of the way. Over a decade has passed since then, but here I am, finally. It's been a long time coming.

Turn the page for a preview of

The Two-Faced Queen

book two of The Legacy of the Mercenary King. . . .

Bound by Fate

It was our birthday, and for the first time in a decade the Princess of Hollow invited me to celebrate it with her.

My mother told me not to go. That it would be a trap. That the princess would use any and every opportunity to get revenge, since I was the primary suspect in her father's death. But my siblings Lyon and Gwen both knew what I would do before I admitted it.

From the very beginning of our lives we had been together. The Princess of Hollow and I had been born on the same day. She was early, while I was late. It had occurred on the last snowfall of the year when spring was in sight, coating the entire city in a heavy white blanket that had kept the midwives from reaching our mothers, forcing our fathers to birth us instead. Fate had decided to replicate that day, as I trudged through the snow toward my destination, wishing it wasn't so far away. The merchants tried to maintain the roads in the city, but in the Upper Quarter it was the Royal's responsibility to clear the snow, and ever since King Isaac's death the castle had gone silent. It might as well have been a mausoleum, because no gossip, rumors, or whispers had come out of it since I had escaped my execution. No doubt the princess was determining whom she could trust and whom she had to dispose of.

According to stories I had heard in my youth, most considered our dual birth to be an omen of good things to come. There was only one other time in Hollow history that a Kingman-and-Hollow bonded pair had ever entered the world together, and it had been Montagne the Remembered and Yuri the Unneeded. They had created a golden age in Hollow together, and without meaning to . . . we had been born with the pressure on our shoulders to do the same. Even if we weren't the heirs. And maybe that was why we became obsessed with our legacies and ancestors.

Because of this supposed destiny, our parents had never been surprised how close we became, even for a bonded pair. There were times that we could communicate without speaking, glances and smiles substituting instead. We were perfect together, inadvertently covering each other's flaws and highlighting our strengths. The princess was intelligent and artistic but quiet and nervous in large crowds, while I was confident and talkative, drawing in people with what she had affectionately dubbed my poisonous tongue. She had also been the only person able to see through my lies—no matter how big or small . . . She always knew the truth. And now, with me being blamed for the king's death, she was about to be my greatest enemy.

If I didn't convince her quickly of my innocence, it was only a matter of time before whatever revenge she had planned came to fruition. My hope was this invitation would prove a chance for me to explain what had happened. So long as she could still see through my lies, she might believe what had happened with her father as the truth. But if this was a trap . . .

I stopped in front of the gates to the King's Garden. The snow was higher here than it was in the rest of the city, with only a single file line of footprints to follow inward. They were smaller than mine, and whose feet they belonged to was clear. The princess had come to the gardens. And judging from the lack of other snow prints . . . it would just be the two of us.

I followed the trail the princess had left behind for me through the snow and slush and flurries around me. Her path led me to a circle of old birch trees, the leaves having been stripped away back when I was an immature brat who couldn't remember anything about his life and thrived on basic things—anger, selfishness, and delusions of grandeur. But I wasn't the same as I had been a month ago. I felt reborn, as if the weight on my shoulders had finally gone away.

Yet, the thing about consequences was that they always caught up eventually. The princess—never one to celebrate in vain—had left me a gift for my birthday. A grave and headstone, to be exact.

There was a large pit big enough to fit my body and then some, along with a crudely chiseled headstone of marble with the words *Here Lies Michael Kingman* carved into it. There were endless groups of four finger marks along the edges, along with dried blood flakes of frozen skin. In the middle of winter, with the ground as hard as diamonds, the princess had dug me a grave with her bare hands. The headstone had been her handiwork, too—bits of marble that hadn't been turned into a fine powder littering the nearby ground. A bouquet of Moon's Tears slightly coated with snow rested at the bottom of the pit. The flowers were pristine and bright, still giving off a faint white glow. They had been picked recently. A few hours ago at most.

I went to the headstone and sat on top of it after brushing off the snow that had accumulated on it. Taking a deep breath, I steadied my heartbeat until I was certain my voice would come out clear and calm. There was no point in shouting at the sky. The princess was around here somewhere. She wouldn't miss the opportunity to watch me admire her threat and declaration of war. But if she wasn't going to stand in front of me herself, I'd take the opportunity to speak un-interrupted.

"Thanks for the gift," I began, running my fingers along the edges of the marble. "It must have taken a long time to do. It definitely makes up for not getting me anything the past ten years." I exhaled and watched as my breath came out white and wispy. "I'm sorry I didn't get you anything as good today. Gift giving has never been a strength of mine—except for Lucky. That gift I was proud of."

The wind answered me, blowing against my face as I returned to my feet. I trudged over to a nearby tree that was just a little bigger than the others, hands still bundled into my pockets to fend off the cold. "But I was good at everyday things, wasn't I? The big moments were always hard for me to get right. Too much pressure. Too many eyes on me. I felt as if everything I did was being watched . . . dissected." I hesitated. "I remember that on your seventh birthday I got you a black leather-bound book that smelt of hidden secrets and bone dust. Everyone I asked for their opinions told me it was a proper gift for a Kingman to give their Royal. It was practical and showed I understand the nature of our bound relationship. That I was maturing and no longer overstepping into something beyond duty."

I kicked at the base of the tree I was standing in front of and watched as snow fell from the branches to the ground. It landed with a soft plop. "It was a lousy gift. Too impersonal for what we were. Even when you smiled sweetly and said thanks through gritted teeth, I knew you hated it. We were best friends, and being a bounded pair was only a part of our relationship—not the base." I took a deep breath. "I should have given you a heart-shaped glass necklace like I wanted to. That was the right gift back then. And although I never got the chance to give you your ninth birthday gift officially . . . better late than never, right?"

Words were carved haphazardly on the tree's trunk in a childish scrawl. *Michael and the Princess—bound by fate but chose each other anyway.*

"That's one birthday gift I missed. Forgive me if it's childish. I was eight when I did it." I returned to the edge of the pit, toes dangling over as if I were about to jump. "Nothing I say right now will make you forgive me or make you believe that I had nothing to do with your father's death. So keep watching until you're satisfied. You won't find the monster you're looking for. Just the foolish boy you once knew."

A voice came from everywhere and nowhere. "I am going to kill you, Michael Kingman."

Unlike my memories of Dawn that returned in a torrent all at once and nearly split my head open . . . my memories of the princess trickled back to me like an offbeat rhythm. It made me wonder if my memories of her had been manipulated or forgotten, or if I had simply pushed them to the back of my mind as a child to save myself from losing another loved one after my father.

I answered her threat with a smile as something in my mind turned open, her name returning to me after a long absence. "Come at me with everything you've got, Serena Hollow." The scrawl on the tree changed. The Princess morphed into Serena. "I promise you that I'm not going anywhere ever again."

There was no response—not that I expected one. Serena had never been good at comebacks under pressure. Actions were her strength and words were mine, and if we were going to be enemies, this would be the last chance I'd have at being in a position of relative power or safety. Serena wasn't careless. I'd have to be better than ever before if I was going to survive her war.

Under the shattered moon and scattered stars I began my walk back to Kingman Keep.

Serena haunted me as I walked through the city she would one day rule. When I passed sweetshops, I recalled how she used to hoard pastries filled with strawberry jam in her room to remind herself of summer. I heard her laugh in my mind whenever I passed wanted posters of myself, knowing she would have made fun of how they depicted my nose jutting out like a bad wart. I smelt her favorite perfume—oranges and lemongrass—as Low Nobles shouted obscenities at me from the windows of homes in Justice Hill. And sometimes I saw her out of the corner of my eye, close enough to feel her breath on the nape of my neck but gone by the time I turned around.

I was so lost in my thoughts . . . I almost didn't notice something that hadn't happened in more than two decades.

There were refugees at the gates of Hollow, begging to get in.

Everyone in the area was caught off guard as a horde of people staggered into the city. Most of them were groaning and fell to their knees clutching at the legs of Advocators. What initially seemed like a dozen or two soon became a few hundred, and people were still coming. Some were bandaged, some bleeding, some had fresh red and flaking burns. Others were missing limbs. A few with red lines covering their bodies spontaneously caught fire the moment their feet touched the cobblestone streets. They died screaming for Celona's mercy while those around them shouted that the Corruption had arrived in Hollow, that a Goldani curse turned magical infection was killing the refugees from the inside out with flames.

There was no indication where they had come from—another city, or a different country entirely. Hollow citizens who had initially stood back to let the refugees pass were suddenly shoving past the healthier ones to reach those more critically injured. All the order had vanished in a singular moment.

Wherever the prince and princess were within the city, they were probably more shocked than I was. It was one thing for King Isaac to deal with the rebellion, and now this—he had decades of experience on the throne. The princess had a month.

What would she do? Would she let them stay? Would she kick them out?

Suddenly I doubted I was Serena's top priority anymore.

MEMORIES OF INK

Morning only brought pain. Whether it was the light in my eyes, the dull ache that covered my body, or the cold that lingered in my bones after a night under a thin, scratchy blanket. I couldn't remember the last time I had slept through the night. Nightmares of the king's suicide usually plagued my mind. They were worse than the ones about the Kingman Keep riots and left me looking for distractions while the city slept. The only good thing to come out of my restlessness was that I had spent that time getting better at shooting guns. I was the scorn of painted-on targets everywhere.

Normally I could take my time getting up, but not today. My mother wanted us to have breakfast together. I realized why the moment I stumbled out of the room I shared with my sister, rubbing sleep out of my eyes. In the middle of the sunlit great hall was a massive maple table that could easily sit thirty. It stood out against the rotten wood, dust, and ruin that was everywhere else, and it was vastly different to the table that had stood here in my youth, but as I ran my fingers over the smooth wood, it still made me remember my father and the elaborate toasts he would give before every meal. I would've cried if I wasn't so tired.

"The Ryders brought it after you fell asleep last night," my black-haired and sun-kissed skin sister said. She had a blacksmith's body with forearms more defined than most soldiers' and had rolled up her sleeves so the crown brand on the back of her left hand was visible. Our mother's red scarf was around her neck. "They said that if we were going to live here, we might as well have a place to eat dinner. Ma and Lyon cried. A lot."

"I forgot how important family meals were to Ma and Da."

"I don't know how you could've," my mother declared, entering behind Gwen. Lyon was at her side, carrying a steaming pot. Unlike Gwen's, the brand above his eyebrow was obscured with the ends of a knit hat. "Without them, none of you would've learned anything about our family history. I don't think I need to say how important that was and how important it'll be in the future."

Lyon put the pot down on the table, gave each of us a spoon, and then a took a place at the table near me and my sister. My mother stopped behind the chair at the head of the table. It had been my father's seat, and now it was hers. After steeling herself mentally, she looked at her amber-eyed children and said, "In the upcoming days, we'll have to make a lot of hard decisions. Some of them none of you will like, and others all of you will."

"Will those decisions include getting beds?" I asked. "Because sleeping on the floor is a pain."

"Michael."

"Sorry, Ma."

Gwen was smiling ear to ear. "It's good to be home again."

"I'm just glad for once it's not me scolding Michael," Lyon said.

"It wasn't that bad, Lyon."

"You two rarely went a day without getting into an argument," Gwen said as she played with her spoon.

"We couldn't be in the same room together," Lyon added.

"That's a little dramatic, don't you think?" I said.

"No," they said in harmony.

"You're both being—"

"Enough," my mother said as she took her seat. "We're all aware of Michael's selective hearing. He's had it since he was a child."

"Ma!"

There was laughter at the table as I flushed.

"Everyone, dig in. After beds, I promise we'll get some plates and bowls."

None of us moved our spoon toward the pot's mysterious red contents. Noticing our hesitation, my mother said, "What?"

"Who made this?" I asked. "And what is it?"

"I did. It's beetroot porridge. Your grandmother made it for me when I was a girl," my mother said. "I was a great cook before I married your father and relied on . . . Just give it a chance."

Bravely, I dipped my spoon into the pot and tried it. "Wish we had some bread to go with it, but I think I like it."

"Seriously? There's no comparison to Ange—" Gwen caught herself before she said his full name, clenching her fists instead.

"Are we going to talk about what he did to us?" Lyon questioned quietly. "Or just keep delaying the inevitable?"

"It's not delaying. It's just . . . we can't move against Angelo openly yet," my mother stated. "So long as the Royals and Efyra think Michael killed King Isaac, they'll react violently to any move we make against them. And that includes Angelo, so long as he works for Scales. They might not be able to come for Michael, but we aren't as lucky."

"What do we do, then?" Gwen asked hesitantly.

"We prepare," my mother said. "After Michael is proven innocent, we'll be able to deal with Angelo Shade. But until we know who he is and what his goals are, we're treading water. Let's use this time to learn."

"*I* know what his goals are," I said. "He wants to destroy all the High Nobles because they did something to his wife and unborn child."

"But what does 'destroy' mean, exactly? Does he want to burn it all down and make himself king? Does he want to stand on the ruins and then walk away? Both have the same end goals, but one is vastly different."

Lyon's face was red, and he picked at a scab on his forearm until it was bleeding. "This is ridiculous. We lived with this man for ten years. How do we know nothing about him? How did none of us realize that we were being manipulated?"

"We were all focused on ourselves," I said. "We have to do better."

If there was anything that could embarrass my siblings, it was when their selfish brother admitted he had been too focused on himself.